Roads of Oku

Journeys in the Heartland

Dennis Kawaharada

Far Roads

2015

ISBN: 978-1500885113

Kalamakū Press
1710 Punahou Street, Apt. 601
Honolulu, HI 96822

Front Cover Photo: Offshore torii at Shirahige Shrine, Lake Biwa, Shiga
Back Cover Photo: Kōtai Jingū (Ise shrine), Mie

Dedication

To Harumi Kawaharada (1899–1998)
and Koyuka Kuwahara (1896–1978), my bridges to the ancestral homeland

To Mom (Matsuko, b. 1925), for a lifetime of support
and for my first visit to Japan in 1970

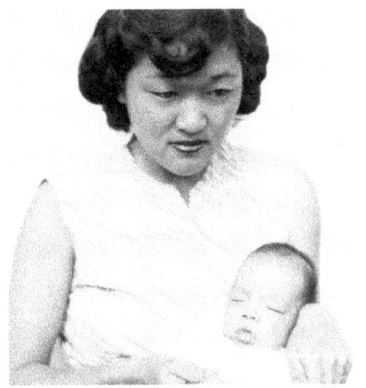

Mom and me, at two months, Agana, Guam, 1952

To Karen Ōno (b. 1952), who traveled the roads of Oku with me—
dōgyō ninin (two people, one path)

Mahalo Píha

Mahalo piha to Richard Hamasaki and Paul Lyons, comrades in literature, whose comments and suggestions on drafts guided revisions for coherence, unity, and clarity.

Roads of Oku

Journeys in the Heartland

Dennis Kawaharada

46 Prefectures of Japan's Four Main Islands

1. Hokkaidō

Chūbu
(Middle Region)
15. Niigata
16. Toyama
17. Ishikawa
18. Fukui
19. Yamanashi
20. Nagano
21. Gifu
22. Shizuoka
23. Aichi

Tōhoku
(Northeast)
2. Aomori
3. Iwate
4. Miyagi
5. Akita
6. Yamagata
7. Fukushima

Chūgoku
(Middle
Provinces)
31. Tottori
32. Shimane
33. Okayama
34. Hiroshima
35. Yamaguchi

Kyūshū
(Nine
Provinces)
40. Fukuoka
41. Saga
42. Nagasaki
43. Kumamoto
44. Ōita
45. Miyazaki
46. Kagoshima

Kantō
(Eastern Gate)
8. Ibaraki
9. Tochigi
10. Gunma
11. Saitama
12. Chiba
13. Tōkyō
14. Kanagawa

Kansai
(Western Gate)
24. Mie
25. Shiga
26. Kyōto
27. Ōsaka
28. Hyōgo
29. Nara
30. Wakayama

Shikoku
(Four
Provinces)
36. Tokushima
37. Kagawa
38. Ehime
39. Kōchi

200 km

100 mi

Kyūshū once had nine provinces; it now has seven prefectures.
Okinawa Prefecture (47) lies 400 miles south of Kagoshima (46). See the map on page 181.

Contents

Essays

Maps

Child of History

Night dew and wind mingle desolately
pine and willow go black,
the sky fills with dark petals of karma

Kenji Miyazawa, 10/5/1924

Scents and flavors of Japan drift through my childhood memories of Kāneʻohe, Hawaiʻi, leaves from a tree far upstream—shoyu and miso, dried seaweed, cuttlefish and abalone. Toys from Japan came in flimsy cardboard boxes, colorful in vivid inks and packed with shredded paper that had a distinct, exotic smell.

Fifty years later, I recall repetitive children's songs:

Chi chi pa pa, chi pa pa
Suzume no gakkō no sensei wa
Muchi o furi furi, chi pa pa

A school of suzume, or sparrows, learns to chirp. A cheerful song, with a stern undertone. The sensei waves his rod. The students are not getting it, so "mō ichidō, issho ni," "once again, all together." The song reminds me of my brief stint in Japanese school: after Ben Parker Elementary released us at 2 p.m., we walked a couple of blocks to the language school at the Honganji (a Jōdo Shinshū Buddhist temple) on Keaʻahala Road. When the bell rang, we lined up in the graveled yard, then filed into the hollow-tile classroom and sat in rows of wooden desks to learn to pronounce and write hiragana: a-i-u-e-o, ka-ki-ku-ke-ko, etc. There was a lot of "mō ichidō, issho ni." Despite the repetition, I never learned to understand spoken Japanese; the syllables seemed to run together, like the babble of water in a stream.

I recall folktales in English, like the one about a woodcutter's cruel wife who cuts off the tongue of a pet sparrow because the sparrow has eaten some of her starching paste. I associate the sparrow's injury with my first cut— accidentally, I nicked my finger on a bread knife and watched blood bead out, feeling queasy.

Another catchy song, from the Taishō Period (1912–1926), was about tanuki, or raccoon dogs. The setting is a garden of a Buddhist temple in

Kisarazu, Ibaraki, where the priests and tanuki sing and dance together on a moonlit night:

Sho-sho-shojo-ji
Shojo-ji no niwa wa
Tsu-tsu-tsuki-yo dan
Minna dete koi-koi-koi

Tanuki inflate their bellies and drum on them (at least the ones in folktales do), producing an entrancing sound—pom-poko, pom-poko, pom-poko—which leads wayfarers astray at night.

Tanuki has a dark side: in one folktale, he's caught stealing vegetables, and the farmer ties him up, planning to cook him in a soup for dinner. But after the farmer leaves, tanuki persuades the wife to untie him, then kills her, cooks her in a soup, and serves her to her husband. The farmer gets revenge with the help of usagi, or rabbit. Rabbit drops a beehive on tanuki's back, then treats the stings with mustard plaster as tanuki writhes in pain. Later, rabbit sets fire to tanuki's load of kindling, scorching his back. He challenges tanuki to a boat race. Tanuki makes a boat out of mud, which disintegrates and sinks. Tanuki drowns. "Mud boat" is proverbial for an enterprise doomed to fail.

Suzume, tanuki, and usagi belonged to a magical, far-off world, unlike home in Hawai'i.

Two grandmothers were my bridge to the ancestral homeland I didn't visit until I was nineteen. My mom's mother, Koyuka Kuwahara (née Kiyokawa), was born in 1896 in Gōnomura, a rice-farming village in north-central Hiroshima.[1] She came to Hawai'i as an eighteen-year-old picture bride in 1914, aboard the SS *Mongolia,* out of Kobe, to join her husband in Hilo (Honolulu Hawaii, Passenger Lists, 1900–1953).

Grandpa Gunichi (1888–1963) was also from Gōnomura. He came to Hawai'i in 1907 on the SS *Korea*, out of Yokohama. Both the *Mongolia* and the *Korea* belonged to the Pacific Mail Steamship Company, which transported mail and passengers between San Francisco and the Far East, with a stop in Honolulu. In the immigration record, grandpa is listed as a farm laborer; a scar on the third finger of his left hand was a mark of identification (Honolulu Hawaii, Passenger Lists, 1900–1953). He had $10, a little more than half of the monthly base-pay ($18) for Asian plantation workers before 1910 (Fuchs 55).

Grandpa and grandma had six children, four boys and two girls; mom was the second daughter and fifth child. She recalls hearing that grandma's introductory letter to grandpa, sent with her picture-bride photo, was written by someone else, so grandpa thought grandma was more educated than she really was. Mom also recalls that grandpa had a mistress.

Grandpa in front of Kuwahara Store on the Hilo waterfront, before World War II

Grandpa prospered selling American and Japanese goods and supplies at Kuwahara Store, on the Hilo waterfront, with branches on Kīlauea Avenue and in Wainaku, a plantation village north of Hilo. Mom doesn't know how grandpa, with just $10, acquired enough capital to establish a store—maybe through tanomoshi, the issei (first-generation) practice of pooling money, then loaning it with interest to contributors to the pool, on a rotating basis.

The family lived on Kaūmana Street in upland Hilo, on the second floor of a two-story building. Grandpa's younger brother, Gunshirō, lived downstairs with his family. Gunshirō's wife was a Honolulu nisei (second generation, born in Hawai'i); the couple also had six children. Gunshirō ran a small store downstairs, next to a barbershop. Mom recalls a man from Gōnomura, not a relative, living with the family for a while. He showed the kids his pornographic photos of geisha and made home brew from berries.

Before World War II, grandpa was active in the community, giving graduation speeches at the Japanese language school run by Yoshio Shinoda. Grandpa also hosted parties for Japanese naval officers when their ships arrived in port. He sent his first son to a college of Waseda University in Tōkyō and his next two sons to colleges in California. (Sending children to college was a dream of the issei, and a major achievement: Hoffman observes that "in 1920 less than half the population [in Japan] got beyond the six years of compulsory schooling, with senior high school, let alone university, accessible to barely one percent of boys and the merest handful of girls.")

Grandpa's first daughter went to finishing school in Japan, returning home just before Japanese planes attacked the American fleet anchored at Pearl

Harbor, on December 7, 1941.

After the attack, grandpa asked a neighbor to hide his projector, along with the films of his parties for Japanese naval officers. But grandpa, like others who associated with Japanese military personnel visiting Hawai‘i, had probably already been identified for arrest by the US military in anticipation of war between the two nations. Kashima notes in his introduction to Soga's *Life Behind Barbed Wire*:

> President Roosevelt in August 1936 wrote to his chief of naval operations: "One obvious thought occurred to me—that every Japanese citizen or non-citizen on the Island of O‘ahu who meets these Japanese ships … or has any connections with their officers or men should be *secretly* but definitely identified and his or her name placed on a *special list* of those who would be the first to be placed in a concentration camp in the event of trouble. (7)

Grandpa was arrested and held at Kīlauea Military Camp near Volcano, then shipped to Sand Island Internment Camp in Honolulu. Around 700 of the internees in Hawai‘i were sent to the mainland in ten groups (Soga 226). Grandpa was in the second group, leaving Honolulu on the USS *Grant* in March 1942 for Camp Livingston, a US Army facility in Louisiana (238). On the way, one of his group, "distraught over leaving his wife and 12 children behind," tried to escape over a barbed wire fence at Fort Sill, Oklahoma, and was shot dead. In 1943, the War Department transferred resident aliens arrested in Hawai‘i to the Justice Department, whose Immigration and Naturalization Service ran eight internment camps—three in Texas, two in New Mexico, and one each in Idaho, Montana, and North Dakota (Burton et al.) Grandpa was detained for the duration of the war. The photos he sent home depicted more than one camp, but mom isn't sure in which locations.

Grandpa's oldest son ran the store in Hilo while grandpa was interned. Two younger sons were drafted: one of them served at Fort DeRussy on O‘ahu and the other in the Military Intelligence Service, which translated Japanese documents and interpreted during the interrogation of prisoners of war. My mom worked to support herself while she attended the University of Hawai‘i. Her youngest brother was drafted after the war was over, and eventually went to Marquette University on the GI Bill.

While grandpa was away, a nisei employee embezzled funds from the store, so it wasn't doing well when grandpa returned with other internees in November, 1945, on the SS *Yarmouth* out of Seattle. On April 1, 1946, a tsunami struck Hilo, damaging the main warehouse and store. Grandpa decided to return to Japan, where, with a female partner, he purchased and ran a hotel at the train station in Hiroshima city, which was rebuilding after the atomic

Kuwahara Store after the 1946 tsunami

bomb attack on August 18, 1945. Grandpa returned to Hilo in the 1950s to retire, having made enough from selling his share of the hotel to give each of his six children a gift of $1,000. He bought a house on Kino'ole Street, and he and grandma lived there with their eldest son and his wife and two daughters.

I met grandpa just once, on a summer trip to Hilo in 1961, when mom took us to see the volcanic eruption at Halema'uma'u crater. When we arrived in the afternoon, grandpa was sitting in a rocking chair on the porch, dressed in a yukata (light cotton kimono). He was apparently ill and didn't join us on any excursions. We drove up to Kīlauea that night and walked in a line of spectators around the deep crater aglow with pools of molten lava. On another night we went to Kaūmana for an Obon dance—a celebration to welcome home ancestral spirits for an annual visit, with music, drumming, dancing, and food. My next visit to Hilo, in December 1962, was for grandpa's funeral at Hilo Honganji. Mom thinks he may have died from liver disease.

After grandpa's death, grandma used her survivor's benefits to travel to Hiroshima and live with her family for eleven months a year, coming back to Hawai'i for a month to maintain her return rights to America. Like other issei, she wasn't eligible for naturalization and US citizenship until seven years after the war ended, in 1952. She remained a Japanese citizen all her life. On her visits home, she took food items that were scarce in post-war Japan (like coffee, cocoa, and chocolate candy) and helped pay bills for her brother and two sisters. She also traveled. In one photo, she is on Itsukushima (Miyajima), with its famous sea torii in the background. Her trips to her homeland continued until she was too old to travel.

Grandma was a small, thin woman who listed to one side and shuffled when she walked, having suffered a stroke. When we were young, she occasionally

Grandma on Miyajima after World War II

stayed with us in Kāne'ohe to babysit us three kids for my working mom. We couldn't speak Japanese, and grandma couldn't speak English, so we hardly communicated. She took us to subtitled samurai and obaké movies at the neighborhood theater. I recall her kintan, a pungent-smelling herbal cure-all wrapped in gold-colored foil. She always packed a bottle. Mom said that grandpa had Hawai'i distribution rights to this medicine, which she recalls using to alleviate a toothache.

Toward the end of her life, grandma moved to O'ahu to live with mom, after mom was widowed and living alone. Lying in bed, grandma listened to Japanese music on her transistor radio and watched Japanese programs on TV. From hearing her music, I developed a fondness for enka, those dreamy, nostalgic ballads of loss, loneliness, and longing for a lover or a hometown. The lyrics feature rainy nights, saké drinking, and rivers of time and destiny flowing ever onward. With orchestral backing, the songs lilt, then swell with emotion and soar, the singers' voices full of tremolo and melancholic tones.

For the issei who settled in Hawai'i, enka must have evoked natsukashimi— deep nostalgia for childhood places, family, and friends left behind. Enka are songs of the nineteenth diaspora of rural people leaving families and hometowns to work in the cities or overseas. I watch the Red and White Song Contest every year, broadcast on television from Tōkyō on New Year's Day, to listen to grandma's enka and remember her. Hilo grandma outlived her husband by fifteen years. She died in 1978 from a stroke, after injuring herself in a fall in mom's apartment. Her ashes are with grandpa's at a cemetery in Nu'uanu.

My dad's mother, Harumi Kawaharada (née Masuda), was born in 1899, in Tomomura, a rice-farming village five miles northwest of Hiroshima city. She arrived in Hawai'i as a seventeen-year-old picture bride in 1916, aboard the *Panama Maru*, a steamship that carried cargo between San Francisco and Japan. Her future husband, Makiso Kawaharada (1887–1953) grew up a ten-minute walk from her house in Tomomura. (The Masuda family were bunkei, a branch of the Kawaharada family.) She was seven in 1906, when grandpa, who was nineteen, left for Hawai'i aboard the SS *Mongolia* to look for an older brother who had come to Hawai'i in the early 1900s and was last heard from on the Big Island. In the immigration record, grandpa is identified as a farm laborer, with $2. His older brother had paid for his

Makiso and Harumi Kawaharada

passage (Honolulu, Hawaii, Passenger Lists, 1900–1953). No one in the family knows what happened to his brother; the family lost track of him. Grandpa settled on Maui and married Tomoe Horio, the nisei daughter of Shimatarō and Shimo Horio of Pā'ia. In the 1910 US Census, grandpa is listed as a 23-year-old son-in-law in the Horio household. Tomoe died in 1911, at nineteen, while giving birth to their first son. The infant was taken to Japan to be raised by the Horio family.

Grandpa got a job at the Pā'ia plantation store of the Maui Agricultural Company, taking orders and delivering goods by truck to communities in Upcountry Maui. Born in 1926, dad was the fourth of ten children and the first son. Grandma fondly remembered the colorful koi (carp) banners that flew over the house for dad's first Boy's Day celebration on May 5 the following year. In 1929, grandpa and grandma bought two acres of gulch land in Kuiaha, across the road from the Pa'uwela Pineapple Cannery (later Libby, McNeil, and Libby). The manager told the couple that if they opened a restaurant there, he would close the cannery's dining hall, and they could count on business from the workers. The M. Kawaharada Restaurant, which eventually included a bakery and small store, prospered for the first two years, but when the Great

M. Kawaharada Restaurant, Kuiaha, Maui, across from the pineapple cannery

Depression set in during the early 1930s, the couple had to let two Chinese cooks go. Grandma ran the restaurant with her children, doing the cooking and baking, while grandpa continued to work for the Pāʻia store. He attended English classes at night.

The family lived in small rooms below the store, which was built on the steep slope of the gulch, overlooking avocado, mango, and lichee trees. A dark, narrow wooden stairway connected the two floors. Beneath the rooms were an outdoor laundry room and concrete shower and bath, where on warm tropical nights, large brown cane spiders clung motionlessly to the walls.

In the mid-1990s, Kayoko, a student of mine from Mihara, Hiroshima, accompanied me to interview grandma about her life with grandpa. Kayoko also translated some of grandpa's documents. One was a 1931 letter from the Japanese community of Hāmākua-poko recognizing grandpa for serving as chairman of the Japanese language school administration board. He raised funds and helped cut costs to keep the school open, in opposition to those who wanted to close the school because it was "un-American." In 1937, the Pāʻia Japanese school, on its thirtieth anniversary, gave grandpa a certificate thanking him for his contribution to school management.

In 1939, he received a certificate of appreciation from the Japanese Empire Board of Education, recognizing the work of its educators in Manchuria, China, Hawaiʻi, and Brazil. The chairman's letter encouraged educators living overseas to become loyal and good citizens of the countries where they lived (if they were allowed to become citizens, which wasn't the case in America), to work hard and uphold the moral values of the ancestors, and to contribute to good relationships between their new home countries and the Empire.

Makiso was able to help the plantation community because he had eight years of education in Japan and could read and write. He served as a liaison to the Japanese consulate on Oʻahu, collecting information from immigrants, explaining and helping them fill out documents, and passing documents back and forth between the consulate and the community. After the attack on Pearl Harbor, grandpa was arrested by four military police officers, who also searched the house and took documents. He was jailed in Wailuku for seven months. After his release, he was allowed to live at home, but until the war ended, had to report his daily activities to a boss at the cannery across the street.

The restaurant did well during the war because the 4th Marine Division was stationed at Camp Maui in nearby Hāʻiku, and the soldiers became customers. In addition to anpan (buns filled with azuki-bean) and pies and saimin, which grandma learned to make from the Chinese cooks, the restaurant starting serving American favorites such as T-bone steaks, hamburgers, and french fries.

Grandpa died from a stroke in 1953, when I was two years old. I never met him. Grandma said that the Kawaharada family were rice farmers and landowners, and also caretakers of Suwa Jinja, the main Shintō shrine of Tomomura. They were responsible for lighting a fire at their farmhouse and taking it to the shrine for the start of the fall harvest festival. Grandpa's one regret was not having returned to Tomomura while his parents were still alive. His parents had asked the couple to return to learn about the family history and traditions to pass on to their children and grandchildren, but grandma and grandpa couldn't afford to go before the war. By the time they returned to Tomomura in 1949, grandpa's parents had passed away. Grandpa and grandma visited their graves.

During the 1950s and 1960s, dad and mom took us kids on summer trips to visit grandma and three of dad's sisters who still lived on Maui. Grandma's house was full of things Japanese—display cases of dolls dressed in kimono and samurai armor, kokeshi dolls, pictures and souvenirs from Japan, and books in Japanese. Like grandpa, grandma had completed eight years of schooling in Japan. She also studied etiquette, sewing, flower arranging, and tea ceremony under the wife of the village headman. In Hawaiʻi, she took lessons in ikebana (flower arranging) from a local instructor with ties to a school in Japan and was active with the Honganji in Paʻuwela. After it closed due to declining membership, she joined the Honganji in Makawao.

We went to summer picnics sponsored by kenjinkai (associations of immigrants from the same prefectures) at Baldwin Park in Pāʻia and Kalama Park in Kīhei, where tablets, pencils, and erasers rather than toys or candies were given out as prizes for games and races. In August, we went to the Obon dance at the Honganji in Pa'uwela. The ancestors must have been surprised by invitations to a celebration over four thousand miles east of the homeland.

Grandma, who spoke a little English, gave us the same advice every time we visited: study hard in school and marry someone Japanese. While her grandchildren took her advice about school, not all took her advice about marriage, and some of her great grandchildren have Mexican, European, and Chinese ancestries.

Like Hilo grandma, Maui grandma outlived her husband, though by much longer—forty-six years. She was eleven days shy of a century when she passed away in 1999, in her small bedroom below the restaurant where she had worked for six decades. Her ashes are housed with her husband's and his first wife's at the urn repository of the Hongan temple in Makawao. When I asked her what she wanted to pass on to her grandchildren and great grandchildren, she said the Kawaharada tradition of helping the community. She recalled a story told in Tomomura of how the family helped small farmers during a drought, and that the farmers remembered the help and continued to express appreciation for many years after.

Japanese emigration to Hawai'i started in the nineteenth century with a friendship between King David Kalākaua (1836–1891), whose mid-Pacific kingdom needed people for a growing economy, and Emperor Meiji (1852–1912), whose East Asian nation had too many people for its depressed economy. In 1881, Kalākaua visited Meiji in Tōkyō, the first stop of a round-the-world tour, to propose repeopling his kingdom with immigrants from Hawai'i. The number of native people in Hawai'i had been reduced by diseases brought by Westerners and Asians who settled in the islands after Captain James Cook accidentally discovered them in 1778. Estimated variously between 300,000 and 800,000 when Cook arrived, the population had fallen to around 57,000 in 1876. Besides diseases, emigration of natives to work on the West Coast also reduced the population. Meanwhile, the Kingdom had entered the global economy and was beginning to prosper from plantations producing sugar for export. To expand its sugar economy, the King needed a larger local labor force. The Chinese were the first plantation workers to come, in 1852, mainly single males, or "coolies," brought to work rather than to settle permanently.

The government under Kalākaua's predecessor, King Kamehameha V (r. 1863–1872), proposed repopulating the islands through immigration of "cognate" races:

> In 1864, in response to the labor crisis, and the monarchy's desire to repopulate the kingdom with a "cognate race," the legislature established a Bureau of Immigration and charged it with the task of finding workers for Hawaii's plantations. Robert Wyllie, foreign

minister under Kamehameha IV and Kamehameha V, augmented bureau initiatives by actively promoting labor migration from Asia and the Pacific. (Okihiro 16)

In 1868, a group of 148 Japanese arrived (six of them women and two children). They were called Gannen Mono, or "First-Year People," because they came in the first year of Meiji's rule in Japan. Following reports of abuse and accusations of contract violations, however, the Meiji government brought home forty who wanted to return and put further emigration on hold (Nordyke and Matsumoto 163). Japanese citizens were considered the emperor's children, and ill or unfair treatment of them was an insult to the nation. Despite the discontent of the forty, the rest of Gannen Mono settled in Hawai'i, and according to Kuykendall, "became merged in the island population":

> By their excellent qualities and good conduct, they did much to foster the idea that Japan was a suitable place from which to obtain both plantation laborers and recruits for the permanent population of the kingdom. (154)

The representatives of the Hawaiian Kingdom in Tōkyō made it known that it would welcome more Japanese workers; however, no more immigrants came for over a decade and a half after the Gannen Mono. At the end of 1884, only 116 Japanese were counted in Hawai'i (Nordyke and Matsumoto 165). According to Kuykendall, one of the reasons the Meiji government was "unwilling to permit its poorer subjects to go abroad as laborers," was "the determination of the authorities to prevent Japanese from being classed and treated as "coolies." (154)

A Hawaiian-Japanese treaty signed in 1871 made it possible for Japanese citizens to apply for passports and travel abroad for work, but the government wouldn't allow any citizen to go unless it was satisfied that "the interests of Japan would not be adversely affected by his going, and also that the laborer's rights and interests would be safe-guarded in the foreign country" (Kuykendall 154). In the meantime, in 1878, Portuguese workers were recruited and came with wives and children to settle; most were from the Madeira and Azores islands, where sugar had been cultivated for four hundred years. (Within a decade, 12,000 arrived.)

Before departing for his visit to Tōkyō, Kalākaua traveled around the islands to inform his people of the purpose of his global tour, one of which was to recruit Japanese immigrants; he "assured his people that the immigrants would be of a 'cognate race' with similar values and hence would be compatible with the Hawaiian character" (Kanahele 326). Perhaps one of the similarities Kalākaua saw between the Japanese and Hawaiians was the determination of both to resist Western colonization. The Japanese were an example for such resistance, as they had defended their sovereignty while other Asian and Pacific nations, including larger nations like India and China, had lost their sovereignty to European powers.

In Tōkyō, Kalākaua made it known that "any Japanese who desired to settle in the Hawaiian Kingdom would be permitted to do so" (Kuykendall 156). The King understood that a revitalized population was essential to build his kingdom's economy and maintain its sovereignty.

In a private meeting with Meiji, Kalākaua addressed his concern about threats to Hawaiian sovereignty from Western nations, such as America, Britain, and France. He proposed the formation of a league of Asian nations to oppose Western imperialism: if Meiji would agree to head the league, Kalākaua offered to promote it to Asian leaders in China, Siam, India, and Persia on his journey around the world. Kalākaua also proposed a marriage between his five-year-old niece and heir, Princess Ka'iulani, and sixteen-year-old Prince Sadamaro, a member of the group escorting the King. Uniting the Hawaiian Throne through marriage with the Imperial Family might help protect Hawai'i from predatory nations (Keene 349).

Interracial marriage was not uncommon in Hawai'i: Ka'iulani was of mixed ancestry—her Scottish father married Princess Likelike, a sister of Kalākaua. But the proposal of an ethnically mixed marriage must have been somewhat of a shock to the Imperial Family. Although modern evidence indicates the Japanese are a mixed race (Jōmon people coupled with settlers from the Korean Peninsula), the Meiji government embraced the myth of Japanese racial purity and superiority, to unify the nation against the West.

Still, Meiji was impressed by Kalākaua. Meiji walked side by side with the king, which the emperor would not do with any of his subjects or other visitors because of his divine descent from the sun goddess Amaterasu (Keene 346). But Kalākaua also had divine ancestry from the Hawaiian gods Papa and Wākea.

That Kalākaua expressed a willingness to sign treaties in which the two nations were considered equals also helped to establish trust and rapport between the two leaders. At the time of the King's visit, Japan was pushing for recognition as an equal with nations of the West; in its 1858 treaties with the United States, the United Kingdom, France, Netherlands, and Russia, it had been forced to concede extraterritoriality, or exemptions of Western residents in Japan from the jurisdiction of Japanese courts.

Before Kalākaua left Japan, the emperor promised to consider the king's proposals and presented Kalākaua with the Royal Order of the Chrysanthemum, Japan's highest honor; in return Kalākaua bestowed on the emperor his kingdom's highest award, the Royal Order of Kamehameha I.

A year later, in 1882, John M. Kapena, a former governor of Maui, made a follow-up visit to Japan and at a dinner in Tōkyō, expanded on Kalākaua's vision for repopulating Hawai'i:

> His Majesty (Kalakaua) believes that the Japanese and Hawaiians spring from one cognate race and this enhances his love for you. He hopes that our people will more and more be brought closer together in a common brotherhood. Hawaii holds out her loving hand and heart to Japan and desires that Your People may come and cast in their lots with ours and repeople our Island Home—with a race which is sent to us by His Imperial Majesty, Your Government and people may blend with ours and produce a new and vigorous nation making our land the garden spot of the Eastern Pacific, as your beautiful and glorious country is of the Western. (Qtd. in Kuykendall 159–160)

While the haole planters in Hawai'i wanted the King to recruit labor so they could increase profits, Kalākaua saw his proposal as recruitment of settlers who would "blend" with native people. Kapena met with Foreign Affairs Minister Inoue and detailed the terms and conditions of the Hawaiian government's immigration proposal, including "full legal protection for the laborer's rights" and "free schooling for their children" (Kuykendall 160).

Kapena brought with him two young ali'i (chiefs), who would study Japanese language and culture at Gakushuin University, also known as the Nobles School (Kuwazoku Gakkō). The two ali'i had the future Emperor Taishō as a classmate. Kalākaua hoped that one day, the two students would conduct Hawaiian affairs with Japan and manage immigration (Quigg 195–198).

The Asiatic league proposed by Kalākaua was never formed. The only record of the proposal is a letter from Meiji to Kalākaua in which Meiji praises the King's "profound and far-seeing views" and notes the common desire of their nations and others in the East to restore their sovereignties and establish "independence and integrity"; but Meiji tactfully declined participation in or leadership of such a "vast undertaking," due to pressing domestic issues that needed his attention (Kuykendall 229). Japan had already embarked on a plan to become a global industrial and military power to defend its sovereignty on its own rather than seek alliances with other nations. Meiji also knew that China wouldn't join a league headed by Japan, because the two nations were already rivals in Asia (Keene 350).[2]

The marriage between Princess Ka'iulani and Prince Sadamaro was also declined in letters from the Prince and the Meiji's Minister of Foreign Affairs;

the prince, it was noted in both letters, was already betrothed (Kuykendall 230).

With economic conditions in Japan worsening, however, the Meiji government eventually reconsidered emigration. Inflation, then deflation, made life difficult for farming families. The price of rice fell by 50% in three years. Unable to pay taxes and forced to sell land, farmers and their tenants were desperate for work. High unemployment and bankruptcies led to riots against the government. In 1884, the Meiji government opened Japanese emigration to Australia, North and South America, Mexico, and the Pacific islands. In 1885, it approved Kalākaua's request for workers and announced the opportunity to its citizens. With a mild climate, "sincere and gentle" people, a good school system, and rice at a price comparable to the homeland's, Hawai'i was appealing. The first recruitment targeted 600 workers; 28,000 applied and 944 were signed to three-year contracts (Odo and Sinoto 21–22).

On February 8, 1885, 676 men, 159 women, and 108 children were welcomed to Hawai'i by the King. The *Pacific Commercial Advertiser* attributed the success of the recruitment to the personal friendship of the Emperor of Japan for King Kalākaua" (Qtd. in Kuykendall 165).

After a second group of immigrants arrived, however, reports of lack of medical care and "unwarrantable and frequent acts of violence that have been perpetrated upon Japanese by overseers on many of the plantations" resulted in the Meiji government putting emigration on hold again, until the Kingdom would assume a role of guardian of the immigrants. An agreement was reached, which read in part: "hereafter no overseer (luna) will be allowed, under any circumstances, to lay hands, in any way, upon any Japanese, and that a violation of this order will be considered sufficient cause by the Government for the removal of any employee" (Qtd. in Kuykendall 169). After the Kingdom hired more Japanese inspectors and physicians to ensure that immigrants would have its full protection and care, emigration was allowed to continue. Between 1885 and 1894, 29,000 Japanese, in twenty-six groups, arrived to settle in the islands (Odo and Sinoto 49).

In 1881, when Kalākaua was in Tōkyō proposing Japanese emigration and an alliance with Japan and other Asian nations, America was competing with Britain and France for political influence, if not control, over Hawai'i. In two letters to the American Minister in Hawai'i, US Secretary of State James G. Blaine expressed support for Hawaiian independence and sovereignty, but noted that "Hawaii is the key to the maritime dominion of the Pacific" and "under no circumstances" would the US allow the islands to fall under the control of any other nation; they must remain a part of "the American system." As if suspecting that Kalākaua might seek assistance in Asia during his global tour, Blaine asserted that "natural law" (as opposed to cognate racial ties) and "political necessity" should and would determine which side of the Pacific the Kingdom aligned itself with:

> The Hawaiian Islands can not be joined to the Asiatic system. If they drift from their independent station it must be toward assimilation and identification with the American system, to which they belong by the operation of natural laws and must belong by the operation of political necessity. (Qtd. in Kuykendall 244–245)

Blaine opposed the immigration of Asians and suggested that the Kingdom be repeopled with Americans instead:

> A purely American form of colonization ... would meet all phases of the problem [of the decline of the native population]. Within our borders could be found the capital, the intelligence, the activity, and the necessary labor trained in the rice swamps and cane fields of the Southern States, and it may be well to consider how, even in the chosen alternative of maintaining Hawaiian independence, these prosperous elements could be induced to go from our shore to the islands, not like the coolies, practically enslaved, not as human machines, but as thinking, intelligent, working factors in the advancement of the material interests of the Islands. (Qtd. in Kuykendall 245)

In 1887, a group of American businessmen serving in the Kingdom passed a new constitution restricting the King's powers and extending voting rights for wealthy noncitizens like themselves while disenfranchising Asians, including the Japanese whom the King had recruited. Kalākaua resisted the restrictions on his authority until he passed away four years later. Liliʻuokalani, his younger sister, succeeded him and continued resisting the attempts of American settlers to control the Kingdom. But the Kingdom didn't have military forces powerful enough to defend its sovereignty, and in 1893, the Americans, with the backing of US Marines, forced the queen to abdicate. The following year, the Americans established the Republic of Hawaiʻi; and in 1895 they put down a counter-revolution to restore the Kingdom and imprisoned the queen.

After the overthrow of the Kingdom, the Meiji government turned over emigration to private labor contractors, who brought 57,000 more immigrants to the islands; the Republic still needed workers, although they had no intention of allowing the immigrants to become citizens (Odo and Sinoto 49). In 1898, America signed a treaty to annex Hawaiʻi and acquired Pearl Harbor as a naval base from which to control the North Pacific. When the islands became a US Territory in 1900, US laws applied to the islands, and contract labor was declared unconstitutional. A period of open immigration followed, during which 71,000 more Japanese arrived in Hawai'i, workers as well as businessmen, professionals, and priests, who provided services for the growing Japanese community (Odo and Sinoto 49). My grandfathers arrived as workers during this period, and within a couple of decades, were running a store and a restaurant.

In 1908, under pressure from American labor and nativist groups to keep foreign workers, particularly Asians, out of the country, the US government limited immigration from Japan. Still, between 1908 and 1924, 61,000 immigrants arrived, including 20,000 picture brides (Odo and Sinoto 49), my two grandmothers among them.

In 1924, anti-immigrant, racist white politicians in America, with support of those in Hawai'i who feared that the Japanese would take over the islands and who also viewed Asians not as cognate races but as inferiors, enacted a ban on immigration from Asia. At that time, there were 116,140 Japanese living in Hawai'i, mainly from the western prefectures of Hiroshima, Yamaguchi, Kumamoto, Okinawa, and Fukuoka, with the largest groups from Hiroshima (30,523) and Yamaguchi (25,878). People of Japanese ancestry made up around 40% of Hawai'i's population (Odo and Sinoto 50). Their children, born in the territory of Hawai'i, became US citizens rather than Hawaiian citizens, as Kalākaua had envisioned.

Before my first visit to the ancestral hometowns in Hiroshima Prefecture in 1970, I knew little about it, except that its main city was the target of an atomic bomb. The war that followed the Japanese attack on Pearl Harbor in 1941 ended after the bombing in 1945. The Pacific war was the climax of a contentious relationship between Japan and America that began with the intrusion of four American ships under Commodore Perry into Edo Bay in 1853. For the previous two and a half centuries, Japan was closed to most foreign shipping. Only the port of Nagasaki in northwestern Kyūshū received foreign ships, and only Dutch and Chinese ships were permitted to enter. The Japanese had a trading post in Pusan, Korea, but only the domain of Tsushima (an island between Kyūshū and the southern tip of the Korean Peninsula) was allowed to trade there. The domain of Satsuma, at the southern end of Kyūshū, traded with the Kingdom of Ryūkyū to the south.

Perry carried a letter from President Fillmore requesting trade with Japan, assistance for crews of shipwrecked American vessels, and permission to provision whalers and merchant ships at Japanese ports. At the time of Perry's arrival, Japan's industry and military were much weaker than those of Western nations. Perry's rigged side-wheel steamer *Susquehanna*, armed with nine cannon, had twenty-four times more tonnage than the largest Japanese vessel. Awed and shocked by Perry's "black ships," the Japanese agreed to open selected ports for trade, hoping to buy time to fortify the country against invasion and colonization. Under Meiji, industrialization and militarization proceeded relatively quickly, and once the country was modernized, it adopted the imperialistic policies and practices of the West to compete against the West for control of resources, labor, and markets in Asia.

In 1869, the Meiji government claimed and colonized the large island to its north and named it Hokkaidō. Ten years later, in 1879, Japan annexed the kingdom of Ryūkyū (Okinawa). After a victory over China at Port Arthur in 1895, it acquired Taiwan and the Pescadores Islands, off the west coast of Taiwan. In 1905, Japan defeated Russia and took the southern half of Sakhalin Island. Russia also agreed to withdraw from Manchuria and to non-interference in Korea. It transferred its Port Arthur lease to Japan.

A 1907 memo on national defense from military leaders to Meiji expressed Japan's growing bellicosity: the country must be prepared to attack "any country that infringed on its rights" and that such readiness "had always been typical of Japan and exemplified the Japanese character" (Keene 650). The militarists began a campaign of national mobilization and predicted that one day Japan would go to war with America over control of Asia and the Pacific. Textbooks in Japanese elementary schools began instilling children with patriotism based on loyalty to a national family, with the Emperor at its head. The myth of the divine ancestry of the emperor became the basis of State Shintō.

The militarization of Japan was opposed by citizens who advocated democracy, social equality, socialism, and pacifism, as well as an end to emperor-rule and imperialism. In 1910, a plot to assassinate Meiji was uncovered; a police roundup ensued, and twelve were hanged, including the anarchist Kotoku Shusui, who was accused of inspiring the plot through his writings.

Under Meiji's son Taishō, Japan joined the Allies in World War I, declaring war on Germany in 1914 and seizing German territory in China. After the war ended in 1918, the League of Nations awarded Japan the former German colonies of Palau, the Marianas, and the Caroline and Marshall Islands. During the so-called Taishō Peace, the Japanese economy grew, and the country prospered.

After Taishō's death in 1926, Hirohito (posthumously, Shōwa) became emperor. When the Great Depression began in 1930, Japan's military leaders advocated expanding the nation's territory to grow the economy. In 1931, while China was embroiled in a civil war between the Nationalists and Communists, the Japanese army dynamited a railroad in Mukden, then used the incident as a pretext to take control of Manchuria.

In 1934, Japan declared China off-limits to the West, a policy modeled on America's Monroe Doctrine, which declared the Americas off-limits to Europe. As part of its so-called East Asian Co-Prosperity Sphere, Japan hoped to rule China one day. In 1937, the Japanese military pushed the Nationalist government to the interior and occupied eastern China. In 1939, Japan turned north against the Soviet Union, as Russia was called after its 1922 Communist Revolution. After losing a battle at Khalkhin Gol, Mongolia, Japan signed a neutrality pact with the Soviet Union in 1941. By 1941, Japan had occupied the French colony of Indochina, with the permission of the Vichy regime, a puppet government put in place by Hitler after Germany occupied France.

Opposed to the Japanese expansion in China and Indochina, the US embargoed scrap iron and steel exports to Japan in 1940, and the following year froze Japanese assets in the US and cut off oil exports. The British and Dutch followed the US lead, with the Dutch stopping oil exports to Japan from its colony of Indonesia. Japan offered to withdraw from Indochina in exchange for American oil, but America wanted Japan to withdraw from China as well.

Desperate for oil and other resources, Japan expanded its East Asian Co-Prosperity Sphere southward. While European forces were engaged in fighting Hitler's Germany, Japan seized the Dutch colony of Indonesia and its oil fields, and the British colony of Malaya, with its rubber plantations and tin mines; it also occupied Hong Kong. To create a buffer on its eastern flank, it took the Bismarck Archipelago, which was under Australian control, then attacked the US naval base at Pearl Harbor and captured the Philippines, Guam, and Wake Island.

The surprise attack on Pearl Harbor by 353 Japanese aircraft from six aircraft carriers damaged or destroyed 188 airplanes and sixteen ships and killed 2,403 (sixty-eight of them civilian). Bombing and torpedoing American warships was the height of glory for the militarists who believed that Japan had been abused by the West for almost a century, ever since Perry's "black ships" had forced their way into the sacred homeland. In the end, though, like Hideyoshi Toyotomi's sixteenth century dream of conquering the Joseon Kingdom on the Korean Peninsula and Ming China, the militarists' dream of defeating America and ruling Asia turned out to be a mud-boat enterprise.

Fear and hysteria after the attack on Pearl Harbor resulted in the incarceration of the 120,000 of Japanese ancestry living on the West Coast of America, including nisei, who were US citizens. The assumption was that everyone of Japanese ancestry was a potential spy or saboteur. Two of my dad's sisters, living on the West Coast, the younger one to attend college, were interned at the Relocation Center in Arizona.

In Hawai'i, the fear was less pervasive. Although prejudice against the Japanese persisted, it didn't prevail, as the Japanese immigrants and their children were generally viewed as loyal to America and essential to the island work force. About 1,200 identified before the war as likely loyal to Japan (mainly issei Buddhist and Shintō priests, Japanese school officials, newspaper editors, and community leaders and businessmen with close ties to Japan, like my mom's father, were arrested and sent to mainland internment camps administered by the US army and Justice Department. An internment camp built for 3,000 at Honouliuli, O'ahu, held, at its peak 320, mainly nisei (Niiya).

Many of the nisei volunteered to fight for America, including the West Coast nisei who were interned along with their families. The nisei served on the battlefield and, like one of my mother's brothers, in the Military Intelligence Service. While friction developed between the issei and nisei loyal to America and those loyal to Japan, the nisei service for America was in keeping with Japanese beliefs and values: the imperial government had encouraged the Japanese settled abroad to be loyal to the countries in which they were living.

Dad was drafted into the US army in 1945. In my talk with her, grandma remembered the party given for her first son before he left for basic training in Alabama. It was a tradition in Japan to celebrate a son's induction into the army because it was an honor to serve the country; passing the army physical exam was also an honor, because it was evidence that a person was healthy and strong. But the war ended before dad was sent into combat. Instead, he went to Japan with the American Occupation force, assigned to do construction work as a private in the army's Quartermaster's Corps. My favorite photo of him shows him as a twenty-year-old in a yukata fastened with an army belt, with Mt. Nantai in Nikkō behind him.

Before dying from lung cancer in May 1970, dad told mom that he wanted her to take us three kids to visit the ancestral homeland. After his stint in the army, he had visited Japan a couple of times for his company (RCA), but never expressed any interest in taking us there, so when mom mentioned his bequest, I was surprised. That fall semester, in preparation for the journey, I took two courses, in Japanese history and language, at the University of Hawai'i—my first formal education about Japan and its language since Japanese school in the mid-1950s.

We landed at Haneda Airport in Tōkyō at night, on Christmas Eve. Having grown up in multiethnic Hawai'i, I was struck by the crowd with only Japanese faces as we exited immigration. We flew to Hiroshima the next day, where Hilo grandma's brother Kiyoshi met us and put us in a taxi to meet the relatives at a family dinner in a small town about thirty miles away. After a night and day visiting the homes of the Hilo side of the family, we took a taxi to Hiroshima city, where we stayed a couple of nights at the Grand Hotel (which wasn't grand). One of my dad's cousins drove us to Tomomura, the Kawaharada hometown. In both towns, we visited family graves and family shrines. In Tomomura, we had lunch with one of Maui grandma's brothers and also went to Sennen-ji, the Buddhist temple where the family was registered, a practice established during the Edo Period (1603–1868) to keep track of and control the population and prevent Christianity from spreading. We also visited Suwa Jinja, the family shrine.

The winter weather was cold and cloudy, which made the city feel drab and dingy. Eichi, a cousin, took us to the Mazda automobile manufacturing plant, where he worked. We watched a morning exercise session for employees. That night, he took my brother and me on a night tour of the city—a pachinko parlor, a bar, a bathhouse, and a late night snack at an oden stand. I remember drunken men standing on a downtown avenue pissing into the gutter. Eichi let me drive his Mazda subcompact, the smallest car I had ever been in, with its steering wheel on the right. What struck me as odd was not driving on the left side of the road, but the way drivers ignored traffic lanes and squeezed through any openings to get ahead.

In 2006, thirty-six years after that first visit, I went back to Hiroshima with Karen. The city was beautiful. The clear November sky was bright blue during the two days we were there, and the slow-moving rivers mirrored the sky. Hiroshima is a city of rivers. The Ōta River flows south from the Chūgoku Mountains and divides into five branches in the city's delta before entering the Inland Sea. During Japan's post-war "economic miracle" in the 1970s and 1980s, the city had been modernized and looked reborn.

Driving across the Aioi Bridge, I had a flashback of driving over it in

Aioi Bridge, where the Ōta River branches into the Motoyasu and Hon Rivers

Eichi's Mazda. The traffic was more organized now, with drivers observing lane markings.

The distinctive T-shaped bridge connects three points of land where the Ōta branches into the Hon and Motoyasu Rivers. I learned later that it was in the airman's bombsight when the atomic bomb was dropped, exploding 1,900 feet overhead. Built in 1932, the bridge buckled but survived the blast. In 1983 a new bridge replaced the original. Just downstream from it, on the east bank of the Motoyasu River is the gutted ruins of the Industrial Promotion Hall, the so-called A-Bomb Dome. Early one summer morning in 2009, on my third visit to Hiroshima, we walked across the Aioi Bridge to the Peace Bell. A middle-aged man and a young woman were sitting on separate park benches alone, quietly staring across the river at the ruins.

I asked mom once whether any of her family died in the bombing. She said no, because they lived outside of the city, over twenty miles away from the area targeted by the bomb. Dad's family lived only five miles away, but Tomomura was protected from the blast by hills. One of Maui grandma's nieces, however, attending school in the city, was killed.

Downstream from the A-Bomb Dome, on the opposite bank, is the Peace Memorial Museum and Park. In 2006, when I saw the long low building in the middle of an open plaza, I recognized its profile from thirty-six years earlier. The museum exhibits, like the city, had been modernized, but the photo of the shadow of a human body burned onto a sidewalk, the body having evaporated

A-Bomb Dome, Hiroshima

in the intense heat, was still on display; so was a piece of keloidal skin, like some ancient reptile's hide. (The following definition of "keloid" is from Ōe, *Hiroshima*, 185–186: "*Keloid* describes an overgrowth of scar tissue on the wound surface during the reparative process following thermal burn. ... In this condition the tissue forms, on the skin surface, an irregularly shaped protrusion which resembles the shell and legs of a crab.")

When I first visited the museum, the atomic bombings of Hiroshima and Nagasaki seemed like ancient history, even though they had occurred only twenty-five years earlier and just six years before I was born. I hadn't read much about the bombings and accepted the simple explanation for them: they were payback for Pearl Harbor and had to be done to end the war and save lives. I learned later, however, that the morality of the bombings is still being debated. Some argue that the Japanese surrender was imminent, so the thousands of civilians who died or suffered from the bombings were unnecessary casualties. Some argue that the America deliberately prolonged the surrender negotiations so that it could test its new weapons of mass destruction (WMDs) in war. Others believe that America used the bomb so it could end the war before the Soviets invaded Japan from the north and could claim territory after the surrender.

The argument that the bombing was needed to end the war and save lives is supported by the surrender speech, in which the emperor cites "the new and most cruel bomb" as a reason for the surrender, in hopes of saving his nation from further attack that "would result in an ultimate collapse and obliteration of the Japanese nation, … [and] also … lead to the total extinction of human civilization."

Some humanitarians argue, however, that WMDs shouldn't be used in war under any circumstances because the destruction isn't limited to military installations and personnel. The area in Hiroshima where the first atomic bomb exploded included the headquarters of the Fifth Division of the Imperial Army, but also civilian neighborhoods. Of the estimated 150,000 deaths, 100,000 were civilians.

If we define terrorism as violence that disregards non-combatants in order to instill fear and demoralize an enemy in a conflict, then the atomic bombings were acts of terrorism. During World War II, the armed forces on both sides resorted to terrorism. The Japanese inflicted civilian casualties in the bombings of Shanghai, Nanking, Chongqing, and other Chinese cities, and the Germans did the same when they bombed London, Coventry, and Liverpool; the Allied forces retaliated with the air raids on German and Japanese cities.

Civilian deaths ran into the millions. In Asia, the most infamous case of terrorism was Japan's bloody assault on Nanking.

Earlier in the twentieth century, with the development of warplanes capable of bombing, the British had pioneered terroristic aerial assaults in Africa, the Middle East, and South Asia:

> Hardly a page goes by [in *Human Smoke*] without [Nicholson] Baker selecting a report of the British bombing of Iraq or India, or Sudan, in some colonial punitive expedition. And this, it becomes clear, is a curtain-raiser for the concept of "area bombing" and Hamburg and Dresden, with all restraint on the inflicting of civilian casualties thrown to the wind. (Hitchens 670)

As casualties mounted in World War II, the Allies used their superior air power to terrorize Germany and Japan into surrender. Before dropping the two atomic bombs, the US Air Force firebombed sixty-seven Japanese cities, from Kagoshima in southern Kyūshū to Aomori in northern Honshū. The strategy was to "bring overwhelming pressure on [Japan] to surrender or to reduce her capability of resisting invasion … [by destroying] the basic economic and social fabric of the country" (Selden).

To address protests by American humanitarians against bombing civilians, the US Air Force dropped flyers warning non-combatants to leave the cities for their own safety; anyone who remained would be at risk. But no flyers were dropped to warn civilians in Hiroshima, or later, Nagasaki, before the atomic bomb attacks.

While the atomic bombings are more widely known, the firebombings of cities in Japan caused more damage and deaths—over 500,000 deaths, mainly civilian. In the firestorm following a night bombing raid on Tōkyō on March 9, 1945, 100,000 people were killed, more than the estimated 80,000 deaths in the atomic bombing of Nagasaki. The firestorm spread over fifteen square miles and left a million people homeless. By the end of the war, half of Tōkyō had been obliterated. Smaller industrial cities, like Tōyama, on the Sea of Japan coast, were almost completely demolished.

General Tasuku Okada, who commanded the Japanese army in Nagoya, declared that downed and captured US airmen who had killed civilians during bombing raids were war criminals under international law. He ordered them beheaded. After the war, he was tried in an American military court and accepted responsibility for the executions. He was hanged.

Firebombing is most deadly when used on dense neighborhoods of wooden houses and buildings, as in Tōkyō. A police cameraman describes the inferno on the night of the March 9th bombing:

> … rivers of fire … flaming pieces of furniture exploding in the heat, while the people themselves blazed like "matchsticks" as their wood and paper homes exploded in flames. Under the wind and the gigantic breath of the fire, immense incandescent vortices rose in a number of places, swirling, flattening, sucking whole blocks of houses into their maelstrom of fire. (Qtd. in Selden)

After the war, in its assessment of the effectiveness of its campaign of terror against Japan, the US government provided a technical description of the Tōkyō firestorm:

> The chief characteristic of the conflagration … was the presence of a fire front, an extended wall of fire moving to leeward, preceded by a mass of pre-heated, turbid, burning vapors…. The 28-mile-per-hour wind, measured a mile from the fire, increased to an estimated 55 miles at the perimeter, and probably more within. An extended fire swept over 15 square miles in 6 hours …. The area of the fire was nearly 100 percent burned; no structure or its contents escaped damage. (Qtd. in Selden)

An American B-29 pilot described the conflagration from the air. Unlike in drone warfare today, a pilot was overhead to inhale the stench of death:

> Suddenly, way off at about 2 o'clock, I saw a glow on the horizon like the sun rising or maybe the moon. The whole city of Tokyo was below

us stretching from wingtip to wingtip, ablaze in one enormous fire with yet more fountains of flame pouring down from the B-29s. The black smoke billowed up thousands of feet, causing powerful thermal currents that buffeted our plane severely, bringing with it the horrible smell of burning flesh. (Thomas)

Ōe reports that at least one US airman involved in the bombing suffered from guilt after the war:

The American pilot who piloted the weather observation plane that flew ahead of the B-29 carrying the atomic bomb [...] was arrested twelve years later for raiding two post offices in Texas. He was found "not guilty by reason of mental derangement." A psychiatrist of the U.S. Veterans Administration testified that his mental disorder was rooted in a sense of guilt toward Hiroshima. (*Hiroshima* 154)

But the pilot and crew of the B-29 *Enola Gay*, which dropped the bomb on Hiroshima, were publicly hailed as American heroes who ended the war. They became celebrities after the war, and autographed photos of the plane and the crew are sold as war memorabilia at auctions and pawn shops today.

Folktales like the ones about the pain inflicted on sparrow and tanuki prepare children for the cruelty we can expect from the enraged, but not for the horror of modern warfare. During the 1943 firebombing of Hamburg (the so-called Hiroshima of Germany), a firestorm ravaged the city, and 40,000, mainly civilians, were killed in one night. An eye-witness describes the corpses:

Some, the obvious victims of exploding bombs, had been terribly torn and dismembered. Fire or heat had killed many more. Most were lying face-down. The flames had shorn their hair and clothes, seared and swollen their buttocks, split their skin and raised their hips a few inches off the ground. Though unmistakably human, they looked like huge bratwursts. The smell of burnt flesh wrenched our stomachs and made us want to cry, but we hadn't enough water in us for tears or throwing up. Instead, I clasped Mother and buried my face in her dress. (Ingram 132)

Some of the burn victims ended up in the Eilbek Canal to escape the firestorm: "Some had faces as swollen and red as Chinese lanterns: their heads had been cooked while their bodies had been under water. Piteous moans, whimpering, and cries of anguish rose from the canal." The ones who had phosphorus burns were in a cruel predicament: "Those still in the canal had discovered that the phosphorus became inactive when it was immersed, but if they left the water it would start burning again as fiercely as before" (133).

One woman reports that Hiroshima A-bomb victims also took refuge in water, as if it could soothe their burns, wash away their injuries or pain, or restore their bodies to health; or perhaps they merely wanted to drown:

> Countless people were struggling to get to the stream under the bridge. I could not distinguish men from women. Their faces were swollen and gray; their hair stood on end. Then, raising both hands skyward and making soundless groans, they all began jumping into the river as though competing with one another. (Ōe, *Notes* 176)

A young Hiroshima woman recalled the aftermath:

> ... some low, dark figures seemed to be sitting in a row .... I could hardly tell man from woman or child, nor could I distinguish their ages. They were all but nude, sitting in a line; and their faces and bodies had swelled up and turned brown .... One had already become blind. Then I noticed a baby on someone's knee; the skin of its back was hanging down, as if a rotten, reddish loquat had been peeled off all around. (Ōe, *Notes* 176–177)

Radiation effects extended beyond the initial blast. Ōe recalls that a clothier from his village on Shikoku, across the Inland Sea from Hiroshima, went looking for his daughter after the pika-don (flash-bang). She had been conscripted to work in a factory in Hiroshima. He never found her. After returning home, he died "an agonizing death" from radiation exposure ("The Day the Emperor Spoke"). Others survived and continued to suffer from physical and psychiatric ailments.

Ōe reports on the research after the war to determine the long-term effects of the A-bomb radiation. The evidence indicates a higher rate of leukemia in bomb victims than in the general population. Other effects, like general sickness, miscarriages, birth defects, depression and other psychiatric disorders, and suicides, while perhaps linked, are harder to attribute with scientific evidence to the bombing ("Chapter 6: An Authentic Man, December 1964," in *Hiroshima*).

But human beings and nature are resilient. The atomic attack didn't bring about "the total extinction of human civilization," as Hirohito feared in his surrender speech. After the attacks on Hiroshima and Nagasaki, the dead were respectfully buried, the injured were treated, and the cities were rebuilt. One woman remembers, "they told us no plants or trees would grow in Hiroshima for ten to fifteen years. ... But the next year the grass grew just the same and the trees bore leaves again" (Booth 210). Ōe presents a more ominous possibility:

> … a certain prophetic voice said that no grass would grow in Hiroshima's soil for seventy-five years. … The prophecy soon proved false when late summer rains washed the wasted land and urged it to new growth. But was not true damage done at a deeper level? I remember the strong physical nausea I felt when through a microscope, I saw the magnified leaf cells of a specimen of *Veronica persica Poir*; the cells were slightly crooked in an unspeakably ugly way. I wonder whether all plants that now grow green in Hiroshima may not have received the same fatal damage. (*Hiroshima* 126)

But Ōe can't be sure that plants, animals, and people had "damage done at a deeper level"; he concludes that, in any case, people need to "believe in the green grass if it sprouts from the scorched earth" (126).

On the grounds of Hiroshima Castle, near ground zero, are two trees that survived the bomb—a eucalyptus and a willow. In late fall, their leafless aged and gnarled trunks and boughs appear to be in agony; but in summer, the trees are leafy green. The wooden castle that was destroyed in the blast was replaced in 1958 by a replica made out of concrete. Strolling around the castle park near ground zero, not knowing the history of the bombing, a visitor wouldn't know that a horrific and tragic event had ever occurred in the area.

While America opposes the spread of nuclear weapons, it has never offered to give up its own arsenal or ban their use. Its armed forces handbooks on the rules of war state that

> [t]here is at present no rule of international law expressly prohibiting States from the use of nuclear weapons in warfare. In the absence of express prohibition, the use of such weapons against enemy combatants and other military objectives is permitted. (Scarry 255)

Not that a law expressly prohibiting the use of WMDs would or could prevent their use. The fact that international law prohibits torture didn't prevent American agents from torturing enemies in its War on Terror.

When push comes to shove, and shoves become punches and kicks, out come the stones, knives, spears, swords, arrows, guns, cannons, tanks, and warplanes, and now, chemical, biological, and nuclear weapons. Prime Minister Eisaku Satō, who won the Nobel Peace Prize in 1974 for his support of Japan's post-war non-nuclear policy, privately asked American Defense Secretary Robert McNamara in 1965 to consider the use of nuclear weapons against China, should China attack Japan.

If Japan had developed an atomic bomb before America, it would have used it. Toward the end of the war, Japan was developing germ agents that it hoped to float to America in paper balloons to avoid detection by radar. High school girls in Gifu, a city known for manufacturing paper lanterns and umbrellas, were set to making the balloons. But the development of an effective germ weapon failed, so instead, the balloons were loaded with incendiary bombs and released in 1944 and 1945. Thirty-six landings in America were reported, and six people (five children and an adult) were killed in Oregon when they tried to move one of the balloons.

Before the war, the area south of ground zero was a business and entertainment district and also housed lumberyards and temples and shrines in the neighborhoods of Nakajima-Honmachi, Tenjin-machi, Motoyanagi-machi, and Nakajima-Shinmachi. The Peace Memorial Museum and Park occupies the land where these neighborhoods once stood, wiped out, along with the headquarters of the Fifth Division and the Second General Army, which was established in 1945 to defend the homeland from an invasion from the southwest.

Today, a citizens' group is interviewing old folks who once lived or shopped in the area and using computers to recreate in virtual reality the neighborhoods that were destroyed in the blast. One member was motivated to join the project after hearing a foreign journalist comment that at least atomic bombing was humanely done because the American military had targeted a park.

After the war, America imposed a pacifist constitution on Japan, prohibiting it from developing or acquiring nuclear weapons or raising an army except for defensive purposes. Since then, there have been discussions in Japan about changing the constitution to allow Japan to rearm, with calls from nationalists to revive bushidō (way of the warrior); but the majority of politicians and people continue to support the pacifist stance. So another consolation of atomic bomb attacks might be that more people would see peaceful coexistence, if not outright cooperation, as a way forward.

In 2004, I published an account of our 1970 Hiroshima Christmas dinner, with Hilo grandma's two sisters, Kosami and Ayame, and Kosami's two daughters and two granddaughters: we sat on the floor around a large table next to the kitchen, our feet warmed by a fire in a pit built into the floor under the table. There was a cozy feeling of family. Tired from travel, we went to bed early, bundled up in futon on the tatami mats of a second-story room. I got up early the next morning, just before sunrise, and slid open the shōji window to look outside. I felt like I was inside a landscape from one of the Japanese folktales I had read as a kid. The narrow streets of the hillside town were still dark, and the tile roofs, the pine and cedar trees, and the rice fields beyond were covered with snow. A river ran through the fields.

After Karen and I began traveling in Japan in 2004, I became curious about whether I could find that house where I spent my first night in Hiroshima. My mother referred to the town as Mukaihara. In fall 2006, driving from Hiroshima to Matsue, we stopped in Mukaihara-machi to look around. Where was the house overlooking the rice fields and river? Where was the family cemetery we visited the next morning? Where was Ayame's house, by a river, where we were driven the next day for lunch? Where was the family shrine on a hilltop nearby, up a stone stairway?

Mukaihara and its surroundings didn't look familiar; it wasn't the town where I spent Christmas in 1970. We ate at a ramen restaurant, then continued north toward Matsue on Route 37. I thought I might recognize a town along the way, but didn't. In the summer of 2009, after visiting Hiroshima again, we drove to Mukaihara, and this time headed south toward Hiroshima airport on Route 29, the way my family must have come by taxi in 1970. Again, nothing looked familiar. (The afternoon taxi ride, which took an hour and a half or so, remains vague in memory: dusky hills, rice fields, farms, and clusters of houses. Night had fallen by the time we reached our destination, with a light snow falling.)

In 2010, I discovered from immigration documents that Hilo grandma was not from Mukaihara, but from Gōnomura, a village on the Gōnokawa (Gō River), just four miles northwest of Mukaihara station, but in a neighboring river valley. I searched Google Maps for shrines in Gōnomura and found a photo of Hokori-no-Miya, whose front steps, porch, and doors and the tiled roof looked like those of the shrine in a dark, faded color photo I took in 1970. In spring 2011, we drove to the shrine; it was raining. The torii, the stone stairway, the shrine, and the hilltop view of the Gō River came back to me, as if in a dream. The shrine had been restored and looked new.

I thought that the house where we had Christmas dinner and where I experienced my first snowfall must be in nearby Akitakata, so we went there and drove up and down its hillside streets; but nothing looked familiar. Had the town changed that much? Could it have burned down and been rebuilt? I felt like Urashima-tarō, the fisherman of folklore who lived in an undersea palace with a princess with whom he had fallen in love. He returned to visit his mother after what he thought was three years, but he couldn't find his house:

There was no house for him to find;
When he sought his village,
There was no village anywhere.

In the rain, at the torii of Hokori-no-Miya, Gōnomura (Photo: Karen Ono)

"How strange!" he thought,
And wondered thereupon
"In the three years
Since the day I left my home
How could the house
Have vanished, the fence be gone?"

Under the spell of the princess, Urashima had lived three hundred years in her palace. Back in this world, everything had changed. His skin wrinkled, his hair grew white, and he passed away (Cranston 144–149, 332–336).

A Hiroshima story tells of an encounter between Seikichi, the young owner of a rice shop, and an enkō (or kappa), an odd frog-faced, shape-shifting water sprite said to drown its victims. On a moonlit summer night, the enkō takes the shape of an old woman and approaches Seikichi on the bank of the Enkō River. She talks about her girlhood and her love for a young man named Seikichi. As she speaks, she turns into a beautiful young girl, puts her arm around Seikichi's waist, and reaches for his hand. But before she can drag him into the river, someone shouts from the road, "There's an enkō!" It dives into the river without Seikichi and disappears ("Kappa").

Memories, beautiful or painful, beckon us to drown in the past; but luckily, the present calls to us, and the past leaps back into the river of time. From Hokori-no-Miya, I knew where Ayame's house was; we had walked from there to the shrine with Eichi (Ayame's son) along Route 54. From another photo I took in 1970, I recognized the bridge over the Gō River behind the house. I could have knocked on the door to ask if anyone recalled a visit by relatives from Hawai'i over four decades earlier.

But a century had passed since Hilo grandma left her family in Gōnomura to come to Hawai'i as a picture bride. When I first visited her hometown, she was still alive, and mom was with us, able to converse with her mother's family because she could speak and understand Japanese. My Japanese is so poor, I avoid asking questions in Japanese, knowing that the answers will be a stream of syllables too slippery for me to grasp. I wouldn't be able to understand the stories told by whoever was living in Ayame's house.[3]

My connection to family in Japan, except in memory, was gone. But at least I had finally found the Gōnomura shrine and the river that ran through grandma's childhood. Taking my bearings from them, we headed for Hiroshima by the same route, through Kaké town, my family had traveled four decades earlier.[4]

Gō River, Hiroshima

NOTES

1. Gōnomura is the old name for Yoshida-chō, in Takata-gun, Hiroshima-ken. Six towns in Takata-gun, including Yoshida, merged to form Akitakata city in 2004.

2. Just before his 1881 visit to Japan and his proposal of an Asiatic league

headed by Meiji, Kalākaua envisioned "gathering all the cognate races of the Islands of the Pacific into a great Polynesian Confederacy, over which he [would] reign" (Kuykendall 311). Hawai'i, after all, was "the most advanced nation in Polynesia, just as Japan was the most advanced nation in Asia. The confederation, which was to include Sāmoa, Tonga, and the Cook Islands, would oppose annexation of the Pacific islands by foreign powers. Kalākaua dispatched an embassy to Sāmoa in 1887; but America, Great Britain, and Germany disapproved of the initiative, so although the Sāmoan king signed the articles brought by Kalākaua's envoy, the embassy was recalled to Hawai'i in the summer of 1887, and the confederation was never realized (See Chapter 12. "Hawaii Seeks Leadership of Pacific Islands," Kuykendall 305–339).

3. On our 2011 trip, after Hiroshima, Karen and I went to Ōshima, in Yamaguchi, to the Museum of Japanese Emigration to Hawaii, to find out where her paternal grandfather, Kichinojo Ōno (1872–1943) came from. In the museum data base, with the help of the museum guide, we found that Kichinojo was from Heigun, an island south of Ōshima, and emigrated to Hawai'i with the last group of government-sponsored contract laborers in 1894, with his wife, Ima Oyama (1884–1953), from Hiroshima. We also met with a distant cousin of Karen's, along with her husband and her daughter, from Yanai, Yamaguchi.

4. In summer 2009, Karen and I drove to the Kawaharada hometown of Tomomura to look for the places I visited on my first trip to Hiroshima in 1970—Sennen-ji (the Buddhist temple where the family is registered), Suwa Jinja (the family shrine), and the family graves. We found Sennen-ji, near the Tomo-chuo stop of the elevated electric train, which was built after I first went to Tomomura in 1970. The front gate to the temple grounds looked as it did in a photo I took of it thirty-nine years earlier, but both the gate and the temple had been restored. In front of the temple was a statue of Shinran, the founder of the Jōdo Shinshū sect of Buddhism.

Tomomura was no longer a small farming village with dusty roads; it was a modern suburb of Hiroshima, just north of the junction of the Hiroshima and Sanyō Expressways. The wide main street of Tomomura was lined with new buildings. The area south of the temple looked familiar, so we drove through it looking for the family shrine and graves, but nothing looked familiar. However, I recently discovered via Google Maps that Suwa Jinja is located less than 900 feet to the west of Sennen-ji; we had driven past it in 2009. Looking at the images of the shrine on Google Street View, I recognized it; it looks as it did in 1970, but restored. I didn't see it while driving past it because it's no longer on the side of a dirt road lined by tall trees, but atop a stone embankment along a paved road cut into a hillside, with a small subdivision of Western-style houses

Left: In 1970, my older brother Michael stands in front of Suwa Shrine, on a dirt road lined with trees. Right: The shrine over forty years later above a street through a sub-division of modern two-story houses.

around it. As the poet Bashō wrote in the seventeenth century:

> … mountains crumble, rivers disappear, roads are altered, stones are buried beneath the earth, trees age and are replaced by saplings. Time passes and the world changes, traces of the past uncertain. (*Oku no Hosomichi*)

The kami worshipped at Suwa Jinja is Takeminakata, a son of the kami Ōkuninushi. The shrine is a branch of the Suwa network headquartered at four shrines around Lake Suwa in Nagano Prefecture ("Suwa Shinkō," *Encyclopedia of Shintō*). The exact date of Tomomura shrine's founding is unknown, but it was sometime during the period when the Takeda clan ruled Aki Province (western Hiroshima), from the late twelfth century to 1541.

Sources

Booth, Alan. *Road to Sata: A 2000-Mile Walk Through Japan.* Tōkyō: Kodansha, 1985.

Burton, Jeffery F., Mary M. Farrell, Florence B. Lord, and Richard W. Lord. *Confinement and Ethnicity: An Overview of World War II Japanese American Relocation Sites.* National Park Service, 2000. Web.

Cranston, Edwin A. *A Waka Anthology, Vol. One: The Gem Glistening Cup.* Stanford: Stanford UP, 1993.

Encyclopedia of Shintō. Kokugakuin U, Sept. 2008. Web.

Fuchs, Lawrence H. *Hawaii Pono: A Social History.* New York: Harcourt, 1961.

Hitchens, Christopher. "Just Give Peace a Chance?" *Arguably: Essays*. New York: Hatchette, 2011. 669–672.

Hoffman, Michael. "The Taisho Era: When modernity ruled Japan's masses." *Japan Times*. Japan Times, 29 July 2012. Web.

Honolulu, Hawaii, Passenger Lists, 1900–1953. *Ancestry*. Ancestry.com, 1997. Web.

Ingram, Marione. "Operation Gomorrah." *The Best American Essays*. Ed. David Foster Wallace. New York: Houghton, 2007. 123–136.

Kanahele, George. *Emma: Hawaii's Remarkable Queen*. Honolulu: U of Hawai'i, 1999.

"Kappa." Interpreters and Guides Association of Hiroshima, 2006–2010. Web.

Keene, Donald. *Emperor of Japan: Meiji and his World, 1852–1912*. New York: Columbia UP, 2002.

Kuykendall, Ralph. *The Hawaiian Kingdom, Volume III, 1974–1893. The Kalakaua Dynasty*. Honolulu: U of Hawai'i, 1967.

Miyazawa, Kenji. *Miyazawa Kenji: Selections*. Ed. Hiroaki Satō. Berkeley: U of California, 2007.

Niiya, Brian. "World War II Internment in Hawai'i." Japanese Cultural Center of Hawai'i, 4 June 2010. Web.

Nordyke, Eleanor C. and Y. Scott Matsumoto. "The Japanese in Hawaii: a historical and demographic perspective." *The Hawaiian Journal of History* 11 (1977): 162–174.

Odo, Franklin and Kazuko Sinoto. *A Pictorial History of the Japanese in Hawaii: 1885–1924*. Honolulu: Bishop Museum, 1985.

Ōe, Kenzaburō. "The Day the Emperor Spoke in a Human Voice." *New York Times*. New York Times, 7 May 1995. Web.

---. *Hiroshima Notes*. New York: Grove Press, 1965.

Okihiro, Gary Y. *Cane Fires: The Anti-Japanese Movement in Hawaii, 1865–1945*. Philadelphia: Temple U, 1991.

Quigg, Agnes. "Kalākaua's Hawaiian Studies Abroad Program." *The Hawaiian Journal of History* 22 (1988). 170–207.

Scarry, Elaine. "Rules of Engagement." *The Best American Essays*. Ed. David Foster Wallace. New York: Houghton, 2007. 234–258.

Selden, Mark. "A Forgotten Holocaust: US Bombing Strategy, the Destruction of Japanese Cities and the American Way of War from World War II to Iraq." *The Asia-Pacific Journal: Japan Focus*. 2 May 2007. Web.

Soga, Yasutaro. *Life Behind Barbed Wire: The World War II Interment Memoirs of a Hawai'i Issei*. Honolulu: U of Hawai'i. 2008.

Thomas, Evan. "Death in the Pacific." *New York Times*. New York Times, 30 Mar. 2008. Web.

Where Kami Alight

The worship of kami—deities venerated at thousands of Shintō shrines—was a mystery to me on my first shrine visit in the winter of 1970. We followed our cousin Eichi through a wooden torii and up a stone stairway to a building on a hill overlooking rice fields and a river in my grandmother's hometown of Gōnomura, Hiroshima. He stood before the steps, bowed, dropped a coin in the wooden offering box, clapped twice, remained silent in prayer, then clapped and bowed again. I walked up the steps to peer inside: no altar or image, just a dark room, unadorned except for framed prints of early twentieth-century warships.

My grandparents worshiped at Shintō shrines before emigrating to Hawai'i, but didn't bring the worship with them, so although there were shrines in Hawai'i, I never visited one while growing up.[1] My family belonged to the Jōdo Shinshū sect of Buddhism, which established its first temple in Hawai'i in 1889. Shinran (1173–1263), the founder of the sect, preached faith in Amida Buddha alone as the way to salvation. Our family went to Honpa Honganji, as the sect's temples are called, mainly for funeral and memorial services.

Hokori-no-Miya, Gōnomura, Hiroshima

After Buddhism was introduced in the sixth century, it became the dominant religion and incorporated Shintō into its beliefs and practices. By the eighth century, kami were worshipped as manifestations of buddhas and bodhisattvas. During the Meiji Period (1868–1912), however, the imperial government ordered a separation of the two religions, declaring Buddhism foreign and Shintō native. Under the slogan "keishin sūso" (reverence for kami, respect for ancestors), the government established Shintō belief as the basis of national unity. The emperor was divine, a descendant of Amaterasu, the sun goddess worshiped at Ise shrine. Shintō rituals and shrine visits were linked to patriotism and, after the nation's military aggressions in Asia began, to victory in war:

> The funeral of the Taishō emperor, the enthronement rites of the Shōwa emperor [1926], and the ritual rebuilding of the Ise shrines were all state rites and ceremonies intimately related to the idea of venerating the deities. They played their part in spreading that ideal throughout Japan. Shrine visits had now become established practice at primary school; there was a growing sense that refusal to visit a shrine disqualified one as a citizen of the imperial nation. This tendency was given added impetus when, with the outbreak of the so-called Manchurian incident in 1931, it became customary to pray for victory at shrines. (Sakamoto 285)

After Japan's defeat in World War II, the Supreme Commander for the Allied Powers (SCAP) that occupied Japan, Douglas MacArthur, abolished state-sponsored Shintō "to prevent recurrence of the perversion of Shinto theory and beliefs into militaristic and ultranationalistic propaganda designed to delude the Japanese people and lead them into wars of aggression" (SCAP memo). On New Year's Day, 1946, at the behest of MacArthur, Emperor Shōwa (Hirohito, r. 1926–1989), in a recorded radio speech, announced to the nation that the emperor was not akitsumi-kami (deity from the spiritual world). However, the emperor was allowed to continue serving as a symbol of the state and unity of the people, and the Imperial Family continued to worship Amaterasu as its ancestor at Ise shrine.

In 2004, while planning a trip to the ancient capitals of Kyōto and Nara, I read that visitors were welcomed at Ise shrine and that everyone of Japanese ancestry should go at least once in a lifetime. I had always assumed that only the Emperor and Imperial Family were allowed to go to the shrine. Also, because of its association with the militarism that led Japan into World War II, Shintō had a vaguely sinister aspect to me when I was growing up in the 1950s. In 2004, however, the war was half a century in the past, and I was returning

Location of places in "Where Kami Alight"

to Japan for the first time in thirty years, and I remembered the mystery of my first shrine visit in Gōnomura. I wanted to find out more about kami and Shintō, and the shrine to Amaterasu Ōmikami (Heavenly-Shining Great August Kami) seemed like best place to start. On our first full day, we drove from Nara to Ise, sixty miles to the east.

Ise shrine is located in a forest of hinoki (cypress) in the hills of Ise Bay. Originally, Amaterasu was worshipped at the palace in Nara, along with a kami named Yamato-no-Okuni-dama, but when pestilence broke out and over half the population died, Emperor Sujin (r. 97 BC–30 BC)[2] "dreaded ... the power of these two Gods" and "did not feel secure in their dwelling together, so he sent them to be worshipped separately elsewhere" (*Nihongi* 151). Princess Yamato-Hime-no-Mikoto was assigned to care for Amaterasu. She moved the kami to a shrine south of Nara, near Mt. Miwa. During the reign of Emperor Suinin (r. 29 BC–AD 70), the kami indicated she wanted to live at Ise, which had everything a kami needs to be happy—rice fields, fresh water (the Isuzu River flows through the shrine), forests, and, from the sea nearby, fish and salt. A shrine was erected there.

The shrine, officially called Kōtai Jingū (Imperial Grand Kami Shrine), is also referred to as Naikū (Inner Shrine). Four miles away is Gekū (Outer Shrine), dedicated to Toyouke-hime (Luxuriant-food-princess), a grand niece of Amaterasu assigned to make food offerings to her. At Gekū, Amaterasu is

The outer gate of Ise shrine, Mie, spring 2004

served two meals daily, in the morning and afternoon, traditional meal times. The food is cooked with sacred fire, started with a drill consisting of a loquat stick spun on a cypress board. Water comes from one of two sacred wells.

A twenty-foot-high torii marks the entrance to Naikū. We arrived on a cloudless spring morning and crossed Ujihashi, a 330-foot wooden bridge over the Isuzu River. The sun rising over the eastern hills shone through the torii. Before proceeding on the pathway to the Goshōden (main sanctuary), we washed our hands and rinsed our mouths at a stone basin with water for purification (temizuya); farther on, on the bank of the Isuzu River is the traditional site for purification. Cleanliness and purity, inner and outer, are at the heart of Shintō worship.

The immaculately kept gravel pathways shaded by towering hinoki led past halls and auxiliary shrines. In the morning, priests sweep the pathways and maiko (shrine maidens) wipe the verandas and steps.

Worshipers stop at the outer gate to thank Amaterasu for her blessings and to pray for the health of the emperor and the nation. The public is not permitted inside to visit the Goshōden, which houses Amaterasu's nigimitama, or "peaceful and calming spirit"; her aramitama, or "ferocious, rough, and violent spirit," which may appear "during times of war or natural disasters," is housed in a nearby sanctuary called Ara-matsuri-no-miya ("Nigimitama" and "Aramitama," *Encyclopedia of Shintō*). As we approached the outer gate, the morning breeze lifted its noren (hanging cloth) above elderly worshipers to reveal another gate within.

The Goshōden is constructed of unpainted hinoki, without nails. Raised on pillars, the rectangular building is thirty-five feet wide along the front and eighteen feet wide on its sides. The roof is thatched with kaya grass. At each end of the ridge pole, bargeboards crisscross and extend above the ridge line. The shrine is modeled after a grain storehouse. Wet-rice agriculture was brought to Japan by settlers from the Korean Peninsula during the Yayoi Period (300 BC–AD 250), and rice kami were eventually worshipped at or in village storehouses.

Robust rice production led to population growth and the political, economic, social, and cultural transformation of the archipelago under the Yamato state, founded by the first emperor, Jimmu, a great grandson of Amaterasu's grandson Ho-no-Ninigi.[3]

Twenty major ceremonies at Ise mark the annual cycle of rice production, with prayers for good weather in spring, offerings of thanks for a bountiful harvest in fall, and rituals to renew the spirit of rice in winter.

The Goshōden houses Yata-no-Kagami (Eight-sided mirror), which is said to have been bequeathed by Amaterasu to her grandson Ho-no-Ninigi before he descended to earth. ("Regard this mirror exactly as if it were our august spirit, and reverence it as if reverencing us." *Kojiki* 131.) The mirror is hidden from view. In 1889, Mōri Arinori, Minister of Education under Emperor Meiji, was severely wounded by a knife-wielding assailant who was enraged by a rumor that Mōri had failed to take off his shoes before entering the shrine and had peeked at the sacred mirror, using his cane to lift the cloth that hid it from his view. Mōri was a reformist from Satsuma (Kagoshima) who had studied in London and served as ambassador to America, China, and Britain and converted to Christianity. He was despised by traditionalists and nationalists for his advocacy of the English language, interracial marriages, and Western culture. After Mōri died from his wound, an official investigation concluded that the rumor of his sacrilege was false (Keene 423).

Naikū and Gekū are rebuilt every twenty years, and the two enshrined kami are moved to new dwellings on lots adjacent to the old ones in a rite called shikinen sengū (transferring the kami to a new shrine in a special ritual year):

> Building a new shrine … takes about eight years, and each stage of the construction is accompanied by a religious ceremony. The carpentry work is carried out by about one hundred men, the majority of whom are local carpenters who set aside their usual work for a privileged period of two to four years. … Although the plans exist for every structure,

the master carpenters must remember and pass on to apprentices their expert knowledge of how to put together the complex joints, using ancient and unfamiliar tools. ("Jingu Shrine in Ise")

Not only are the buildings reconstructed according to their original forms, but over a thousand sacred objects and apparel pieces are duplicated by contemporary artisans to traditional specifications. The main pillar of the old Naikū is used to restore the torii at the entrance to the shrine, and other pillars are distributed to shrines around Japan for their torii.

Shikinen sengū promotes both cultural and environmental preservation. Originally, trees from the 13,590-acre forest around the shrine were used in the reconstruction. Since 1391, due to deforestation, trees from the Kiso Mountains in Gifu and Aichi Prefectures have been used. In 1923 a reforestation program with a 200-year plan was established, so that trees from the shrine precinct could be harvested once again to rebuild the shrine. Around 10,000 trees are needed for the reconstruction, the largest four-and-a-half feet in diameter, equivalent to roughly 400 years of growth.

Restoring the dwelling of Amaterasu every twenty years is intended to keep her spirit (and the spirit of the nation she embodies) toko-waka, "forever young." The sixty-second rebuilding of Naikū was completed in 2013. We returned to Ise for a visit in spring 2014 to see the new shrine: fresh cypress wood and kaya made the Goshōden gate appeared miraculously reborn.

Akima writes, "the founding of the Grand Shrine of Ise was the most important factor in the creation of the myth of Amaterasu Ōmikami, and … marked an important step in the centralization of Japan under the Yamato leadership" (172–173). In the fifth or sixth century, the imperial court began sending princesses as priestesses to serve at Ise. The first shikinen sengū took place in 690, during the reign of Empress Jitō (r. 686–697), the first imperial head to visit the shrine, in 692.

Before Amaterasu became the main kami worshipped by the Imperial Family, prayers for the accession of emperors and empresses were addressed to two other kami associated with musubi, or "birth and growing": Takami-musubi-no-kami (High August Producing Kami) and Kami-musubi-no-kami (Divine August Producing Kami). These two kami were among the first to appear after the creation of Heaven and Earth. Takami-musubi-no-kami was recognized as the head of Shintō pantheon (Akima 175–176).

The two earliest historical texts in Japan, *Kojiki* and *Nihongi*, elevate Amaterasu to the head of the Shintō pantheon. The texts establish the Imperial Family as the rightful rulers of Ō-ya-shima-kuni (Country of the Eight Great Islands). The narratives are based on oral traditions, recorded in kanji-writing adapted from the Chinese. *Kojiki,* or *Records of Ancient Matters* (711), contains a single version of events. *Nihongi,* or *Chronicles of Japan,* also called *Nihonshoki* (720), provides variants for some events, from sources that include documents from Baekje, a kingdom on the Korean Peninsula once allied with Yamato.

The selection of a solar deity as the ancestress of the Imperial Family was influenced by Asian tradition: Matsumae remarks that "the royal families [of China and Korea] were believed to have been the direct descendants of the solar deity" (11). The sun has a universal presence, not limited to a single locale or region, like a river or a mountain (e.g., Mt. Fuji, which is also worshipped as a kami). The sun passes overhead daily, shining from horizon to horizon, and thus serves as a fitting symbol for an imperial house claiming to rule "all under heaven."

Two other characteristics make the sun a fitting symbol of a family whose role is to preserve the life and health of the nation: the sun also disappears at night, but is reborn every morning, eternally young; and the movement of the sun's rising and setting points along the horizon determines the annual cycle of death and rebirth in nature, its increasing warmth and light in spring and summer bringing forth bountiful harvests of rice.

While there were male and female sun kami, Matsumae believes that Amaterasu was originally a male sun kami named Amateru, worshipped by a fishing clan at Ise. ("Amaterasu" is the honorific form of "Amateru," "Shining in heaven," neither name gender specific.) There were shrines to Amateru in various places in Yamato, and also on Tsushima, an island lying between the northwest coast of Kyūshū and the southeastern tip of the Korean Peninsula (3).

Amateru was worshipped as a sacred pillar, which suggests a male fertility symbol, but also the axis mundi, or World Pillar, connecting heaven and earth. This pillar is represented by the central pillar of the Goshōden.

The choice of a kami from Ise as the imperial ancestress may have been influenced by the location of Ise, to the east of the capital in Nara, in the direction of the rising sun. Matsumae suggests that the Imperial Family also wanted an ancestral deity that no other family could claim, as it sought to elevate itself above the rest:

> there was no powerful nobility in [Ise] that had served this deity. If any powerful nobles such as the Kii Clan in the Hinokuma Shrine had served the deity of the Ise Shrine, the Yamato nobility would have found it difficult to regard this deity as their only ancestor. (10)

Matsumae cites Orikuchi's opinion on Amaterasu's gender change from male to female, asserting that the male kami began to be identified with his priestesses, after which "the male elements of this deity faded away while the female elements gradually increased" (7).

That Amaterasu was originally a priestess is supported by her association with silk weaving. Amaterasu is overseeing the weaving of garments when her brother Susa-no-ō breaks a hole in the roof and dumps a flayed colt through it (*Kojiki* 63–64, *Nihongi* 41). The role of a priestess was to serve as wife to a kami and to weave his garments as offerings. Matsumura notes that during the Daijō sai (the imperial accession ceremony) "divine garments woven from raw white silk were placed on the divine seat, while silk was also placed in the bamboo baskets located to either side of the seat" (Section 8. Rice and Silk).

That the imperial ancestress is associated with silk weaving suggests its importance to the Yamato court. Silk was produced since the Yayoi Period, but its production increased in both quality and quantity after new techniques were introduced from the Korean Peninsula in the fifth century. The improvements have been linked to the Hata family, "one of the most famous peninsular families to make the Eight Great Islands their home in the ancient period" (Farris 97). (The Hata are also said to have introduced new methods of brewing saké.) By the Asuka Period (538 -710), sericulture was a major source of wealth for the Imperial Family and the Yamato nobility.

A strange tale of marriage between a maid and a horse provides a link between the origin of silkworms and the flayed horse that Susa-no-ō dumps into Amaterasu's weaving hall:

> the story relates that "the horse and maid were of the same mind and love, and at last became united as husband and wife. When the horse's owner learned the awful truth, he killed the horse by hanging it from a mulberry tree. But when he skinned it, the hide wrapped itself around the young woman and flew away. The young woman appeared in a dream and said she had become a horse-headed silkworm, and that her parents should feed it mulberry leaves to raise it, then sell the silk to live on. And in this way, the horse and the young woman became the oshirasama who is the god of silkworms." (Matsumura Section 7. Silkworm Cultivation)

Matsumura summarizes a similar story from fourth-century China, noting that "the sinuous body of the silkworm was compared to that of a woman, while the head was thought to resemble that of a horse."

Before he dumps the horse into Amaterasu's weaving room, Susa-no-ō, like the horse's owner, flays it. In the uproar that follows, either Amaterasu

(*Nihongi* 41) or the weaving maids (*Kojiki* 64) are wounded in the genital(s) by the shuttle(s). Mortified, Amaterasu hides in a cave, symbolically dying, until she is called out ritually for rebirth, like the rising sun. The rebirth of the maid as a silkworm goddess after she is wrapped in the skin of her horse lover parallels Amaterasu's rebirth as sun goddess after Susa-no-ō dumps a flayed horse into her weaving room. Both the silkworm and the sun are reborn annually, in spring, following the short, cold, dark days of winter. On the first full moon of spring (1.15 by the lunar calendar), "silkworm goddesses were called out using imagery based upon the silkworm's ability to 'die' as it enters a cocoon only to reemerge as a transformed being capable of flight [i.e., a moth]" (Como xx). (Lunar calendar dates are given in two numbers, the first indicating one of the twelve annual moons and the second identifying one of thirty moon phases.)

The goddess Oshirasama is worshipped in Tōhoku (northern Honshū) as a kami of both sericulture and agriculture. The object of worship is made from a pair of mulberry sticks wrapped in cloth and topped with a human face or a horse's head. The first Oshirasama festival of the year is held on 1.16, the day after the first full moon of the year ("Oshirasama," *Encyclopedia of Shintō*; cf. Yanagita 42–43).

Akima believes that Amaterasu is a conflation of two female kami rather than a priestess transformed into a goddess. The two females are associated with male sun kami: (1) Sarume, a sea kami of Ise, is either a wife or sister of the sun kami Saruta-hiko; and (2) Yamato-toto-hime is the wife of Ōmononushi, the sun kami of Mt. Miwa, a small mountain south of Nara (141). Akima identifies the wife with Yamato-hime-no-Mikoto, the princess who transfers Amaterasu from the palace in Nara to Ise shrine.

As evidence that Amaterasu was once a sea kami, Akima states that "the mirror symbolizing Amaterasu at Ise was placed in a coffin-like container named mifune-shiro, or 'the boat substitute'" (141). The sky and the sea were closely affiliated in Japanese tradition, with the sun traveling west through the sky during the day and east under sea at night, reappearing each morning at the eastern horizon. According to Akima, in early Japanese, "the word 'ama' meant both the sea and the sky" (146).

As rice became the primary source of food, the new imperial ancestress was identified mainly with agriculture rather than fishing. Akima suggests that Amaterasu's loss of her association with the sea is reflected in the transfer of the shrine at Ise from near the seashore to an inland forest (169–171)—closer to the source of the Isuzu River, which feeds rice paddies along its banks. But the Imperial Family's control over the sea is asserted when Amaterasu's grandson Ho-no-Ninigi descends to rule on earth: Sarume, the sea kami of Ise, asks all things living in the sea to promise to "respectfully serve him" (*Kojiki* 137). (This episode suggests that Sarume is a separate kami, not absorbed into Amaterasu, as Akima suggests.)

Kojiki begins with the appearance of kami and the procreation of the Eight Great Islands, followed by (1) the birth of more kami, including Amaterasu and her brother Susa-no-ō; (2) a quarrel between Amaterasu and Susa-no-ō; (3) Susa-no-ō's descent to the Eight Great Islands and his good works in the province of Izumo, where he rules; (4) the unruliness of the land under Susa-no-ō's descendants and the appointment of Amaterasu's grandson Ho-no-Ninigi to rule the Eight Great Islands; and (5) the establishment of Yamato by Ho-no-Ninigi's great grandson Jimmu. *Kojiki* continues the story of the imperial line after Jimmu to Empress Suiko, the thirty-third imperial head (r. 592–628); *Nihongi* extends the record by eight generations, to Empress Jitō (r. 686–697).

The two narratives embody the principles and values of Shintō, whose rituals and prayers are aimed at managing the seasonal and generational flux of life and death, and fortune and misfortune, to ensure that good health and fortune prevails over suffering, illness, and death. The first kami appear self-generated in Takama-no-hara (Plain of High Heaven): seven emerge alone, including Takami-musubi-no-kami and Kami-musubi-no-kami, after which five pairs of older brothers and younger sisters appear. The last of the pairs, Izanagi-no-kami (male-who-invites kami) and Izanami-no-kami (female-who-invites kami) are assigned to make islands (*Kojiki* 17–21).

The couple descend to an island they create by stirring the waters with a spear, after which they procreate more islands. The first two births are "not good." The failures are attributed to a breach in protocol: the younger female, Izanami, speaks before the elder male, Izanagi. After the couple reverse their order of speaking, eight healthy islands are born, followed by six smaller ones. The episode establishes the priority of male and age in Yamato culture and Shintō tradition (21–29).

Izanagi and Izanami procreate a couple of dozen nature kami until a misfortune occurs: giving birth to the fire god Hi-no-kagu-tsuchi (Fire-shining elder," Kagutsuchi for short), Izanami's vagina is scorched, and the injury causes her death. From her vomit, feces, and urine more kami are born. Izanagi buries his sister and, in grief and anger, slays the fire kami from whose blood eight additional kami are born and from whose head, chest, belly, private parts, hands, and feet, eight mountain kami are born (29–40).

The grief-stricken Izanagi descends to Yomi (the underworld), where his sister has gone after her death, to ask her to return, as "the lands that I and thou made are not yet finished." She's honored by his request and goes back in to confer with the underworld kami, but warns her brother not to look at her, as she has eaten food in the underworld. Izanagi is impatient, however, and enters the palace with a torch made from the tooth of his comb. He sees his sister's putrefying corpse, full of maggots, and flees in horror (*Kojiki* 40–42).

Shamed, enraged, and vengeful, Izanami sends in pursuit the ugly female of Yomi and the eight thunder kami born from her decaying body. Near the opening to the world above, Izanagi picks three peaches and hurls them at the thunder kami, driving them back. (In Chinese tradition, peaches are believed to ward off harmful spirits. At an archaeological site associated with the Imperial Family in Nara, peach pits were found in abundance and are believed to be the remnants of peaches used in rituals.) Izanami follows in pursuit, but Izanagi reaches the exit from the underworld and blocks it with a huge rock. From behind the rock, Izanami vows to kill 1,000 of his offspring every day; he responds that 1,500 women will give birth every day, ensuring population growth (42–46).

The Shintō scholar-poet Motoori Norinaga (1730–1801) identifies Izanami's death with the origin of evil:

> Until [Izanagi and Izanami] produced the Fire God, there were only good things and no evil. As a result of giving birth to the Fire God, Izanami passed away, and evil began in the world. (*Poetics of Motoori Norinaga* 109–110)

By evil, Norinaga doesn't mean sin, but suffering and death; good, on the other hand, is whatever protects life, health, and well-being. Shintō is not so much a religion of morality as a set of practices and prayers to maintain the blessing and protection of kami with prayers and to propitiate angry kami to prevent them from harming the living. Every kami has both creative and destructive aspects, with a changeable character explained by the concept of ichirei shikon—one spirit with four tama, or souls:

1. aramitama (rough, violent, destructive, invasive soul)
2. nigimitama (calm, peaceful soul)
3. sakimitama (soul bringing blessings & prosperity in hunting & fishing)
4. kushimitama (wondrous soul, with mysterious powers of healing)

Each of the four souls may be manifested in a kami's actions. Norinaga sees sakimitama and kushimitama as aspects of nigimitama rather than as separate souls. Aramitama manifests itself when a kami is unhappy or angry; nigimitama may be restored through pacification rituals and proper worship (*Encyclopedia of Shintō*).

After escaping from Yomi, Izanagi washes off the pollution from his encounter with his sister's corpse: "So he went out to a plain [covered with] ahagi at a small river-mouth near Tachibana in Himuka in Tsukushi and purified and cleaned himself" (*Kojiki* 46–47; cf. *Nihongi* 26; ahagi is bush clover; Himuka is the old name for Miyazaki Prefecture; Tsukushi is the old name for Kyūshū island.) This act of water purification is re-enacted in the washing of hands and mouth at the temizuya at the entrance of a Shintō shrine.

As he removes his clothing and washes himself, Izanagi engenders twelve kami, then another fourteen, the last three being Amaterasu, from the washing of the left eye, and two brothers, Tsukiyomi-no-kami (Moon-night-possess-or Kami), from the washing of the right eye, and Take-haya-susa-no-ō-no-mikoto (Brave-swift-impetuous-male-augustness), from the washing of the nose. Amaterasu is assigned to rule the Plain of High Heaven; Tsukiyomi the Night; and Susa-no-ō the Sea Plains (Unabara; perhaps a reference to oversea colonies) (*Kojiki* 51–52).

Susa-no-ō is unhappy with his assignment, and his aramitama takes over: he cries and weeps, causing the green mountains to wither and the rivers and seas to dry up. He tells Izanagi that he wants to join his mother in Yomi. Before going there, however, he ascends to Heaven to bid his sister farewell. Her brother's intrusion into her domain arouses Amaterasu's aramitama: she "brandished and stuck her bow upright so that the top shook, ... stamped her feet into the hard ground up to her opposing thighs, kicking away [the earth] like rotten snow, and stood valiantly like unto a mighty man" (55).

Standing across from his sister on a bank of Ame-no-yasu-kaha (Tranquil River of Heaven), Susa-no-ō calms her by explaining he has come to bid her farewell and offers to prove his good intent by producing children with her. Amaterasu asks for her brother's sword and breaks it into fragments, chews them, blows them out, and from the mist of her breath produces three female kami. Susa-no-ō asks for his sister's jewels, chews them, blows them out, and produces five male kami. Amaterasu claims the five male children and gives Susa-no-ō the three daughters (55–59).

In a sudden fit, Susa-no-ō's aramitama emerges, and he starts destroying Amaterasu's rice fields and desecrating her property:

he broke down the divisions of the rice fields laid out by Amaterasu, filled up the [irrigation] ditches of her rice paddies, and moreover strew excrements in the palace where she partook of the great food [i.e., the ritual tasting of the first rice of the season]. ... As Amaterasu sat in her weaving-hall seeing to the weaving of the august garments of the Deities, he broke a hole in the top of the hall, and through it let fall a heavenly piebald horse, which he had flayed. (63–64)

Kojiki explains the destruction by describing Susa-no-ō as "impetuous with victory" (62) since, true to his word, he has produced children with his sister and gained three daughters in their contest of pledges (ukehi). According to *Nihongi*, Susa-no-ō destroys his sister's rice fields because he is jealous that they are productive "and never suffered even after continuous rain or drought," while his rice fields are in "barren places … [i]n the rains, the soil was swept away, and in drought, it was parched up" (48).

Amaterasu retreats into Ama no Iwaya (Rocky Cave of Heaven), blocks the entrance with a large boulder, and refuses to come out. The Plain of High Heaven and the Country of the Eight Great Islands turn dark, "eternal night" prevailing.

The sun's retreat into the heavenly cave has also been associated with the sun disappearing behind storm cloud; the coming of winter; and a solar eclipse or ash from a volcanic eruption blocking the sun, both omens of disaster. It also suggests Amaterasu, like the silkworm, wrapping herself in a cocoon.

The kami meet in the bed of the Tranquil River of Heaven to devise a plan to bring Amaterasu out. After divination with a stag shoulder blade and tree bark, they adorn a sakaki (a sacred evergreen) with a mirror fashioned from stones of the River of Heaven and iron from the Heavenly Metal Mountain; an eight-foot-long string of curved jewels; and pacificatory offerings of paper mulberry and hemp cloth (*Kojiki* 66–68).

Liturgies are recited, and Ame-no-uzume-no-mikoto (Heavenly Alarming-august-female), dancing on a sounding board, performs a comic striptease. Laughter erupts, and Amaterasu peers out of her cave to find out why they are rejoicing when the world is dark. Ame-no-uzume tells her that they are rejoicing because "there is a Deity more illustrious than Thine Augustness." The mirror is brought forth, and Amaterasu, peering at it, becomes "more and more astonished," and then is drawn by the hand from the cave and prevented from going back in (68–79).

Allegorically, the cave is a tomb/womb/cocoon. As tomb, the cave is equivalent to the underworld, and Amaterasu's retreat into the cave re-enacts Izanami's descent to the underworld after her death. But unlike Izanami, Amaterasu doesn't die; she is reborn, the tomb becoming a womb, and with her rebirth, she turns night into day again, winter into spring, and death into life; she is a moth emerging from a cocoon.[4]

The ritual actions for bringing Amaterasu out of the cave are the basis of

Ama-no-Yasukawara cave, associated with the Amaterasu myth, near Ama-no-Iwato Shrine, Takachiho, Miyazaki. See note 4.

Chinkon sai (Settling-of-the-spirit Ritual), a rite for pacifying the "restless spirit" of the imperial head, to prevent the spirit from leaving the body and bringing on death ("Chinkon sai," *Encyclopedia of Shintō*). The Chinkon sai was held annually on 11.22, the twenty-second day of the eleventh moon of the year, around winter solstice, when the spirit of the imperial head is at a point of departure.[5]

The ritual was conducted by shrine virgins/priestesses (mikannagi) and kagura dancers, or Sarume, who are descendants of Ame-no-uzume:

> a Sacred Maiden ... standing on top of an overturned tub taps it with a spear counting from one to ten, imitating the dance of the goddess Ame no Uzume in front of the Heavenly Rock-Cave. (Naumann 54–55)

Chinkon sai strengthens "the spirit-soul of the emperor before he performed the major rituals of Daijō sai and Niiname sai, to renew the world at the end of the year" (*Encyclopedia of Shintō*).

On 11.23, the day after the Chinkon sai, Niiname sai (Celebration of the First Tasting), a harvest festival, was held. At the palace, the imperial head

> partook of first fruits from the recent harvest in a shared meal with the deities and was thus revived as a new-born 'rice king' fully prepared for the new growing season. (Inoue et al. 41)

At the accession of a new imperial head, Daijō sai (Celebration of Great Tasting) replaced the Niiname sai for that year and marked the start of a new reign.

Today Niiname sai is celebrated on November 23 (11.23 on the Gregorian calendar) as a national holiday for labor and thanksgiving. The Daijō sai was performed in 1990 for Emperor Akihito, the one hundred twenty-fifth imperial head in succession from Jimmu. The details of the ceremony are kept secret, but the general belief is that the emperor re-enacts the descent of Amaterasu's grandson, Ho-no-Ninigi, to rule on earth, and "thus re-embodies Ninigi's imperial spirit" in the new head of state (Inoue et al. 33).

While traveling in eastern Kyūshū in 2006, to places associated with the story of Amaterasu and her descendants, we stopped on November 23 at Udo Shrine, located in a cave overlooking the sea on the Nichinan coast south of Miyazaki city. Rain and wind swirled around us and waves surged against the sea-sculpted rocks as we descended the stairs to the cave entrance. Sheltered from the storm outside, the cave was full of people celebrating the thanksgiving festival. The shrine had on display offerings of first "fruits": rice, saké, and oranges. A group of elderly men in suits and other worshipers sat on chairs facing the altar and stage. Soon priests dressed in ceremonial garb filed in. Chanting followed, along with flute, drum, and samisen music; children performed court dances.

Udo (Cormorant House) is said to be the location of the birth hut thatched with cormorant feathers, where the sea goddess Toyo-Tama-Hime (Luxuriant

Entrance to Udo Jinja, in a rainstorm, Miyazaki (Photo: Karen Ono)

Jewel Princess) gave birth to the father of the first emperor, Jimmu. The shrine is dedicated to the father. On the ceiling of the cave in back of the shrine are breast-like bulges called Ochichi-iwa (Breast Stone), said to be breasts Toyo-Tama-Hime left behind to feed her child.[6] The shrine sells a milk candy called ochichi-ame (breast drops), infused with water drippings from Ochichi-iwa.

People visit the shrine to pray for easy childbirth, healthy children, and happy marriages, as well as safety at sea. From the vermilion railing next to the sea, worshipers may toss small round ceramic charms purchased at the shrine into a squarish depression in a rock just beyond; landing a ball in the depression is said to bring fulfillment of one's wish.

After Susa-no-ō is expelled from the Plain of High Heaven for his rude, destructive behavior, the events of his life on earth become the focus of the *Kojiki* and *Nihongi*. One version in *Nihongi* records that Susa-no-ō dwelt in Silla, a kingdom in Kara (Korean Peninsula), before crossing the sea to Izumo, on the north coast of western Honshū (57), in a rice-growing region watered by the Hii River. His story reprises the motifs of destruction and creation in nature and of death and rebirth in passing generations—the basic organizing principles of the two mythic-historical narratives. Susa-no-ō continues to display both his violent and beneficent tama (souls): while he is known as a storm kami for his violent tantrums and destructive behavior, he is also remembered for his good works in the Eight Great Islands.

The Hii River, sandy and shallow near Lake Shinji, Shimane

On his way to Izumo, his aramitama emerges again: Susa-no-ō begs food from Ō-ge-tsu-hime-no-kami (Princess-of-great-food Kami), then slays her because she serves him filth taken from her nose, mouth, and anus. But from her head, silkworms are born; from her eyes, rice; from her ears, millet; from her nose, small beans; from her vagina, barley; and from her anus, large beans (*Kojiki* 71). The seeds from these plants are disseminated by the creation deity Kami-musubi-no-kami.[7]

In Izumo, Susa-no-ō saves Kushi Inada Hime (Wondrous Rice-field Princess) from an eight-headed, eight-tailed serpent named Yamata-no-Orochi (Eight-forked giant serpent), who has devoured seven of eight daughters of an earth kami named Ōyama-tsu-mi-no-kami (Great-mountain-possessor Kami, a son of Izanagi and Izanami). Susa-no-ō slays the serpent and takes from one of its tails a sword symbolizing authority over the Hii River region. He sends the sword back to the Plain of High Heaven, marries the rice-field princess, and becomes the ruler of Izumo.

The story suggests a nature allegory. The eight-forked serpent is the Hii River: the eight heads are the river's tributary sources in the Chūgoku Mountains, and the eight tails are branches in its delta on the western side of Lake Shinji. The maidens devoured are rice fields destroyed by the river's annual flooding. (Shirane takes the myth literally: a maiden was sacrificed annually to placate the destructive river-serpent kami until the worship of Susa-no-ō was established "to control the unruly waters of the river" [14]).

In summer 2009, when we drove along the river into Oku Izumo to visit an iron and steel manufacturing museum, a flood-control channel was being dredged near the town of Izumo, along the sandy west bank of the wide, shallow riverbed.

The sword taken from the serpent's tail has been linked to the swordsmithing of Oku Izumo ("Remote Izumo"). While iron ore is scarce in Japan, iron sand is abundant, and the Hii River is a major source. *Kojiki* notes that after Susa-no-ō slays Yamata-no-Orochi, "the River Hii flowed on changed into a river of blood" (75), suggesting red flood waters, colored by oxidized iron sand particles found in and along the riverbed. To extract the particles, sand was sluiced, leaving behind the heavier iron sand, which was layered with charcoal, then subjected to intense heat in a clay furnace—a process called tatara-buki (air-blowing furnace). The intense heat reduced the iron sand to kera (iron bloom); from the kera came tama-hagane (jewel steel), which was forged to produce swords. Steel from the iron sands of the Hii River is said to be the best in Japan and is sought after by contemporary master swordsmiths for fashioning their works of art.

In addition to being revered as a savior of rice fields from flooding,

Susa-no-ō is also noted as a creator and planter of trees. In an episode in *Nihongi*, he produces trees from hair plucked from his body: from his beard comes cryptomeria (cedar); from his chest hair, thuja (a conifer); from his buttock hair, makinoki (black pine); and from his eyebrows, kusunoki (camphor). He teaches the proper uses of these woods: cryptomeria and camphor for ship-building, thuja for shrines, and black pine for coffins. He also sows eighty kinds of fruit trees (58). His son Isotakeru (Fifty-courageous) and two daughters, Ōya-tsu-hime and Tsuma-tsu-hime, also plant trees (58–59). His children are worshipped at shrines in Wakayama, on the west coast of Kii (Trees), a heavily forested mountainous region south of Nara ("Isotakeru" and "Ōyatsuhime, Tsumatsuhime," *Encyclopedia of Shintō*).

Susa-no-ō's ability to control flooding may be associated with his role as a creator and planter of trees. Deforestation was recognized as a cause of floods and erosion, as well as drought:

> … as the Yamato state took on ever larger dimensions in the seventh and eight centuries and palaces and large temple complexes were erected throughout the Nara basin, the upper reaches of the Yamato and Yodo Rivers became deforested. As a result, floods and droughts became more frequent and the loss of top soil in these areas became severe. (Sonoda 38)

Hence, "[t]he Imperial court reacted at a relatively early stage by taking measures against over-exploitation of the natural ecosystem and by protecting forests and improving rivers." In 821, the court decreed that "the felling of trees along streams, springs and ponds that irrigate paddy fields will henceforth be forbidden both on private and public lands" (Sonoda 39).

The children of Susa-no-ō with Kushi Inada Hime include Yashima-shi-nu-mi (Eight Island Ruler). With another wife, Kamu-ō-ichi-hime (Divine-Princess-of-Great-Majesty), Susa-no-ō produces Ō-toshi-no-kami (Great-harvest Kami) and Uka-no-mi-tama (August Spirit ofFood), whose names suggest their roles in food production (*Kojiki* 79). His most illustrious offspring, six generations after him, is Ō-kuni-nushi-no-kami (Master-of-the-Great-Land Kami), who, with a kami named Sukuna-bikona no Mikoto (Honored-small-one), is venerated for kuni-tsukuri, or "country-building":

> Now [Ōkuninushi] and Sukuna-bikona no Mikoto, with united strength and one heart, constructed this sub-celestial world. Then, for the sake of the visible race of man as well as for beasts, they determined the method of healing diseases. They also, in order to do away with the calamities of birds, beasts, and creeping things, established means for their prevention and control. (*Nihongi* 59)

Despite Ōkuninushi's good works, the land becomes unruly, so Amaterasu sends a warrior named Take-mika-zu-chi-no-wo-no-kami (Brave-Awesome-Possessing-Male Kami) to persuade the descendants of Susa-no-ō to turn over the governance of the Eight Great Islands to her family. Takemikazuchi defeats Ōkuninushi's son Take-mi-nagata-no-kami (Brave-August-Name-Firm Kami) in a contest of strength (said to be the first sumo match), thus opening the way for Amaterasu to send her grandson Ho-no-Ninigi to rule the islands.

Before he descends, Amaterasu presents him with three sacred treasures: the sword taken from Yamata-no-Orochi's tail by Susa-no-ō, and the mirror and jewels used by the kami to draw Amaterasu out of the heavenly cave.[8]

Ho-no-Ninigi alights on Mt. Takachiho (High-Thousand-Rice-Ears), a 5,146-foot-tall volcano in the Kirishima Mountains, in southeast Tsukushi (Kyūshū), in the province of Himuka (Facing the Sun). He declares the land good:

> This place is opposite to the land of Kara [Korean Peninsula]. One comes straight across to the august Cape of Kasasa [at the southwest corner of Kyūshū]; and it is a land whereon the morning sun shines straight, a land which the evening sunlight illumines. (*Kojiki* 135–136)

His declaration suggests a migration route from Kara via Cape Kasasa. At Cape Kasasa, Ho-no-Ninigi meets and marries Konohana-sakuya-hime (Flowers-of-the-blooming-trees Princess), who like Susa-no-ō's wife Kushi Inada Hime, is

Mt. Takachiho in spring mist, Kirishima, Miyazaki

a daughter of Ō-yama-tsu-mi (Great-mountain-possessor) (*Kojiki* 138; *Nihongi* 70-71).

A fertility kami, Konohana-sakuya-hime appears pregnant and ready to give birth after only one night. Her husband questions her fidelity. To prove herself true, Konohana-sakuya-hime encloses herself in a hall and has it set on fire, declaring that if she and her children die, the children are someone else's, but if they live, they are Ho-no-Ninigi's. She gives birth to Ho-deri-no-mikoto (His Augustness Fire-shine), Ho-suseri-no-mikoto (His Augustness Fire-climax), and Ho-ōri-no-mikoto (His Augustness Fire-subside), the grandfather of Jimmu, the first emperor (*Kojiki* 141–143).[9]

Shintō venerates a bewildering number of kami in its pantheon. Along with Amaterasu and her family, the creation kami Izanagi and Izanami and kami in the imperial line after Amaterasu have shrines dedicated to them. Amaterasu's younger brother Tsukiyomi (the moon kami) has a shrine near his sister's in Ise. Susa-no-ō is worshipped as a kami of marriage and fertility at Kumano Taisha, the highest ranking shrine in Izumo, as well as shrines like the famous Yasaka, in Kyōto.

The three princesses born from Susa-no-ō's sword are worshipped at the Munakata shrines in northwest Kyūshū: Ichikishima-hime (Lovely Island Princess), at Hetsu-gū, in Fukuoka; Tagitsu-hime (Rough Water Princess), at Nakatsu-gū, on Ōshima, an island offshore of Fukuoka; and Tagori-hime (Fog Princess), at Okitsu-gū, on Okinoshima, another island offshore. These shrines were established to provide protection for travel, fishing, and trade between Kyūshū and the Korean Peninsula and China ("Ichikishimahime," "Tagitsuhime," and "Tagorihime," *Encyclopedia of Shintō*). The three daughters are also enshrined at Itsukushima (Miyajima), an island near Hiroshima, to protect seafarers and vessels in the Inland Sea. The shrine was supported by the Taira, a samurai clan, and its leader Taira no Kiyomori (1118–1181), who once served as governor of Aki (Hiroshima) and later became the head of the Taira family and chief minister of the imperial government. In 1168, Kiyomori restored and expanded Itsukushima Shrine to promote trade with Asia.

Amaterasu's grandson Ho-no-Ninigi is enshrined at Kirishima, near Mt. Takachiho, in Kyūshū, where he descended to earth. On November 11 each year, at the original site of Kirishima Shrine on Mt. Takachiho, his descent is celebrated with a bonfire, kagura dancing, and taiko drumming. Established in the sixth century, the original shrine was destroyed several times by volcanic eruptions, so it was moved to its present location, three and a half miles southwest of Mt. Kirishima.

Ho-no-Ninigi's wife Konohana-sakuya-hime, who gave birth to three sons, is venerated as a fertility kami; and because her fidelity made her impervious to the flames, she is prayed to for protection from fire. During the Muromachi Period (1338–1573), she became identified with Asama, or Sengen, the kami of Mt. Fuji, who protects worshipers from volcanic fire. The deities are worshipped at Sengen shrines established around Fuji. Ho-no-Ninigi's son Ho-ōri is enshrined at a mausoleum on the west side of Mt. Takachiho. Ho-ōri's son, Ama-tsu-hi-daka-hiko, is enshrined at Udo Shrine, south of Miyazaki city. Ho-ōri's grandson, the first emperor, Jimmu, is enshrined at Miyazaki Shrine in Miyazaki, from where he began his eastern journey, and at Kashihara, in Asuka, Nara, where he established the first capital of Yamato.[10]

Kojiki describes the original location of Jimmu's mausoleum: "on the top of the Kashi Spur on the northern side of Mount Unebi." Its actual location is unknown, but a mausoleum was established for him at a site designated in 1863, in a grove of trees at the end of a gravel road north of Kashihara Shrine and Mt. Unebi. We drove there in 2006: A low outer fence surrounds the tomb; beyond the gated torii, about thirty yards off, is another fence and gated torii. Visitors aren't allowed to enter the grounds.

A note in *Nihongi* describes the site and a rite associated with it:

there are here two enclosures, the inner of which contains two low mounds each about 18 feet in diameter and 2 feet in height. A Chokushi

Gates of the two enclosures around Emperor Jimmu's mausoleum, Kashihara, Nara

or Imperial Envoy visits this Misasagi [imperial tomb] annually on the 3rd of April with offerings of products of mountain, river, and sea, viz. tahi [tai or sea bream], carp, sea-weed, salt, water, saké, mochi [rice cakes], warabi (fern flour?), pheasants and wild ducks. (137)

Amaterasu's warrior Takemikazuchi, who defeated Ōkuninushi's son Takeminakata, is worshipped as a kami of martial arts at Kashima Shrine in Ibaraki, on the Pacific coast, where he is said to have pinned the head of a giant mythical catfish named Namazu whose movement in an underground pond causes earthquakes.[11] Takeminakata, who fled to Suwa (Nagano) after his defeat (*Kojiki* 123), is worshipped at four shrines around Lake Suwa as a kami of wind and water, hunting, agriculture, and warfare, along with Yasakatome, his female counterpart and consort ("Suwa Shinkō," *Encyclopedia of Shintō*).

Dangerous kami are also venerated, to prevent their destructive spirits from harming the living. For example, the flood-causing eight-headed river kami Yamata-no-Orochi, slain by Susa-no-ō, is worshiped as a rain god in Shimane.

Kagutsuchi, the fire kami whose birth caused his mother Izanami's death, is enshrined at Akihasan Hongū on a mountain slope in western Shizuoka. Up a steep trail or a narrow, winding road, it offers from its golden torii a spectacular view of the Tenryū River valley and the Pacific Ocean. In fall the maple trees along the long stone stairway to the shrine are ablaze with red leaves; and in

Akihasan Hongū, Hamamatsu, Shizuoka

December a fire festival is held to pray for a good harvest and protection from fire in the coming year.

Susa-nō-o's most illustrious descendent, Ōkuninushi, is enshrined at Izumo Taisha (Grand Shrine of Izumo), in Shimane, and worshipped as a kami of agriculture and medicine and also, like Susa-no-ō, as a kami of marriage and fertility. In exchange for relinquishing government affairs to her grandson Ho-no-Ninigi, Amaterasu places Ōkuninushi in charge of family affairs. Every fall, from all over Japan, kami gather at Izumo Taisha to match couples and review marriages, deaths, and births. The starting date of the six-day gathering, called Kami-Ari (Kami-present), is set by the lunar calendar on 10.10, the tenth day of the tenth moon of the year; the ceremonies continue on as the moon waxes auspiciously full (10.15).

Karen's family meets at a branch shrine of Izumo Taisha in Honolulu for annual blessings on New Year's Day.[12] I started joining them in 2002 and became interested in visiting the main shrine in Shimane. Planning a trip to western Honshu in fall 2006, I read the public was welcome to attend the opening ceremony of Kami-Ari, which takes place at Inasa Beach, where the kami come ashore after sunset. We decided to attend. In 2006, 10.10 fell on November 30. We drove to Izumo Taisha from Matsue as the sun set behind clouds above Lake Shinji. The shrine appeared deserted, and I began to doubt that we had come on the right night. Then small groups of people began emerging from the dark streets leading to the beach. We parked and followed the groups along the sidewalk, then down a path through pine trees to the beach. A tent had been set up facing the shore, where small wavelets were breaking. Overhead the ten-day-old moon shone through patches of passing clouds. Soon several hundred people had gathered. Four fires were lit in front of four two-foot-high cones of sand. Drum and flute sounded, and priests marched through the crowd to the fires, clapping four times and chanting.

A gust of wind blew down from Yakumo Hill, welcoming the arriving kami. The priests clapped four more times to end the ceremony, then accompanied the kami in procession to the shrine, holding upright a branch of the evergreen sakaki, on which the kami had alighted. White cloth screened the sakaki from the crowd, which held up wands of folded paper (shi-de) to attract the blessings of the kami and take them home. The crowd followed the procession from the beach to the shrine, where the ceremonies (closed to public) would continue over the next week.

Shrines dedicated to the most potent kami branch into networks, with the kami's spirit divided (bunrei) and shared among the branches. Amaterasu's

Priests entering Izumo Taisha during Kami-Ari (Photo: Karen Ono)

shrine at Ise presides over a network called Shinmei (Kami-Shining) with 18,000 branches. The Munakata shrines dedicated to her three daughters number 8,500. The worship of Ōkuninushi's son Takeminakata, headquartered at four shrines around Lake Suwa, has 5,000 branches, in Nagano and the neighboring Prefectures of Saitama, Niigata, Gunma, and Toyama. ("Suwa Shinkō," *Encyclopedia of Shintō*).

Two kami not mentioned in *Kojiki* and *Nihongi,* Hachiman and Inari, have larger shrine networks than Amaterasu. Hachiman shrines, headquartered at Usa Hachiman-gū in Ōita, in northern Kyūshū, form the nation's second largest shrine network, with 25,000 branches. Hachiman worship has its roots in local kami cults and shamanistic traditions brought by settlers from the Korean Peninsula. Kanda cites its eclecticism as a reason for its widespread appeal:

> One of the distinguishing features of the Hachiman cult is its all-embracing quality. The cult worships: kami of both mountain and sea; local clan deities of northern Kyushu; deities of Korean origin; and deities associated with the Yamato clan. From the very outset it had a strong shamanistic undercurrent on which Buddhist elements were superimposed. This unique and powerful amalgam of beliefs and practices at the Usa Shrine explains Hachiman's meteoric rise to national prominence during the early decades of the eighth century. The cult's adaptability, but especially its responsiveness to the religious needs of all strata of society, has assured it success over the centuries. (37)

One of the three priestly families at Usa worships Hime-gami, a kami of sea travel and agriculture; a second family, of Korean ancestry, worships Kara Kuni Okinaga Ohime no Mikoto, a mountain kami associated with mining and metal-working; the third family, originally from Yamato (Nara), may have been "devotees of the Empress Jingū and her son Ōjin" (Kanda 37–38). Around the ninth century (or by one account, much earlier, in 584), Hachiman declared through an oracle that he was the spirit of Emperor Ōjin (r. 270–310), the fifteenth imperial head (Kanda 43). Ōjin is said to have been in the womb of his mother, Empress Jingū (r. 201–269), when she led an invasion of the Korean Peninsula and made its three kingdoms tributaries of Yamato. (The invasion is considered apocryphal.) To prevent Ōjin from being born before she could return home to Kyūshū, she inserted a stone into her womb (*Nihongi* 229).

At Usa Shrine, as early as the sixth century, kami and Buddhist rituals and deities were syncretized. Hachiman rose to national stature in 749, when his divided spirit was transported in a sacred cart from Oita to Nara by Emperor Shōmu (r. 724–749), after an oracle declared that Hachiman would assist in casting the giant bronze statue of Dainichi (Great Sun), the Japanese name for Vaicorana, the cosmic Buddha sitting in meditation at the center of the Universe. (The esoteric sects of Tendai and Shingon Buddhism worshipped Dainichi as the Buddha from which the myriad other buddhas emanated.) Shōmu wanted the statue cast after prayers to Buddha seemed to end a smallpox outbreak in 743. Before proceeding with the work (and before Hachiman agreed through his oracle to assist), Shōmu sent an emissary to Ise to ask for Amatersu's

Usa Hachiman-gū, Ōita

permission to cast the statue; her oracle approved, declaring that Amaterasu and Dainichi to be one and the same deity.

The giant statue, housed at Tōdaiji, was completed in 751. Subsequently, Hachiman was recognized as a guardian of both the nation and Buddhism, with shrines dedicated to him often located next to temples. Tamukeyama, as the Hachiman shrine at Tōdaiji is known today, was moved in 1250 to its present location just east of the huge wooden building housing the Daibutsu; the shrine was rebuilt in 1691 after it was destroyed by fire.

In 859, based on another oracle, Iwashimizu Hachiman Shrine was constructed south of Kyōto, in Yawata (an alternative reading for the two kanji for Hachiman), to protect the Imperial Family and Heian (Kyōto), which became the capital of Yamato in 794. At Iwashimizu Shrine, Hachiman is worshipped as an avatar of Amida Buddha ("Hachiman Shinkō," *Encyclopedia of Shintō*).

Hachiman eventually became the tutelary kami of the warrior class. The samurai Genji (Minamoto family) claimed imperial descent through Emperor Ōjin and began worshiping Hachiman in the eleventh century, crediting him with a series of military successes. In 1180, Minamoto no Yoritomo (1147–1199) established Tsurugaoka Hachiman Shrine in Kamakura. In 1191, the Genji defeated the Heike for control of the government, and Yoritomo became Yamato's first permanent shogun, with his bakufu (military government) headquartered in Kamakura. Hachiman worship spread among the samurai clans:

> In the medieval period, Hachiman developed from the Genji clan's ujigami into the guardian kami of the warrior class, and many Hachiman shrines were established (kanjō) on estates (shōen) in various regions as the "tutelary guardian of those areas" (chinjugami). ("Hachiman Shinkō," *Encyclopedia of Shintō*)

Hachiman is credited with delivering the kamikaze, or divine winds, that buffeted and weakened fleets of invading Mongols in 1274 and 1281, allowing the samurai clans to repel both invasions.

Broader in appeal than either Amaterasu or Hachiman worship is Inari worship, with 32,000 shrines, the largest network in Japan. Inari worship has no centralized authority or orthodox beliefs or class affiliation. Smyers remarks that "Inari worship may be conducted by Shintō or Buddhist priests, by nonclerical religious specialists, by lay worship group leaders, or by devotees themselves" (5). Worshipers may seek help with personal matters (good fortune, prosperity, protection) or pray for wider benefits, such as world peace.

Torii pathway at an Inari shrine branch in Takayama, Aomori

The name "Inari," which first appears in an eighth-century document, is said to be derived from "ine," or "rice" (Smyers 16). But while Inari was originally a kami of agriculture, identified as the spirit of rice, people from all vocations and avocations pray to her today. Worship sites include shrines "without full-time resident priest, home and company shrines, tiny field and roadside shrines." Inari shrines are found "in famous large shrines and temples, on factory rooftops, in lay religious establishments, in alleys of major cities, on sacred mountains, in rice fields" (Smyers 1).

The original shrine was established in 711, at the foot of Mt. Inari, in Fushimi, just south of Kyōto, an area settled by the Hata, an immigrant family from the kingdom of Silla. According to the shrine's origin legend, a member of the prosperous clan was practicing archery one day, using a rice cake as his target. After it was pierced, the rice cake changed into a white bird and flew to the mountain top. The archer found a rice plant where the bird landed (Smyers 15). He felt contrition over his abuse of a precious rice cake, and the Inari shrine was built. Inari has been identified with Uka-no-mitama, a kami of food and a child of either Susa-no-ō (*Kojiki*) or Izanagi and Izanami (*Nihongi*). Four other kami are venerated with her at the Fushimi shrine, which serves as headquarters for the shrine network.

Inari worship spread widely during the Heian Period (794–1185) after Kōbō Daishi (774–835), the founder of Shingon Buddhism, declared Inari to be the guardian kami of a new temple built to protect the nation. In the tenth century, the shrine at Fushimi was awarded imperial patronage. Mt. Inari became a popular pilgrimage site and remains so today (Smyers 17–18). By the Edo period (1603-1868), Inari shrines were so common, one wit commented that in the capital, they were "as numerous as dog droppings" (20).

The shrine at Fushimi is noted for its tunnels of red torii, paid for by donors in thanks for blessings and future considerations and protection. The shrine is also noted for its statues of pairs of foxes. Foxes, which appear in rice fields, are believed to be messengers of Inari. One of the pair holds in its mouth a cylindrical key to a rice storehouse, symbolic of wealth; the other holds a wish-fulfilling jewel. The pair represent Inari's powers to increase wealth and to grant wishes. A proverb advises worshipers to pray to Kōbō Daishi for protection against illness and to Inari for fulfillment of desires (Smyers 22). Under Buddhist-Shintō syncretism, Inari has been identified with the Buddhist deity Dakiniten, originally an East Indian demon-deity who fed on corpses, but was converted to Buddhism. In Japan, Dakiniten is depicted as a bodhisattva riding a white fox and is worshipped at Buddhist Inari temples (Smyers 82).

The fourth largest shrine network, with 10,500 branches, is dedicated to the worship of ninth-century scholar and bureaucrat Sugawara no Michizane (845–903), also known as Tenjin (Heavenly Deity) and Tenman (Heavenly Fullness). Falsely accused of plotting against the sixtieth imperial head, Emperor Daigo (r. 897–930), Michizane was banished from Kyōto to Kyūshū in 901. After his death, a series of disasters attributed to his angry spirit struck the capital. Lightning strikes at the palace in 930 killed four courtiers, including one involved in the accusations against Michizane. From this incident, he was identified with kaminari, a kami of lightning and thunder. (The deification of "spirits of the dead" and "ancient sages and masters" was introduced from China [Kuroda, Dobbins, and Gay 8].)

In 947, Kitano Tenman-gū, in Kyōto, was dedicated to Michizane to placate his spirit and protect the capital. The shrine at Kitano is considered one of the two headquarters of Tenjin worship (Borgen 310-311). The other headquarters is a religious complex that developed from an altar erected at Michizane's grave site in Dazaifu, nine miles southeast of Fukuoka, in Kyūshū. The complex once included a Buddhist monastery, but with the separation of Buddhism and Shintō during the Meiji Period, the site became exclusively a shrine, known today as Dazaifu Tenman-gū. Michizane was a noted scholar and poet. During the Edo Period (1603–1868), his spirit became a kami of scholarship, and students began praying to him for success in school.

In May, 2010, we were in Tsuruoka, Yamagata, on the day of its annual Tenjin festival, sponsored by the local shrine. The parade includes a re-enactment of Michizane's procession into exile, guided by two men dressed as Tengu (Heavenly Dog)—a long-nosed, red-faced mythical trickster and patron of the martial arts who targets misbehaving Buddhist priests, as well as those who misuse their knowledge or authority to advance themselves, as did Michizane's accusers. Onlookers and passers-by are served saké by bakemono (people with their faces hidden by large straw hats and towels), based on the story that Michizane's followers offered each other saké while commiserating over their lord's exile, but disguised themselves so the authorities couldn't identify them.

An animistic religion involving kami worship existed in Japan before the kami were personified in narratives like *Kojiki* and *Nihongi*, and kami worship was institutionalized by the imperial court. The hunters and gatherers who inhabited the Japanese archipelago during the Paleolithic and Jōmon Periods (before 30,000 BC–300 BC), like hunters and gatherers worldwide, would have prayed to nature spirits for successful hunts and protection. The Ainu, descendants of the Jōmon, call such spirits kamuy. The sun and moon, clouds, lightning and thunder, rain, wind, mountains, hills and peaks, rocks, waterfalls, rivers, plants, and animals—all are animated by spirits that can both benefit or harm people. Ancestral spirits were also worshipped, with villages built around grave sites.

In Japanese folk tradition, kami also inhabit the house—the hearth, the sleeping room, and the toilet (Yanagita 19–20). Man-made objects, such as weapons, mirrors, tools, and clothing, also embody kami. While everything has a spirit, "kami" denotes "superior," "worthy of respect or awe," and "venerable"; so outstanding manifestations of humanity or nature (sages and shoguns, as well as tall mountains, bizarrely shaped rocks, aged trees) are particularly revered as kami. Natural objects of worship may be marked by shimenawa (rice-straw rope) hung with shide (white, folded paper streamers).

When settlers from the Korean Peninsula brought rice agriculture during the Yayoi Period, they worshipped spirits of nature that contributed to nurturing and protecting the crops and producing good harvests. At first kami were prayed to and petitioned at natural sites around the villages—at large rocks (iwasaka or shiki) or "at springs, waterfalls, river banks and by large trees, mostly in places that were important for the water supply of farming communities":

> [S]acred spaces were created and marked off, kami were temporarily invited to descend and attend, and rites relating to the agricultural calendar were performed. For the purpose of such rites, objects known as yorishiro were placed in the sacred space to which the kami were invited to descend. At this stage kami were imagined as invisible spirits, without permanent dwelling places. (Inoue et al. 15)

A reconstructed kura at Toro Ruins, Shizuoka

Tree branches, particularly evergreens like sakaki or matsu (pine), or animals may serve as yorishiro. Also, "geological features such as waterfalls, streams, hills, or islands served as objects of worship" (Inoue et al.), and kami were thought to dwell permanently in them. Writing in 1922, Yanagita notes that in Tōno, it "is quite common to find large rocks by the side of the road with the words 'mountain kami,' 'kami of the fields,' and 'kami of the village entrance' engraved on them" (58).

When rice agriculture began to produce surpluses that could be stored, rites for the kami were performed at the village granary (kura) or at the dwelling of the local chief (miya). These sites developed into permanent shrines, the oldest ones dating to the third or fourth centuries, toward the end of the Yayoi Period. The kura, which housed the rice spirit in the stored rice grains, developed into the shinmei-style shrine, exemplified by Ise shrine, with an entrance on the long side of the building. The chief's dwelling developed into the taisha-style shrine, exemplified by Izumo Taisha, with its entrance on the short side of the building. Shirane sees the movement of the sites of worship from the periphery of the village to sites within the village as indicating "greater technological control over nature, particularly management of water and irrigation" (14).

After Buddhism was introduced in the sixth century, the building styles of Chinese temples began to influence shrine architecture, so that now many shrines, with curved tile roofs and vermilion painted buildings, no longer look like kura or miya.

Kamosu Shrine, Shimane, dedicated to Izanami, is said to be the oldest taisha-style shrine in Japan. (Photo: Karen Ono)

While animism may be the basis of an early form of kami worship, scholars like Kuroda have pointed out that many of the ceremonies and beliefs of Shintō were borrowed from Taoism (6). (Shintō, or "Way of the Gods," is written with the same two kanji as "Tao" or "Dao.") During the Asuka Period, the Imperial Family adopted Taoist beliefs and practices from China to bolster its claim of a divine right to rule:

> 'Teachings, rituals, and even the concepts of imperial authority'—
> everything from the veneration of swords and mirrors to religious titles
> and the physical structure of the most sacred shrine of Ise—all spring
> from Taoism; so too were local beliefs defined by Taoist influence.
> Taoism totally pervaded early Japan's religious milieu, obliterating
> what indigenous practices may have existed prior to that foreign
> creed's advent. 'Shinto,' in its earliest known usage, was then nothing
> but a Chinese cultural import. (Breen and Teeuwen 5)

Starting around the late eighth century, kami worship was absorbed into Buddhism, under the theory of honji suijaku, that "the *kami* are simply another form of the Buddha, and their form, condition, authority, and activity are nothing but the form and the acts by which the Buddha teaches, guides, and saves human beings" (Kuroda 12). Kuroda adds that the secular functions of kami were complementary to Buddhism's other-worldliness: "as a general rule matters of this world were addressed to the *kami* and those of the coming world to the Buddha. In times of wordly difficulty one might pray for the protection of the kami and the Buddha, but first and foremost for that of the kami" (16).

Toward the end of fifteenth century, Shintōists began to differentiate Shintō from Buddhism, with the rise of Shintō-only schools of thought. By the seventeenth century, scholars in Japan began to distinguish Shintō as a religion separate from Taoism, Buddhism, and Confucianism and declared Shintō indigenous. At the start of the Meiji Period, in 1868, the government forced the separation of Shintō from Buddhism (shinbutsu bunri). Buddhism was attacked as foreign in order to weaken the sects and temples and promote Shintō as the basis of national unity, in preparation for economic competition and military conflict with the West (Kuroda *passim*).

Since the banning of the nationalistic state-sponsored Shintō at the end of World War II, the main function of Shintō for the ordinary worshipper has been to secure blessings and protection for himself and his family. The frequency of shrine visits depends on an individual's level of interest or strength of belief. Worshipers may visit shrines to renew the blessings of the kami at the start of each year (hatsu-mōde, or first visit); the more devout might pray at a shrine at the start of each month, or even daily.

To keep a declining number of worshipers engaged and making donations, Shintō promotes the traditions of blessings deemed necessary at particular stages of life. The stages-of-life observances were originally practiced by the court nobility, then spread among the samurai after they rose to power, and to artisans and merchants in towns and cities during the Edo Period.

Parents may take newborns to shrines to receive their first blessings from the uji-kami, or clan deity. Thereafter, children may be blessed in ceremonies at the ages of three, five, and seven, celebrating important stages of growth. Traditionally, before age three, children had their heads shorn because of a belief that harmful spirits could enter the body through hair; at three, children were considered strong enough to grow their hair out. At five, boys were given hakama, or formal trousers; at seven, a ceremony called "tateage" (standing up) was held, when banners were raised on bamboo poles, marking the passage from childhood to boyhood (Casal 70). At seven, girls were allowed to use obi (ornamental sashes) rather than cords to tie their kimono, as a sign that they had entered girlhood. These childhood blessings took place traditionally on 11.15, the full moon of mid-winter, in December, around winter solstice, at the start of the cold season, to prevent illness. Today, celebrations of shichi-go-san (seven-five-three) are held at shrines in November.

Traditionally, individuals were blessed in ceremonies for coming of age between twelve and sixteen for girls and between eleven and seventeen for boys, when adult hair-styles and clothing were worn for the first time. Today coming of age, at the legal age of twenty (twenty-one by Japanese reckoning), may be acknowledged secularly, with a ceremony at city hall on Seijin no Hi (Adulthood Day), in January.

Priests also bless couples who marry. (The prime ages traditionally were being nineteen for women and twenty-five for men.) A generation ago, 70% of weddings featured Shintō rites, but now less than 20% do, with Western-style wedding ceremonies gaining in popularity. The choice is a matter of fashion rather than of religious belief (French).

Worshipers ask for blessings for other important events, such as an entrance exam, the opening of a new business, or the purchase of a home or car; and after a successful event, a shrine visit may be made to thank the kami. As life progresses, worshipers seek protection in years considered dangerous: for women, age thirty-three ("sanzan," a homonym for "disaster"), and for men, age forty-two ("shi-ni," a homonym for "to die"). Travel is also considered a risky event, requiring a blessing.

In the Chinese calendar introduced to Japan in the mid-sixth century a sixty-year cycle was considered a lifetime, when the combinations of ten heavenly stems and twelve earthly branches return to the combination of the a person's birth year. If a person lives past sixty, the sixty-first year, kanreki, or "calendar return," is celebrated as a rebirth. Beyond sixty, longevity might be recognized in auspicious years identified by numerology: seventy, seventy-seven, eighty, eighty-one, eighty-eight, ninety, ninety-nine, one hundred, one hundred and eight, and one hundred and eleven.

Shrines are also associated with other spiritual services like fortune-telling, exorcism, or contact with the dead, although such services may not be officially recognized or sanctioned.

For rites of death, the majority of Japanese turn to Buddhism. One reason is that Shintō views contact with the dead as pollution: when Izanagi sees Izanami's maggot-infested corpse, he flees in fright and purifies himself by bathing afterwards. On the Shintō island of Miyajima, near Hiroshima, both funerals and burials were banned, with corpses transported to the mainland for cremation and burial. Also, the Shintō afterlife is not very appealing: the spirits dwell in Yomi, a dark, cold underground place, essentially the grave, where decaying corpses are quarantined. Buddhism, on the other hand, promises the faithful spiritual rebirth in the Pure Land and hope of eternal Bliss in Nirvana. After Buddhism and Shintō were separated during the Meiji Period, the main activity of Buddhist temples became funeral and memorial services.

The annual festival for the dead, called Obon, like many Japanese spiritual traditions, is a curious mix of Shintō, Taoism, Buddhism, and Confucian ancestor worship. Introduced from China during the Nara Period (710–794), Obon was celebrated at Buddhist temples or Shintō shrines for three or four days around the first full moon of autumn (7.15, usually in August), based on the Chinese belief that the gates of the underworld open for fifteen days after mid-year (7.1 to 7.15). (The gates also open for the first fifteen days of the year, 1.1 to 1.15; Como 99–100). During Obon, families welcome ancestral spirits back to the furusato (family home village or town).

At the start of Obon, mukae-bi (welcoming fires, including candles lit on altars) guide the ancestral spirits home for the celebration. In honor of the returning spirits, families clean the graves, set out favorite foods of the deceased, and burn incense (the scented smoke serves as nourishment for the spirits). Unhappy or angry spirits are placated. On the evening of 7.15, families dance in lantern-lit streets or fields, to taiko drum, samisen, and bamboo flute music, cheering the spirits up and showing them that all is well in the world of the living, so they can depart and rest peacefully in the afterworld for another year. Fireworks follow. The spirits are then sent back to the afterworld under the light of the full moon, so they don't lose their way. Bonfires or floating lanterns serve as okuri-bi (sending-off fires), also to light the way. Spirits who don't return to the underworld wander the earth, a potential hazard to the living.

When the Gregorian calendar replaced the lunar calendar during the Meiji Period, 7.15 was translated as July 15, and some temples and shrines began holding Obon around July 15 (or alternately, August 15) rather than around the first full moon of autumn.

"Obon" is from the Sanskrit "Ullambana" (which became "urabon-e" in Japanese, or "bon" for short), meaning "hanging upside down," a reference to the torments suffered by sinners in the Realm of Hungry Ghosts, one of the six Buddhist realms in which the unenlightened are trapped in endless cycles of birth and rebirth. Mokuren, a disciple of Buddha, saw his mother's spirit suffering in this position and secured her release by making offerings to Buddhist monks completing their summer retreat on 7.15. In celebration of his mother's release, Mokuren danced for joy, the original bon dance.

In Buddhist practice, the spirits of the dead, like the living, should strive to break their attachments to this world. But the living want ancestral spirits to return home once a year, to feed and thank them, or to appease them, or to ask for their blessings. Thus, they are shuttled back and forth annually, between this world and the next.

Attending Obon festivals at Buddhist temples while growing up, I had no idea that we were supposed to be welcoming, feeding, and entertaining ancestral spirits. On warm summer nights in Hawai'i, we went to bon dances for fun, looking for girls in the crowd under paper lanterns lit with electric bulbs, as folk music blared over the sound system, and dancers circled a taiko drum stage. The food sold at stalls—saimin, teriyaki beef sticks, and corn on the cob—was for the living. Originally attended mainly by Japanese immigrants and their descendents, today Obon in Hawai'i has turned into a secular summer festival open to everyone in the multiethnic community.

Shrines attract their largest crowds for matsuri, or festivals. Traditionally, festivals were agricultural. Non-agricultural festivals were introduced to the Yamato court from China during the Classical Period (538–1185) and later spread to the samurai and commoners. During the Edo Period, the Five Sacred Festivals were established as national holidays. The original date for each festival was based the numerology of the lunar calendar, in which the doubling of odd digits (e.g., 3.3, 5.5, 7.7, or 9.9) were days to ward off harmful spirits and ask for blessings and protection. The five festivals are still celebrated at shrines today, in various ways, on days set by lunar or Gregorian calendar.

The first festival, at the start of the year, with the first moon of spring, is Nanakusa no Sekku, or Festival of Seven Grasses, held on 1.7 (seventh day of the first moon, in late January or February by the lunar calendar). This festival day serves as the culmination of the New Year's celebration that begins on 1.1. Seven wild herbs are gathered and used to make a rice porridge, which is offered to the kami, then eaten by participants "so that their fresh life force could be absorbed into the body" (Shirane 136) to ward off illness in the coming year.

At the start of the last moon of spring, on 3.3, in late March or early April, when peach trees are in bloom, Momo no Sekku (Peach Festival) is held. Like the seven grasses, the peach is believed to ward off harmful spirits and enhance health and fertility.

3.3 was a day of purification, when pollution was transferred to dolls of grass or paper, which were burned or tossed into a river to be carried away to the sea. One such ritual was conducted at Ise shrine, on the banks of the Isuzu River, in the reign of Emperor Suinin (r. 29 BC–AD 70) (Casal 37). Eventually, "the custom of playing with elaborately dressed dolls emerged from this ritual, and in the Muromachi Period ... [it] evolved into the Doll's Festival (Hinamatsuri)" (Shirane 156). The Peach Festival and Doll's Festival merged into Girls' Day, as the 3.3 celebration is known today.

The third festival, Tango no Sekku, is celebrated at mid-summer, on 5.5, which, like 3.3, was a day for warding off harmful spirits. "Tan" means "start of," and "go" refers to the horse, the Chinese zodiac animal associated with the fifth moon. Tango marks the start of the summer rainy season, or the fifth-moon rains (samidare). Shirane explains why festivals were held at this time:

> summer in early medieval Kyōto was in reality a time of extreme heat, pestilence, and death [and also heavy rains and flooding due to the fifth-moon rains]. The result was a large number of local major festivals in the capital (such as the Gion Festival and the Hollyhock [Aoi] Festival) and in the provinces intended to appease the gods and to exorcise sin and dangerous elements. (12)

The plant used to drive away pestilence and death on this occasion was ayame, the mountain iris, which was attached to eaves and fences around houses, scattered on roofs, or stuffed in pillows. Thus, the festival is also known as Ayame no Sekku. Baths or saké infused with ayame was considered both prophylactic and medicinal. Growing in ponds, ayame takes on water's life-giving power. Its long, pointed leaves resemble swords, and its sharp smell were weapons to "defeat the goblins of darkness" (Casal 64). Mock battles among boys armed with the pointed leaves took place, and by the Edo Period, the festival became Boys' Day, an occasion to pray for the health and success of sons, who are encouraged to become strong and bold, like warriors, in their endeavors. Swords, helmets, and other warrior regalia became popular gifts. Carp banners were hung above houses to celebrate the birth of a first son, a tradition based on a Chinese legend about a carp swimming upstream past rapids known as the Dragon Gate. In recognition of the fish's perseverance and strength, the gods turned the carp into a dragon.

Boys' Day carps, Shirakawa-gō, Gifu

The fourth festival, Tanabata, is celebrated on 7.7, at the start of autumn, a time to pray for clear skies for harvest. Around this date, two stars, Vega (Orihime Boshi or

"Weaving Princess Star") and Altair (Kengyū Boshi or "Cowherd Star") begin to appear together in the eastern sky in the evening, just after sunset, separated by the River of Heaven (Milky Way). The legend of romance between the two stars encourages young people to wish for hard-working spouses, like the weaving princess and the cowherd, who live apart for the year working, but are allowed to join each other for an annual reunion on 7.7. In the urban adaptation of the festival during the Edo Period, girls prayed for better skills in sewing and other crafts, while both girls and boys practiced their calligraphy by writing poems praising the star lovers or expressing personal wishes. The seventh moon of the year is known as Fu-zaki, "moon of literary composition," and the wishful writings, on slips of colored paper, are hung from bamboo poles as part of the festivities.

The fifth and last sekku, Kiku no Sekku (Chrysanthemum Festival), was traditionally celebrated on 9.9 during the last moon of autumn (October), to strengthen the body for the cold, dark winter months ahead. Chrysanthemum, like the seven grasses, peach tree, and mountain iris of the first three sekku, is thought to promote good health. Celebrants may drink saké infused with kiku for longevity. Because of the flower's shape (with petals radiating from its center) and its hardiness (it's a perennial that can withstand cold weather), chrysanthemums are believed to embody the life-force of the sun (Casal 96–97). Starting with Emperor Go-Toba (r. 1183–1198), the Imperial Family, worshipers of the sun kami, has used a sun-like kiku emblem as its crest. Today, shrines host chrysanthemum festivals in October and November.

Kiku festival display, Yahiko Shrine, Niigata

Spring Sengen festival, Shizuoka

Three spring festivals we attended in 2008 illustrate how Shintō mythology has been woven into shrine celebrations. On the first Saturday of April, Shizuoka city holds a flower-viewing procession to Sengen Shrine, dedicated to the kami of Mt. Fuji, Konohana-sakuya-hime, the wife of Amaterasu's grandson Ho-no-Ninigi. The procession was established by Shogun Ieyasu Tokugawa (1543–1616), who grew up in and retired to Sumpu (Shizuoka).[13] The modern procession is a touristy affair, featuring adults and children costumed in traditional outfits, joined by high school marching bands and pompom girls. In the afternoon wooden floats are stationed in front of the moat and outer walls of Ieyasu's former castle to provide music for groups of mainly elderly women performing folk dances. The urban setting of Shizuoka's spring matsuri (festival), with numerous spectators lining the streets between Sumpu and Sengen Shrine, has changed its character from matsuri into what Yanagita calls seirei, or spectacle: "the shift took place when the crowd emerged as mere observers rather than active participants in the events" (Inoue et al. 128).

On the second Saturday in April, Tejikaraō Shrine in Gifu hosts a 300-year-old fireworks festival to welcome back the fertility kami to the fields after their winter hiatus in the mountains. The town and its shrine are named for Ame-no-Te-jikara-ō, "Heavenly-hand-strength-male," the kami who is said to have opened the rock door of the cave in which Amaterasu hid (or he held onto her hand and drew her from the cave).

In the afternoon, when we arrived, a crowd was gathering outside the

Mikoshi bearers, Tejikaraō fire festival, Gifu

shrine, in a narrow street where booths sold grilled foods, toys, and gold fish. As twilight fell, the kami of Tejikaraō town and eleven neighboring towns arrived in mikoshi (portable shrines) hoisted on the shoulders of young men. Shouting and chanting to the beat of cylindrical metal gongs, the mikoshi bearers thrust the mikoshi up and down, to invigorate the kami inside. (At other festivals, to rouse the kami, mikoshi are dropped on the ground, bumped into each other in competition, or immersed in a river or the ocean.)

On the west side of the shrine courtyard was a long stage decorated with sprays of sakura and figures from myth and history, including Tejikaraō hoisting a rock over his head in front of Amaterasu's cave. As the mikoshi bearers danced in succession around each town's lantern pole, gunpowder packs atop the pole were ignited, and sparks cascaded down. The dancers worked themselves into a state of ecstasy, possessed by the divine energy of the kami. Like miniature volcanoes, the mikoshi spewed fountains of flames and sparks into the air through pipes on their roofs. Aerial hanabi, or "flowers of fire," streaked skyward and exploded.

Three days later, on April 14 and 15, we attended the spring festival in Takayama, also in Gifu. The festival was established in the seventeenth century, in honor of Sanno-sama, the kami of the south, to pray for a good rice harvest. An autumn harvest festival is held on October 9 and 10, to thank Hachiman-sama, the kami of the north.

The spring festival features twelve twenty-foot-tall, ornate floats, lacquered and embellished with carvings, banners, and paintings on silk. In the morning,

73

Puppeteer and puppet, Takayama festival, Gifu

the floats are wheeled out of their storehouses, paraded through town, and displayed in the central plaza near the train station. Around noon, karakuri-puppet performances take place. Manipulated by a master and assistants, the small, multi-stringed puppets perform stately nō dances on planks projecting from the floats. (The karakuri were invented in China in the tenth century and introduced to Japan during the Muromachi Period. The town of Inuyama, just south of Takayama, is famous for its karakuri manufacturing.)

The Takayama festival is among the most famous in Japan, and the puppet performances attract crowds of local and international spectators and media. In the early afternoon, after the puppet performance, several hundred locals dressed in Edo-period costumes paraded through the town, with a group of lion dancers performing in front of shrines along the way.

After the Takayama festival, we spent a night at Hirayu Onsen, in the Hida Mountains. The next morning, just after sunrise, I was relaxing in the rotemburo (outdoor hot spring), surrounded by granite peaks still streaked with snow. Head above water, body floating below the surface, images of sakura blooming and spring festivals adrift in my pool of memories, I felt the nigimitama of Amaterasu in the glowing sun-lit steam rising from the water and swirling in a light breeze, then vanishing. Her spring warmth and light are a blessing on the land and people, calling forth the bloom of sakura that sweeps across the archipelago, from Okinawa to Hokkaidō, and quickening leaves of the forest trees and rice plants in her radiance.

Through the summer rains, the droughts, and the fierce winds, with the constant care and toil of farmers, the rice fields flower and ripen:

At their tips, which waited patiently in the rain,
tiny white flowers glisten
and above the quiet amber puddles reflecting the sun
red dragonflies glide.
Ah, we must dance, dance like children
and that's not enough.
…
we must dance, clapping our hands, like the innocent gods of the past,
and that is not enough.

(Kenji Miyazawa, "The Breeze Comes Filling the Valley." 7/14/1927)

The worship of Amaterasu and other kami is thanksgiving for the rebirth and flourishing of all that's vital, robust, and beautiful in the world.

It's remarkable that after over a century and a half of Westernization and globalization, with so many local religions in other places losing their vitality and purpose, Shintō remains alive. It has co-existed over the centuries with Buddhism, which has profoundly influenced it, and Christianity, which hasn't. (During the Edo Period, Christianity was banned and converts were persecuted as part of the shogunate's anti-foreign policies.) Shintō's endurance may be due to the fact that lay worshipers don't have to study theologies or take sides in sectarian disputes over doctrines or follow rigid moral rules; they mainly visit shrines to thank the kami or ask for blessings, protection, or forgiveness.

But shrine visits are declining in Japan with the secularization of society after World War II and depopulation. Small rural shrines may be neglected or abandoned after their support communities die out or move away, and large city shrines pay expenses by renting their lands (French). When we went to Yasaka Shrine in Kyōto on New Year's Eve in 1970, a crush of people pushed up the stairs to light straw ropes from the shrine's herbal fire, taken home to cook the first meal of the year or light a candle on the altar, for protection from illness and disaster in the coming year. Over forty years later, in 2013, the crowd was sparser and more orderly, waiting patiently in lines to light their ropes.

Most Japanese say they have no formal religious affiliations, and the majority don't believe in Shintō or Buddhism. A survey of visitors to Kamigamo Shrine in Kyōto revealed that less than 5% came with a religious purpose; the rest were there to go for a walk or enjoy the well-kept shrine grounds, because they happened to be in the area or lived nearby or read or heard about the shrine in a tourist guide or on TV. The most common response to the question of why they were visiting was "no special reason." Eighty-six percent didn't know the name of the kami—Wake Ikazuchi—to whom the shrine is dedicated (Nelson 30-31). Inoue et al. comment that although "veneration is never entirely absent [from shrine visits], it is subordinated to the pleasure, entertainment dimension":

> Such practices as senja mōde (thousand-shrine pilgrimage) which involves visiting multiple shrines, especially those dedicated to Inari, and shichi fukujin mairi (tours of temples and shrines that venerate one or more of the seven gods of good fortune, Ebisu, Daikokuten, Bishamon, Benzaiten, Hotei, Fukurokuju and Jurōjin) are popular among young people today, but their abiding concern seems to be collecting the stamps available from the railway stations on the pilgrims' routes. (196)

But enjoyment of life is the goal of Shintō worship.

Superstitious as shrine activities may be, praying for wealth, health, love, marriage, children, and longevity, expressing thanks for good fortune, asking for guidance and protection, placating angry spirits, communicating with the dead or having one's fortune told—all fulfill human needs rooted in anxieties and fears about the future. As the poet Miyazawa suggests in "The Breeze Comes Filling the Valley," we suspect that whatever we do is "not enough." Many visitors to shrines may be skeptics like me, but feel it's worthwhile to purchase amulets and charms, just in case. I have a couple of dozen at home.

NOTES

1. Japanese immigrants established Yamato Shrine, dedicated to Amaterasu, in Hilo, in 1898. The shrine is known today as Hilo Daijingū.

Amaterasu worship was established on O'ahu in 1916 by Hawaii Daijingū, (Inoue et al. 172). According to the organizations's website, the shrine's founder was Masasato Kawasaki and "[i]ts initial site was Liliha Street. The fund [sic] came from the sale of personal property Masasato had owned in Japan." The daughter-of-law of Masasato reminisces:

> The outbreak of the War between Japan and the United States saw the closure and confiscation of the [shrine] as an enemy alien's property. Within several months my mother-in-law, children and I were sent to a camp in the mainland. After several months in the camp we were all shipped to Japan as part of the exchange program of the detainees.

When the war ended, the [shrine] was in a state of ruin. But upon the request of the congregation Kazoe [Bishop Kawasaki, son of the founder] and I returned to Hawaii to rebuild the [shrine] and resume our missionary activities.

The shrine is presently located in Nu'uanu.

Other Shintō sects, dedicated to other kami, were introduced. In 1906, Izumo Taisha-kyō, based on the worship of Ōkuninonushi, was established in Honolulu by Katsuyoshi Miyao.

A branch of Kotohira-gū a famous shrine atop Mt. Zōzu in Kagawa, Shikoku, was established in Kapālama, Honolulu, in 1920. Kotohira-gū promotes the worship of Ōmononushi-no-kami, a kami of fishing, seafaring, and trade worship, along with the spirit of Emperor Sutoku. Before the war, two other shrines brought their kami to the shrine in Kapālama, including Shirasaki Hachiman-gū of Yamaguchi-ken and Otaki Jinja, which enshrines the guardian kami of Otake city, Hiroshima, near its border with Yamaguchi.

After the war, more shrines and kami joined the the Kapālama shrine, including Dazaifu Tenman-gū of Saifu city, Fukuoka; Suiten-gū of Kurume, Fukuoka; and kami from an Inari Jinja and Watatsumi Jinja.

2. The dates given for the reigns of first fourteen imperial heads, including Sujin (the tenth) are considered mythical; and the dates of reigns up to the twenty-eighth head are considered historically inaccurate. While there was a shrine at Ise as early as the third or fourth century, the shrine at its present location is believed to have been built in the sixth or seventh century

3. The names of the kami in *Kojiki* and *Nihongi* are often very long: for example, Ho-no-Ninigi's full name is Ame-nigishi-kuni-nigishi-ama-tsu-hi-daka-hiko-ho-no-ninigi-no-mikoto, translated as "His-Augustness-Heaven-Plenty-Earth-Plenty-Heavenly-Sun-Height-Prince-Rice-Ear-Ruddy-Plenty. The first emperor's full name is Kamu-yamato-ihare-biko-no-mikoto (His-Augustness-Divine-Yamato-Ihare-Prince). Jimmu is his posthumous name. Here and elsewhere, I use shortened forms of the full names.

4. Near Takachiho, in Kyūshū, is a cave on Iwato stream, said to be the one in which Amaterasu hid herself. It's located across from the main building of Ama-no-Iwato (Heavenly Rock Door) Shrine. Another cave, upstream, known as Ama-no-Yasukawara, is said to be the cave where the kami met to devise their plan to bring Amaterasu out of the cave where she hid. Ama-no-Yasu-kawara, unlike the cave where the goddess hid, is accessible to visitors, down a path that goes to the river, then upstream along the bank, for about a third of a

mile. Inside the wide-mouthed cave is a small shrine. At a shrine in Takachiho town, the story of Amaterasu's retreat into the cave and Ame-no-uzume's dance to bring her out is re-enacted for visitors.

5. Cultures around the world recognized winter solstice as a dangerous time of the year. The days around solstice are the shortest of the year, and the rising sun appeared to linger at the same position on the horizon, as if winter might last forever. (Solstice means, literally, "sun standing still.") Thus, ritual action was needed to arouse the sun and get it moving again. The songs and dances known as Oku Shareh, or Turtle Dance, performed around solstice at San Juan Pueblo, New Mexico, is an example of ritual action intended to awaken the sun's spirit and beckon it to return from the dead of winter. Alfonso Ortiz writes in the liner notes to *Oku Shareh: Turtle Dance Songs of San Juan Pueblo*:

> The Turtle Dance is easily the most important public religious ceremony of the San Juan calendar, defining as it does the end of one year and the beginning of a new one. The dance is named for the turtle, believed to be the first hibernating being that moves about after the year has turned; thus the turtle is seen as a symbolizing the beginning of each new annual cycle.

6. Toyo-Tama-Hime is a daughter of Ōwata-tsumi-no-kami (Great-ocean-possessor Kami). She comes ashore to marry Jimmu's grandfather, Ho-ōri. When she's ready to give birth to a child, she builds a birth hut of cormorant feathers and tells Ho-ōri not to look at her because she will assume her native form during childbirth. He can't resist peeping, however, and sees that the princess is a wani (wani-zame, a kind of shark; Akima 149, note 3). He flees in terror. Shamed, she returns to her father's undersea palace after giving birth and closes up the road between the shore and the palace (*Kojiki* 154). The child born, Jimmu's father, is named Ama-tsu-hi-daka-hiko-nagisa-take-u-gaya-fu-ki-ahezu-no-mikoto (His Augustness Heaven's-sun-height-prince-wave-limit-brave-cormorant-thatch-meeting-completely).

7. The story of Susa-no-ō's slaying of a food kami from whose body animals and plants emerge is a variant of a myth distributed worldwide: food (plants and animals) is produced from the corpse of a deity who is killed or sacrifices herself or himself to provide sustenance for her or his descendants.

In an episode in *Nihongi*, the moon kami Tsukiyomi, Amaterasu's other brother, is assigned the role of slayer of a food kami. When Amaterasu sends him to earth to serve Ukemochi no kami (Food-possessing Kami), Ukemochi vomits boiled rice, fish, and animals and offers them to Tsukiyomi. Offended by the "filthy" food, Tsukiyomi slays her. Angered by his violence, Amaterasu sends Tsukiyomi to dwell separately from her, in the night sky.

From Ukemochi's corpse emerges animals and plants: from her crown the ox and horse; from her forehead millet; from above her eyebrows silkworms; from her eyes panic grass; from her belly rice; from her genitals wheat and large and small beans. Amaterasu rejoices and plants millet, panic grass, wheat, and beans in dry fields and rice in wet fields. She also puts silkworms in her mouth and spins thread from their cocoons (32–33).

8. The names given the three sacred imperial treasures are as follows:

Yata-no-Kagami. The eight-sided (or eight hand-span) mirror used to bring Amaterasu out of the cave where she hid. The mirror is said to be housed at Ise shrine.

Yasakani-no-Magatama. The eight-foot long string of jade stones used to entice Amaterasu out of the cave. The jewels are said to be housed at Kokyo, the Imperial Palace in Tōkyō.

Kusanagi. The sword taken by Susa-no-ō from one of the eight tails of Yamata-no-Orochi. According to *Nihongi*, Susa-no-ō sent the sword sent back to the Plain of High Heaven (53, 58).

The mirror and sword, traditional Taoist symbols of rule, indicate that Amaterasu worship developed after they were introduced to Japan from China and the Korean Peninsula.

During the Heian Period, a mirror, a string of jewels, and a sword were designated as the ones given to Ho-no-Ninigi by Amaterasu.

The mirror, Yata-no-Kagami, was originally kept in the Imperial Palace. In 960, a fire destroyed most of the palace, but the mirror was "miraculously unscathed," having flown to safety (Inoue et al. 82). During the Gempei War (1180–1185), as the Genji forces closed in on Kyōto, the Heike fled with their child Emperor Antoku (r. 1180–1185) and the three sacred treasures. In the sea battle of Dan-no-ura, near Shimonoseki, the mirror was almost lost: a Heike court lady was about to leap into the sea with the Chinese chest containing the mirror when a Genji warrior pinned her skirt with an arrow, and she tripped. The Genji warriors seized her and the chest; when they opened it: "darkness blinded their eyes instantly and blood gushed from their nostrils" (*The Tale of the Heike* 378–379). The mirror was brought back to Kyōto and was later placed at Ise shrine.

The story of the imperial sword is more complicated. According to *The Tale of the Heike*, "three sacred swords [were] handed down since the age of the gods": (1) Tozuka (Ten hand-breadths), "deposited at Iso-no-kami Furu Shrine in Yamato Province"; (2) Kusanagi (Grass-cutter), taken from Yamata-no-Orochi's tail; and (3) Ama-no-hayakiri (Heavenly Dragon Killer), enshrined at Atsuta, in Nagoya (383).

The name Kusanagi, "Grass-cutter," comes from an event in imperial history generations after Susa-no-ō slays the serpent Yamata-no-Orochi: Yamato Takeru, the son of Emperor Keikō, the twelfth imperial head (r. 71–130), was sent to subdue the eastern barbarians with the sword. He used it to escape death in a burning field by cutting the grass around him to create a safe area, then setting a counter fire that killed his attackers (*Kojiki* 255–256; *Nihongi* 205). According to *The Tale of the Heike*, Kusanagi-no-Tsurugi was lost at sea in the sea battle at Dan-no-ura. The emperor's grandmother (widow of the former head of the Heike family, Taira no Kiyomori) took the child emperor and the sacred sword and jewels and leapt into the sea. Both the grandmother and the child drowned. The jewels were recovered after the box they were in floated to the surface, but the sword was lost forever. One diviner claimed that Antoku was a reincarnation of Yamata-no-Orochi, the sword's original owner, and the serpent reclaimed the sword when it sank into the sea (383–386).

After Kusanagi was lost, Ama-no-hayakiri, at Atsuta Shrine, was designated as the imperial sword.

In one variant in *Nihongi*, the sword used to slay Yamata-no-Orochi is called Ama no Hayekiri, "Fly-cutter" (57). In other variants, the sword is called "Orochi no Ara-masa" (Rough-true), "now at Isonokami," Nara (56); and "Orochi no Kara-sabi" (Korea blade), housed in Kibi, Okayama (57).

9. The area where Ho-no-Ninigi's family settled after migrating to Japan is east of Mt. Takachiho, in the province of Himuka (or Hyūga, now Miyazaki Prefecture) in southeastern Kyūshū. Like Ise, where Amaterasu is enshrined, Himuka is situated on a coast facing the rising sun.

Himuka is a region of plateaus and alluvial plains, good for wet-rice cultivation. Three rivers—Ōyodo, Hitotsuse, and Komaru—flow east into the sea of Hyūga. In this area, archaeologists have identified about 140 kofun, the key-hole-shaped tumuli associated with the burial of clan chieftains. Eight of the ten largest kofun in Kyūshū are located in Himuka.

At Saitobaru, an archaeological site on the Hitotsuse River, 311 burial mounds have been identified, dating from the Kofun to Nara Periods (250–794), the highest concentration of such mounds in Japan. The mounds include thirty-one kofun. The two largest kofun on Kyūshū are located here: Mesa-hozuka (key-hole shaped, 577 feet long) and Osa-hozuka (scallop-shaped, 547 feet long). Assumed to be associated with the Imperial Family, neither has been excavated.

According to Inoue et al., kofun were eventually used as the sites for the transfer of power from one emperor to the next. The ceremony of transfer took place on the high round portion of the tomb, in which the deceased ruler was laid to rest. The lower square platform was used for the proclamation establishing the authority of the new ruler. After the transfer, the round portion was surrounded by haniwa, or unglazed terra-cotta cylinders and sculptural forms (19).

The largest kofun in Japan, located in Sakai, just south of Ōsaka, belongs to Nintoku, the sixteenth imperial head (r. 313–399). Nintoku's reign is described in *Kojiki* (324–346): his public works included granaries, flood control projects, and a port close to Naniwa (Ōsaka). At 1,594 feet long, 1,000 feet wide, and 115 feet high, Nintoku's kofun is much larger than the largest kofun found on Kyūshū, suggesting the increase in power and authority achieved after the Imperial Family migrated from Kyūshū east to the Nara-Kyōto-Ōsaka region, led by Ho-no-Ninigi's great grandson Jimmu, who remarks that while his family has "accumulated happiness and amassed glory" in Himuka,

> the remote regions [to the east] do not yet enjoy the blessings of Imperial rule. Every town has always been allowed to have its lord and every village its chief, who, each one for himself, makes division of territory and practises mutual aggression and conflict. (*Nihongi* 110)

He has heard that

> in the East there is a fair land encircled on all sides by blue mountains. … I think that this land will undoubtedly be suitable for the extension of the Heavenly task, so that its glory should fill the universe. It is, doubtless, the center of the world. … Why should we not proceed thither, and make it the capital? (110-111)

After a long journey and a series of battles, in one of which his oldest brother Itsuse is mortally wounded, Jimmu arrives at Kashihara (Oak-field)in Asuka, Yamato (Nara Prefecture), and builds a palace:

> So having thus subdued and pacified the savage Deities, and extirpated the unsubmissive people, Kamu-yamato-ihare [Jimmu] dwelt at the palace of Kashibara near Unebi [hill] and ruled the Empire. (*Kojiki* 175)

Jimmu reigns for seventy-five years (660 BC–585 BC). His youngest son by his consort I-suke-yori-hime succeeds him to the throne after a struggle against the eldest son from Jimmu's first wife.

10. Asuka was the imperial capital of Yamato from 538 to 710. During these years, Japanese emperors erected seven palaces. In 710, under Empress Gemmei (r. 707–715), the capital was moved fourteen miles north to Nara, which was modeled after the capital of T'ang China, Chang'an (Xi'an). In 794, under Emperor Kammu (r. 781–806), the capital was moved twenty-three miles north to Kyōto, so the imperial court could escape the influence of the powerful Buddhist temples that had established themselves in Nara.

11. A catfish's movements are associated with earthquakes because catfish are said to get excited and swim wildly when they sense an earthquake, before the ground starts noticeably shaking. One theory is that rocks under extreme stress emit charged particles that alert the catfish to the impending quake. During the Edo Period, the catfish Namazu was venerated as a symbol of world renewal by the poor, who believed upheavals like earthquakes would bring opportunities to escape poverty and obtain wealth (Ashkenazi 220-221, 266–267).

12. Izumo Taisha-kyō was founded during the Meiji Period in Japan by Takatomi Senge (1845–1918) to promote religious freedom. The sect opposed the government's efforts to place Shintō worship under government control. Izumo Taisha-kyō espouses the divine virtues of Ōkuninushi, the kami enshrined at Izumo Taisha in Shimane. In 1882, Izumo Taisha-kyō was recognized as an independent sect, with a formal body of teachings separate from State Shintō. The sect spread by proselytizing in Japan and overseas, in Sakhalin, Korea, Taiwan, Manchuria, and Hawai'i ("Izumo Ōyashirokyō," *Encyclopedia of Shinto*).

The first Izumo Taisha worship hall in Hawai'i was near 'A'ala Park, on the outskirts of downtown Honolulu. In 1907, a temporary shrine was erected, followed by a permanent shrine in 1922. During World War II, the Honolulu head priest, Shigemaru Miyao (a son of Katsuyoshi, who brought the worship to Hawai'i), was arrested, interned on Sand Island, then sent to an internment camp on the continent for the duration of the war. The shrine organization was dissolved, and its property, including the shrine building, was gifted to the city. In 1961, after a long legal battle, the property was returned to the shrine organization. The shrine was moved to its present site alongside Nu'uanu Stream to make way for a redevelopment project. It was restored in 1969.

13. Ieyasu Tokugawa (1543–1616), whose family ruled Japan for fifteen generations, from 1603–1858, was a supporter of Sengen Fuji Shrines, dedicated to Sengen or Asama and Konohana-sakuya-hime, kami worshipped for protection from the eruptions of Mt. Fuji.

Fujisan Hongū Sengen Taisha, the head shrine, was originally established in its present location in Fujinomiya during the reign of Emperor Keikō (r. 71–130). In 1604, Ieyasu constructed the inner and outer shrine buildings and tower gate to commemorate his victory over his rivals for control of the government. Located on Fuji's southwest side, the buildings house the spirits of Sengen/Asama/Konohana-sakuya-hime, as well as Ho-no-Ninigi and Asama/Konohana-sakuya-hime's father, Ōyamatsumi, a son of Izanagi and Izanami.

The Kanda River is fed by spring water from Mt. Fuji emerging at Wakutama Pond at the shrine. The water is considered sacred and purifying, and people come to fill containers to take home for cooking and purification. Ducks, salmon, and carp inhabit the pool.

There are around 1,300 Sengen Fuji branch shrines, concentrated in Shizuoka and Yamanashi Prefectures, around Fuji. Most of these shrines have views of the mountain; those without views have replicas of the mountain built on their grounds from its volcanic rocks.

SOURCES

Akima, Toshio. "The Origins of the Grand Shrine of Ise and the Cult of the Sin Goddess Amaterasu Ōmikami." *Japan Review* 4 (1993): 141–198.

Ashkenazi, Michael. *Handbook of Japanese Mythology*. Santa Barbara: ABC-CLIO, 2003.

Borgen, Robert. *Sugawara no Michizane and the Early Heian Court*. Cambridge: Harvard UP, 1986.

Breen, John and Mark Teeuwen, eds. *Shinto in History: Ways of the Kami*. Honolulu: U of Hawai'i, 2000.

Casal, U.A. *The Five Sacred Festivals of Ancient Japan*. Rutland: Tuttle, 1967.

Como, Michael. *Weaving and Binding: Immigrant Gods and Female Immortals in Ancient Japan*. Honolulu: U of Hawai'i, 2009.

Encyclopedia of Shintō. Kokugakuin U, Sept. 2008. Web.

French, Howard W. "Japan Has Little Time for Its Old-Time Religion." *New York Times*. New York Times, 13 Sept. 2001. Web.

Farris, William. *Sacred Texts and Buried Treasures: Issues in the Historical Archaeology of Ancient Japan*. Honolulu: U of Hawai'i, 1998.

Inoue, Nobutaka, Satoshi Itō, Jun Endō, and Mizue Mori. *Shinto—A Short History*. Trans. and adapters Mark Teeuwen and John Breen, London: Routledge Curzon, 2003.

"Jingu Shrine in Ise." *Japan Atlas*. Web Japan, n.d. Web.

Kanda, Christine Guth. *Shinzō: Hachiman Imagery and its Development*. Boston: Harvard UP, 1985.

The Kojiki: Records of Ancient Matters. Trans. Basil Hall Chamberlain. Boston: Tuttle, 1981.

Kuroda, Toshio, James C. Dobbins and Suzanne Gay. "Shinto in the History of Japanese Religion." *Journal of Japanese Studies* 7.1 (1981): 1–21.

Matsumae, Takeshi, "Origin and Growth of the Worship of Amaterasu." *Asian Folklore Studies* 37.1 (1978): 1–11.

Matsumura, Kazuo. "Ancient Japan and Religion." *Nanzan Guide to Japanese Religion*. Eds. Paul L. Swanson and Clark Chilson. Honolulu: U of Hawaiʻi, 2006. 131–142.

Miyazawa, Kenji. *Miyazawa Kenji: Selections*. Ed. Hiroaki Satō. Berkeley: U of California, 2007.

Naumann, Nelly. "The state cult of the Nara and early Heian periods." Breen and Teeuwen 52–67.

Nelson, John K. *Enduring Identities: The Guise of Shinto in Contemporary Japan*. Honolulu: U of Hawaiʻi, 2000.

Nihongi: Chronicles of Japan from the Earliest Times to A.D. 697. Trans. W.G. Aston. Boston: Tuttle, 1972.

The Poetics of Motoori Norinaga: A Hermeneutical Journey. Trans. and ed. Michael F. Marra. Honolulu: U of Hawaiʻi, 2007.

Sakamoto, Koremaru. "The structure of state Shinto: its creation, development and demise." Breen and Teeuwen 272–294.

Shirane, Haruo. *Japan and the Culture of the Four Seasons*. New York: Columbia U, 2012.

Smyers, Karen A. *The Fox and the Jewel: Share and Private Meanings in Contemporary Japanese Inari Worship*. Honolulu: U of Hawaiʻi, 1999.

Sonoda, Minoru. "Shinto and the natural environment." Breen and Teeuwen 32–46.

The Tale of the Heike. Trans. Helen McCullough. Palo Alto: Stanford UP, 1988.

Yanagita, Kunio. *The Legends of Tono*. Trans. Ronald A. Morse. New York: Lexington, 2008.

Tracking Mankai

Driving along the Kumano coast in mid-March 2004, I noticed amid the grays and greens small patches of faint pink and white on the mountain slopes:

sakura starting to bloom on high peaks
don't they look like wispy clouds? (Saigyō)

A week later, at Momoyama Castle in Ōsaka and along the streets, canals, and river banks of Kyōto, sakura trees were blooming.

Not a flower enthusiast (though I like flowers), I hadn't planned for hanami (flower viewing) on our first springtime visit to Japan. We returned to Hawai'i before mankai, or full bloom. But seeing the bloom in the ancient capital evoked a nostalgia for something I'd heard in song, but never experienced while growing up:

Sakura, sakura –
In fields and villages
As far as the eyes can see …
Mist or clouds?
Fragrant in the morning sun.

Four years after our spring visit, I planned a two-week journey through central Honshū in the first two weeks of April, on average, the best time for hanami there. The bloom lasts about three weeks:

in sakura's house, from start to finish, around twenty days
hana o yado ni / hajime owari ya / hatsuka hodo (Bashō, spring 1688)

Mankai occurs a week after kaika (first bud opening) and lasts for a week or so before the bloom diminishes through the final week. During mankai, only a few days might be considered full bloom, before gusts of spring winds sweep the branches, and the small petals come swirling down.

Starting in Okinawa in January and ending in Hokkaidō in late May, the sakura bloom moves from southwest to northeast, earlier in warmer years, later in cooler ones. It's hard to predict which sites will be in bloom when. We planned to follow the routes of two historic roads between Tōkyō and Kyōto, traveling the Tōkaidō (Eastern Sea Road) west to Kyōto, into the oncoming bloom along the coast; then returning along the Nakasendō (Central Mountain Road), east through the inland mountains, where the trees bloom later than they do along the coastal plains.

For scholar and poet Norinaga Motoori (1730–1801), yamazakura (mountain cherry trees, what we saw in the Kumano hills) represents the essence of the Japanese spirit:

> Asked what is the Yamato-Spirit of old Japan:
> It's the mountain sakura
> Fragrant in the morning sun.

Since ancient times, farmers have taken the blossoming yamazakura as a sign that the fertility kami, who retreat to the mountains in winter, are ready to return to the fields.

> sakura in sunlight,
> somehow look like frogs' eggs. (Miyazawa 115)

Before planting, farmers went to the mountains and made offerings under the trees, then carried the kami in blossoming branches to the rice fields. A full bloom was an auspicious sign for a good rice harvest to come.

There are about 400 varieties of sakura, in shades of white, pink, or yellow, with five or more petals, and branches upright or weeping. Different varieties bloom at different times, mainly in spring and summer, but even in winter.

In 1860, a Tōkyō horticulturist developed Somei-Yoshino, a hybrid whose flowers appear before its leaves, so at mankai, the trees have full crowns of white-pink blossoms with no greenery. Somei-Yoshino has been planted along roads and river banks, in parks, and around castles, temples, and shrines to create spectacular scenes when all the trees come into full bloom at the same time.

On our hanami journey, we hoped to hit one or more spots at mankai, and that one of those spots would be Yoshino, a mountain south of Nara considered the most spectacular full bloom. In the eighth century, Yoshino became the headquarters of Shugendō, a syncretic Buddhist-Shintō sect practicing mountain asceticism. The sect regards sakura blossoms as offerings to Zaō, the deity enshrined at Mt. Yoshino, so worshipers have planted the mountain with 30,000 trees. The blossoms help worshipers enter a spiritual state:

> Cherry blossoms in full bloom were considered to be intoxicating

and to draw the adherent's spirit into the world of gods and buddhas. When the cherry blossoms bloomed at Mount Fudaraku [the mythical Buddhist Pure Land said to be located] to the south of Mount Nachi [south of Yoshino on the Kii peninsula], … the distance to the Pure Land was believed to disappear, and this world became that world. (Shirane 152)

Yoshino's remotest viewing area, oku-senbon, was the site of a meditation hut belonging to Saigyō (1118–1190) a samurai who became a priest and poet, and whose waka (traditional five-line syllabic poems) express his enchantment with the beauty of sakura, especially around Mt. Yoshino:

Mt. Yoshino: since the day I saw blossoming branches of sakura, my heart has wandered from my body.

Mt. Yoshino: I change my path every year, searching for blossoms in forms I've never seen.

If only I could divide myself, not miss a single tree, see the blossoms at their best on all ten thousand mountains! ("Sanka: Saigyo's Mountain Home")

In one waka, Saigyō expresses his wish to die when the world was at its most beautiful—at mankai under the full moon of Kisaragi (second moon of the year, around March). His wish was fulfilled when he passed away in 1190, at 73, at Hirokawa Temple in Kawachi (eastern Ōsaka). It was on the sixteenth day of Kisaragi, a day after full moon (March 23 that year) with sakura in bloom.

The practice of hanami was introduced from China as an aristocratic pastime during the Nara Period (710–794). Initially, the flower of hanami was ume, or plum blossom, which blooms before sakura, in the first moon of spring. *Manyōshū* (Collection of Ten Thousand Leaves), the earliest anthology of Japanese poetry, compiled around 749, contains four times more poems about ume than about sakura:

Superb is the fragrance
Of the plum blossoms
So no matter how far you are,
I will think of you
Until my heart fades away.

Sakura became the flower of hanami during the Heian Period (794–1185).

Emperor Saga (r. 786–842) established the practice of holding parties with saké and food to celebrate the blossoming of the trees. Shikibu Murasaki's eleventh-century *Genji Monogatari* (*Tale of Genji*) describes a hanami party at which the guests wrote poems in honor of the sakura:

> It was a lovely day, with a bright sky and birdsong to gladden the heart, when those who prided themselves on their skill—[p]rinces, senior nobles, and all—drew their rhymes and began composing Chinese verses. (Murasaki 155)

When the daimyō (feudal warlords of the samurai class) rose to power, they adopted the practice of hanami to establish that their aesthetic sensibilities were equal to those of the nobles. Hideyoshi Toyotomi (1536–1598), a farmer who climbed the ranks of Nobunaga Oda's army to control the government as Regent, hosted lavish hanami celebrations. In spring 1594, he invited five thousand guests to Yoshimizu Shrine in Yoshino. It rained for three days, and, according to legend, Hideyoshi threatened to torch the mountain unless the monks's prayers could bring good weather. Fortunately for both the monks and the guests, the rain stopped (Lindelauf).

Four years later, in the year he died, Hideyoshi held a grand hanami at Daigo Temple in Kyōto. He refurbished the temple, redesigned the garden, and transplanted seven hundred sakura from Ōshū and Kawachi to create a tunnel of blossoms through which he led a parade of fifteen hundred participants. Hideyoshi composed a waka about the renewal of the shrine and the blossoming of sakura, metaphorically expressing his hope that his son Hideyori (1593–1613) would rule after him:

> Renovated, change your name, Miyukiyama: the buried flowers have reappeared.

Hideyoshi's wish didn't come true: his son committed ritual suicide in Ōsaka Castle after his army was defeated by the forces of Ieyasu. But the Daigo hanami lives on in the Hideyoshi Hanami Parade held annually on the second Sunday in April (Ikeda).

By the Edo Period (1603–1868), merchants and trades people had joined the nobles and samurai in the celebration of sakura, with eating, drinking, and singing under blossoming trees:

> at the base of the trunk, soup and fish salad, and of course, sakura!
> ki no moto wa / shiru mo namasu mo / sakura kana (Bashō, spring 1690)

Of the revelry of commoners, aesthetes commented contemptuously "hana yori dango" (more than flowers, rice-dumplings). For some of the celebrants, saké, not hana or dango, was the essence of the celebration:

saké cup in my sleeve, ready for flowers! (Kūga, 1699)

beneath the flowers, ruling the world for seven days: drinkers! (Ōemaru, 18th century)

without saké, viewing sakura is a kappa's fart. (Yanagidaru, 19th century)

The urban crowds at hanami could be boisterous, not just drinking and singing, but gambling, thieving, and fighting:

stirring up quarrels, scattering flowers, they pass by (Issa, 1817)

The Dutch, who were the only Europeans allowed into the country during the Edo Period, were the first Europeans to participate in hanami:

a dutchman, too, comes to view sakura, from the saddle of his horse oranda mo / hana ni ki ni keri / uma ni kura (Bashō, spring 1679)

Today, the hanami tradition continues. Kayoko, a student of mine who grew up in Mihama, Hiroshima, describes late twentieth-century hanami:

The TV news reports how far the blossoms have moved every day. People watch the report to find out when the blossoming will reach their town so that they can go sakura viewing on the right day.

Whole families or whole companies will go to view cherry blossoms together. Picnic mats are spread under the trees. We eat, drink, sing and dance. ... Pink cherry blossoms are beautiful under the baby blue of the spring sky; so are the somewhat darker-colored blossoms in the white moonlight. The sakura watchers keep on coming until past midnight. (Norton 20)

On our flight from Honolulu to Narita on April 3, 2008, I read in a newspaper that the best day for hanami in Tōkyō was the day before. The flowers had opened about a week earlier than predicted. (In 2009, prime bloom in the capital was even earlier, after the earliest blooms on record in southern and western Japan. By chance, on March 31, 2014, we were in Tōkyō at the start of mankai and caught a train to crowded Ueno Park to stroll beneath the trees.)

Our first stop in 2008 was Kamakura, twenty-eight miles southeast of

Sakura on the approach to Tsurugaoka Hachiman Shrine, Kamakura

Tōkyō, where the avenue up to Tsurugaoka Hachiman Shrine is planted with sakura. It was a sunny afternoon, ideal for hanami. As we walked with the crowd along the avenue of fully-bloomed trees, a few petals fluttered down with each light breath of wind. Beneath the trees around the shrine's ponds, petals floated on the surface.

Farther west, the sites we visited were in various stages of bloom. At Odawara Castle, the sakura around the entrance and along the moat were peaking, and the park and square in front of the castle grounds were crowded with people enjoying picnics and strolling around an open market.

We detoured off the Tōkaidō to tour the Izu peninsula; at a mountain flower park, the sakura had yet to bloom; but when we got to the port of Shimoda, the flowers along the Inozawa River were fully bloomed. We walked along the bank in the morning, the blossoms tinted with a soft yellow glow by the sun rising above the hills. Along the cliff-side road on the west coast of Izu, rows of trees sprinkled the asphalt with petals.

We stopped in Shizuoka city for its spring festival, held on the first Saturday of April. The trees along the street were past mankai, already sprouting green leaves. (The bloom comes to Shizuoka a week before it arrives in Tōkyō.) The festival features a hanami procession to Sengen Shrine, dedicated to Asama or Sengen, the kami of Mt. Fuji. Around the fifteenth century, Asama was identified with Konohana-sakuya-hime (Flowers-of-the-blooming-trees Princess), who married Ho-no-Ninigi, the grandson of Amaterasu sent from the Plain of High Heaven to rule the Eight Great Islands.

The story of her marriage to Ho-no-Ninigi establishes flowers as the quintessential metaphor for transient human life, the passing of generations, the rise and fall of ruling families. The princess's father, Ō-yama-tsumi (Great-mountain-possessor) agrees to Ho-no-Ninigi's proposal to marry his daughter, but sends along with the beautiful flower princess her uglier older sister, Iha-naga-hime (Rock-long Princess). Ho-no-Ninigi sends the older sister back. Ō-yama-tsumi explains he offered the rock princess so that [their offspring] might live eternally immovable like unto the enduring rocks." Because Ho-no-Ninigi marries only the flower princess, "the august offspring of the Heavenly Deity shall be but as frail as the flowers of the trees" (*Kojiki* 138–140).

West of Shizuoka, at Lake Hamana, our ryokan (inn) provided a shuttle for yozakura (night sakura) at the nearby Hamamatsu City Flower Park. Yozakura features the blossoming trees illuminated by paper lanterns. When we went back the next day to see the sakura in daylight, amid fields of red, yellow, and white tulips, sakura petals were swirling down and driven along the paths in cold gusts of wind; a thick layer of pink petals floated at the edges of the ponds.

To get to Yoshino from Lake Hamana, we drove off the Tōkaidō, at Seki, and into the mountains of Iga-Ueno, the hometown of the seventeenth-century haiku poet Bashō. After moving to Edo, Bashō returned to Iga-Ueno in the summer of 1687 and went to Yoshino the following spring for hanami:

> During my three-days' stay in Yoshino, I had a chance to see the cherry blossoms at different hours of the day—at early dawn, late in the evening, or past midnight when the dying moon was in the sky. Overwhelmed by the scenes, however, I was not able to compose a single poem. My heart was heavy, for I remembered the famous poems of Sesshōkō, Saigyō, Teihitsu and other ancient poets. (Bashō 84)

When we arrived at Yoshino on the morning of April 7, the valley and ridges weren't covered with blossoming yamazakura as I had imagined and anticipated. Too early or too late? Photos posted later on the internet suggest we were too early, mankai arriving on the hillsides around April 12. Still, some fully bloomed trees along the street to Kinpusen Temple were impressive.

We drove eleven miles north to Ishibutai (Stone-stage), in Asuka. This empty crypt is believed to belong to Soga no Umako (551–626), a powerful aristocrat who, with Prince Shōtoku, fought to establish Buddhism in Japan. The roof of the tomb is formed by two massive elongated rocks. On the south

The entrance into Ishibutai, Nara

side, sakura trees were just past full bloom. Walking to the dead-end of the dark, damp, cold, empty chamber with walls and ceiling of massive stones, I felt a chill inside me, a gust of centuries passing.

In Kyōto, along the Kamo River and its canals and on the grounds of the old Imperial Palace, mankai was fading, and in the chilly breeze, petals fluttered down like swarms of small white butterflies.

After a couple of nights in Ōtsu, just east of Kyōto, where the Tōkaidō and Nakasendō join, we drove to Hikone Castle, which is far enough north to be blooming later than Kyōto. It turned out to be the highlight of our hanami: the bloom of trees along a wide moat was fuller than at Kamakura or Odawara a week and a half earlier. The small, well-preserved Edo-period castle, situated on a low hill, was surrounded by pink clouds of blossoming trees under an overcast spring sky. Trees blooming along the pathway to the castle were framed, like a painting, by a wide dark gateway through a massive stone wall, just past a wooden bridge. In the courtyard in front of the castle keep (brought from Ōtsu Castle), trees with curving branches were thick with swirls of blossoms.

Three days later, when we arrived in the mountain town of Takayama for its spring festival on April 14, the sakura trees along the Miya River were still in bud. After we returned home to Hawai'i, a blogger from Takayama, dated April

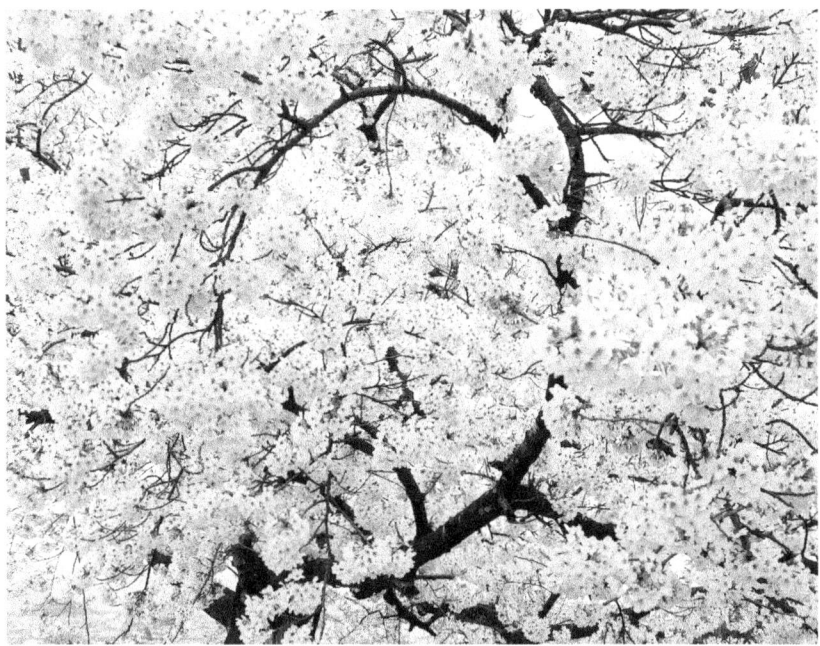

Swirl of sakura at Hikone Castle, Shiga

28, 2008, reported, "The peak was actually during last week, and with the rain we had over the weekend most of the petals are now gone."

Other flowers appear before sakura to signal the arrival of spring. In the first moon of spring by the lunar calendar (late January or February), fukuju-sō bloom amid snow and dried leaves, at the fringes of bare deciduous forests. Like the Adonis plant of the Mediterranean, which is a relative, fukuju-sō signifies the rebirth of nature. (Adonis is the beloved hunter of the moon goddess Aphrodite. After he is killed by a boar, she brings him back to life as the flower named after him.)

Ume (plum trees) flower next:

> People go plum viewing, but it is not warm enough for a picnic yet. Instead of going in a large group, we usually go with a few people and walk around under the trees with our hands deep in coat pockets. If it gets too cold to be walking, we can stop at a nearby tea room for hot drinks. (Norton 19)

In late March, 2004, we were walking to Kasuga Shrine in Nara on a cold, rainy morning, with our hands in our rain-jacket pockets. We came across some blossoming trees with small white flowers. "Sakura?" I asked an elderly couple walking by. "Perhaps ume" was the wife's polite reply.

> after the fragrance of ume: a mountain path where the sun appears
> (ume ga ka ni / notto hi no deru / yamaji kana (Bashō, spring 1694)

After ume, momo (peach) and sakura bloom at about the same time:

> in two hands, peach and cherry blossoms with mugwort-flavored rice cake
> ryō no te ni / momo to sakura ya / kusa no mochi (Bashō, spring 1692)

Peach blossoms are associated with Girls' Day, originally Momo no Sekku, or Peach Festival, celebrated on 3.3 (around early April), at the beginning of the last moon of spring:

> Peaches are pale pink like a little girl's cheek; compared to plum, peaches are much more feminine. The petals are softer and the branches are more curved. (Norton 20)

Norinaga refers to a poem in *Kokinshū* (905–920) to explain why he prefers sakura to ume:

> It is because they scatter
> Without leaving a trace
> That sakura flower delights us so,
> Since to linger in the world to the end
> Is depressing. (Poem 2:71)

In contrast to sakura, Norinaga explains:

> [Ume blossoms] do not know how to scatter by the time the cherries have bloomed, … they age and shrink. When I look at them surviving, every spring, I am reminded of the pain of lingering in the world, a pain that is associated with everything. (*Poetics of Motoori Norinaga* 125)

Norinaga remarks that humans are able to see themselves as sakura because of their capacity for what he calls mono-no-awaré, "to be stirred deeply by external things" (*Poetics of Motoori Norinaga* 174–175), an ability he associates with kokoro, or heart (172). The awareness of the transiency of life seen in the brief flowering of sakura each spring developed into a paradoxical appreciation of life and death intertwined, with death intensifying the beauty of life.

Among the samurai, the belief that to die young was better than lingering into old age was embraced as a way of coming to terms with death in battle.

During World War II, the first four units of kamikaze (divine wind) that crashed their planes into American warships on suicidal missions took their names from words in Norinaga's poem equating the Japanese spirit to mountain sakura at dawn: Shikishima (Deer Islands, a poetic name for Japan), Yamato (Japan), Asahi (morning sun), and Yamazakura (mountain sakura).

Kayoko recalls her last hanami in Japan before coming to America with her American husband:

> I knew I couldn't come back for another hanami for a long time. That day, I woke up at five o'clock in the morning. I packed the best lunch I had ever cooked. It was the finest day of that April. Hundreds of cherry trees in the park were blooming in full. The air was colored with blossoms. I wished I could be dyed pink, too. I wished that that wouldn't be my last hanami. I wished everything would be fine in the States. I wished… I wished… Maybe, I shouldn't have made any wishes under the tree. So far, none of my wishes have come true. (Norton 20)

Her memory of leaving home reminded me of my two grandmothers, who emigrated from Japan to Hawai'i a century ago, as picture brides, to marry my grandfathers. Only two sakura varieties have been planted here, an Okinawan variety in Wahiawā, O'ahu, and a Taiwanese variety in Waimea, on the Big Island (these two upland areas having relatively cool rainy seasons).

I hope that the wishes that my two grandmothers had when they left the homeland had been fulfilled. They both had large families (six and ten children, with grandchildren and great grandchildren). Like many of the immigrants, they wanted to educate their offspring, so the family could rise from the farming and merchant class to become professionals, the equivalent of Confucian scholars. Many of their children and grandchildren graduated from college.

Both grandmothers outlived their husbands by many years before passing on. My mother's mother, less rigid and more accepting of life and change, seemed the happier of the two; my father's mother, because she had strong expectations of her children and grandchildren and resisted change, was more susceptible to disappointment. Kayoko's essay concludes with a melancholy characteristic of Japanese writings about spring and autumn:

> Cherry blossoms are the last sign of spring. They tell us spring is evaporating under the recovering sun. Usually, strong winds will come and wipe out the remainders of spring. When the wind blows the last petal of cherry blossom away, spring is officially over.
>
> Spring has a mind of cherry blossom, impermanence. We wait and wait for it but as soon as it comes, it is already going. There are no sure

moments of it. This is why, though it is the time for new lives to be born, spring also implies death. Spring reminds us that time is always running away. (Norton 20)

By the time we drove back down to the Kantō plains and Tōkyō after two weeks, the hanami season there was over. Our journey felt disjointed, a mosaic of sites in various states of bloom. One day, I hope to stay in one place to experience the anticipation of spring during the last days of winter and the excitement of watching sakura day by day come into full bloom, followed by the sadness of blossoms falling:

a cloud of blossoms, a temple bell—at Ueno? or Asakusa?
hana no kumo / kane wa Ueno ka / Asakusa ka (Bashō, spring 1687)

SOURCES

Bashō. *The Narrow Road to the Deep North and other Travel Sketches*. Trans. Nobuyuki Yuasa. New York: Penguin, 1966.

Ikeda, Janet. "Memorialized in Verse: Hideyoshi's Daigo Hanami in 1598." *Obaegaki: Newsletter of the Early Modern Japan Network*. 5.1 (1995). Np.

The Kojiki: Records of Ancient Matters. Trans. Basil Hall Chamberlain. Boston: Tuttle, 1981.

Lindelauf, Perrin. "Yoshino: Hanami among the mountains gods." *Japan Times*. Japan Times, 14 Mar. 2008. Web.

Miyazawa, Kenji. *Miyzawa Kenji: Selections*. Ed. Hiroaki Satō. Berkeley: U of California, 2007.

Murasaki, Shikibu. *The Tale of Genji*. Trans. Royall Taylor. New York: Penguin, 2003.

Norton, Kayoko. "Signs of Time Running Away." *Horizons, A Journal of International Writing and Art* 3 (1995): 19–20.

The Poetics of Motoori Norinaga: A Hermeneutical Journey. Trans. and ed. Michael F. Marra. Honolulu: U of Hawai'i, 2007.

"Sanka: Saigyo's Mountain Home." *Hermitary: resources and reflections on hermits and solitude*. Hermitary and Meng-hu, Sept. 2008. Web.

Shirane, Haruo. *Japan and the Culture of the Four Seasons*. New York: Columbia UP, 2012.

Fujisan and Mountain Worship

In "One Hundred Views of Mt. Fuji," Osamu Dazai (1909–1948), taking an outsider's point of view, questions the Japanese adulation of Fujisan (Mt. Fuji):

> If I were living in India … and were suddenly snatched up and carried off by an eagle and dropped on the beach at Numazu in Japan, I doubt if I'd be very much impressed at the sight of this mountain. (71)

Viewing Fuji from a window in Tōkyō, he remarks:

> That small white triangle poking up over the horizon: that's Fuji. It's nothing; it's a Christmas candy. What's more it lists pathetically to the left, like a battleship slowly beginning to founder. (71–72)

He points out that Fuji's slopes are not as steep and its cone is not as symmetrical as depicted in art, so the mountain is not as impressive as its image: "… the real Fuji is unmistakably obtuse, with long leisurely slopes; by no means do one hundred twenty-four degrees east-west and one hundred seventeen north-south make for a very steep peak" (71).

In the end, though, he's unable to resist the beauty of the most distinctive and striking geographical feature in the six thousand islands of his homeland. After seeing the mountain from Misaka Pass, he confesses, "It occurred to me that I was no match for Fuji. I was ashamed of my own fickle, constantly shifting feelings of love and hatred. Fuji was impressive. Fuji knew what it was doing" (76).

Mt. Fuji is celebrated in the first anthology of Japanese poetry, *Manyōshū* (Collection of Ten Thousand Leaves), compiled in 759. Akahito Yamabe proclaims its glory in a waka: "since the separation of heaven and earth, Fujisan has towered above Suruga, lofty, noble, and divine."

Among the most-cited poems about Fuji is one by the eighth-century court poet Mushimaro Takahashi:

> There, the peak of Fuji soars skyward
> At the border of Kai and wave-washed Suruga,
> Halting the heavenly clouds,
> Blocking birds in flight.

Snow quenches its fire.
Falling snows dissolves in its flames.
No words can describe
The mystery of this living kami.

The mountain embraces
The waters called Se,
The torrential river we cross
Is called Fuji.
Fuji is at the source of the sun,
The guardian of the land of Yamato,
A living kami, a treasure in Suruga.
Our eyes never grow weary gazing up
At the lofty peak of Fuji.

Envoy:

On Fuji's peak
The fallen snow vanishes in mid-summer
Only to appear again that very night.

At the border of Kai (Yamanashi) and Suruga (eastern Shizuoka), Mt. Fuji lies
in the direction of the rising sun from Yamato (Nara). The meaning of the name
"Fuji" is lost in time, with various etymologies suggested, none conclusive.

During the Edo Period (1603–1868), when the center of political and
commercial power shifted from Kyōto to Tōkyō, the already legendary
mountain seventy-five miles west of the new capital became the nation's
central landmark and symbol. Fuji was a favorite subject of Edo poets. During
the sixth moon (around July) of 1676, on his first trip home to Iga-Ueno after
moving to Edo in 1672, Bashō (1644–1694) marveled at the summer greenery:

rooted in clouds, Fuji is cedar-shaped and thickly forested
kumo o ne ni / fuji wa suginari no / shigeri kana

That summer in Ueno, at a poetry session in his honor, the poet offered a
fan to provide relief to his friends from the heat and humidity:

Fuji's wind: carried in this fan, a gift from Edo
fuji no kaze ya / ōgi ni nosete / Edo miyage

Whether seen or shrouded in mist, Fuji fascinated:

To be honored with a view is special: fifth-moon Fuji
me ni kakaru / toki ya kotosara / satsuki fuji (Summer 1694)

misty shower: a day when Fuji can't be seen still enchanting
(kiri shigure / fuji o minu hi zo / omoshiroki (Autumn 1684)

Fuji was also a favorite subject of Edo woodblock-print artists: in 1827,
Katsushika Hokusai (1760–1849) published "36 Views of Mount Fuji"; and
two decades later, Andō Hiroshige (1797–1858) produced two collections
of "36 Views," one in landscape format, then a year later, another in portrait
format. As these woodblock prints spread to the West, Fuji became internationally famous.

In the late nineteenth and early twentieth century, when Japanese began
traveling abroad and returning home by steamship, as they approached Tōkyō
Bay, the summit of Mt. Fuji might be the first land sighted. In "Feelings of One
Born in Honolulu," Naoto Nakashima describes his first view of Fuji, in 1917,
from the deck of an arriving ship: the snowy summit, lavender-colored, in the
hazy light of an autumn dawn. As the other passengers gaze in wonder at the
mountain, the teenager from Hawai'i attempts to sketch it, but is overwhelmed
by emotion. Finally, he writes simply: "I am a boy who was born in Hawai'i.
For the first time in my sixteen years I'm visiting Japan. This isn't a dream ....
In several hours, splendidly dressed, I will be able to step onto my mother's
homeland." He recalls seeing Fuji in a painting at a Hongan temple in Honolulu.

At 12,288 feet, Mt. Fuji is Japan's tallest mountain. It grew in three stages:
Komitake, the oldest mountain, is 700,000 years old; Old Fuji, which formed
atop Komitake, is 100,000 years old; and Young Fuji, the conic mountain we
know today, is 11,000 years old. In the last two thousand years, it has erupted
over seventy times. The most recent eruption occurred three centuries ago, in
1707. After an earthquake, cinder and ash (but no lava) spewed from vents
on the southwest slope and drifted east-northeast over Edo. The mountain is
considered a low risk for eruption today, although seismic activity continues.

The kami of Fuji is Asama-no-Ōkami. "Asama" (the two kanji are also
read "Sengen") may be Ainu in origin, her name meaning "mountain spouting
fire." During the reign of Emperor Kōrei (r. 290 BC–215 BC), people living
near the mountain fled from eruptions. Emperor Suinin (r. 29 BC–AD 70),
enshrined Sengen at the base of Fuji to pacify the kami. (Suinin is also said to
have enshrined Amaterasu at Ise.)

When Yamato Takeru (Brave One of Yamato), son of Emperor Keikō (r.
71–130), came to Suruga to subdue the eastern barbarians, he was trapped by a
fire set in a field of grass. He prayed to Sengen and was saved, so he built her a
shrine at Yamamiya, on the southwest side of Fuji.

Between 781 and 1083, Fuji erupted nine times. In 806, Emperor Heizei

(r. 806–809) ordered Sakanoue no Tamuramaro (758–811), the shōgun who pacified northern Honshū, to move the Sengen Shrine four miles south to its present location in Fujinomiya, at the limit of a lava flow. Despite the presence of the shrine, another major eruption occurred in 864, spewing cinder, ash, and lava for ten days and causing deaths. The lava flowed down the northwest slope and divided a large lake into two smaller lakes, Lake Sai and Lake Shōji.

During the Muromachi Period (1338–1573), Sengen became identified with Konohana-sakuya-hime (Flowers-of-the-blooming-trees Princess), the daughter of Ōyamatsumi no Kami (Great-mountain-possessor Kami). The basis of this identification is the story told in *Kojiki*, of princesss' marriage to Amaterasu's grandson Ho-no-Ninigi. Ho-no-Ninigi questions her fidelity when she becomes pregnant and is ready to give birth in one night. She encloses herself in a hall and has it set on fire, declaring that if she has been unfaithful she and her children would perish in the fire; if not, they would survive. She and three newborn sons—named Ho-deri (Fire-shine), Ho-suseri (Fire-climax), and Ho-ōri (Fire-subside)—emerge unharmed. The princess's fidelity and purity are credited with making her and her children impervious to fire, and she is worshipped as a protector against fire. Konohana-sakuya-hime, along with Ho-no-Ninigi and Ōyamatsumi, are venerated at Fujinomiya Shrine. This shrine, officially called Fujisan Hongū Sengen Taisha, is the headquarters of 1,300 Sengen shrines, the majority located in areas from where Fuji can be seen.

In Buddhism, Mt. Fuji is symbolic of zenjō, the state of perfect concentration in meditation, when worshipers rise above worldly illusions. Mountain ascent is equated with spiritual ascent.

Prince Shōtoku (576–622), an early patron of Buddhism, is said to have flown over the summit on a black horse. En-no-Gyōja (En the Ascetic, b. 634), the founder of Shugendō, a syncretic Buddhist-Shintō sect practicing mountain asceticism, engaged in nightly austerities on Fuji after flying there from Izu (Earhart 208–209). Earhart explains the purpose of nyūbu, the practice of "mountain entry," of which mountain ascent was one form:

> to leave the ordinary world, purify and transform oneself through contact with the sacred mountain and the performance of ascetic and devotional practices, and return to the ordinary world in a renewed state. (212)

In 1149, Matsudai Shōnin, a shugenja (practitioner of Shugendō), ascended the summit of Fuji and built a temple dedicated to Dainichi (Great Sun), the cosmic Buddha sitting in meditation at the center of the Vairocana mandala.

In a vision aided by a quartz rock shaped like Fuji, he saw the female Sengen as a manifestation of the male Dainichi, a single god, Sengen-Dainichi, who transcended the division between kami and Buddha, and female and male. Matsudai established the headquarters for Fuji Shugendō in Murayama (now Fujinomiya). He and his followers climbed the mountain on proxy visits, to deposit scriptures offered by retired emperors and nobles. In 1930, a cache of scriptures dating from the early thirteenth century was discovered at the summit (Earhart 209–211).

In the early fourteenth century, Raison, another Murayama shugenja, established a Fuji-climbing pilgrimage and encouraged people of all social classes to make the ascent, visit sacred sites, and perform rituals and austerities. The dates of the ten-day confinement at the summit were set by the lunar calendar, from 7.22 to 8.2 (ten or eleven days around the end of August). Eventually, Murayama Shugendō gained control of access to Fuji from Murayama and charged climbers a fee (Earhart 211–214).

Murayama Shugendō also set up purification sites along rivers around Fuji. The period designated for these purification rites, 5.25 to 6.2 on the lunar calendar, preceded the period of summit ascent. (The mountain was still considered too cold to climb.)

During the Warring States Period (1467–1573), Murayama Shugendō became allied with Yoshitomo Imagawa, the lord of Suruga Province, with shugenja serving as his spies. In 1560, after Imagawa was defeated and killed by the forces of Nobunaga Oda, Nobunaga had the shrine at Fujinomiya destroyed. The Takeda clan was given control of the province, and Murayama Shugendō went into decline.

Fujinomiya was rebuilt in 1604 by Ieyasu Tokugawa, who became shōgun in 1603. Ieyasu grew up in Sumpu (Shizuoka city), to the west of Fuji, and was a supporter of Sengen worship. In 1606, Ieyasu dedicated Okumiya (the summit) to Fujinomiya Shrine. In a prolonged legal suit (1655–1679), Murayama Shugendō was deprived of its control of summit access, which was given to the Fujinomiya Shrine. The temples and adherents of Murayama Shugendō declined in numbers, although the sect endured until 1930 (Earhart 214–215).

By the end of the fifteenth century, interest in the summit ascent had spread beyond Murayama Shugendō. Climbing routes from Suyama, Subashiri, Kawaguchi, and Yoshida were established. Fuji-kō (societies for Fuji worship) sponsored annual pilgrimages. After Edo became the capital in 1603, Yoshida, the closest and most convenient access site, became the headquarters of the Fuji-kō movement (Tyler, "The Book" 253).

Fuji-kō reached its peak of popularity in the late eighteenth and early nineteenth century. Most of the worshipers were Edo artisans and merchants (Tyler, "The Book" 253). They built mounds around the Kantō region from Fuji volcanic rocks (kuroboku) to serve as sites for worship when the mountain was closed to climbing ("Fuji/Sengen Shinkō," *Encyclopedia of Shintō*).

Although the kami of the mountain was female and associated with childbirth, women were not allowed to climb the summit until the Meiji Period (1868–1912). The ban on female climbers was rooted in the bias against females in religious worship based on such factors as "the Shintō aversion to blood defilement [e.g., during menstruation], the Buddhist association of women with bad karma, a persvasive contempt for women in Buddhist scriptures, and local folk traditions" (Nenzi 59).

According to Yanagita, one such local tradition was intended to protect women from female mountain kami: "Women in Tono [in rural Iwate] are told, even today [c. 1910], not to climb [the three mountains surrounding Tōno] lest they arouse the jealousy of [their female] kami" (12). Others say that women were banned from sacred mountains so as not to distract male pilgrims who were trying to escape from worldly desires.

While influenced by the ascetic practices of Murayama Shugendō, Fuji-kō developed along its own lines. One of its seminal figures was an ascetic from Nagasaki named Kakugyō (1541–1646). While meditating in a cave in Mutsu (northern Honshū), he received a revelation from the spirit of Shugendō founder En-no-Gyōja, who directed him to Hitoana (Human Cave), located on the western side of Fuji, ten miles north of Fujinomiya. This cave has thirty-one steps leading down to a small chamber with a twelve-foot-high ceiling, from which the water of Fuji drips. A stone is enshrined inside, ten yards from the entrance; to the left of it is a small, narrow passageway. A sign outside the cave tells visitors not to touch, approach, or enter the historic site, due to dangerous conditions.[1]

Hitoana is mythic. A sixteenth-century text, *The Tale of Fuji's Hitoana*, describes how Minamoto no Yoriie, a thirteenth-century shōgun sent a retainer, Nitta Tadatsune, to explore the cave, where Nitta finds

> a wondrous world containing a fantastic palace: the abode of the Great Asama Bodhisattva, the resident deity of Mount Fuji. Appearing at first as an enormous snake, the Bodhisattva rages at Nitta for Nitta's violation of his sacred space. However, the Bodhisattva is quickly mollified by a gift of Nitta's swords, and changing his appearance to that of a teenage boy, he offers to lead Nitta on a grand tour of the Six Realms of Transmigratory Existence (the realms of hell, hungry ghosts, animals, ashura, humans, and heaven) before returning him to his home in the human world. (Kimbrough 3)

Entrance to Hitoana, Yamanashi

The tale describes the tortures of sinners in hell—flogged, skewered, suffering in waves of fire and water, etc. Nitta was warned not to reveal what he saw for three years and three months, but the shōgun ordered him to tell all, and Nitta fell dead after he recounted his vision.

When Kakugyō arrived at Hitoana in 1560, the villagers told him that the cave was cursed and anyone who entered it would die. They directed him to meditate at the nearby Shiraito Falls instead. He went to the waterfall and prayed for seven days, until a celestial child led him to Hitoana and gave him permssion to enter the cave (Tyler, "The Book" 286–287).

After Kakugyō meditated another seven days, the dark cave was illuminated by the sun, an embodiment of Sengen-Dainichi. Kakugyō was instructed to stand in mediation on tiptoe, his two toes on a square block of wood five-and-a-half inches on each side, and to bathe in cold water of Shiraito Falls six times a day to purify his six senses. After a thousand days of this practice, Kakugyō received a vision from Sengen-Dainichi that Fuji was the cosmic pillar of the universe and the source of all life.

In this revelation, Kakugyō was told that the social disorder of his times (a period known as Sengoku, or Warring States) was due to disharmony between heaven and earth. Pilgrimages to Fuji would enlighten worshipers to the true way of living and restore peace and well-being to the nation. Because harmony required ethical behavior by all four social classes (aristocrat-scholars, farmers, artisans, and merchants), Kakugyō, like Raison, encouraged everyone to make the summit ascent.

Kakugyō revered the mountain not as a paradise of Buddha, but as a god in itself, along with the sun, moon, and stars (sankō, or three lights). He advocated the Murayama Shugendō practice of bathing in the waters of Fuji to purify oneself and increase one's spiritual powers and preached reverence for rice as the staff of life. The influences of Buddhism, Shintō, Taoism, and Confucianism, along with Shugendō, are evident in his teachings (Earhart, 218–221; Tyler, "The Tokugawa Peace" 103–106).

The cult of Fuji grew even more popular after Jikigyō Miroku (1677–1733), a follower of Kakugyō, fasted to death in one lunar cycle (thirty days), in a three-foot-tall portable shrine that he had transported on horseback up the north slope. His goal was to become one with Sengen-Dainichi and serve as a savior for all sentient beings. A cave near where he fasted to death, at a place called Eboshi-iwa, just above the seventh station, became a meditation site for pilgrims. It's depicted in a Hokusai print of pilgrims ascending the mountain. Jikigyō originally wanted to fast to death on the summit, but the Sengen Shrine at Fujinomiya forbade him to do so.

During the Edo Period, the shogunate tried to ban Fuji-kō, as its calls for world renewal were seen as a threat to the social order, but Fuji-kō survived, and their pilgrimages continue today.

The spiritual presence of Fuji in every aspects of Edo life is captured in the scenes of Hokusai's woodblock prints in *Thirty-six Views of Mt. Fuji*: in the foreground, commoners (roofers, barrel makers, fishermen, clam diggers, tea pickers, lumbermen, mail carriers, and ferry steersmen) go about their daily actitivies, while in the background, Fuji appears at a distance, an eternal protective presence.

"Rainstorm below the Summit" depicts a bolt of lightning in darkness suggesting the fallen world, with Fuji rising serenely above it. In the "Great Wave off Kanagawa," the turbulent sea is ready to engulf three boats and their crews, while Fuji, in the background, framed by the wave, stands as a stable reference point.

In "View from Umezawa Manor, Sagami Province," Fuji appears above a landscape of cloud-shrouded hills studded with pines and inhabited by cranes, both symbols of longevity. The scene identifies Fuji with Mt. Hōrai, one of three islands in the Eastern Sea, like Japan itself. According to a note in *Nihongi*, the spirits who inhabit this mythic paradise maintain an eternal vigor from

> the waters of the fountain of life which flowed for them in a perpetual stream. The pine, the plum, the peach-tree and the sacred fungus grow for ever upon its rocky shores; and the ancient crane builds its nest upon the giant limbs of its never-dying pine. (368)

My first view of Fujisan was on a flight from Tōkyō to Hiroshima in the winter of 1970—a tiny snow-capped peak above the sea of clouds just off the starboard wing. I have no recollection of seeing Fuji from the ground when we returned to Tōkyō on the Shinkansen; the mountain was probably hidden by the winter clouds.

My first land view was in 2005, on a drive from the castle-town of Matsumoto to Kawaguchiko, one of five lakes on the northern side of Fuji. We got off on the wrong expressway exit, before Kōfu, and ended up driving up and down the narrow, winding Shōji Blueline Road over the mountains west of Misaka Pass. As we descended toward Lake Shōji, Fuji was suddenly there.

Fuji is said to be shy. On our first day in Kawaguchiko, in early June, only a part of a slope of her snowy summit appeared through the clouds.

At 3 a.m. the next morning, we drove eighteen miles up to the Kawaguchiko fifth station to watch the sunrise, at 4:30. The clouds around the summit were gone. I was expecting at least a small crowd on such a famous mountain, but no one was there. We walked to a viewing platform in the dark, then onto a gravel road that led to the summit trail. The sun, a tiny yellow ball, rose at the far eastern edge of the cloud-sea. Later, from Lake Saiko, the slopes of Fuji appeared whole, rising gently upward and floating, a kami, above the dark landscape around it.

If Ōyamatsumi had offered Fuji rather than Iha-naga-hime (Rock-long

Mt. Fuji, above Lake Saiko, Yamanashi

Princess) in marriage to Amaterasu's grandson Ho-no-Ninigi, he might have married both the mountain and the blossoming tree, instead of just the tree, so that his offspring "might live eternally immovable like unto the enduring rocks" (*Kojiki* 139–140).

Today, hundreds of thousands of people climb Fuji each year—pilgrims, recreational hikers, and tourists, many of them from outside of Japan; and more are expected after the mountain was designated a World Heritage Site by UNESCO in 2013.

To shorten the ascent, climbers can go by car or bus and start their climbs at four stations, three of them over half-way up the slopes. Once at the top, climbers may circle the crater rim (ohachi-meguri, "circling the bowl"). Around the crater (known as Dainai-in, "Great Palace," or Yukyu, "Shrine of the Depths") are eight sacred peaks and two pools of holy water fed by melted snow: ginmei-sui (silver-shining water), on the southwest rim; and kinmei-sui (gold-shining water), on the north rim.

The official climbing season lasts two months, from roughly July 1 to August 31. On June 30, at Kitaguchi Hongū Fuji Sengen Jinja in Fuji-Yoshida (the northern entrance), priests pray for the safety of climbers, and groups of worshipers carry two mikoshi (portable shrines), one shaped like Fuji, through the town. After an overnight stop, they take the mikoshi back to the shrine the next day. On July 1, a yama-biraki, or mountain-opening ceremony, is held. At the close of the climbing season, on August 26, the shrine conducts a fire festival based on a 500-year-old ceremony to placate Asama/Sengen and prevent eruptions. At night, over seventy torches on nine-foot-tall wooden towers are lit along the main street to the shrine in honor of the kami.

The priests at Fujisan Hongū Sengen Taisha, the southwest entrance, open and close the climbing season about a week after the shrine at the northern entrance: on July 7, the priests pray for the safety of climbers, and on September 7 hold a ceremony to thank the kami for her protection.

Dazai, for one, wasn't interested in making the ascent: "Climb a mountain and you just have to come right back down again. It's so pointless." (Dazai committed suicide at age 38, in 1948.) In modern times, an old saying "You are wise to climb Fuji once, and a fool to climb it twice" has been recast into "He who climbs Fuji once is a fool; he who climbs Fuji twice is twice a fool."

The tradition of mountain asceticism that developed into Fuji pilgrimages has its roots in the rugged mountains south of Nara on the Kii peninsula, around Ōmine (Big Peak), the tallest peak on Sanjō-ga-dake. During the Nara Period (710–794), Buddhism and Taoism from Asia coalesced with the native worship of kami and mountains into Shugendō. Kami were worshipped as local manifestations of buddhas and bodhisattvas. The mountains around Ōmine became a training ground for shujenja, or yamabushi (those who retreat to the mountains), who entered the sacred mountain space to achieve enlightenment and acquire supernatural powers. ("Shugendō" is formed from three kanji: shu, "to discipline oneself"; gen, "to benefit from austerities"; and dō, "religious pathway.")

En no Gyōja (En the Ascetic), also known as En no Ozunu, is recognized as the founder of Shugendō. En was born in the seventh century in the Katsuragi Mountains, between Yamato (Nara) and Kawachi (eastern Ōsaka). He was revered for his knowledge of medicinal plants and magical spells. In 699, during the reign of Emperor Mommu (r. 697–707), En was accused of sorcery by a disciple and exiled to an island offshore of the Izu peninsula. According to one legend, the disciple was possessed by the kami of Mt. Katsuragi who was angry at En ("En no Ozunu," *Encyclopedia of Shintō*).

The source of En's power to subdue harmful spirits was the fierce blue-black Zaō, depicted in statuary scowling, his left hand forming the sword mudra (hand gesture) and his right hand holding a vajra (thunderbolt scepter). Zaō was the kami of Mt. Kinpu, identified as a manifestation of Shakyamuni (historical Buddha), Maitrya (future Buddha), and Kannon (bodhisattva of compassion). En enshrined Zaō at Kinpusen Temple, on Mt. Yoshino, which served as the headquarters of Shugendō.

En also enshrined Zaō at the temple-shrine complex of Ōminesan-ji on Ōmine, a training area for yamabushi. The climb to the summit is restricted to males; an area below is open to women practitioners. En's mother is said to have transformed herself into a turtle to visit him, near a rock known as Kame Ishi, or "Turtle Rock" (Swanson 70).

The Ōmine Mountains developed as a Shugendō training ground during the Heian Period (794–1185) and Kamakura Period (1185–1333). The northern entry was Mt. Yoshino; the southern entry was Kumano Sanzan, "Three Mountains of Kumano," a cluster of three taisha (grand shrines) dedicated to three kami avatars of Buddhist deities.[2]

Along the forty-mile route between Yoshino and Kumano, sacred sites were established commemorating places where local kami submitted to En's authority (Swanson 63).

Pilgrimages went in both directions, from Kumano to Yoshino and from Yoshino to Kumano. Honzan-ha (Original Mountain School), affiliated with Tendai Buddhism, established a ritual center at Kumano during the Kamakura Period, and conducted pilgrimages to Yoshino; Tōzan-ha (This Mountain

School), affiliated with Shingon Buddhism, established a ritual center near Sanjō-ga-dake during the following Muromachi Period and conducted pilgrimages to Kumano (Swanson 58, 63).

Often shrouded in mist and rain, the sparsely populated region of steep peaks and deep gorges at the center of the Kii peninsula was envisioned as sacred Buddhist space: Ōmine, like the mythic Mt. Meru, is said to sit atop a giant turtle, with the axis of the universe situated north-south, along the Yoshino-Kumano Trail. The landscape north of Ōmine represents the Diamond Realm, where Five Wisdom Buddhas reside; the south side represents the Matrix or Womb Realm, inhabited by the Five Guardian Kings who protect the Five Wisdom Buddhas (Swanson 63; "Yoshino, Kumano Shinko," *Encyclopedia of Shintō*). The Kii Mountains are also said to represent the Pure Land of Amida Buddha; and in another tradition, the Pure Land of Kannon, Fudaraku, is located offshore and reachable by an ocean journey from Kumano.

Shugendō training areas developed around other mountains, for example, Dewa Sanzan (The Three Mountains of Dewa) and Mt. Chōkai in northern Honshu; Mt. Nikkō near Edo; Mt. Ishizuchi on Shikoku; Mt. Daisen in western Honshu; and Hikosan, in northern Kyūshū.

On pilgrimages, yamabushi recite sutras and perform a fire ritual that involves burning 108 prayer sticks to signify release from 108 human desires and attachments. Austerities include fasting or eating sparingly; climbing peaks and rock towers; walking along the ledges of steep cliffs; crawling up narrow ridges and through tunnels; meditating and chanting under icy waterfalls or in secluded caves; and hanging face forward over steep cliffs while confessing sins and promising to live by the precepts of Buddhist law. Such practices are intended to focus the mind on the moment and clear it of distractions, so yamabushi can glimpse the state of nothingness (mu) that leads to enlightenment (Swanson 72).

Pilgrimages are structured as enactments of spiritual rebirths, guiding participants through the ten

Nachi Falls, Wakayama

ascending states of being to enlightenment (tormented souls, hungry demons, beasts, half-human and half-demon ashura, human beings, rapturous beings, seekers after truth, finders of partial truth, bodhisattvas, and buddhas) (Swanson 59).

A legendary austerity took place in the winter of 1160 at Nachi Falls, near Nachi Taisha. (See note 2.) The wandering monk Mongaku vowed to remain standing under the icy 440-foot waterfall for twenty-one days while reciting 300,000 invocations to the fierce Buddhist guardian deity Fudō-myō-ō, who converts anger into salvation, subdues demons, and terrifies unbelievers into accepting Buddhist law:

> It was past the Tenth day of the Twelfth Moon [the last moon of the year]. The snow was deep, the ice was thick, the valley streams had fallen silent, a freezing gale blew from the peaks, icicles had formed in the waterfall, and all the surroundings were perfectly white, even to the branches of the trees. Mongaku entered the pool below the torrent, submerged himself to the neck, and set about reciting a fixed number of invocations to Fudō. (*The Tale of the Heike* 178)

Mongaku endured the icy water for several days before he lost consciousness and floated downstream. A young man pulled him to shore. After regaining consciousness, he was angry at having failed and returned to the waterfall to continue his recitation. On the second day, two divine messengers of Fudō floated down from the top of the waterfall to warm him and give him strength, and he was able to fulfill his vow.

During the civil wars of the sixteenth century, the number of shugenja decreased and continued to decline in the Edo Period. Some became less focused on austerities and spiritual matters and more concerned with worldly matters, influenced by the growing secularism and pursuit of wealth and pleasure in emerging cities like Edo and Ōsaka:

> there were many instances of shugen attaining higher rankings without the need to undertake any practice. Village shugen … were strongly characterized as magico-religious practitioners and providers of prayer rituals for this-worldly benefits. ("Shugendō," *Encyclopedia of Shintō*)

At the beginning of the Meiji Period, as part of its promotion of nationalism and the Shintō-based worship of a divine emperor, the government ordered a separation of Shintō and Buddhism (shinbutsu bunri), declaring Shintō native and Buddhism foreign.[3] This declaration was a blow to Shugendō, as it was based on the amalgamation of the two religions. In 1872, Shugendō was banned as superstition and its temples converted into Shintō shrines. Shugendō priests were given the choice of becoming either Shintō or Buddhist priests, or returning to lay life; most chose to become Shintō priests.

After World War II, when religious freedom was re-established, Shugendō practices were revived at Ōmine and Kinpusen as well as other mountains, such as Hakusan, at the border Ishikawa, Fukui, and Gifu Prefectures, and at Dewa Sanzan (Three Mountains of Dewa) in Yamagata.

Dazai's assessment of Fujisan ("not really remarkable"), while not true about Fuji, may be said of Japan's other mountains. The mountains of Ōmine are not particularly outstanding in shape or size. Still, mountains in all parts of Japan are venerated as shintai, or sacred bodies, of kami. What makes a mountain worthy of worship is not its appearance, but stories about the kami associated with it. For example, Mt. Miwa, in Nara, at 1,532 feet a hill rather than a mountain, is said to be the shintai of Ōmononushi (Great Master of Things), one of the kami who pledged to support Amaterasu's grandson Ho-no-Ninigi after he was sent to rule Japan.

On the trail to Miwa summit, an area of broken stones called Okitsu-Iwakura is designated as the spot where Ōmononushi entered Mt. Miwa. The kami also takes the form of a white snake, which inhabits an ancient cedar tree on the grounds of Miwa Shrine, one of the oldest in Japan, located at the base of the mountain. During a disorderly, pestilence-plagued period, Ōmononushi's son Ō-tata-neko was put in charge of Ōmononushi worship and restored health, peace, and prosperity to the land (*Nihongi* 152–153). Another story connects Ōmononushi with saké brewing, so brewers worship him at Miwa Shrine.

Dazai, from Kanagi, a town in Tsugaru in northern Honshū, describes affectionately his home mountain, Mt. Iwaki (Stone-tree), the tallest mountain of the region:

> Where the view across the irrigated rice fields dissolved into the horizon, there was the gently floating figure of the Tsugaru Fuji— Mount Iwaki, 1,625 meters high. The mountain really did seem to be floating, unencumbered by weight. A lush deep green, it hovered silently in the blue sky, more feminine than Mount Fuji, its lower slopes like a gingko leaf standing on its wavy edge or like an ancient court dress folded open slightly, the symmetry of the folds exactly preserved. The mountain resembles a woman of an almost translucent grace and beauty. (*Return to Tsugaru* 121)

"For all that," he adds, "it's not very high." At 5,330 feet, it's half the height of Fuji. And although Mt. Iwaki looks "classically graceful" from the Tsugaru plains, Dazai concedes, "[s]een from the coast, the mountain looks totally worthless—in tatters, no longer even the shadow of a beautiful woman" (122). Earlier, he quotes Tsugaru novelist Kasai Zenzō:

> Mount Iwaki looks so beautiful because there are no high mountains around it, but go look in other parts of the country and you'll find plenty of others like it. It's such a wonderful sight only because it stands there all by itself.... (17)

Still, after mountain asceticism spread from Yamato to northern Honshū, Iwaki, like Fuji and Ōmine, became a center of worship. Standing west of Hirosaki, Mt. Iwaki is said to guard the city from winter storms. It serves as a landmark, guide, and protector of fishermen and mariners. A fishing boat caught offshore in a winter storm was reportedly saved from capsizing in heavy seas by prayers to the kami of Akakura, the northern slope of Mt. Iwaki (Schattschneider 43).

The Edo-period *Iwakisan Engi* (Mt. Iwaki Origin Tale) identifies Tatsubihime no mikoto, a princess whose form is a dragon or a snake, as the original kami of the mountain. The princess is also known as Akakura-sama, Iwaki-sama, and Onigami-sama. When the kami Ōkuninushi came to Mt. Iwaki, the dragon princess emerged from a pool of mud and offered him a tama (jewel or spirit). Ōkuninushi gave the princess the name Kuniyasu-tama-hime and married her: "Henceforth they shared the mountain and the rule over the country which, thanks to this combination, thrived and prospered" (Liscutin 193). The story, Liscutin observes,

> follows a common pattern in Japanese mythology according to which a male deity related to the central Yamato state ... ventures out to expand its territory, to pacify the country, and to bring ... civilization to these "uncultured" territories. (193)

Tōhoku, the northern region of Honshū around Mt. Iwaki, was once inhabited by Ezo (pre-Yamato settlers, considered barbarians). The region was brought under the control of the imperial court between the seventh and ninth centuries. The history parallels the mythical story of Ōkuninushi's arrival: during the Heian Period, a shōgun named Sakanoue no Tamuramaro (758–811) came to Tsugaru from Yamato and, with the help of the female dragon kami of Iwaki, pacified the area. The victory is celebrated in the festivals known as Nebuta in Aomori and Neputa in Hirosaki, during which huge paper floats, illuminated from within, are paraded through the streets. In *Return to Tsugaru*, Dazai describes Hirosaki's Neputa festival and its connection to the area's history:

> This is an annual Tsugaru festival, held around the seventh day of the seventh month of the lunar calendar. Young people, dressed up in all sorts of costumes, dance through the streets in a parade pulling huge lanterns, which are shaped like warriors, dragons, or tigers painted in brilliant colors and mounted on wagons. Part of the excitement always consists in bumping into lanterns made by other neighborhoods and fighting it out. Tradition has it that Sakanoue no Tamuramaro used this kind of lantern on his expedition against the Ezo to lure the barbarians out of their mountains before massacring them, though such explanations are largely apocryphal. Similar parades are held not only in Tsugaru but all over the northeast, so the Nebuta lanterns should probably be considered a local variation of the floats used in the other summer festivals of the north, and not so different from those of Tōkyō's summer festival. (63–64)

During the Kamakura Period, syncretic Shintō-Buddhist beliefs spread to northern Japan, and the kami of the three peaks of Mt. Iwaki were paired with Buddhist deities. By the Edo Period, the following pairings had been established. Gankisan (Mt. Ganki, the northern peak) is inhabited by a female kami, Tatsubihime no mikoto (the so-called "shining dragon princess), identified with Kannon, bodhisattva of mercy. Iwakisan (Mt. Iwaki, the middle peak) is home to a primordial kami, genderless or male, Kuni-toko-tachi no mikoto, identified with Amida. Chōkaisan (Mt. Chōkai, the southern peak) belongs to the kami Ōkuninushi, identified with Yakushi, the buddha of medicine and healing.

On the northern half of the mountain, considered wilder and rougher in terrain than the southern half, oni-kami, or demon-gods dwell. "Ganki," the northern peak, is written with the kanji for "rock" (gan), and "demon" (ki). Its steep, rocky slope is called Akakura (Red Storehouse), which is also the name of a deep gorge below the slope.

Akakura is a center for the ascetic practices and activities of shugenja and female shamans, or itako, and kamisama (divine being), also called gomiso (mystic healers). Itako, blind from birth, make their living summoning the dead to communicate with the living. Kamisama, like shugenja, go through ascetic training to acquire the ability to perform cures and exorcisms and to tell fortunes. Particularly inspiring kamisama establish personal followings. For example, the Akakura Mountain Shrine, located above Ōishi (Big Rock) shrine on the northeast slope of Mt. Iwaki, is home to a religious community based on the teachings of a kamisama born in 1888, a peasant woman named Kawai. From an impoverished family, Kawai had a recurrent dream of a dragon rising from the mountain, entering a hole in the roof of her house, and standing

Akakura Gorge on the northeastern side of Mt. Iwaki, Aomori

next to her, then turning into a beautiful woman who introduced herself as Akakura Daigongen (Great Avatar of Akakura). The kami instructed Kawai to climb the slope of Akakura. Based on this vision, Kawai established a religious practice involving mountain austerities on Akakura in order to purify and heal practitioners physically and spiritually and make them kami-like (Schatt-schneider, *passim*).

Chōkaisan, the southern peak, is associated with the male-dominated political and religious establishment of Tsugaru. In 1610, at the beginning of the Edo Period, Nobuhira (1586–1631), the son of the founder of the Tsugaru clan, took over Hyakutaku-ji, the Buddhist-Shintō complex on the southern side of Iwaki, and used it to bolster his rule with sacred authority. He enlarged the complex, and enshrined in the main temple the three Buddhist deities of the mountain (Kannon, Amida, and Yakushi). Priests conducted state rituals, such as praying for rain during droughts and for protection against floods during the storm season.

At the birth of the fourth Tsugaru daimyō, Nobumasa (1667–1710), a bright light is said to have shone forth from Mt. Iwaki, and colored clouds came to Hirosaki Castle, indicating that the newborn child was an incarnation of the mountain kami. After his death, Nobumasa was buried on Iwaki, deified as a gongen (kami manifestation of a buddha) and enshrined at Takateru Shrine, just east of Hyakutaku-ji (Liscutin 195). Like Ieyasu Tokugawa, who had himself deified as a gongen and enshrined at Nikkō after his death, Nobumasa hoped

Iwakiyama Shrine below the southern side of Mt. Iwaki, Aomori

his deification would ensure the continuity of his family's rule.

During the Meiji-period separation of Shintō and Buddhism, the Buddhist halls at Hyakutaku-ji were dismantled or converted to Shintō halls, and Buddhist images were removed. The site was renamed Iwaki-yama Jinja and designated as the northern gate protecting the nation against foreign invasion.

The Tsugaru lords were sponsors of the practice of ōyama mōde, or pilgrimage to the summit. The annual pilgrimage is still held in fall as part of Ōyama sankei (Big Mountain Ritual). The festival takes place between 7.28 and 8.1 by the lunar calendar (around the beginning of September). Dressed in white robes, wrist coverings, and leggings, men from the surrounding villages gather on the day before 8.1 at Iwaki-yama Shrine to make the climb via the skyline road to a small shrine at the summit of Chōkaisan. Accompanied by flutes and drums and carrying poles decorated with paper streamers, the pilgrims chant "Saigi, Saigi" (Cleansing, Cleansing) for purification during the ascent. They reach the summit on the night of the new moon, offer their streamers to the kami, and stay till dawn to worship the rising sun ("Ōyama sankei," *Encyclopedia of Shintō*). Climbing the mountain in three consecutive years is considered an initiation into manhood (Schattschneider 35).

Until the Meiji Period, women were barred from participating in this pilgrimage, and even after the ban was lifted, few women went against the belief that they should not enter the mountain by this route. An Edo-period rationalist was puzzled by the ban on women:

> Since they worship a woman, Anjuhime, as the goddess of the mountain, how can they forbid women to enter the mountain? How strange indeed! If the mountain path is treacherous, they should forbid women to climb it; but there certainly exists no kami or Buddha who hates women. (Qtd. in Liscutin 196)

However, Anjuhime (a local female kami), identified with the female kami (Tatsubihime no mikoto or Akakurasama), is worshipped at the northern peak, Gankisan (Liscutin 194), not at Chōkaisan, where Ōkuninushi, a male kami, is venerated.

Gankisan is open to climbing by female ascetics, like those who worship at Akakura Mountain Shrine. The route to the summit takes the worshipper up a ridge (the body of the dragon kami) lined with thirty-three statues of Kannon (bodhisattva of compassion). Halfway up is a sacred boulder called Ubaishi (Wet-nurse Stone), a twenty-foot-high triangular rock, where the worshipers crawl through a narrow tunnel simulating rebirth, three, four, or six times, depending on the needs of the pilgrim. At the summit is a statue of Kannon. An ascent in itself doesn't guarantee a vision of the deity or rebirth into a higher state, because the demons living on the mountain may possess a worshipper, leading her astray, into confusion or depression (Schattschneider 162–165). Believers must work continuously toward becoming more kami-like through prayers, offerings, rituals, and mountain treks.

Shamanistic activities at Akakura survived the Meiji-period ban on such practices, and itako and kamisama continue them today. Akakura Mountain Shrine sponsors an annual cycle of thirteen rites on and around Mt. Iwaki, including a late-spring ceremony to open Akakura slope, when a shimenawa (rice-straw rope) is strung across the gorge, inviting the ancestral spirits and kami down to the human realm for the summer. The ceremony also opens the summit to ascent by worshipers.

During summer, a tour of thirty-three Kannon temples around Tsugaru takes place, followed by ascents of Mt. Taihei, in Akita, south of Iwaki, and Mt. Hakkōda, east of Iwaki. In autumn, an ancestral memorial ceremony and a mountain closing ceremony are held, sending the ancestral spirits and kami back to their mountain abode for the winter. Sacred fires are lit and prayer sticks are burned at the memorial ceremony to carry messages and prayers up the mountain with the ascending spirits. The thirteen rites after the ceremony to open the mountain are associated with three cycles: (1) events in the life of the founding kamisama; (2) the birth, death, and rebirth of the year; and (3) the spiritual births and rebirths of each individual worshipper and the congregation as a whole. A cooking pot rite is performed three times a year, at the New Year's festival, the summer festival, and the autumn festival: a boiling pot of sacred water from Akakura Stream begins to "hum" (the dragon's voice), and rice grains and salt are thrown in and cooked. The partially cooked rice is then packaged and distributed to the congregation and their families for healing and protection. A Fudō-myō-ō sword ritual is held four times a year, in May, June, September, and October: the sword of this fiery deity is passed around the bodies of those seeking help, to cut and burn away the passions, encumbrances, and pollution that are the causes of suffering (Schattschneider *passim*).

Worshipers of Mt. Iwaki say that just looking at the mountain brings them "blessings of health and serenity" (Schattschneider 32). The mountain is essential to the identities of the congregation at Akakura Mountain Shrine:

> Over time, each worshiper comes to associate the variegated mountain landscape with her personal biography, the life histories of certain exemplary antecedents and ancestors, and the collective biography of the extended congregation. (6)

Some Hirosaki migrant workers say that the first thing they do when they return home is to gaze at Iwaki or climb its summit (32). Schattschneider speculates that the adoration of the mountain and participation in the shrine community express a nostalgic longing for the close-knit extended families that once gave individuals their identity. The close bonds of extended families have been loosened in the modern industrial state, because mechanized agriculture doesn't require many hands working together; family members leave their rural hometowns to take jobs in cities and towns, either seasonally or permanently:

> In this sense, the Akakura system functions as a compensatory home, a symbolic bulwark against the vast social and economic pressures breaking up extended multigenerational agrarian houses. To this day, my informants strongly feel that farming, land, and locality matter, and that ancestral veneration must continue in some form, even if the idealized extended households no longer exist. (Schattschneider 221–222)

Whatever their sizes, shapes, or locations, mountains are the largest and most imposing, enduring, and recognizable forms in our landscapes. If not who we are, mountains tell us where we are, which, for some, is the same thing. Those that rise recognizably by height or shape, or both, from the land around them are revered as kami: in addition to Fujisan and Iwakisan, famous mountains include Chōkaisan (Bird Sea Mountain), in Yamagata; Tateyama (Standing Mountain), in Toyama; Hakusan (White Mountain), on the borders of Ishikawa, Fukui, and Gifu; Daisen (Big Mountain), between Tottori and Shimane; and Ishizuchi (Stone Hammer), in Ehime, on Shikoku.

When driving to Makiki, in Honolulu, after returning from overseas trips, I feel at home when I see Keahiakāhoe, Lanihuli, and Kōnāhuanui, the three highest peaks in the Koʻolau Mountains on the north side of the city, above Nuʻuanu. In Hawaiʻi, as in Japan, mountains are sacred places, home of the gods (wao akua). On Kōnāhuanui, the highest of the three peaks, lives a moʻo, or water-lizard, who like Akakura's dragon, captures rain clouds and oversees the water that collects in the reservoirs inside the mountain and flows out in the streams of Kāneʻohe on its koʻolau (windward) side and Nuʻuanu and Mānoa Valleys on its kona (leeward) side.

Fascinated by mountains, I spent three summers in college with some high school friends hiking the ridges and peaks of Oʻahu. It's the best way to get to know a place; as Schattschneider writes about climbers on Mt. Iwaki, it "taught me through my body." Hiking brings a deeper understanding of how to move within nature, like wind, clouds, and water, following contours up a mountain ridge or down mountain streams.

Experiencing the land in this way, one becomes accustomed and attached to it:

> Just as the topographical contours of the mountain direct a stream along its course, so should the worshiper surrender to the higher forces of the benevolent kami and follow the true pathways the mountain has laid down for her. (Schattschneider 159)

A description by Gary Snyder of descending "rocky ridges and talus slopes" in the Sierras reminded me of the experience of rock-hopping down streams:

> It is an irregular dancing—always shifting—step of walk on slabs and scree. The breath and eye are always following this uneven rhythm. It is never paced or clocklike, but flexing little jumps—sidesteps— going for the well-seen place to put a foot on a rock, hit flat, move on—zigzagging along and all deliberate. The alert eye looking ahead, picking the footholds to come, while never missing the step of the moment. The body-mind is so at one with this rough world that it makes these moves effortlessly once it has had a bit of practice. (113)

Schattschneider describes Mt. Iwaki's rugged slopes, from a human point of view:

> [We are] only temporary sojourners, perhaps even trespassers, in an alien and frightening territory. The mountain … belongs to the gods, ancestors, and demons; it is not the natural abode of human beings who traverse it at their peril in order to partake of its life-giving flows and qualities. As guests on the mountain, we must not stay there indefinitely; we must, when the time comes, leave the mountain and return to the world below. (159)

I experienced this "frightening territory" when we hiked up the Castle Trail, which ascends the steep face of the mountains above Punaluʻu Valley on the windward side of Oʻahu. At the top was a desolate landscape, a grass-covered slope studded with rocks. The trail continued over a ridge to a stream flowing down a narrow ravine, eventually tumbling down the cliff at Kaliuwaʻa. I never returned to that place, but remember the cold wind blowing mist toward the summit, and the mist merging into cloud banks shrouding the peaks.

Locations of famous mountains in Japan

NOTES

1. Hitoana is on the grounds of Hitoana Jinja, a mile north of Hitoana Elementary School, on Route 71-Route 75. When we visited the cave in 2012, a class of middle school students was there. In front of the shrine, the teacher was narrating the story of Kakugyō to her students, standing on her toes to demonstrate the difficulty of his meditation technique and asking them to try it.

2. Kumano Sanzan is still a popular pilgrimage destination today. Hongū Taisha (Original Grand Shrine) was once located on a sandbar on the Kumano River. After it was destroyed by a flood in 1889, it was rebuilt at its present location, nearby, on higher ground. Roofed with cedar bark and unpainted, the shrine embodies the simplicity, purity, and natural harmony of the original Shintō architecture, before continental influences introduced images and vermilion paint. The shrine's symbol is a three-legged crow, associated in Chinese myth with the sun and in Japanese myth with Yata-garasu (Eight-foot-long or Eight-headed Crow), which guided the first emperor of Yamato, Jimmu, through the Kumano Mountains on his way to establishing his capital in Kashihara, just south of Nara city. Hongū enshrines Ketsumiko no mikoto as a kami manifestation of Amida Buddha. (Ketsumiko is identified with Amaterasu's brother Susa-no-ō.)

Hongū Taisha, Wakayama

119

The second Kumano shrine, Hatayama Taisha, at Shingū (New Shrine), is dedicated to Hayatama-no-ōkami, an avatar of Yakushi, the buddha of medicine and healing. Hayatama is the first kami to be born from the spittle of creation kami Izanagi after he returned from his underworld visit to his sister Izanami. Founded in the twelfth century, the shrine is located about twenty miles south of Hongū, on the Kumano River near where it enters the sea, on the southwest

Karen walking down the steps below Gotobiki rock at Kamikura Shrine

coast of the Kii Peninsula. On its grounds is an 800-year-old nagi (a kind of evergreen tree) venerated as a kami.

On the cliff of Mt. Gongen near Hatayama Taisha, at the top of a steep stone staircase of 538 steps, is a subsidiary shrine known as Kamikura. Perched above the small shrine and encircled by a shimenawa (rice-straw rope placed around sacred objects) is Gotobiki, a huge spherical rock worshipped as a kami. Bronze bells from the third century have been found in the area. The shrine is said to mark a place where kami descended to earth. On February 6 each year, two thousand men and boys gather at the shrine to light torches and descend in single file, forming a flaming dragon-like body.

The third Kumano shrine, Nachi Taisha, houses the twelve kami of Kumano, including Fusumi no ōkami, an avatar of Kannon. Fusumi is associated with forestry, fisheries, and marriage and is identified with the creation goddess Izanami. Because it enshrines this goddess, women are allowed to participate in rituals at the shrine. Nachi Taisha is located near Nachi Falls, the tallest single-stage waterfall in Japan (440 feet high). Nachi Falls is the shintai (kami body) of the dragon Hiro, who is also worshipped at Nachi Shrine. At a small shrine in front of the falls, visitors pray for Hiro's blessings and also drink his water, said to promote longevity.

3. The attacks on Buddhist temples was most severe in areas where anti-Buddhist and/or pro-Shintō sentiments were strongest, such as in Okayama, Mito (Ibaraki), Aizu (western Fukushima), Yamashiro (southern Kyōto), Nara, and Satsuma (Kagoshima). A factor in the attacks on Buddhism (aside from the rejection of Buddhism as foreign) was resentment over the wealth and power that Buddhist temples had acquired. During the Edo Period, in order to prevent Christianity from spreading, the Tokugawa Shogunate required all families to affiliate and register with a Buddhist temple, which certified that they were not Christian. For this certification, families had to donate money to the temples. The burden was heavy, with over 100,000 temples for a population of 30 million, or 300 people per temple. Thus, the temple closings during shinbutsu bunri were a financial relief for people.

SOURCES

Dazai, Osamu. "One Hundred Views of Mt. Fuji." *Self Portraits*. Tōkyō: Kodansha, 1991. 69-90.

---. *Return to Tsugaru: Travels of a Purple Tramp*. Tōkyō: Kodansha, 1985.

Earhart, Byron H. "Mount Fuji and Shugendo." *Japanese Journal of Religious Studies* 16.2-3 (1989): 205–226.

Encyclopedia of Shintō. Kokugakuin U, Sept. 2008. Web.

Kimbrough, R. Keller. "Travel Writing from Hell? Minamoto no Yoriie and The Politics of Fuji no Hitoana Shōshi." *Proceedings of the Association for Japanese Literary Studies* 7 (2007): 1–11.

The Kojiki: Records of Ancient Matters. Trans. Basil Hall Chamberlain. Boston: Tuttle, 1981.

Liscutin, Nicola. "Mapping the Sacred Body: Shintō vs. Popular Beliefs at Mt. Iwaki in Tsugaru." *Shinto in History.* Eds. John Breen and Mark Teeuwen. Honolulu: U of Hawai'i, 2002. 186–204.

Nakashima, Naoto. *Hawaii Monogatari.* Translated Manuscript. (Published in Tōkyō in 1936).

Nihongi: Chronicles of Japan from the Earliest Times to A.D. 697. Trans. W.G. Aston. Boston: Tuttle, 1972.

Nenzi, Laura. *Excursions in Identity: Travel and the Intersection of Place, Gender, and Status in Edo Japan.* Honolulu: U of Hawai'i, 2008.

Schattschneider, Ellen. *Immortal Wishes: Labor and Transcendence on a Japanese Sacred Mountain.* Durham, NC: Duke UP. 2003.

Snyder, Gary. "Blue Mountains Constantly Walking." *The Practice of the Wild.* New York: North Point, 1990. 97–115.

Swanson, Paul L. "Shugendō and the Yoshino-Kumano Pilgrimage." *Monumenta Nipponica.* 36.1 (1981): 55–84.

The Tale of the Heike. Trans. Helen McCullough. Palo Alto: Stanford UP, 1988.

Tyler, Royall. "'The Book of the Great Practice' The Life of the Mt. Fuji Ascetic Kakugyō Tōbutsu Kū." *Asian Folklore Studies* 52 (1993): 251–331.

---. "The Tokugawa Peace and Popular Religion: Shōsan, Kakugyō Tōbutsu, and Jikigyō Miroku." *Confucianism and Tokugawa Culture.* Ed. Peter Nosco. Honolulu: U of Hawai'i, 1997. 92–119.

Yanagita, Kunio. *The Legends of Tono.* Trans. Ronald A. Morse. New York: Lexington, 2008.

Roads of Oku

Days and months go by, travelers for countless generations, and so, too, are the passing years. Aboard a boat, a lifetime drifts away; for someone leading a horse by the mouth, facing old age, traveling onward day after day, the journey itself is home.

– Bashō, Oku no Hosomichi

You cannot travel on the path before you have become the Path itself.

– Buddha (qtd. in Chatwin, 179)

Possessed by wanderlust, beckoned by Dōsojin, dual guardian gods of the road, imagining the moon over Matsushima, haiku poet Matsuo Bashō left Edo for Oku at the end of spring in the second year of Genroku (1689).[1] *Oku no Hosomichi*, his prose-poetry account of the five-month, twelve-hundred-mile journey, is his most famous and beloved work.

Oku refers to Mutsu and Dewa, two provinces of northern Honshū through which Bashō traveled.[2] The "Oku" of the title has been translated "Deep North," "Far Towns," "Far Province," and "Interior." "Oku" is used as a prefix for place names to suggest "at the far end of" or "deep within." It also means "inside" or "heart." Far from the capital of Edo, it was a rural rice-growing region where agricultural and folk traditions endured, and the poet could feel the presence of the people of old.

I read Nobuyuki Yuasa's *The Narrow Road to the Deep North,* the first English translation of *Oku,*[3] in 1971, in my second year of college, when I was nineteen. Like the calligrapher Soryū, who copied the text for Bashō, I was "stirred to the core. Once I had my raincoat on, I was eager to go on a like journey" (*Back Roads* 123). But back then, my future was full and open—so many places to go, so many things to do, so much time to do it in. I had a lifetime ahead of me. The journey was put on hold and eventually forgotten.

Over thirty years later, while planning a three-week trip to northern Honshū in summer 2005, I recalled my intention to retrace Bashō's journey. Bashō traveled "to inquire into the truth of poets" (*Oi no Kobumi*) and to see places whose names had become uta-makura, or "poetic headrests"—allusions to places made famous in ancient poetry and historical texts. I included in our itinerary some of the places he describes. Like Bashō, I wanted to visit these "places ears had heard of, eyes never seen" (*Back Roads* 19), to stand in the presence of the ancients, Bashō himself now among them. I thought his narrative and poetry would make more sense to me if I saw the newly planted rice fields of early summer along the Abukuma River, the gilded mausoleum known as the Hikaridō in Hiraizumi, and the cliffs and caves of Natadera; and if I heard the chorus of cicada filling the summer woods and smelled the redolent waters of Yamanaka hot spring.

In 2005, I was fifty-four, older than Bashō when he made his journey at forty-five, older than he was five years later, in 1694, when he completed *Oku* and died from dysentery. I felt the finity of days more strongly than when I first read the narrative. My aging allowed me to see more clearly that for Bashō, feeling the effects of illness and aging, travel was a spiritual undertaking, a way of letting go of attachments to this world:

> ... recurring illness nagged, but what a pilgrimage to far places calls for: self-abandonment, resignation to the transient flow of life, to die on the road, heaven's decree. (*Back Roads* 51)

The narrative is about impermanence and homelessness in an illusory world, as Buddhism teaches its followers to see human existence. Living in accord with the "transient flow of life" was a form of enlightenment, as was accepting disappointments and separations along the way. The Buddhist context gives a spiritual depth to Bashō's conventional use of the seasonal imagery of classical Japanese court poetry, which was more often about worldly love.

At the start of his journey, the poet crosses the Sumida River by boat, then bids farewell to his friends at Senju, on the other bank. In his haiku on the event, "yuku haru" (spring passing) is a reference to the date, the twenty-seventh phase of the last moon of spring (3.27)[4]:

> spring almost gone—birds cry, fish eyes are tears
> yuku haru ya / tori naki uo no / me wa namida

Given the far roads he planned to travel, Bashō wasn't sure if he would return to see his friends again. His river crossing might be like a spirit's crossing the river Sanzu at death, from shigan, this side, to higan, the other side.

The last haiku of the narrative (dated 9.6, the sixth phase of the last moon of autumn, October 19) is not about homecoming, but another departure. Bashō boards a boat at Ōgaki to travel to Ise for the dedication of the rebuilt shrine to Amaterasu, which takes place once every twenty years. Given the life expectancy of his time and his weakening health, Bashō senses that this

Locations of places in "Roads of Oku"

rebuilding might be (and it was) his last[5]:

> clam shell and body separating: autumn passing
> hamaguri no / futami ni wakare / yuku aki zo

Yuku aki (autumn passing) and yuku haru (spring passing) frame the narrative. The haiku puns on the name of a cove near Ise, Futami, known for its clams: "futa" (lid, i.e., of the shell) and "mi" (body). Bashō is once again departing the shelter of a house (shell) for naked life on the road. In 1690, after his journey to Oku, he describes himself in two similar figures of homelessness:

> I gave up city life some ten years ago, and now I'm approaching fifty.
> I'm a mino-mushi (moth larva) without its cocoon, a snail without its

125

shell. ("The Hut of the Phantom Dwelling")

Since "mi" means "soul" as well as "body," a clam's body separating from its shell also represents the spirit departing from the body with the passing of life.

Between yuku haru and yuku aki are other partings. When Hokushi, a friend from Kanazawa, leaves him at Maruoka, Bashō composes a poem on a fan and tears it in two; he offers the poem to his friend as a parting gift. It's also a gesture marking the passing of summer (with fall's cool weather coming on, he no longer needs a fan) as well as a gesture of unburdening himself of another worldly possession:

> poem composed, fan torn in two—parting
> mono kaite / ōgi hikisaku / nagori kana

At Yamanaka, in Kaga (Ishikawa), he says goodbye to his traveling companion Sora, who suffers from a stomach ailment and decides to abandon the journey to recover at a relative's house in Ise (Mie).[6] Bashō's poem on their separation refers to the inscription on their kasa (broad-brimmed, conic hats woven from straw, sedge, bamboo, or cypress bark):

> from today on, inscription wiped away, kasa's dew
> kyō yori ya / kakitsuke kesan / kasa no tsuyu

Even today, kasa is standard gear for a pilgrim, a portable roof providing protection against sun and rain. Pilgrims write on the broad brims inscriptions like "dōgyō ninin" (two travelers), referring to a solitary traveler and Buddha. Before traveling from Edo to Akashi and Kyōto in 1687–1688, Bashō and his companion Tokoku ink on their kasa "kenkon, mujyū / dōgyō ninin" (in heaven and on earth, no home / two people on the same path; *Oi no Kobumi*). He and Sora must have written something similar on their kasa for the trip to Oku. Wiping away the inscription is a way of acknowledging that the companionship of two travelers, like dew, is ephemeral.[7]

Bashō saw life on the road as the heart of his poetry:

> staying at inns, know my poems—autumn wind
> tabine shite / waga ku o shire ya / aki no kaze (Autumn 1687)

His homelessness was both metaphysical and real. He attributes his physical homelessness to "the magic spell of poetry":

> Because of this spell, I abandoned everything and left home; almost

penniless, I have barely kept myself alive by going around begging. How invincible is the power of poetry, to reduce me to a tattered beggar! (Ueda 168–169)

Home was Ueno, in Iga (Mie), where Bashō was born in 1644. His father was "probably a low-ranking samurai who farmed in peacetime" (Ueda 20). He passed away when Bashō was twelve. From boyhood, Bashō served Tōdō Yoshitada, a relative of the lord of Ueno. Although Tōdō was two years his elder, they were close, sharing an interest in poetry. In 1666, however, when Bashō was twenty-two, Tōdō died, and a younger brother took over the household. Perhaps because his prospects under a new master weren't promising, or wanting to improve his education and pursue his interest in literature and art, Bashō began frequenting Kyōto, thirty miles to the northwest, where he "studied philosophy, poetry, and calligraphy under well-known experts" (Ueda 21).

Bashō began publishing poetry in anthologies and moved to Edo in 1672, giving up his samurai status, as he was required to do when he left the domain of his lord. In Edo, he gained a reputation as a poet and became a teacher, living on donations, including housing, from his students and friends.

In the winter of 1682, his house in Edo was destroyed by a fire that swept through his neighborhood. He escaped the flames by immersing himself in the Sumida River. A few months later his mother passed on. When he returned to Ueno in the fall of 1684, his older brother showed him a lock of their mother's gray hair, which moved Bashō to tears:

in my hand, my burning tears would melt it: autumn frost
te ni toraba / ki-en namida zo atsuki / aki no shimo

His 1684–1685 journey from Edo to Ueno and Kyōto and back produced the first of his prose-poetry narratives: *Nozarashi Kikō* (Weather-Beaten-in-Fields Journal). He spent the last ten years of his life on various journeys, producing four more narratives: *Kashima Kikō* (Kashima Journal), about a moon-viewing visit to Kashima Shrine in Ibaraki, in autumn 1687; *Oi no Kobumi* (Bamboo Back-Pack Notebook), about a journey from Edo to Akashi and Kyōto, from autumn 1687 to autumn of the following year; *Sarashina Kikō* (Sarashina Journal), about another moon-viewing journey, from Nagoya to Sarashina in Shinano (Nagano), in autumn 1688; and finally *Oku no Hosomichi*.

Walking great distances, away from home, was a way to remove a pilgrim from the distractions of life and to focus on purifying the spirit. Like John Bunyan's *Pilgrim's Progress* (1678), Bashō's *Oku* is a religious allegory. In a Buddhist context, the traveler is striving to enter the Western Paradise or

Pure Land of Amida Buddha, whose Sanskrit name, Amitābha, means "Infinite Light." After becoming a Buddha, Amida offered salvation to anyone, including sinners, who had faith in him; in the Western Paradise, he would teach them to achieve Nirvana.

Pilgrimages to temples and shrines were a popular form of travel since the Heian Period (794–1185), when set routes and destinations were first established. For example, one pilgrimage in the Kinki region (provinces around the capital of Kyōto) made a circuit of thirty-three temples dedicated to Kannon. (Kannon was introduced to Japan in the late sixth century from China, where she is known as Kuan Yin. Her name, translated "watchful listening," suggests her nature, which is to listen to all who suffer and to offer them comfort and salvation. Kannon and Amida are the two most widely venerated deities in Japan.)

In Bashō's time, during the Edo Period (1603–1868), pilgrimages were the only kind of travel allowed to the general population by the restrictive Tokugawa Shogunate, which set up barriers, or checkpoints, on major roads to control the movement of its citizens. Bashō records that on the way from Narugo hot spring in Mutsu to Obanazawa in Dewa, the guards at the Shitomae barrier eye them suspiciously before allowing them to continue on.

Bashō and Sora visit both Buddhist temples and Shintō shrines. The Shintō kami were considered manifestations of buddhas and bodhisattvas, and deities of both religions were worshipped together, often at temples and shrines built next to each other.

While living in Edo, Bashō studied Rinzai Zen under the priest Butchō (1642–1715) and was designated heir to his teaching; but like many lay worshipers, the poet was non-sectarian and eclectic in his beliefs. In a haiku on his visit to Zenkō Temple in Shinano (Nagano) in autumn 1688, he points out that four sects—Tendai, Jōdo, Zen, and Ji (an off-shoot of Jōdo)—worshipped there as one:

> beneath moonlight, four gates, four sects, just one
> tsuki kage ya / shimon shishū mo / tada hitotsu ("Sarashina Journal" 48)

Four days after departing Edo for Oku, Bashō arrives in Nikkō, on the first day of summer (4.1, May 20). His haiku marks the transition from spring to summer: wakaba, "young leaves," is a spring kigo (season word), and aoba, "green leaves," a summer kigo:[8]

> glorious! green leaves, young leaves in sunlight
> ara tōto / aoba wakaba no / hi no hikari

Mt. Nantai (right) above Lake Chuzenji and Chuzenji Falls, Nikkō, May 2004

"Sunlight" puns on the name Nikkō, which is composed of two kanji, "sun" and "light." The haiku praises the enlightenment brought to the nation by Buddhism: the summer leaves symbolize the land and people flourishing under the light emanating from the holy mountain, "the splendor now gracing our skies and the blessings extended to the eight directions and the four classes of citizens living in peace" (*Back Roads* 25).[9]

A haiku by Sora, who joins Bashō at Nikkō, refers to the custom of koromogae, changing into summer clothing, on 4.1. In preparation for the pilgrimage, Sora shaves his head and dons a pilgrim's garb:

cut my hair and cast it away, at Mt. Kurokami, changing clothes
sori sutete / kurokamiyama ni / koromogae

Mt. Kurokami (Black Hair), another name for Mt. Nantai, the highest peak in Nikkō, is changing for summer: its melting snow will begin to reveal granite cliffs. Typically, Shirane notes, in court poetry, koromogae was a time of regret over the passing of the flowers of spring, symbolic of lost love or youth (38). Sora's haiku alludes to a tanka in which snow falling on Mt. Kurokami suggests white hair and aging (*Bashō's Narrow Road* 48). In a Buddhist context, with the snow soon to begin melting in summer, Sora's haiku expresses hope. He, like Bashō, sees their pilgrimage as a way to redemption and rebirth, and he changes "the characters in his name from *sōgo* (all five) to *sogō* (religious enlightenment)" (*Bashō's Narrow Road* 49).

Following Sora's poem, Bashō describes Urami Falls, on the trail from Nikkō up to Lake Chuzenji:

> After climbing uphill for over a mile, we came to a cascade falling a hundred feet over a cliff-cave and into a rocky green pool. Entering the cave, our bodies hidden, we could see out from behind the falls, hence its name. [Urami means "see from behind."]

Another haiku commemorating the first day of summer follows:

> for a while, confined behind the waterfall: summer's start
> shibaraku wa / taki ni komoru ya / ge no hajime

The Buddhist practice of summer confinement for meditation and copying sutras started on 4.16, a day after the fourth full moon of the year (U-tsugi), which was the first summer moon. Originally, in India, this retreat was called "rain retreat" because it took place during the monsoon: "the Buddha did not want his followers to wade up to their necks in floodwaters," so "the homeless pilgrims were to congregate on higher ground and live in huts of wattle and daub. It was from these sites that the great Buddhist monasteries arose" (Chatwin 180). Bashō's haiku about confinement behind a waterfall foreshadows Japan's summer rains, the samidare, during the fifth moon of Satsuki.

From Nikkō, the travelers head east, spending most of the fourth moon in the towns of Kurobane and Sukagawa. At the start of the fifth moon, they head north down the Abukuma River valley toward sea coast town of Matsushima. The imagery of the samidare—heavy downpours, muddy roads, and swollen rivers—represent the misery of humanity in a fallen world. In the town of Iizaka (5.2, June 19), Bashō and Sora bed down on "thin mats over bare earth" in a "ramshackle sort of place .... All night, thunder, pouring buckets, roof leaking, fleas[,] mosquitoes in droves: no sleep (*Back Roads* 51).

In the district of Kasashima (on 5.4), between Shiroishi and Sendai, they search for the town of Kasashima (Rain-Hat or Umbrella Island) to find shelter:

> Kasashima: where is it, on the fifth-moon's muddy roads?
> kasajima wa / izuko satsuki no / nukarimichi

At the border of Mutsu and Dewa (5.15, July 2), during three days of stormy winds and rain, the travelers take shelter in a shack, an experience which elicits Bashō's famous complaint:

> fleas, lice, horse pissing on the head-rest
> nomi shirami / uma no bari suru / makura moto

On the way west through Dewa (6.3, July 19), they ride a boat down the rain-swollen Mogami River, a culminating image that suggests the fleeting passage of their lives:

> fifth-moon rains gathering swift Mogami River
> samidare o / atsumete hayashi / mogamigawa

From the suffering in this transient world, Buddhism provides otherwordly shelter. On 4.5, near the town of Kurobane, in Nasu, Bashō and Sora visit Unganji, a temple founded in the twelfth century. Here, "perched on a ledge up against a cave," Bashō finds a mediation hut used by his Zen teacher Butchō:

> even a woodpecker can't destroy this hut: summer grove
> kitsutsuki mo / io wa yaburazu / natsu kodachi

Buddhism was a gift to the imperial court in 552, brought by an envoy from the kingdom of Baekje, which was seeking the help of the Yamato emperor against the rival kingdom of Silla. "Woodpecker" alludes to the angry spirit of Mononobe no Moriya (d. 587), who opposed the new religion. Blaming it for an outbreak of disease, Mononobe and his allies, with the support of the Emperor Bidatsu (r. 572–585), burned a Buddhist temple, destroying the statue of Buddha it housed. Despite the opposition, Buddhism took root and flourished, supported by the next emperor, Yōmei (r. 585–587), and his son Prince Shōtoku (572–622). Allied with the Soga clan, Prince Shōtoku defeated the anti-Buddhist forces in a battle in which Mononobe was killed. After his death, Mononobe's angry spirit is said to have taken the form of a woodpecker to continue to destroy Buddhist temples; but the new religion, as Bashō's haiku suggests, gained so much strength and influence, it was impervious to a woodpecker's attack.[10]

In Nasu, Bashō and Sora visit two places associated with a story illustrating the spread of enlightenment to this former area of darkness: first, the tomb of Tamamo-no-mae, a concubine of the retired Emperor Toba (r. 1107–1123); then Sesshō-seki, "Killing Stone," in a sulphur field below Mt. Nasu.

The story of the stone is told in the nō drama *Sesshōseki*: while traveling through Nasu, the priest Gennō sees birds fall from the sky above a stone, and the spirit of Tamamo-no-mae appears to tell her tale: after Emperor Toba falls ill, an onmyōji (a taoist diviner) recognizes Tamamo-no-mae as an incarnation of a fox spirit. The evil spirit flees from Kyōto to Nasu, where it is hunted down by archers on horseback and killed. Its negative karma congeals into a toxic stone that becomes known as the Killing Stone because any living being that approaches it dies.

Gennō performs a memorial service to release the fox spirit. The stone breaks apart, and the fox spirit emerges, accepts Buddhist Law, and vows to kill no more. The spirit then turns into a rock memorializing its vow not to kill.

Bashō notes "a pile of dead bees[,] butterflies[,] and other bugs" covering the ground around the stone (*Back Roads* 35), killed perhaps by toxic volcanic gases emitted from the ground. Apparently, the folk belief persisted that the stone was deadly, despite the happy ending suggested by the nō play.

North of Nasu, Bashō and Sora visit another legendary site of Buddhism's triumph over darkness—Kurozuka (Black Mound), near Kanze-ji (Adachigahara Temple), in Nihonmatsu. Kurozuka is the grave of an oni-baba (a demon possessing an old woman). Her story is told in the nō drama *Adachigahara* or *Kurozuka,* attributed to Zeami (1363–1443). Yūkei is a priest from Nachi traveling with a fellow priest and a temple servant. They arrive on a cold autumn night at an isolated, run-down cottage on the plains of Adachi. Yūkei asks the old woman living there for lodging for the night. Reluctant at first to allow them to stay, she finally yields. While demonstrating a spinning wheel for making hemp thread, she laments her bitter karma and the transiency of life. After she leaves to gather firewood, the travelers discover a room full of foul-smelling bones and human corpses: the old woman is a demon who kills and eats travelers. As the priest and his companions flee, the oni-baba pursues them, enraged that her shame has been revealed. The holy travelers rub their rosaries and pray to Buddha, driving off the oni-baba, who fades away into the stormy night.

On the way north to Matsushima, Bashō and Sora also stop at places recalling the Gempei War (1180–1185), in which the Genji (Minamoto family) defeated the Heike (Taira family) to gain control of the government. The downfall of the Heike is told in the fourteenth-century Buddhist narrative *Heike Monogatari* (*The Tale of the Heike*). Brought up in a samurai family, Bashō is deeply moved at the sites associated with the warriors in this heroic, tragic struggle.

At a shrine in Kurobane dedicated to Hachiman, the guardian kami of samurai, the poet recalls Yoichi, a Genji archer who hailed from Nasu. On 5.1 (June 18), the travelers arrive in Iizaka, a hot spring town near Fukushima, and visit the ruins of the hilltop castle of Satō Motoharu and the cemetery of the Satō family at Ioji. Motoharu's two sons Tsugunobu and Tadanobu died during the Gempei War serving as substitutes for Minamoto no Yoshitsune (1159–1189), who led the Genji forces against the Heike. (Substitutes dressed in battle gear like their lords to confuse the enemy.) Bashō's haiku at Ioji celebrates Boys' Day, on 5.5:

backpack and sword—display them in the fifth moon: paper streamers
oi mo tachi / mo satsuki ni kasare / kami-nobori[11]

The sword belonged to Yoshitsune and the bamboo backpack to Benkei, a warrior-priest who served him. The two warriors brought locks of hair from the slain Satō sons to Ioji and left the sword and back-pack as offerings in honor of the sons. At the graves of the widows of Tsugunobu and Tadanobu, Bashō recalls the widows' story and weeps: the widows went to console their husbands' grieving mother, Otowa, appearing before her dressed in their dead husbands' armor and telling her, "Mother, we have returned in triumph and glory." The camellia tree (tsubaki) in the cemetery at Ioji is known as Otowa, because camellia flowers drop suddenly from their stems before their petals fall. (Yasunari Kawabata once wrote, "Camellias are said to be bad luck because the flowers drop whole from the stem, like severed heads.")

Farther north, at Myōjin Shrine in Shiogama, Bashō finds a stone lantern donated in 1187 by Saburō no Izumi, also known as Fujiwara no Tadahira, another warrior loyal to Yoshitsune. Tadahira was the third son of Hidehara Fujiwara (1122–1187), whose family ruled Dewa and Mutsu from the town of Hiraizumi.

After Yoshitsune led the Genji to victory, he lost the favor of his older brother Yoritomo, head of the Genji. In 1187, Yoshitsune fled north, taking refuge at Hiraizumi, under the protection of Hidehira. Before dying that year, Hidehira instructed his sons to protect Yoshitsune.

Tadahira remained loyal to his father and Yoshitsune, but Tadahira's older brother Yasuhira sided with Yoritomo and attacked Yoshitsune, who committed suicide after killing his wife. Yasuhira also had his brother Tadahira killed. Ironically, Yasuhira was killed by Yoritomo, who invaded the domain of the northern Fujiwara in 1189 and crushed its forces to eliminate a rival.

Five hundred years after the Gempei War, when Bashō visits Hiraizumi, Yasuhira's fort is gone and the outer gates of Hidehira's manor house is in ruins. Borrowing imagery from the eighth-century Chinese poet Tu Fu ("The country devastated, mountains and rivers remain; in the castle in spring, the grass green"), Bashō composes a haiku on war from a Buddhist perspective:

summer grasses: all that's left of warriors' dreams
natsukusa ya / tsuwamonodomo ga / yume no ato

Just north of Hiraizumi, at Chūson Temple, the poet sees the Konjikidō (Golden Hall), also known as Hikaridō (Hall of Light), a small, beautifully gilded and lacquered mausoleum inlaid with mother of pearl and precious stones.[12] The Hikaridō houses the mummified remains of the three Fujiwara rulers—Kiyohara, Motohira, and Hidehira. Noting that the "glory of the three generations lasted only as long as a single nap" (*Bashō's Narrow Road* 85), Bashō praises the survival of the mausoleum:

Hikaridō, unscathed in the fifth-moon rains
samidare no / furinokoshite ya / hikaridō

The gilded mausoleum represents Amida Jōdo, the Pure Land of Amida, the Western Paradise beyond time, change, and suffering, where the spirits of the faithful go after death, to be instructed by Amida in achieving Nirvana.

While Bashō was brought up to admire warriors like Yoshitsune and Tadahira, Buddhism taught him to see the glories of the samurai as illusions. The culminating poem on the vanity of war is in the second half of the narrative. At Tada Shrine, in Komatsu:

heartless: under Sanemori's helmet, a cricket
muzan ya / kabuto no shita no / kirigirisu

A native of Echizen (Fukui), Saitō no Bettō Sanemori (1111–1183) served the Genji under Yoshitsune's father, Yoshitomo, who gave him the helmet. But later Saitō switched sides, joining the Heike. At seventy-three, intent on dying a warrior's death in his homeland, he rode into battle, his white hair dyed black so he wouldn't suffer the humiliation of being dismissed as an over-the-hill warrior by a younger opponent. After he was slain and beheaded, a Genji warrior recognized the face and cried out, "Ana muzan ya" (How heartless!). The narrator comments, "How piteous that his empty name alone should have survived, impervious to corporeal decay, while his mortal remains have become one with the northern soil!" (*The Tale of the Heike* 234).

The helmet that once protected the head of this legendary warrior now shelters a katydid, to which a heroic warrior's life and death has no more meaning than a rock tumbling down a hillside in a deserted forest.

Bashō and Sora arrive at Matsushima on 5.9 (June 25). The bay was known as the most scenic place in the country in Bashō's time, comparable to Lake Seiko in China. Bashō praises the wind-and-wave-sculpted islands as "the face of a beautiful woman," an allusion to Xi Shi, a legendary fifth-century Chinese beauty said to have been reincarnated in Lake Seiko.

But meditation sites and recluses on Ōjima, an island just offshore, draw his attention back to Buddhism:

On the island are the ruins of Zen master Ungo's retreat and his meditation rock. And here, too, in the shade of trees were a scattering

Meditation cave on Ōjima, Matsushima, Miyagi

of recluses, living peacefully in thatched huts, with smoke rising from fires of fallen needles and cones.

Ungo (1582–1659), a Rinzai Zen master from Tosa (on Shikoku), was a teacher of Bashō's teacher, Butchō. Ungo was invited to Matsushima to revive Zuigan-ji, a Zen temple in Matsushima. Zen advocated meditation in seclusion as a way to enlightenment.

While Bashō anticipates seeing the moon over Matsushima before leaving Edo, the climax of his journey occurs later, in two ascents he makes while crossing the central mountains on his way west to the Sea of Japan. After resting at Obanazawa, he travels twenty miles south to Ryūshaku-ji, also known as Yamadera (Mountain Temple). Founded in 860, the temple was an "unusually well-kept quiet place," atop a hill of "rocky steeps, ancient pines and cypresses, old earth and stone and smooth moss" (*Back Roads* 81). Climbing to the temple, Bashō finds the halls deserted and locked. The lonely isolation clears his heart and mind:

untroubled: cicada shrills soaking into stone
shizukesa ya / iwa ni shimiiru / semi no koe

Cicadas emerge from the ground in warm summer weather to mate

Buddhist carvings on a cliff at Yamadera   *Trail through cedars to Haguroyama*

and lay eggs, then die, symbolizing transient human life. Membranes on their bodies vibrate during their mating, saturating their surroundings with a dense, high-pitched chorus. In a haiku composed a year later, Bashō describes the cicada's ironic existence:

> soon to die, but showing no sign: cicada voices
> yagate shinu / keshiki wa miezu /semi no koe (Summer 1690)

But the cicada also represents rebirth: after it appears, it molts, shedding its old self and becoming a new being (green before darkening), like a spirit disengaging from its body at death.

Bashō's climb up Yamadera is a prelude to his ascent of Dewa Sanzan, the Three Sacred Mountains of Dewa: Haguro-yama (Black-feather Mountain); Gassan (Moon Mountain); and Yudono (Hot-spring Chamber). During the sixteenth and early seventeenth centuries, the three mountains developed into a pilgrimage destination for followers of Shugendō, a syncretic Buddhist-Shintō sect practicing mountain asceticism. The ascent of Dewa Sanzan was a physical form of spiritual rebirth:

> During the ritual period known as natsu no mine (Summer Peak) when shugenja traveled between the various sacred sites in the three mountains, they prayed for peace and tranquility in the present at Haguro, attained assurance of buddhahood in the future at Gassan,

and reached the Mitsugon Pure Land, the paradise of Dainichi, at Yudono, traversing the barriers of the everyday and the sacred realms, experiencing the unity of the everyday and the sacred, and achieving the Enlightenment of buddhahood in this very body. ("Dewa Sanzan Shinkō," *Encyclopedia of Shintō*)[13]

On 6.3 (July 19), Bashō and Sora arrive at Haguro-yama. Founded at the end of the sixth century, this Tendai temple is dedicated to Kannon, who comforts the living as they struggle to escape from earthly desires and suffering. Her Shintō manifestation at Haguro-yama is Tamayorihime, "Divine Bride," also known as Uganomitama, a kami of food, or the spirit of rice, and identified with Inari, a kami of rice.

Lodging at Minamidani (South Valley) on the southwest side of Haguro-yama, Bashō expresses his gratitude for the refreshing coolness from Gassan, whose snows last into August:

thank you—scented by snow, Minamidani
arigata ya / yuki o kaorasu / minamidani

Bashō uses "suzushia" (coolness), an autumn kigo, in his summer haiku at Haguro-yama to suggest the escape this mountain retreat offers from the muggy heat of the lowlands—symbolically, the relief Kannon offers to suffering humanity:

coolness: faint crescent moon, Haguro-yama
suzushisa ya / hono mikazuki no / haguro-yama

On 6.8 (July 24), Bashō and Sora make the eleven-mile trek to the summit of Gassan, at 6,509 feet, the tallest of the three peaks:

I walked through mists and clouds, breathing the thin air of high altitudes and stepping on slippery ice and snow, till at last through a gateway of clouds, as it seemed, to the very paths of the sun and moon, I reached the summit, completely out of breath and nearly frozen to death. (*Back Roads* 87)

The haiku on Gassan contrasts the ever-changing summer clouds (that is, the transient world below the summit) with the permanence of the mountain rising above them:

cloud peaks, countless, collapsing: moon mountain
kumo no mine / ikutsu kuzurete / tsuki no yama

The temple on Gassan is dedicated to Amida. His Shintō manifestation at

Gassan is Tsukiyomi, the moon kami, brother of Amaterasu, the sun goddess. While Kannon assists worshipers to overcome their worldly desires, Amida helps them to enter the Pure Land, where free from distractions and suffering, they can focus on achieving Nirvana.

After the ascent, the travelers descend to the temple-shrine at Yudono (Hot -spring Chamber), the inner shrine (oku-no-in) of Dewa Sanzan, considered the holiest of the three places. The temple is dedicated to Dainichi, the cosmic Buddha (the principle deity of Shingon Buddhism) who sits in meditation at the center of the Universe. His Shintō manifestation at Yudono is Ōyamatsumi (Great-mountain-possessor). A triad of conic rocks is venerated at the shrine, the tallest rock flanked by two smaller rocks, just as Gassan is flanked by the lower peaks of Haguro-yama and Yudono. Hot spring water pours over the three rocks, and its mineral content (limonite, or hydrated iron oxide) has given the rocks an ochre coloring. As pilgrims walk over the rocks bare-footed, the warm water soothes their feet and washes away the impurities and dust of this world (jōkuse jindo).

After the heights of Yamadera and Dewa Sanzan, Bashō and Sora descend again to the realm of human suffering. A two-day rest in the port town of Sakata on the Sea of Japan coast is followed by an eighteen-mile walk north to Kisakata, a bay that in Bashō's time was filled with ninety-nine pine-covered islands, said to rival Matsushima in beauty.[14] The weariness of the journey and the oppressiveness of the sweltering heat and rain imbues Bashō's writing with gloom: "Whereas Matsushima seemed to smile, Kisakata droops in dejection. The lonely, melancholy scene suggests a troubled human spirit." At Kisakata, Bashō recalls the legendary Chinese beauty Xi Shi (Seishi in Japanese), just as he did in his praise of Matsushima, but now with sadness:

Kisakata: in the rain, Seishi, a sleeping-tree flower
kisakata ya / ame ni seishi ga / nebu no hana

Seishi sacrificed herself for her homeland, the Kingdom of Yue, to help free it from the domination of Wu; the flowering tree in the rain suggests to Bashō her tragic beauty. Nemu-no-ki (sleeping-tree), a summer kigo, has flowers with thin pink stamens radiating, like silk threads, hence its common English name, "silk tree." "Sleep" refers to the fact that its bipinnate leaves close at night or when touched by rain.

The most oppressive part of the journey follows: 260 miles from Sakata through Echigo (Niigata) and Etchū (Toyama), to the town of Kanazawa in Kaga (Ishikawa). The trek takes place during the last moon of summer and the first moon of autumn, the hottest period of the year. Bashō sums up the oppressive conditions: "clouds gathering over Hokurikudō (North Land Road). Felt miserable at the thought of 130 li[15] to Kaga; crossed the Nezu barrier into Echigo; arrived at the Ichiburi barrier in Etchū: nine days of heat and humidity made my body toil; became sick; could barely write."

On the first day of autumn (7.1, August 16), in Echigo (Niigata), Bashō's haiku features Sado Island offshore, and two autumn kigo, "araumi" (rough seas) and "Ama-no-gawa" (River of Heaven, or Milky Way):

rough seas: leaning over Sado, River of Heaven
araumi ya / sado ni yokotau / amanogawa

In a prose work, he describes Sado as a place of exile and imprisonment, which, along with the rough seas, represents the realm of human suffering:

from past to present, a place of exile for felons and traitors, [Sado] has become a distressing name. As the evening moon sets, the surface of the sea becomes quite dark. The shapes of the mountains are still visible through the clouds, and the sound of waves is saddening. (Qtd. in *Bashō's Narrow Road* 148)

On the approach to Kaga, with its fertile rice fields, the humid air of early autumn is heavy with the aroma of ripening grain, which Bashō contrasts to the rough seas (ariso umi, a variant of araumi) offshore:

the scent of ripening rice, pushing on: to the right, rough seas
wase no ka ya / wake-iru migi wa / ariso umi

The travelers arrive in Kanazawa on 7.15, the first full moon of autumn (August 30), and the last night of Obon, the festival of the dead. They attend a memorial service for a local tea merchant and poet named Isshō (One Laugh), who died at thirty-six the previous year. The two haiku use the kigo "autumn wind" to represent both time passing and the world's cry of sadness.

burial mound, move: my crying voice is the autumn wind
tsuka mo ugoke / waga naku koe wa / aki no kaze

red red sun unrelenting, autumn wind, too
aka aka to / hi wa tsurenaku mo / aki no kaze

Shirane describes the transitional weather of this period at the beginning of autumn in meteorological terms:

At the start of fall, the Ogasawara high-pressure system begins to retreat to the south and the cool winds from the continent start to arrive, but the atmosphere remains hot—a long lingering summer—until the third week of August. (11)

In the haiku on Nikkō at the beginning of the journey, the sun signifies enlightenment; now the sun, relentlessly hot, belongs to the realm of human suffering, the travelers finding relief in the sun's setting, as in this poem, composed on their way back from Kisakata to Sakata:

scorching sun entering the sea: Mogami River
atsuki hi o / umi ni iretari / mogamigawa

With the sun associated with suffering rather than enlightenment, the River of Heaven and the moon at night replace it as symbols of the wisdom and compassion of Amida and Kannon. In the haiku on Sado, the River of Heaven leans over Sado, as if sheltering it from the rough seas. In a haiku composed earlier, at an inn in Ichiburi, the moon blesses the two pilgrims along with two yūjo (prostitutes, literally, "good-time girls"):

one house: prostitutes sleep here, too, bush clovers and moon
hitotsu ya ni / yūjo mo netari / hagi to tsuki

Bashō overhears the two yūjo talking about their profession and describes their fate with an image of rough seas borrowed from a classical tanka (*Bashō's Narrow Roads* 110): "On the strand where white waves crash," we wander, children of the sea, thus fallen, to every chance relation, every day *karma*, shame (*Back Roads* 97).

The two women are from Niigata, a port town with an entertainment district in whose brothels destitute families placed their daughters under contract for cash advances. Using two conventional autumn kigo (bush clovers and the moon), Bashō gives his haiku a Buddhist perspective expressing compassion for the two yūjo. The hagi (bush clover) represents the transient world in which pilgrims and prostitutes, both wanderers and dwellers at the margins of society, are caught in the illusory cycle of desires and suffering. A poem in *Kokinshū* links the bush clover to worldly love: "The stag has come to my hill, looking for his flower wife—the first bush clover" (Shirane 42). Shirane remarks that hagi, like sakura (cherry blossom), embodies "impermanence, fragility, and vulnerability" (134).

In the second-to-the-last haiku of *Oku*, at Tsuruga bay, Bashō reprises hagi and waves as symbolic of the transient world and its inhabitants:

between waves, mixed with small shells, hagi litter
nami no ma ya / kogai ni majiru / hagi no chiri

The moon shining on the bush clovers at Ichiburi, like the River of Heaven above Sado, represents the all-encompassing compassion of Kannon and Amida. A passage from *The Tale of the Heike*, about the tragic Gempei War, details the Buddhist symbolism of the moon:

> ...the moon of divine responsiveness shone cloudless on the riverbank where the Lotus Sutra was studied; no dew of false thought settled in the courtyard where the sins of the six sense organs were repented. There was promise everywhere of hope for the life to come. (347)

The man traveling with two yujō is returning to Niigata. Uncertain of the way to Ise, the two ask Bashō to allow them to follow behind, at a distance, and to grant them the blessing of Buddha. His practical reply is that he and Sora plan to stop here and there along the way, so the two women should follow others going directly to the shrine, a response that suggests that he sees himself as a wanderer rather than a guide. He encourages the prostitutes on their pilgrimage by assuring them that Amaterasu will protect them.[16]

Twenty miles south of Kanazawa, Bashō and Sora visit Natadera, a Kannon temple located in a valley beneath cliffs pitted with caves.[17] Bashō again evokes the autumn wind, linked, through synesthesia, to the white limestone-silicate cliffs:

whiter than Ishiyama's stones: autumn wind
ishiyama no / ishi yori shiroshi / aki no kaze

Limestone-silicate cliffs of Natadera, Ishikawa

White is the color of the tiger spirit of autumn, associated with death. Ishiyama (Stone Mountain), another temple dedicated to Kannon, is also known for its whitish limestone-silicate rocks.

Seeking relief from the cold autumn wind, and to help them recover from the exhausting trek from Sakata to Kanazawa, Bashō and Sora spend a week (7.27 to 8.5, September 12–18) at Yamanaka hot spring, near Natadera:

Yamanaka! kiku unfallen, redolent water
yamanaka ya / kiku wa taoranu / yu no nioi

The poem alludes to Kiku no Sekku (Chrysanthemum Festival), the last of five annual seasonal festivals, held on 9.9, in the last moon of autumn. The festival is still over a month away and falls outside the narrative, whose last entry is on 9.6; but the Kiku Festival and Hinamatsuri (the second annual festival), alluded to in the first haiku of *Oku*, frame the year as the passage of an individual's life: Hinamatsuri, or Girls' Day (3.3), is associated with springtime and youth, and Kiku no Sekku with autumn and old age, leading to winter and death. (In between, the third and fourth festivals go by—Boys' Day, on 5.5, associated with boys becoming warriors, and Tanabata, on 7.7, associated with love and marriage.)

Kiku is a perennial, known for its hardiness; it can withstand cold weather, and remains in bloom for an extended period, its petals never falling (Shirane 44). Traditionally, in China, celebrants of the kiku festival drank rice wine infused with the flower's petals to fortify the spirit against the coming winter. Poem 470 in *Kokinshū* (an anthology of poems compiled during the Heian Period) suggests the flower's promise of longevity:

Let me break off this chrysanthemum, still wet with dew, and place it in my hair, so that never-aging autumn lingers on.

tsuyu nagara / orite kazasamu / kiku no hana /oisenu aki no / hisashikarubeku

The gist of Bashō's haiku is that he feels like the unfallen kiku when bathing in Yamanaka's sulphate waters, which are said to sooth aching muscles, fatigue, and digestive problems, from which he and Sora suffer.[18]

In another prose piece, he describes how the hot spring revived him to the point where he felt reborn:

Certainly as I bathed often, my skin and flesh were moisturized, muscles and bones softened. Heart and mind relaxed, and I truly felt my complexion revived. I did not care whether the boat to the earthly paradise or the marker for Tz'u-t'ung's chrysanthemums was lost. (Qtd. in *Bashō's Narrow Road* 150-151)

Tz'u-t'ung, an exiled young Chinese courtier, is said to have become an immortal by drinking the dew from kiku petals and leaves (Casal 102).

But the redolent hot spring waters provide only temporary relief. Still suffering from a stomach ailment, Sora leaves the pilgrimage after Yamanaka. In Fukui, Bashō seeks out Tōsai, a poet whom he hasn't seen in ten years, and the two decide to go to Tsuruga bay to view the mid-autumn full moon (8.15, September 28), considered the brightest and most beautiful moon of the year.

Autumn is considered the best time for tsuki-mi, or moon viewing, because of its clear, cool weather. Bashō composed haiku about his obsession with moon viewing:

autumn moon: I circle the pond all night long.
meigatsu ya / ike o megurite / yomosugara (Autumn 1686)

awakening nine times so far: the moon at four a.m.
kokono tabi / okite mo tsuki no / nanatsu kana (Autumn 1691)

In autumn 1688, the year before traveling to Oku, Bashō walked 160 miles in five days up the mountainous Kiso Road to view the moon over Mount Obasute near Sarashina village in Shinano (Nagano), a journey he describes in "Sarashina Journal."

Two years before his journey to Oku, in the autumn of 1687, Bashō goes on a moon-viewing journey to Kashima Shrine, fifty miles east of Edo. When he and his two companions arrive in the afternoon, it starts to rain, and the rising moon is hidden. Near dawn, a break in the clouds allows some light from the setting moon to shine through. Excited, Bashō rouses the others, but the full moon never appears: "We sat for a long time in utter silence, watching the moonlight trying to penetrate the clouds and listening to the sound of the lingering rain." In the end:

It was really regrettable that I had come such a long way only to look at the dark shadow of the moon, but I consoled myself by remembering the famous lady who had returned without composing a single poem from the long walk she had taken to hear a cuckoo. (*The Narrow Road to the Deep North* 67–68)

Bashō and Tōsai arrive in Tsuruga on 8.14. But like the moon viewing at Kashima, this one is a disappointment. While the nights before and after are clear, the night of 8.15 is rainy, the moon hidden by clouds:

full-moon! north country weather is unpredictable
meigetsu ya / hokkoku biyori / sadame naki

Bashō realizes that this might be (and it was) his last opportunity to see the autumn moon over Tsuruga bay. The haiku also suggests the uncertainties of attaining, or holding on to, enlightenment.

The disappointment at Tsuruga recalls an earlier disappointment in his journey: Bashō searches the marshland around the town of Hiwada in Mutsu (Fukushima) for flowering katsumi (water-oat), made famous in poetry. He wanders around the marsh, asking those he meets if they can show him katsumi, without luck.

His disappointments give his writing a tone of sorrow and resignation that is integral to the aesthetics of living in a transient world. As Saigyō (1118–1190)[19] remarks ironically:

Were the world without
falling blossoms
or the clouded moon,
I could no longer live
in sad longing. (Qtd. in Barnhill)

Before arriving at Matsushima at mid-journey, Bashō visits Tsubo no Ishibumi, a stone monument erected in the reign of Emperor Shōmu (r. r. 724–749). The monument was made famous by earlier travelers to Oku, including Saigyō, and Bashō is elated to be standing before it:

… finally arriving here at this memorial that had undoubtedly survived a thousand years, I peered into the hearts of the ancients, as if they were standing now right before my eyes. One reward of a pilgrimage is the ecstasy of such experiences; forgetting the hardships of the road, I simply wept.

The religious purpose of his journey, to detach himself from this world in preparation for the next, is often at odds with his worldly attachments—his desire to visit "places ears had heard of[,] eyes never seen" (*Back Roads* 19); his love of nature's beauty (moon and flowers); his delight in poetry; and his admiration for those whose actions and works have provided the passing generations with models of living. While Buddhist aesthetics suggest that enlightenment can be found in nature or "in this very body," it also makes clear that nature and this body are transient.

At times, Bashō expresses a wish to adopt the Zen ideal of becoming a recluse, as when he sees hermits on Ōjima, in Matsushima; or earlier, at Sukagawa, when he admires a man living alone in a hut at the edge of town, next to a chestnut tree, its plain flowers in bloom at the eaves of his hut:

unnoticed by the world, a flowering chestnut tree his neighbor
yo no hito no / mitsukenu hana ya / noki no kuri

Bashō notes that the kanji for kuri (chestnut) includes the kanji for "tree," with the kanji for "west" above it, suggesting a symbolic guidepost to Amida's Western Paradise.

Following his journey to Oku, he lives as a hermit for a while in the hills south of Lake Biwa, at Genjū-an (Hut of the Phantom Dwelling), which was named after a monk who lived there and who was known as Elder of the Phantom Dwelling. Bashō explains his motivation for becoming a recluse:

troubled by frequent illness and weary of dealing with people, I've come to dislike society. Again and again I think of the mistakes I've made in my clumsiness over the course of the years. There was a time I envied those who had government offices or impressive domains, and on another occasion I considered entering the precincts of the Buddha and the teaching rooms of the patriarchs. Instead, I've worn out my body in journeys that are as aimless as the winds and clouds, and expended my feelings on flowers and birds. But somehow I've been able to make a living this way, and so in the end, unskilled and talentless as I am, I give myself wholly to this one concern, poetry. … we all in the end live, do we not, in a phantom dwelling? ("The Hut of the Phantom Dwelling" 294–295).

But despite this inclination to become a recluse, the poet is also reluctant to let go of company. Letters to his friends indicate his longing to see them again. He travels to Oku and on other journeys with companions, rather than alone, as Saigyō did; after Sora leaves, Bashō seeks out Tōsai in Fukui.

In "A Visit to the Kashima Shrine," he expresses his uncertainties about his attachments metaphorically:

neither a priest nor an ordinary man of this world was I, for I wavered ceaselessly like a bat that passes for a bird at one time and for a mouse at another (*The Narrow Road to the Deep North* 65)

The pen name he adopted, "bashō" (banana plant), suggests his flexible, fragile, wavering nature:

> Its leaf is wide enough to cover a koto. At times, blown down midway, it pains you like the phoenix's broken tail or, like a torn green fan, it sorrows in the wind. From time to time its flowers bloom but they are not florid, and though its stalk is thick, it is never axed. Comparable to "useless trees in the mountain," it is noble in character. Monk Huai-su ran his brush on it, while Chang Heng-chu, looking at its new leaves, gained strength for greater learning. I do neither; simply idling beneath its leaves, I admire the way they tear easily in wind and rain. (Qtd. in *Bashō's Narrow Road* 48)

Shirane writes that the bashō, the subject of a plant-spirit nō play by Konparu Zenchiku (1405–1468), "not only becomes a symbol of the impermanence of all things, but represents those beings (such as women) who are thought to have difficulty being saved"; he quotes a line from the play:

> The mountain wind, the wind through the pines, sweeps through, sweeps through; the flowers and plants scatter and scatter; the [bashō] leaves are torn and left broken. (124)

After Bashō returns to Edo from Oku, he tries to stop writing poetry, realizing it's an attachment to the illusory world Buddhism urges him to escape; "but every time I [stopped], a poetic sentiment would solicit my heart and something would flicker in my mind" (Ueda 169). He continues writing, and till the end, his wavering spirit plagues him. One of his last haiku, written while he was ill, expresses his feeling of being in limbo rather than on his way to the Pure Land of Amida:

> on a journey, ailing, dreams on a withered field running in circles
> tabi ni yande / yume wa kare no o / kakemeguru (Autumn 1694)

In 1694, on a journey from Edo back to his hometown of Iga-Ueno, Bashō fell ill from dysentery in Ōsaka. Facing death, he asked to be buried not at the isolated hermitage of Genjū-an, but at nearby Gichū Temple, on the shore of Lake Biwa, next to Lord Kiso: "Genjūan, where I found my first prop in a pasania tree, is too far from any human abode. I would rather have my grave by the side of Lord Kiso" (Takarai).

Lord Kiso died during the Gempei War, at the battle of Awazu, south of Lake Biwa. Born Minamoto no Yoshinaka (1154–1184), he was taken to the Kiso valley as an infant after his father was killed by a cousin, and later changed his name from Minamoto to Kiso. He was also known as Gichū (alternative reading of the two kanji in Yoshi-naka).

Gichū-ji was built on the southern shore of Lake Biwa during the Muromachi Period (1338–1573) to honor Lord Kiso's spirit. At the temple, in 1691, Bashō's students constructed for their master a hut called Mu-myō-an (Nameless Hut). After Bashō passed away from dysentery, they carried his remains there and buried him next to Lord Kiso; a bashō tree was planted at his grave.

According to *The Tale of Heike*, Lord Kiso was "the son of a prostitute" (15–16). Osamu Dazai includes a note about him in *Return to Tsugaru*:

Minamoto no Yoshinaka (1154–1184), a cousin of Yoritomo and Yoshitsune, had been brought up in the rural Kiso region and was not familiar with the finer points of etiquette as observed in the capital. He once offered plain, unsalted mushrooms to an Imperial vice-councillor, but the refined nobleman was so horrified at Yoshinaka's display of rustic courtesy that he could hardly force himself to touch his food and finally fled in confusion. (57)

Like Lord Kiso, Bashō was a rustic samurai who felt out of place in society.

Kikaku, a disciple, notes the appropriateness of Bashō's final resting place, given Bashō's fondness for beautiful landscapes:

Our master had a particular love for scenic places. His grave is graced by Mount Nagara and Mount Tanokami and the waves of Lake Biwa that come right up to the temple gate. The boats going out leave their traces on the water, reminding us of the short span of our life. Deer on the woodcutters' paths, wild geese flying over farm houses, the moon shining over the lake—all these add beauty to his grave. (Takarai)

If all that's beautiful in life is fleeting, the poet's consolation was to be buried in a landscape beautiful in every season.

NOTES

1. 1689 was the second year of Genroku (Original Happiness), a nengō, or "name of years." Genroku marked the start of the reign of Emperor Higashiyama (r. 1687–1709) and is considered a golden age of the Edo Period, when art and architecture flourished. Nengō years are numbered consecutively until a new nengō is established.

2. The Meiji government renamed the provinces of Bashō's time as prefectures in 1885, when it dismantled the feudal system of the Edo Period.

3. Nobuyuki Yuasa's translation of *Oku no Hosomichi* (*The Narrow Road to the Deep North and other Travel Sketches*) was published in 1966; others followed, including Cid Corman's *Back Road to Far Towns* (1968); Earl Miner's "The Narrow Road through the Provinces" (in *Japanese Poetic Diaries*, 1969); Dorothy Britton's *Haiku Journey: Basho's Narrow Road to a Far Province* (1980); Helen Craig McCullough's "The Narrow Road of the Interior" (in *Classical Japanese Prose: An Anthology*, 1990); Hiroaki Satō's *Bashō's Narrow Road: Spring & Autumn Passages* (1996); Donald Keene's *The Narrow Road to Oku* (1996); Haruo Shirane and James Brandon's "Narrow Road to the Deep North (Oku no Hosomichi 1694)" (in *Early Modern Japanese Literature: An Anthology, 1600–1900*, 2002); and David L. Barnhill's "The Narrow Road to the Deep North (Oku no Hosomichi)" (in *Bashō's Journey: The Literary Prose of Matsuo Bashō*, 2005). I quote from various of these translations; when there are no citations for quoted passages, I've translated the lines myself.

Completed in summer 1694 after over four years of revision following the journey, *Oku no Hosomichi* is considered a classic of haibun, or a genre that combines poetry and prose. Bashō first used the genre term in 1691, in a letter to a friend.

Bashō also wrote renga, or "linked verse," composed by multiple poets led by a master/critic who composed the first verse and applied the rules and conventions of composition to judge each poet's subsequent contribution. The participants took turns composing alternating triplets of 5-7-5 syllables and couplets of 7-7 syllables, based on the traditional waka form (five lines, in a pattern of 5-7-5-7-7 syllables). Originally, a hundred verses made up a renga composition; the number was later reduced to fifty or thirty-six.

On his journey to Oku, Bashō hosted thirty or so renga sessions for students interested in his style of composition (*Bashō's Narrow Road* 29).

Haiku, a poem of three lines in a pattern of 5-7-5 syllables, developed from the opening triplet of renga (called hokku, or opening verse). Bashō's canon contains about a thousand haiku.

Keene provides a literary-social context for Bashō's poetry in "Haiku and the Democracy of Poetry as a Popular Art." During the Edo Period, new arts and aesthetics were established outside of the courtly tradition of poetry, among poets and artists supported by merchants in the towns and cities. Unlike courtly poetry, which was limited to the archaic vocabulary and hackneyed subjects and images of ancient works, the new poetry had its roots in haikai (comic linked verses), and allowed for a broader range of content and the use of colloquial language.

Bashō's life and development as a poet is summarized in Makoto Ueda's biography *Matsuo Bashō*: "… he began with a witty, pedantic style and gradually became more serious and somber" under the influence of Zen Buddhism and Chinese Taoist poetry (70); in a late phase, he advocated "lightness" as a way for poets to avoid heavy sentimentalism and moralizing.

4. Bashō's narrative records the passage of time by the lunar calendar introduced from China during the Nara Period (710–794). The dates have two numbers, the first referring to one of twelve annual moons and the second to one of the 29 or 30 moon phases per cycle. A "month" begins at midnight of the new moon and ends 29 or 30 days later at midnight on the night of the next new moon.

1.1 is the first day of the year, which begins on the night of the new moon after the moon that follows the moon of winter solstice, the date falling between Jan. 22 and Feb. 20 on the Gregorian calendar. In 1688, the year before Bashō's journey, the last moon of the year waxed and waned from January 21 to February 19. Thus, 1.1 in 1689 was on February 20.

Each of the four seasons has three moons (1689–1690 dates):

Spring Moons: *Mu-tsuki* (Harmonious Moon, Feb. 20–Mar. 21); *Kisaragi* or *Kinusaragi* (Changing into New Clothes, Mar, 22–Apr. 19); *Yayoi* (Grass Grows Dense or New Life, Apr. 20–May 19).

Summer Moons: *U-tsugi* (Moon of the U-flower, May 20–June 17); *Sa-tsuki* (Moon of Rice-sprouts, June 18–July 16); *Mina-tsuki* (Moon of Water, July 17–Aug. 15).

Autumn Moons: *Fu-tsuki* (Moon of Literary Texts, Aug. 16–Sept. 13); *Ha-tsuki* (Moon of Leaves, Sept. 14–Oct. 13); *Naga-tsuki* (Long Moon, Oct. 14–Nov. 12).

Winter Moons: *Kami-na-tsuki* or *kan'na-tsuki* (Moon of Gods, Nov. 13–Dec. 11); *Shimo-tsuki* (Frosty Moon, Dec. 12–Jan. 10, 1690); *Shi-wasu* (Priests-run; so called because priest run around blessing everything for the New Year, Jan. 11–Feb. 9).

With the adoption of the Gregorian calendar in 1873, a lunar date like 3.27 was translated to March 27, so the Gregorian dates were about a month earlier than the lunar calendar dates. The change caused some confusion. For example, a couple of translations of *Oku no Hosomichi* describe sakura in bloom as Bashō left Edo:

The faint shadow of Mount Fuji and the cherry blossoms of Ueno and Yanaka were bidding me a last farewell. (Yuasa)

Mount Fuji just a shadow, I set out under the cherry blossoms of Ueno and Yanaka. (Hamill)

But 3.27, or May 16, is too late in the year for sakura to be blooming in Edo. The bloom occurs earlier in late March or April. However, Bashō doesn't write that he saw sakura or walked under them as he left Edo, only that he was uncertain that he would ever see the sakura of Ueno and Yanaka again.

Along with the lunar count, the annual solar cycle was used to track the seasons. This cycle is generally aligned to, but not exactly coincident with the lunar seasons. Twelve moon cycles take about 354 days to complete, while one solar cycle takes 365 days, so an intercalary moon was added every three years to maintain the alignment of the lunar and solar calendars.

The solar seasons in the Chinese calendar are determined by equinoxes and solstices, but unlike in the West, these solar events mark the middle of the seasons rather than their beginnings and ends. Thus, the first days of the solar seasons by the Chinese calendar occur forty-five days earlier than the seasons in the Gregorian calendar:

Haru / Spring: Feb. 4–May 4 (Spring Equinox: Mar. 21)
Natsu / Summer: May 5–Aug. 6 (Summer Solstice: June 21)
Aki / Autumn: Aug. 7–Nov. 6 (Autumn Equinox: Sept. 23)
Fuyu / Winter: Nov. 7–Feb. 3 (Winter Solstice: Dec. 22)

In 1689, the lunar New Year on February 20 was sixteen days later than the solar New Year on February 4; the next lunar new year (1690) began six days after the solar New Year, on February 10.

5. Pilgrimages to Ise shrine were popular during the Edo Period. However, Buddhist pilgrims were not allowed to pray at the shrine. About his visit to Ise in spring 1685, Bashō writes: "I resemble a lay person, but my head is shaven. Although I am no priest, here those with shaven heads are considered to be Buddhist friars, and I was not allowed to go before the shrine" ("Journal of Bleached Bones" 15). The ban on Buddhist priests was lifted in the Meiji Period (1868–1912).

6. Sora (1649–1710) joined Bashō in Nikkō and the two traveled together until Sora's ailment forced him to abandon the journey. Sora was his neighbor in Edo; of him, Bashō wrote:

Sora is from the Kawai family; his common name is Sōgorō. With our eaves side by side under the lower leaves of plantain [bashō], he helps me in the labor of acquiring firewood and water. This time he was delighted to share with me the views of Matsushima and Kisakata. (Qtd. in *Bashō's Narrow Road* 49)

7. Along with kasa, pilgrims wear waraji, or straw sandals. Bashō writes after six months of travel between Edo and Nagoya during fall and winter of 1684:

> year gone, kasa still on, straw sandals, too
> toshi kurenu / kasa kite waraji / hakinagara

In Sendai, north of Shirakawa, Bashō receives a parting gift of sandals from an artist named Kaemon, with straps woven from ayame leaves. The occasion was the approach of the summer festival of Ayame no Sekku (which later became Boys' Day), when ayame (mountain iris) was hung from the roofs to ward off evil and disease:

Waraji

> iris-grass: binding the feet to straw-sandals
> ayamegusa / ashi ni musuban / waraji no o

The feet represent the travelers, and the sandals are protection from the impurities and dust of this world (jōkuse jindo).

At temples around Japan, pilgrims hang their worn-out waraji at the gates, where some temples display giant waraji.

8. Haiku records moments in the passing of a year using kigo, or season words, referring to plants, animals, and celestial and weather phenomena associated with the each season. The summer haiku of *Oku* contain summer kigo: aoba (green leaves), hototogisu (cuckoo), samidare (fifth-moon rains), semi (cicada), and summer flowers, such as katsumi (a species of iris), kuri no hana (chestnut flowers), and ayame (mountain iris). The haiku of autumn contain autumn kigo: wind, moon, River of Heaven (Milky Way), rough seas, dew, and hagi (bush clover).

9. Nikkō was opened as a site for Buddhist worship by Shōnin (735–817), who went there in 766 and climbed Mt. Nantai, at 8,150 feet the highest of Mt. Nikkō's three peaks. Shōnin built a hermitage on the east shore of Lake Chuzenji, below Mt. Nantai. In 784 the hermitage became a religious training center.

Originally, Mt. Nikkō was called Futara-yama, possibly a Japanese rendering of a Sanskrit name for Fudaraku-sen, the Pure Land of Kannon, the bodhisattva of mercy. The kanji characters for Futarayama can also be read "Nikō-zan," or "Mt. Two-Disasters," alluding to a tradition that two violent storms per year came from a cave to the northeast (a direction associated with harmful spirits and disasters in Chinese tradition). According to Bashō, the kanji were changed to Nikkō (Sun-light) by Kūkai (774–835, posthumously Kōbō Daishi), the founder of Shingon Buddhism, to suggest the enlightenment that emanated from the mountain.

In Buddhist tradition, Nikkō and his sister Gakkō (Moon-light) accompany Kannon and Yakushi (the Buddha of medicine and healing). Together, the two heavenly sources of light symbolize wisdom, virtue, and compassion.

By the Muromachi Period (1338–1573), Nikkō had developed into a training center for mountain ascetics. Eventually, a pilgrimage route of over one hundred temples and shrines was established in the mountains around Nikkō. The ritual ascent of Mt. Nantai and a circuit by boat around Lake Chūzenji are still practiced today.

10. After Buddhism was established as a state religion by Prince Shōtoku (572–622), temples were established throughout Yamato, to conduct ceremonies to prevent epidemics, earthquakes, and floods and to ensure an abundant harvest.

Early in the Heian Period, two schools of Buddhism were introduced from China: Tendai, established by Saichō (767–822) and headquartered at Enryakuji, on Mt. Hiei, northeast of Kyōto; and Shingon, established by Kūkai (774–835) and headquartered on Mt. Kōya, south of Nara. These two priests went to China in 804 to study Buddhism.

Both sects developed esoteric rituals and practices to achieve enlightenment, through trance aided by mantra (sacred sounds, vocalized in chants); mudra (symbolic hand gestures and body positioning); and mandala (concentric diagrams used to visualize sacred space). Both schools were also syncretic and considered the kami of Shintō as suijaku, or manifestations of buddhas and bodhisattvas, who were honji, "original ground."

During the Kamakura Period (1185–1333), the Jōdo (Pure Land) school was established by Hōnen (1133–1212). Jōdo opened Buddhism to the masses, offering salvation to anyone who called on Amida Buddha by chanting "Namu Amida Butsu" (I take refuge in Amida). Salvation was based on the Primal Vow of Amida to renounce Nirvana until all who called on him had entered the Pure Land, where they would learn to unburden themselves of their negative karma and achieve Nirvana.

Jōdo Shinshū, founded by Shinran Shonin (1173–1263) was an offshoot of Jōdo, based on the beliefs that salvation was a gift from Amida rather than the result of an individual's effort and that chanting Amida's name was not the cause of salvation, but a form of thanks. Jōdo eventually became the most widely practiced form of Buddhism.

Zen was also established during the Kamakura Period, advocating a path to enlightenment through zazen, or sitting in meditation, and other austerities, which include living simply, often as a recluse at a monastery or in a remote location.

Eisai (1141–1215) founded Rinzai Zen after his return from China in 1191. Its rigorous training in artistic activities (tea ceremony, flower arranging, calligraphy) and its use of kōan (enigmatic words, grasped intuitively) appealed to aristocrats and scholars. Zen monks also provided training in warrior skills (e.g., archery and swordsmanship), so Rinzai became popular among the samurai.

One of Eisai's disciples, Dōgen (1200–1253), after study in China, established Sōtō Zen around 1227. This school had a broader appeal than Rinzai, emphasizing shikantaza, "nothing but sitting" (that is, meditation), as a simple, but rigorous practice to recognize the Buddha within.

11. "Kami-nobori," "paper streamers," may refer to paper carps, koi-nobori, or carp streamer, hung from bamboo poles on Boys' Day, a tradition established during the Edo Period, based on a Chinese legend about a carp swimming upstream past rapids known as the Dragon Gate. In recognition of the fish's perseverance and strength, the gods turned the carp into a dragon.

Casal remarks that there was another kind of paper streamer displayed on Boys' Day: "multicolored, long and rather broad streamers gathered around a circlet, the *fuki-nagashi* pennons. The flutterings and crossings of these ribbons were intended to entangle or shoo away evil" (71). Swords, helmets, armor, and other warrior regalia became popular gifts on Boys' Day; these were put on display, as were figures representing Yoshitsune and Benkei (75).

12. In 1337, a fire destroyed most of the Chūsonji complex, but the Hikaridō was saved by its protective building. The temple complex was rebuilt in the seventeenth century. Today, Hikaridō, a national treasure, is housed in an air-conditioned concrete building. In 2011, Hiraizumi, including the Chūsonji complex, was designated a World Heritage Site by UNESCO.

13. Shugenja gather at Hagurosan three times a year (summer, autumn, and winter) to go through rituals of symbolic death and rebirth through ten successive realms, the six realms of suffering and the four realms of enlightenment. The aim of the participants is to become bodhisattvas, ready to return to the everyday world to assist others along the path toward Nirvana. The pilgrims perform rites and austerities at sacred sites around Gassan, including a rock pinnacle and a cave. Enlightenment is also said to come from understanding the

sounds of wind, birds, and insects as voices of the kami and buddhas (*Haguro Shugendo: The Autumn Peak*).

14. In 1804, an 7.1-magnitude earthquake raised the floor of Kisakata Lagoon almost eight feet, so what were once small pine-covered islands are now small hills surrounded by rice fields. Kanmanju Temple, where Bashō and Sora stayed, is still there, in the rice fields near shore, just off the coastal highway.

15. Bashō gives distances in li, a traditional Chinese measure that varied in length. During the Edo Period, when traditional units of measure were converted to meters, the li became fixed at 3.927 km, or 2.44 miles.

16. Bashō's reply is in keeping with his statement earlier in *Oku no Hosomichi*, that traveling the road of life requires "self-abandonment, resignation to the transient flow of life, to die on the road, heaven's decree" (*Back Roads* 51).

On a journey from Edo to Kyōto in autumn 1687, while walking along the Fuji River, Bashō and his companion Chiri came upon an abandoned two-year-old child ("Journal of Bleached Bones" 14). He gave the child his food, then left it to its destiny, remarking it was heaven's will. But his reflection on the child's fate results in a self-mocking haiku:

saddened by a monkey's cries: what of a child left to the autumn wind?
saru o kiku hito / sutego ni aki no/ kaze ika ni

Ueda sees Bashō's objectivity as a "return to nature": "A poet observes each object of nature quietly following its predetermined course of life, and makes that observation a basic lesson in living his life as a man" (168). However, applied to an abandoned child, Bashō's detachment seems "muzan," pitiless.

17. Natadera's name was given by Emperor Kazan (968–1008), from the first syllables ("Na" and "Ta") of the first and last Kannon temples in the thirty-three-temple tour in Kinki (the area around the capital, Kyotō): "Na" is from Nachi Temple in Kii (Wakayama) and "Ta" from Tanigumi Temple in Mino (Gifu).

The founder of Natadera was Taichō (682–767), a mountain ascetic who climbed Hakusan (White Mountain), a sacred mountain twenty-two miles east-southeast of Natadera. At a pond below its peak, he had a vision of the mountain kami Kikuri Hime emerging from the waters and transforming herself into Kannon. He enshrined an image of the eleven-headed, thousand-armed Kannon in one of the caves at Natadera.

Today, Natadera is dedicated to world peace and natural harmony. Its main hall houses a statue of the eleven-headed Kannon. Visitors can enter womb-like caves to light candles in worship and be symbolically reborn. Below the cliffs is a garden with a swan pond representing the Pure Land of Kannon. In mid-January, when we visited, there were few visitors. The spiritual aura was intense.

18. The founding legend of Yamanaka associates the hot spring with a medicine Buddha. The hot spring was opened during the Nara Period by Gyōki (668–749), a traveling monk remembered for building bridges, dams, roads, temples, and monasteries and nunneries that served as hospitals for the poor. Gyōki dug at a spot pointed out by old man and released the hot spring waters from underground. The old man later appeared to him in a dream, saying, "I am an incarnation of the healing Buddha." Gyōki carved a statue of Buddha out of wood and enshrined it next to the spring.

During a period of civil unrest the hot spring at Yamanaka was forgotten. Lord Hasebe of Noto rediscovered it during the Heian Period: while hunting, he saw a white heron bathing its injured leg in a stream. A young woman appeared to Hasebe and said, "I am an incarnation of the healing Buddha. There is a hot spring here which will cure illnesses." The lord dug into the ground and rediscovered the hot spring and the statue, after which he built twelve ryokan (inns) nearby for travelers who came to use the waters for healing ("History of Yamanaka Onsen").

19. Saigyō (1118–1190), a samurai who served the Genji before the Gempei War, became a priest when he was 23 and a wanderer, mountain recluse, and poet. He traveled to Oku. At Ashino, Bashō writes a haiku that echoes the following tanka by Saigyō:

> at the roadside, clear water flowing and a willow's shade: I stopped, telling myself to rest a while.

> michonohe ni / shimizu nagaruru / yanagi kage / shibashi tote koso / tachidomari-tsure. (*Bashō's Narrow Road* 56)

Bashō places the willow tree in a farming scene next to a stream, suggesting how the area might have changed in the 500 years between Saigyō's time and his, and also illustrating Bashō's interest in people as well as nature:

> one rice paddy planted, got up and left the willow tree
> ta ichimai / uete tachisaru / yanagi ka na

SOURCES

Barnhill, David Landis. "Sorrow and Blossoms: The Poety of Saigyō." *David Barnhill*, 2011. University of Wisconsin. Web.

Bashō. *Back Roads to Far Towns*. Trans. Cid Corman and Kamaike Susumu. New York: Grossman,1968.

---. *Bashō's Narrow Road: Spring & Autumn Passages*. Trans. Hiroaki Satō. Berkeley: Stone Bridge, 1996.

---. "The Hut of the Phantom Dwelling (Genjūan no Ki, 1690)." *From the Country of Eight Islands: An Anthology of Japanese Poetry.* Trans. Hiroaki Satō and Burton Watson. New York: Doubleday, 1981. 293–296.

---. "Journal of Bleached Bones in a Field." *Bashō's journey: the literary prose of Matsuo Bashō.* Trans. David Landis Barnhill. Albany: SUNY P, 2005. 13–22.

---. *The Narrow Road to the Deep North and Other Travel Sketches*. Trans. Nobuyuki Yuasa. New York: Penguin, 1966.

---. *Oi no Kobumi*. Japanese Text Initiative. U of Virginia Library. 2006. Web.

---. "Sarashina Journal." *Bashō's journey: the literary prose of Matsuo Bashō.* Trans. David Landis Barnhill. Albany: SUNY P, 2005. 45–48.

Chatwin, Bruce. *The Songlines*. New York: Penguin, 1987.

Casal, U.A. *The Five Sacred Festivals of Ancient Japan*. Rutland: Tuttle, 1967.

Dazai, Osamu. *Return to Tsugaru: Travels of a Purple Tramp*. Tōkyō: Kodansha,1985.

"History of Yamanaka Onsen." *Welcome to Yamanaka Onsen*. Yamanaka Tourism Association, n.d. Web.

Keene, Donald. "Haiku and the Democracy of Poetry as a Popular Art." *Sources of Japanese Tradition: 1600–2000.* Eds. William Theodore de Bary, Carol Gluck, and Arthur E. Tiedermann. New York: Columbia UP, 2005.

"Kurozuka." *The NOH-com*. the-NOH.com, 2013. Web.

Haguro Shugendo: The Autumn Peak. Dir. Kitamura Minao. Trans. Gaylord Sekimori. Visual Folklore Inc., 2004. Film.

"Sesshōseki." *The NOH-com*. the-NOH.com, 2013. Web.

Shirane, Haruo. *Japan and the Culture of the Four Seasons*. New York: Columbia UP, 2012.

Takarai Kikaku. "An Account of Our Master Bashō's Last Days." Trans. by Nobuyuki Yuasa. *Simply Haiku: A Quarterly Journal of Japanese Short Form Poetry* 4.3 (2006). Web.

The Tale of the Heike. Trans. Helen McCullough. Palo Alto: Stanford UP, 1988.

Ueda, Makoto. *Matsuo Bashō*. Tōkyō: Kodansha, 1970.

In Snow Country

On our way to the New Year's fire festival in Nozawa in 2008, we made our first visit to yukiguni (snow country), the mountainous interior of Honshū, where winter cold fronts from Siberia sweep across the Sea of Japan, bringing snowfall that piles as high as twelve or thirteen feet in villages and towns. Snow country had been on my mind ever since I read Yasunari Kawabata's novel *Snow Country* in the winter of 1970, on my first trip to Japan. Kawabata (1899–1972) was the first Japanese writer to win the Nobel Prize for literature, in 1968. I knew little about his writing or its cultural traditions, but the lyrical imagery of seasons in the story, set in a hot spring village, stayed with me, dream-like, in memory.

Snow Country opens with a train from Tōkyō coming out of a long tunnel into a snowy landscape. In 1931, four years before Kawabata published the short story that he later expanded into his novel, the six-mile-long Shimizu Tunnel was completed after nine years of construction. The tunnel was on a railroad route connecting the capital, on the Pacific side of Honshū, through snow country, to Niigata Prefecture, on the Sea of Japan side. The rail was part of a nation-building effort in preparation for war, but it also made snow country more easily accessible to well-to-do travelers who wanted to escape the crowded, industrialized capital for summer mountain climbing, autumn-foliage viewing, and winter skiing. The village in the novel, based on one that Kawabata visited in the mountain valley where the tunnel emerges on the Niigata side, also offers hot springs baths and geisha.

The passing seasons provides a conventional frame for the story of a doomed relationship between Shimamura, a wealthy middle-aged idler and dreamer from Tōkyō, and Komako, a nineteen-year-old he meets when he requests a geisha at his inn.

The geisha at mountain hot springs served as both entertainers and prostitutes. Commodified sex was established in Japan during the Medieval Period (1185–1573) when a market economy developed around castle towns. In 1587, to control the sex trade and collect taxes from it, the government created a licensed pleasure quarters in the capital of Kyōto. Edo (Tōkyō) opened its own sex and entertainment district in the early seventeenth century when it became the capital under the Tokugawa Shogunate. In the eighteenth century, geisha emerged as entertainers after "women in the districts began to specialize in the sex business and lost their artistic repertoires and skills" (Matsugu 244). But eventually geisha also engaged in the sex trade.

In 1872, after Britain and America criticized Japan for promoting sexual slavery by allowing male heads of families to contract daughters to brothels, the Meiji government freed geisha and prostitutes from their contracts. However, it allowed local governments to license females who wanted to offer sex services, either as geisha and prostitutes; the licensing included periodic tests for syphilis:

> While geisha were also tested in shamisen-playing and dancing, for geisha who specialized in selling their services to all but the highest classes in Tōkyō, such skills were less important than sex appeal when it came down to getting the license and making money for the geisha house. (Matsugu 244)

The Meiji-period sex trade embodied the sexist attitudes and priorities of the male-dominant state, and the taxes and licensing fees on geisha provided funds for its nation-building:

> In the later nineteenth century authorities exploited geisha's labor to promote state policies of industrialization and militaristic expansion. "Sake, women, and shamisen are privileges for men as well as symbols of local economic prosperity," said supporters of a policy to increase licensed pleasure districts in the 1890s. National development denoted the promotion of the capitalist economy together with the military invasion of other Asian countries such as Taiwan, Korea, and China. (Matsugu 245)

As Japan colonized east and southeast Asia in the late nineteenth and early twentieth centuries, the military provided "comfort women" to "boost the morale of officers and soldiers" stationed overseas. While the soldiers went to brothels, the officers were serviced by geisha, whose "'Japaneseness'— in costume, hairstyle, makeup, and artistic skills" made them preferable to "Japanese prostitutes or non-Japanese women" (Matsugu 245). The brothel sex workers, whether Japanese or non-Japanese, were purchased from poor families or simply forced to work.

During Kawabata's time, although it was illegal, the pre-Meiji practice of indenturing daughters to brothels continued in Japan. Kawabata's ironic sketch "Thank You" (made into a film in 1936) depicts a mother on a bus taking her daughter to sell as "a plaything" for strangers (*Palm-of-the-Hand Stories* 41–43). Poverty among the lower classes was widespread. The government taxed farmers heavily to pay for industrialization and militarization, forcing farmers "to give up their lands and become tenant farmers or leave villages. Many of these abjectly impoverished families had to sell their daughters into prostitution" (Matsugu 245). In poor rural areas like Tōhoku (northern Honshū), crop failures ("major ones occurred in 1902, 1905, 1913, 1926, 1929, and 1931") made life even harder for farmers, and while the national government intervened to stave off starvation, the selling of "young daughters to brothels" was "openly, and widely, practiced" (Satō 15).

After a week of mountain climbing at the end of May, Shimamura asks for a geisha at his inn, but the dozen or so licensed geisha are working at a celebration for the opening of a new road. The maid calls Komako, who is not licensed, but has worked as a geisha previously, in Tōkyō. A patron paid her debts to free her from her contract, and she now earns a living by helping the other geisha at large parties at the hot spring, playing the samisen and dancing; but she "almost never came alone to entertain a guest at the inn" (17).

Shimamura is attracted to Komako but decides not to drink and sleep with her because she isn't a professional. He's married and wants to avoid "drawn-out complications from an affair with a woman whose position was so ambiguous" (23–24). Komako is attracted to Shimamura by what she feels is his honest heart (he tells her "it couldn't last") and by his talk about kabuki theater: having lived in Tōkyō, she longs for cultured conversations, which is hard to come by in a mountain village.

When Komako drops by the next day, Shimamura asks her to call a geisha for him. Komako feels humiliated and refuses, so the maid calls one, and Komako leaves. However, Shimamura is disappointed by the teenager who arrives: she is "dark" and unappealing, and he sends her away. That night Komako arrives drunk at his room; she goes and comes back, calling out to him, "the naked heart of a woman calling out to her man" (34). Then she vacillates: "I'm not that sort of woman. It can't last. Didn't you say that?" (34). In the end, she spends the night with Shimamura.

What appeals to Shimamura about Komako are her qualities of cleanness and freshness:

> The impression the woman gave was a wonderfully clean and fresh one. It seemed to Shimamura that she must be clean to the hollows under her toes. (18)

> With her skin like white porcelain coated over a faint pink, and her throat still girlish, not yet filled out, the impression she gave was above all one of cleanness, not quite one of real beauty. (32)

In the aesthetics of Shintō, a religion based on the worship of kami (natural and deified spirits), the qualities of cleanness, freshness, and luminosity, associated with youth, are esteemed; the ideal is toko-waka (forever young). Darkness and dirtiness, associated with illness and death, are shunned. In the Shintō creation story, the kami Izanagi flees in horror and disgust when he sees the maggot-infested corpse of his sister Izanami (*Kojiki* 42).

Drawn back to the mountain village by the memory in his finger of his sexual relationship with Komako (7), Shimamura returns in early December, when snow has already fallen in the village. He learns that Komako has become a licensed geisha to help pay medical bills for the son of the music teacher in whose house she lives; the son is dying of tuberculosis. Komako also reveals that after becoming a geisha that summer, she thought she was pregnant by a man from Hamamatsu, who wanted to marry her. She felt nothing for the man and declined the offer (64).

As Shimamura prepares to return to Tōkyō, the complications he initially feared begin to develop. Komako becomes petulant: "it's not easy for me. Go back to Tōkyō" (78). But when he tells her he may leave the next night, she snaps back: "No! Why are you going back?" His reply—"What can I do for you, no matter how long I stay?"—angers her, but in the end she agrees: "You really must go back tomorrow" (79).

On his third visit, the following year, amid the falling leaves and dying insects of late autumn and the roar of the freezing mountains as winter approaches, Komako needles him about a broken promise—he promised to return for the bird-chasing festival earlier that year, in February, but didn't show up:

"I dislike people from Tōkyō because they're always lying." …
"I'll know better than to believe you next time" (94).

She gives him her assessment of his character:

"You have plenty of money, and you're not much of a person. You don't understand at all." (102)

Shimamura decides that it would be better if he doesn't return.

Kawabata contrasts Komako's busy, impoverished life as a geisha with Shimamura's life of privilege and leisure in Tōkyō. She rushes from party to party with her heavy samisen and rents dingy attic rooms; Shimamura, on the other hand, doesn't work. When he's back in Tōkyō researching Western ballet as a hobby, he indulges in reveries on a dance he has never seen, while writing a book that would probably "contribute nothing to the Japanese dancing world" (131):

> Nothing could be more comfortable than writing about a ballet from books. A ballet he had never seen was an art in another world. It was an unrivaled armchair reverie, a lyric from some paradise. He called his work research, but it was actually free, uncontrolled fantasy. He preferred not to savor the ballet in the flesh; rather he savored the phantasms of his own dancing imagination called up by Western books and pictures. (24)

Shimamura also indulges in reveries on young women, rendering their beauty otherworldly and forever young in his imagination, before the passage of time can destroy it. Windows and mirrors help him create his illusion. In a railcar on the way to the mountain village for his second visit, he is attracted to another snow country maiden, Yōko. He observes her reflection in the window, ethereal over the landscape visible beyond the glass. Yōko is traveling with a man who's ill and who turns out to be the son of the music teacher with whom Komako lives:

> In the depths of the mirror the evening landscape moved by, the mirror and the reflected figures like motion pictures superimposed on the other. … the figures, transparent and intangible, and the background, in the gathering darkness, melted together into a sort of symbolic world not of this world. Particularly when a light out in the mountains shone in the center of the girl's face, Shimamura felt his chest rise at the inexpressible beauty of it. (9)

The imagery of reflection, landscape, and beauty recurs when Shimamura views Komako in a mirror one morning:

> The white in the depths of the mirror was the snow, and floating in the middle of it were the woman's bright red cheeks. There was an indescribably fresh beauty in the contrast. (48)

The window and the mirror allow Shimamura to set Yōko and Komako apart, pure and inviolable, like eternal beauty in nature or myth:

> Always ready to give himself up to reverie, he could not believe that the mirror floating over the evening scenery and the other snowy mirror were really works of man. They were part of nature, and part of some distant world. (57)

The disparity between the lives of working people like Komako, who produce goods and services, and the wealthy, like Shimamura, who consume them, is accentuated when on his third visit Shimamura decides to take a train trip down the valley alone, thinking it might "set him on his way toward breaking away from this hot spring" (155). He goes to a town where he imagines a fabric called Chijimi might have been woven during the dark months of winter, when the dry cold air made it easier to work with hemp fibers finer than animal hair.

Shimamura collects old Chijimi—another of his self-indulgent hobbies. Chijimi became popular in the seventeenth century after a new weaving technique made creases in the cloth so that it felt "cool to the skin in the hottest weather" (154). The cloth was bleached toward the end of winter and spread over the snow in fields and gardens, the thought of which evokes another reverie on cleanness:

> The thought of the white linen, spread out on the deep snow, the cloth and the snow glowing scarlet in the rising sun, was enough to make him feel that the dirt of the summer had been washed away, even that he himself had been bleached clean. (152)

The best cloth was produced by young girls:

> The girls learned to weave as children, and they turned out their best work between the ages of perhaps fourteen and twenty-four. As they grew older they lost the touch that gave tone to the finest Chijimi. (151)

However, like Komako, the Chijimi workers lived drably and labored tediously for long hours: "the weaver maidens, giving themselves up to their work here under the snow, had lived lives far from as bright and fresh as the Chijimi they made" (157). The narrator adds ironically, "[t]he nameless workers, so diligent while they lived, had presently died, and only the Chijimi remained, the plaything of men like Shimamura, cool and fresh against the skin in the summer" (157).

On his second visit, in early winter, Shimamura promises Komako to return for the village's bird-chasing festival, on the first full moon of spring (1.15 by the lunar calendar), in February, at the start of the New Year. The Shintō festival captures the "spirit of this snow country." Children build a kamakura (snow house) "six yards square and more than ten feet high":

> Since the New Year was celebrated here early in February, the traditional straw ropes were still strung up over the village doorways. On the fourteenth, the children gathered the ropes and burned them

in a red bonfire before the snow palace. They pushed and jostled one another on the roof and sang the bird-chasing song, and afterwards, setting out lights, they spent the night in the palace. At dawn on the fifteenth, they again climbed to the roof to sing the bird-chasing song. (94–95)

Still celebrated in snow country today, the bird-chasing festival is an occasion to pray for abundant crops and the health and well-being of the family, particularly the children; and to thank the kami for the snow, which would melt into water under the spring sun. In Yokote, in Akita Prefecture, the festival is called the Kamakura Snow Festival:

This 400-year-old festival is said to have its origins in the traditional event of returning New Year decorations to the gods by burning them, and also in the custom of children chasing away birds damaging crops. Inside the kamakura, an altar is set up to honor the water gods and to pray for plenty of clear water, while saké and rice cakes are offered to the gods. ("Kamakura Snow Festival, Yokote")

In Tokamachi, a snow country town "blanketed with snow for almost half of every year," "children parade through the city beating wooden clappers while singing traditional songs in order to chase away birds that might damage crops" ("About Tokamachi").

Traditionally, bird chasing was just one ritual action performed at the start of the year: "farmers, treating the temple-shrine grounds as a rice field, imitated hoeing paddies, planting seedlings, driving away harmful birds, and so forth, thereby praying for a rice harvest" (Shirane 22).

On Shimamura's first visit in early summer, he and Komako walk together in a shrine grove, with the scent of new leaves in the air, two yellow butterflies fluttering about, and cedars soaring high into the late May sky. But Shimamura's failure to come for a festival to celebrate the return of spring the following year suggests that he's no fertility kami and his relationship with Komako is sterile.

The legend underlying *Snow Country* is from another Shintō festival, Tanabata, celebrated on 7.7, the seventh phase of the seventh moon of the year, in the first moon of autumn (usually in August by the lunar calendar). Autumn is the season of Shimamura's last visit, and his reverie on Chijimi weaving links it to the Tanabata legend, originally a festival of silk weaving.

In early autumn, two bright stars, Altair and Vega, appear in the eastern evening sky, separated by the River of Heaven (Milky Way). The three celestial bodies figure in the festival legend: a cowherd boy (Altair) and a silk-weaving princess (Vega) fall in love and are married. But because the princess neglects her weaving, the King of Heaven separates them, on opposite banks of the River of Heaven. They work through the year and are allowed to meet only once, on 7.7, crossing the river either by boat (the seven-day-old crescent moon) or by a bridge formed by magpies or crows. Customarily, children chant on the morning of 7.7 for good weather ("Tenki ni nare!") and throw stones at the magpies and crows to remind them of their duty to fly to heaven to form the bridge for the lovers (Casal 82).

While the festival was originally an occasion to pray for silk-weaving skills, by the Edo Period (1603–1868), when the celebration became an official holiday and spread to the common people in the towns and cities, girls prayed for the more common domestic skill of sewing. And because the legend features love and marriage between the two stars, girls also wrote wishes for a future husband, who, like the cowherd, was hardworking and faithful.

Kawabata links both Komako and Yōko to the girl in the legend. When Shimamura visits Komako's attic room in the music teacher's house, he notices her "vermilion sewing-box" (55). Later, she says that the quiet inn would be a good place to "work on my sewing" (115). In addition to this domestic skill, Komako also practices her geisha skills at the inn, playing the samisen and producing music as beautiful as silk to captivate Shimamura:

> A chill swept over Shimamura. The goose flesh seemed to rise even to his cheeks. The first notes opened a transparent emptiness deep in his entrails, and in the emptiness the sound of the samisen reverberated. (71)

Earlier, when Shimamura sees Yōko on the train, she strikes him as "a character out of an old, romantic tale" (11), like the weaving princess. Imagery connects Yōko to the princess's star form, Vega: a light from the mountains shines through the reflection of her eye in the train window, rendering the eye star-like:

> As it sent its small ray through the pupil of the girl's eye, as the eye and the light were superimposed one on the other, the eye became a weirdly beautiful bit of phosphorescence on the sea of evening mountains. (10)

Later, after hearing Yōko singing in the bath at the inn, Shimamura imagines her as a Chijimi weaver: "had she been born long ago, she might have sung thus as she worked over her spools and looms, so exactly suited to the fancy was her voice" (154).

As with the reference to the bird-chasing festival, Kawabata uses the Tanabata legend for thematic contrasts: Komako and Shimamura aren't two lovers who will marry and meet eternally once a year in autumn. And Shimamura is no hardworking cowherd, but someone who indulges himself in pleasant, but useless, pastimes:

> He pampered himself with the somewhat whimsical pleasure of
> sneering at himself through his work, and it may well have been from
> such a pleasure that his sad little dream world sprang. (131)[1]

Yōko's self-sacrificing relationship with the music teacher's tubercular
son, who once worked in a watch shop before falling ill, is also transient: he
dies in his mid-twenties after Shimamura's second visit, leaving Yōko on the
verge of insanity.

The silk weaving of the Tanabata legend also underlies the novel's imagery
of silkworms and moths (the adult form of silkworms). Pollack describes
the silkworm in the aesthetic terms of the novel: "In its juvenile phase the
silkworm is inscribed with the attributes of youth, translucence, vitality" (112).
He also points out that the silkworm suffers two possible fates. Some are boiled
to death in their cocoons, "both to degum the thread for reeling and to kill the
moths inside before they emerge from the cocoon and so ruin the thread"; some,
"however, are allowed to hatch normally in order to produce future silkworms;
they mate immediately after hatching and die soon after laying their eggs (112).
  Shimamura imagines Komako as a silkworm when he visits her attic room
and learns that the room was once used to raise silk worms:

> For a moment, he was taken with the fancy that the light must pass
> through Komako, living in the silkworms' room, as it passed through
> the translucent silkworms. (54)

On his third visit, however, he notices changes in Komako's body; she
is losing the beauty of the translucent silkworm: "[t]he fat on her abdomen
was heavier" now that she's quit smoking (104), and she has developed the
"low, bunched-up hips so common with geisha" (105). After reflecting on how
"human intimacies have not even so long a life" as Chijimi cloth, Shimamura
imagines Komako "as the mother of another man's children" (154).
  In contrast, at the end of the novel, like the silkworm boiled to kill
it and preserve the beauty of its silk, Yōko is burned in a fire in a cocoon
and rice warehouse being used as a movie theater. Although the translator's
introduction notes that readers aren't told "whether Yōko is alive or dead" (ix),
she is apparently dead: "Yōko's face hung vacantly, as at the moment of the
soul's flight (175). The warehouse contains no cocoons at the time of the fire,
but "mixed in with the smoke was a smell like boiling cocoons" (170).

Kawabata has said that he "used Shimamura only as an instrument to bring out the portrait of Komako" (Liman 284). Of the two characters, Komako is portrayed more sympathetically. While Shimamura is self-indulgent and weak, Komako is spirited, strong, and resourceful. When Shimamura visits Komako at the house of the candy shop whose owner has contracted her services as a geisha, he sees the owner's family sleeping downstairs, with "five or six children" and senses in them, despite their "drab poverty," "an urgent powerful vitality" (142). Komako has the same vitality, which Kawabata describes using animal imagery. Her attic room strikes Shimamura as "a fox's or badger's lair" (143). Earlier in the narrative, at dawn, as Komako prepares to leave his room, Shimamura sees her as "some restless night beast that fears the approach of the morning. It was as though a strange, magical wildness had taken her" (47).

The self-indulgent Shimamura lacks this vitality. As Komako plays the samisen, he is overwhelmed:

> Taken by a feeling almost of reverence, washed by waves of remorse, defenseless, quite deprived of strength—there was nothing for him to do but to give himself up to the current, to the pleasure of being swept off wherever Komako would take him. (71)

Later, he contrasts Komako's aggressiveness to his own hollow core and lack of emotion:

> He had simply fallen into the habit of waiting for those frequent visits. And the more continuous the assault became, the more he began to wonder what was lacking in him, what kept him from living as completely. He stood gazing at his own coldness, so to speak. ... All of Komako came to him, but it seemed that nothing went out from him to her. He heard in his chest, like snow piling up, the sound of Komako, an echo beating against empty walls. (154–155)

Talking about a hiker who has fallen to death, "broken into a pulp, ... skull bones and all," Komako comments, "People are delicate, aren't they," adding, "a bear could fall from a higher ledge and not be hurt in the least" (111). Shimamura reflects, "If man had a tough hairy hide like a bear his world would be different indeed." Later he imagines Komako as having such a hide: her "full flesh under ... the white powder" suggests a woolen cloth ... or the pelt of some animal" (130). She will be able to handle the hurt when he abandons her.

Toward the end of the narrative, Komako mocks Shimamura's weak character, challenging him to experience something she doesn't believe he could endure, the deep winter of snow country. She compares him to two timid animals:

"Come sometime when we have a real blizzard, and the snow drives along the ground all night long. But you won't, of course. Rabbits and pheasants come running inside the house to get out of the storm." (169)

Komako contrasts herself with an older geisha, Kikuyu, who ends up in a sad situation because she "found someone she liked and was going to marry him, but he ran off and left her" (97); Komako adds, "You can't go losing your head over every man that likes you" (98). She may waver, but maintains control in the end to ensure she has choices in life. She tells Shimamura about her current patron, an old man living on the coast of the Sea of Japan. It wasn't convenient for him to keep her there, so he housed her with the music teacher in the mountain village when she was sixteen. She isn't particularly attached to him, but maintains a relationship out of gratitude for his kindness. This revelation helps Shimamura understand her "lack of caution that had at first so puzzled him" (106).

In his Nobel Prize lecture ("Japan, the Beautiful and Myself"), Kawabata describes the influence of Zen Buddhism on Japanese art and literature, including his own writing. *Snow Country* belongs to this tradition of Buddhist literature: while portraying Komako sympathetically, Kawabata invites his readers, through Shimamura's eyes, to see both her and Shimamura (and themselves) as insects caught in the illusory cycle of desires and suffering, trapped by their karma. The wealthy Shimamura is fated to shallowness and useless reveries on dance and women. Komako has the karma as the two prostitutes from Niigata described by the seventeenth-century Zen poet Bashō on his journey along the sea coast in Hokuriku: in a room next to his at an inn in Ichiburi, he overhears the two women lamenting their fate (which reminds him of a tanka in which a prostitute compares herself to a fisherman's daughter).

"On the strand where white waves crash" we wander, children of the sea, thus fallen, to every chance relation, every day *karma*, shame ….
(Bashō 97)

Shimamura calls Komako's life "beautiful but wasted" (127) and uses the phrase "wasted effort" in reference to her longing for city life (43), her selling her services to pay the medical bills of a dying man (61), and her practicing to sharpen her samisen playing without a teacher (72). And he applies the phrase to his own mountain climbing—"almost a model of wasted effort" (112). The term also fits his longing to preserve girls forever young and his writing a fanciful book on Western dance.

Both their lives are vacant and in vain. Born into unenlightened lives, they face the destiny of the insects Shimamura observes, aging to death after a brief passage on earth:

> Each day, as the autumn grew colder, insects died on the floor of his room. Stiff-winged insects fell on their backs and were unable to get to their feet again. A bee walked a little and collapsed, walked a little and collapsed. It was a quiet death that came with the change of seasons. (131–132)

The final scene is dominated by two images: the raging warehouse fire and the River of Heaven of the Tanabata legend, arching above. The climactic fire suggests the bonfires lit at New Year's festivals to burn the straw ropes hung from houses to protect them from malevolent spirits at the year's end and return them to the kami. But the burning warehouse isn't dedicated to the life-giving kami: it kills Yōko and turns the pure snow that nurtures Shimamura's reveries into slush and mud.

Shimamura struggles till the end to see Yōko and Komako as unreal, beyond life and death. As he and Komako run toward the fire, Komako becomes a masked character in a mythic drama: "Komako's face floated up like an old mask" (168). When Yōko's body plunges downward from the second floor, she is "doll-like," like a puppet in bunraku theater:

> He saw the figure as a phantasm from an unreal world. That stiff figure, flung out into the air, became soft and pliant. With a doll-like passiveness, and the freedom of the lifeless, it seemed to hold both life and death in abeyance. (173)

Not wanting to witness her death, Shimamura hopes that her body will remain "a perfectly horizontal line" when it hits the ground; however, "there was a suggestion of a spasm in the calf of Yōko's leg" and "a chill passed down his spine to his very feet. His heart was pounding in an indefinable anguish" (173). Still, "Shimamura did not see death in the still form. He felt rather that Yōko had undergone some shift, some metamorphosis" (174).

With the River of Heaven overhead, the narrator wonders, "Was this the bright vastness the poet Bashō saw when he wrote of the River of Heaven arched over a stormy sea?" (165)[2]. For Bashō, the celestial river symbolizes the eternal compassion of the Buddha, leaning above Sado Island, where humanity huddles in exile, encircled by a stormy sea. Buddhism offers salvation from the illusory cycle of suffering to those who have faith in bodhisattvas or who free themselves from worldly illusions through meditation, achieving Enlightenment. On his excursion to Chijimi country, Shimamura sees Buddhist nuns crossing a bridge to their nunnery, a refuge from heavy snows.

But Shimamura, Komako, and Yōko don't have any spiritual aspirations. They inhabit the secular, materialistic world that became the norm for the majority of Japanese in the twentieth century. Shimamura sees the River of Heaven not as a Buddhist symbol, but as a heavenly geisha:

> The River of Heaven came down just there, to wrap the night earth in its naked embrace. There was a terrible voluptuousness about it. (165)

The embrace leaves her lover, the mountains, in a spiritual abyss:

> The River of Heaven spread its skirts to be broken by the waves of the mountain, and, fanning out again in all its brilliant vastness higher in the sky, it left the mountain in a deeper darkness. (168)

In the final scene, Shimamura feels buoyant at first, "floating into the River of Heaven" (165). The fire, too, draws him skyward: "The sparks spread off into the River of Heaven and Shimamura was pulled up with them" (171). Liman interprets the final scene as a blissful fusion, a "purifying immersion into the Milky Way ... the fusion of mind, self, and all things in the 'one'" (285). But the image is one of drowning rather than of bliss or enlightenment: Yōko's corpse belies Shimamura's dream-world where beautiful young women shine eternally as stars. In reality, they die young; or they age and die old.

When Shimamura tries to join Komako and Yōko, like the cowherd going to join the weaving princess, he is pushed back by the crowd (itself a kind of river) and loses his footing, his head falling back, as "the River of Heaven flowed down inside him with a roar" (175). The "roar," like "the roaring at the center" in the mountains (159), announces the coming of winter, darkness, and death. Shimamura swallows the river of time, and at the same time is swallowed by it and goes under.

Witnessing Yōko's death, Shimamura suffers from the anguish that the kami Izanagi experiences when he see a dead body for the first time—his sister's maggot-ridden corpse. Izanami, like Yōko, is killed by fire (*Kojiki* 34). Toko-waka belongs only to Izanami's spirit, restored and worshiped as a kami at various shrines, and to kami like the sun goddess Amaterasu, who is reborn daily at sunrise and annually in spring. Humans, on the other hand, are doomed to bloom, wither, and die, like flowers in spring (*Kojiki* 139–140); physical renewal comes only with children born in a new generation.

Planning our route to the Nozawa fire festival, I read that Echigo-Yuzawa, the first stop in snow country on the Jōetsu Shinkansen line from Tōkyō, was the village where Kawabata met the geisha on whom he modeled Komako. I booked an overnight stay to walk in the landscape in which Kawabata's novel is set.

Yuzawa, along the Uono River, Niigata

We emerged from a tunnel into a snowy landscape in the evening twilight—not the Shimizu Tunnel of Kawabata's opening scene, but the newer, longer Daishimizu Tunnel (almost fourteen miles long), completed in 1978. Yuzawa is no longer the village of Kawabata's novel; it's a modern resort town, with sixteen ski slopes and high-rise condominiums along the expressway and rail lines from Tōkyō. The three-story wooden inn where Kawabata stayed has been rebuilt as a modern concrete hotel featuring a room with artifacts and memorabilia associated with *Snow Country*.

Our ryokan (inn) was a short walk from the Shinkansen station. We soaked in its hot spring bath before dinner and bed. The next morning, with a couple of hours before boarding a local train, we wandered around the town. It was early, so everything was closed. The ropeway to the Yuzawa Highlands opened at 8 a.m., so we rode up, walked around the snow-covered slopes overlooking the town, then descended, just in time to check out and board our train. The snowfall in town wasn't deep—only a couple of feet and melting. Snow country gets its heaviest snowfalls in February, and we were still in the second week of January.

Kawabata's model for Komako was Kiku Kodaka (1915–1999). Kiku came from a poor family and had nine siblings; her father was a blacksmith (Matsugu 248). Kiku was nine when her parents placed her under contract to a geisha house in Nagaoka. She was trained as a geisha and, at thirteen, went to work at the most expensive inn in Yuzawa. Her geisha name was Matsue. The thirty-five

Karen in front of our ryokan in Yuzawa

-year-old Kawabata met her there in 1934, when she was nineteen, Komako's age when she meets Shimamura.

Kiku told a reporter she recalled incidents with Kawabata that were depicted in the novel, such as the visit to the shrine grove (Roscoe 132). Like Komako, Kiku enjoyed reading in her spare time, historical romances and detective fiction (Roscoe 236).

Free of her geisha contract in 1940, she returned to her hometown of Sanjō,

and two years later, married a successful tailor and became a kimono tailor herself. When she married, she burned her copy of *Snow Country*, which was filled "with red ink marks, including comments such as 'I did not say that' and curse words in the margins" (Matsugu 249).

Although the couple had no children, they adopted Kiku's niece. According to a neighbor, Kiku "was kind to children in the neighborhood," and she and her husband lived together happily until Kiku passed away in 1999, at eighty-four. Her husband died soon after (Roscoe 236).

Snow Country endowed Kawabata's fictive version of Kiku with literary immortality. A beauty contest named after Komako is held in Yuzawa annually during its snow festival in early March. Each year, three new beauties are given the title of Miss Komako, who, like the character in the novel, remains forever young, embodying the town's spirit and promoting tourism.

After our stop in Yuzawa, we continued on via Kanazawa and Nagano to Nozawa for the fire festival celebrated on January 15 every year. The town is just twenty-five miles from Yuzawa, but in a different river valley. Kawabata's *Snow Country* felt close there: like the bird-chasing festival, the fire festival features a bonfire for burning protective straw ropes and other New Year's decorations to return them to the kami. Established in 1863, Nozawa's festival is dedicated to Dōsojin, a pair of male and female kami who protect the village from malevolent spirits and to whom worshipers pray for happiness in marriage, childbirth, and family life, as well as a good harvest. Dōsojin is represented in

Dōsojin figures near the Nozawa fire festival grounds

Shaden, Nozawa fire festival   *Forty-two-year-old men in a pine nest*

Nozawa by two tree trunks, placed next to each other, one painted as a male and the other as a female. The pairs are set up at the entrance to the village, the festival grounds, and around town; smaller pairs are displayed inside houses and hotels, and miniatures are sold at souvenir booths.

When we arrived in the early afternoon, a Shintō priest from Kosuge Shrine[3] was consecrating the shaden for Dōsojin. The shaden is a structure made from beech trees cut in the mountain forest in October and brought down to the village just before the festival. The wood is lashed together with rice-straw rope. Above a square base the size of a small hut is a nest of pine boughs and five beech trees soaring skyward, about fifty feet high. The pine and beech symbolize fertility and longevity.

In the evening, the forty-two-year-old village men gather in the pine nest, while the twenty-five-year-old men station themselves around the base to protect them from attack by the rest of villagers, who will try to set the shaden on fire with reed torches. The festival is enacted to ward off the dangers of the critical forty-second year of male lives: "shi-ni" (forty-two), is a homonym for "to die." The twenty-five-year-olds, also in a critical year in their lives, defend their elders in a rite of passage into manhood.

Around the shaden, lantern poles are raised and hung with streamers with prayers for the health and good fortune for first sons born in the preceding year. The infants are brought under the umbrellas of the lantern poles while the villagers stop by to offer best wishes.

Father and son, Nozawa fire festival   *Lantern pole hung with with prayers*

At 7 p.m., the festival's bonfire is lit from a fire started using two flint stones. At around 8, aerial fireworks go off, and taiko drums begin pounding rhythmically. The villagers, fueled by saké and armed with flaming bundles of reeds lit at the bonfire, move down a lane through the crowd to attack the shaden. Children go first, followed by adults. Holding on to short ropes attached to the base, the twenty-five-year-olds ward off the attacks with pine branches. Full of confidence and saké, the forty-two-year-olds egg on the attackers, tossing down to them unlit bundles of reeds for more attacks.

The vitality of the villagers that Kawabata describes in *Snow Country* was evident at the festival. A crowd of several hundred pushed to get near the shaden, and a couple of drunken young Japanese men started fighting with each other. A foreigner, also drunk, got upset at being shoved about and started swearing in English. While the villagers pray for both a good harvest and more tourists for the ski slopes, the *Snow Japan* website reported that tourists who tried to take part in the ritual were attacked by locals in 2007. In 2008, a foreign visitor blogged after the festival that he joined the attack when he was invited to do so, but after he made one run with a torch and reached up to catch another for a second run, he "heard an angry scream": "I looked over to see spit flying and teeth gnashing as an open hand connected with the side of my face. A large drunken local punched me in the head."

Villagers with reed torches preparing to attack the shaden

The visitor reflects good-naturedly on the lesson learned, while praising the vitality of the participants in perpetuating tradition:

> Never had I seen a Japanese person stand up for something as fiercely as those men had, drunk and violent or not. Never in this country have I experienced such anger and commitment. I immediately gained a great deal of respect for those who stand up for tradition and loyalty. That was not my place to be. That was not my event.

A flyer in our hotel room when we checked in informed visitors that only villagers are allowed to participate in the festival; outsiders should remain spectators.

Around ten, the attacks ended. The forty-two-year-olds declared victory as they chanted and clapped in their nest, their leader waving a pine branch overhead; then they climbed down the ladder for their safe passage through the next year. Meanwhile, the twenty-five-year-olds, exhausted, their faces and clothes blackened with ash, but having proven their ability to protect their elders, moved off, and the villagers pushed burning logs against the shaden, using poles as levers. The shaden was consumed in a huge bonfire, after which the townspeople headed home through the dark snow-lined streets, and visitors returned to their inns for a warm soak in the sulphurous hot spring baths, said

The shaden burning at the close of the fire festival

to be good for fatigue and rheumatism.

Unlike the accidental warehouse fire at the climax of *Snow Country*, the bonfires set in Nozawa are controlled, with fire fighters on hand for emergencies; bad spirits are driven off and no one is killed. The festival, after all, is a comedy, not a tragedy like Kawabata's novel.

In 2008, only two first sons were honored at the Nozawa fire festival, down from an average of five in previous years. (The resort town has a population of about 5,000.) For Children's Day 2014, the national government reported that the number of children under age fifteen fell in Japan for the thirty-third consecutive year. Despite the good health and longevity of its people, Japan's population is shrinking due to a low birth rate: at the current rate, its population of 127 million people in 2000 is projected to be down to 100 million by mid-century, and 64 million by the end of the century. The promise of the Shintō creation kami Izanagi that 1,500 children would be born for every thousand that his sister Izanami killed (*Kojiki* 45) no longer holds true.

The decline of the traditional values of labor-intensive agriculture, which favored marriages and large families, is cited as one cause of the population decline. In the urban industrial economy that replaced the agricultural economy, marriage and parenthood preferences and practices have changed dramatically: once arranged by families to ensure offspring, marriages have become a matter of individual choice, which has led to fewer marriages and a higher rate of divorce. Though still socially stigmatized, divorce is more accepted now than in the past, and the rate, although about half of the US rate, increases every year. In 2014, the number of single adults in Japan, as in other developed nations, was at its highest level ever (Haworth).

After World War II, women began entering the workforce in greater numbers. Those pursuing careers may choose to stay single or single longer and to delay childbirth or not have children. A friend (single, childless) told me that she and her friends feel that there is not much social support for working mothers, so they are forced to choose between careers and motherhood. One young woman says that she turned down a marriage proposal because she decided she "cared more about her job"—if she married and had a child, she couldn't manage "long, inflexible hours"; and "being a housewife with no independent income" is "not an option for women like me" (Haworth).

Urban life in Japan and elsewhere promotes individualism over families. Status is acquired by education, careers, wealth, and conspicuous consumption and leisure. Expending time, energy, and resources on acquiring this status, with so many possibilities and distractions, real and virtual, an individual may have little time left for marriage or raising children. Working couples sometimes elect to have just one child in whom they invest their limited time and resources to create optimum advantages for the child. Singles and childless couples can pay for social services when they grow old—or hope that the government will provide services to them.

Shimamura's detached, sterile reveries on women via windows and mirrors has morphed and spread to the masses with new technologies and media. In animé, manga, and video games, child-like female characters are sexually objectified, forever young and beautiful. Unlike Shimamura, who suffers because his lust draws him into a relationship with a geisha, some new-age voyeurs understand that if they want to preserve the objects of their desires forever young and enjoy relationships without complications, they have to forego real relationships and engage with characters in a fantasy world. In "Japan Shrinks," Eberstadt cites an example: "In 2009, a 27-year-old Japanese man made history by 'marrying' a female video game character [from Nintendo's "Love Plus"] while thousands watched online" (34). This new-age Shimamura told CNN, "Nene is better than a human girlfriend. 'She doesn't get angry if I'm late in replying to her. Well, she gets angry, but she forgives me quickly'" (Lah). While the young man is aware that he can't "physically or legally" be married to Nene, he takes her with him wherever he goes, on his portable video game player.

Celibacy is relatively common among the young today, enough so that it's acquired a label: "sekkusu shinai shokogun" (celibacy syndrome). The Japan Family Planning Association reported in 2014 that over 25% of males in the 16–24 age group "were not interested in or despised sexual contact"; 45% of the women in that age group felt the same way (Haworth). The reasons for the attitudes are, no doubt, complex and varied. The young man who married Nene belongs to a social group mocked as "herbivores," as opposed to the "economic animals" of the previous generation. Herbivores lack "their elders' willingness to toil for endless hours at the office, or even to succeed in romance" (Fackler). They have supposedly lost their initiative and sexual vitality during Japan's prolonged economic stagnation and deflation, which has lingered for over two decades, making it difficult for them to get high-paying, full-time, permanent jobs in order to buy homes and start families. Fackler adds that herbivores have been blamed, if "only half jokingly, for the country's shrinking population."

NOTES

1. Male longing for young, untouchable beauty is one of the obsessively recurrent motifs in Kawabata's writings. In "The Dancing Girl of Izu" (1925), the narrator looks back on his college years, when hiking on the Izu peninsula, he meets a group of traveling entertainers, one of whom is a young beauty named Kaoru. Her hair arranged elaborately for performance, she looks to be about seventeen and arouses his desires: "my daydreams began a vivid, reckless dance." Later, however, when she stands naked on a rock at an onsen (hot spring) and waves innocently to him from across the river, he recognizes her behavior as that of a child, whose purity appeals to him more than the "reckless dance":

> I felt pure water flowing through my heart. I breathed a sigh of relief and laughed out loud. She's a child—a child who can run out naked in broad daylight, overcome with joy at finding me, and stand tall on her tiptoes. I kept laughing with delight. My head was clear as though wiped clean. I could not stop smiling. (14)

His desire is also tempered by the mother of the other girl in the troupe, who forbids her to go with the student narrator to a movie after they arrive in Shimoda. Kaoru's brother, the only male in the group, tells the student that his sister is fourteen. As the student parts from the group to take a ferry back to Tōkyō, he resigns himself to the fact that he'll probably never see Kaoru again. Alone, he is surprised by the pleasure of his memory: "My head had become clear water, dripping away drop by drop. It was a sweet, pleasant feeling, as though nothing would remain." That he would never see Kaoru again allows him to preserve the purity of her beauty in memory.

In "The House of the Sleeping Beauties," completed in 1961 when he was sixty-two, Kawabata depicts the longing for untouchable young beauty in the context of old age. Eguchi, a lonely, unattractive sixty-seven-year-old man, begins visiting a house where elderly, impotent clients are allowed to sleep next to, but not violate in any way, naked young beauties who have been drugged to sleep. Eguchi, who is not impotent, is tempted by the sleeping beauties—but before he can act out his lust, one of the young girls dies in her sleep from an overdose of the drug.

2. In the quotations from Seidenstecker's translation of *Snow Country*, I change "Milky Way" to "River of Heaven."

3. Located a couple of miles southwest of Nozawa, Kosuge Shrine is known for its tradition of mountain asceticism (shugendō). The inner shrine, dating in its present form from the sixteenth century and housing eight kami, is approached up a pathway lined with 180 tall cedar trees, including one 300 years old and over 100 feet tall. Based on a legend about a lord of Kaga meeting a beautiful girl at the shrine and marrying her, and the couple being blessed with a healthy child, the shrine is associated with match-making, marriage, and easy childbirth, and has become a popular site for proposing to a future spouse ("A Walk in Kosuge Village").

Sources

"About Tokamachi," *Web Japan.* Web Japan, 2012.

Bashō. *Back Roads to Far Towns.* Trans. Cid Corman and Kamaike Susumu. New York: Grossman, 1968.

Casal, U.A. *The Five Sacred Festivals of Ancient Japan.* Rutland: Tuttle, 1967.

Eberstadt, Nicholoas. "Shrinking Japan." *The Wilson Quarterly.* Spring 2002. 30–37.

Fackler, Martin. "Japan Goes From Dynamic to Disheartened." *New York Times.* New York Times, 16 Oct. 2010. Web.

Haworth, Abigail. "Why have young people in Japan stopped having sex?" *The Guardian / The Observer*. Guardian News and Media, 19 Oct. 2013. Web.

"Kamakura Snow Festival, Yokote." Japan National Tourism Organization, n.d. Web.

Kawabata, Yasunari. *The Dancing Girl of Izu and Other Stories*. Trans. J. Martin Holman. Washington, D.C.: Counterpoint, 1997.

---. "Japan, the Beautiful and Myself." *Nobelprize.org*. Nobelprize.org, 12 Dec. 1968. Web.

---. *Palm-of-the-Hand Stories*. Trans. Lane Dunlop and J. Martin Holman. New York: North Point Press, 1988.

---. *Snow Country*. Trans. Edward G. Seidenstecker. New York: Vintage International, 1956.

The Kojiki: Records of Ancient Matters. Trans. Basil Hall Chamberlain. Boston: Tuttle, 1981.

Lah, Kyung. "Tokyo man marries video game character." *CNN World*. CNN, 17 Dec. 2009. Web.

Liman, Anthony V. "Kawabata's Lyrical Mode in *Snow Country*." *Monumenta Nipponica* 26.3/4 (1971): 267–285.

Matsugu, Miho. "In the Service of the Nation: Geisha and Kawabata Yasunari's *Snow Country*." *The Courtesan's Arts: Cross Cultural Perspectives*. New York: Oxford UP, 2006. 243–253.

"Number of children in Japan drops for 33rd year." *Japan Times*. Japan Times, 4 May 2014. Web.

Roscoe, Bruce. *Windows on Japan: A Walk through Place and Perception*. New York: Agora, 2007.

Pollack, David. "The Idealogy of Aesthetics: Yasunari Kawabata's *Thousand Cranes* and *Snow Country*." *Reading Against Culture: Ideology and Narrative in the Japanese Novel*. Ithaca and London: Cornell UP, 1992. 110–120.

Miyazawa, Kenji. *Miyazawa Kenji: Selections*. Ed. Hiroaki Satō. Berkeley: U of California, 2007.

Shirane, Haruo. *Japan and the Culture of the Four Seasons*. New York: Columbia UP, 2012.

"A Walk in Kosuge Village." Shinshu-Iiyama Tourism Bureau, N.d. Web.

Hokule'a in Yokohama

In summer 2007, a modern replica of a traditional double-hulled Hawaiian voyaging canoe docked in Yokohama, the last stop on a cultural exchange and goodwill tour of Japan. Known for her role in reviving Polynesian voyaging and navigation, *Hōkūle'a* sailed from Hawai'i in January to the Marshall Islands, Micronesia, Palau, and Yap, then north to Japan, visiting Okinawa, Kumamoto, Nagasaki, Fukuoka, Yamaguchi, Hiroshima, and Ehime Prefectures. I joined the crew of fifteen in Uwajima, a fishing town in Ehime, on the west coast of Shikoku, for the passage to Yokohama. I was on board to document the Yokohama arrival for the Polynesian Voyaging Society (PVS), which built *Hōkūle'a* in 1975 and maintains and sails the canoe for cultural education.

The night after arriving in Uwajima, I heard some Japanese *Hōkūle'a* fans had invited the crew to a music festival in the mountains. I had to post a backlog of reports and photos on the PVS website, so I skipped the gathering, but a

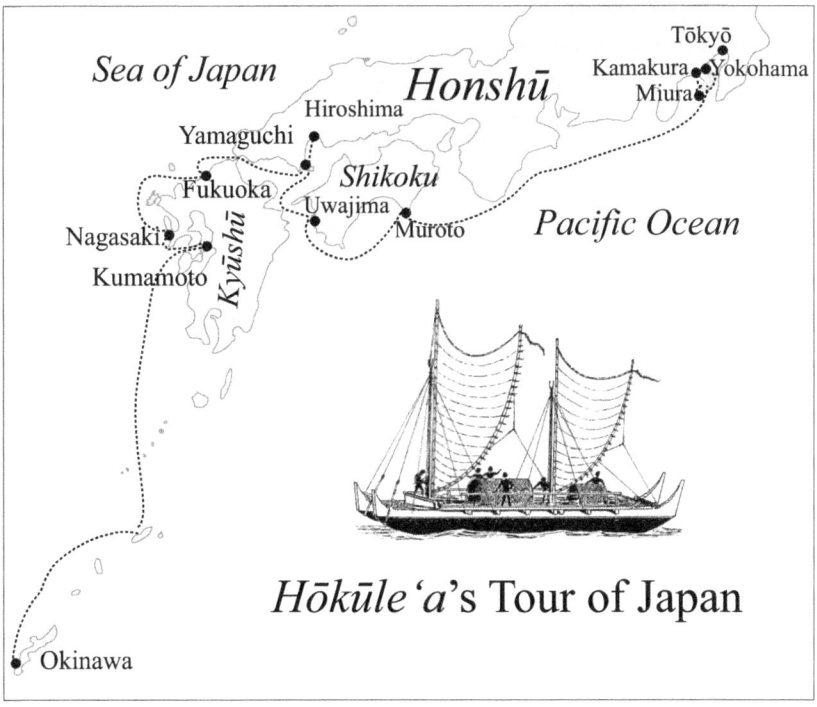

Hōkūle'a's Tour of Japan

crew member told me the next day that it was a 60s kind of happening, with food, music, and free-form communal dancing. Our medical officer, Cherie Shehata, described the festival in her blog:

> Tonight we attended a concert to celebrate the full moon and the arrival of *Hōkūleʻa*. This concert took place up in the mountains, in a secluded forest. Even Kana [one of two Japanese crew members] and her Japanese friends had not seen anything like it before. It was "new age" to them. The first performance was some singing and dancing. As it got dark, we heard the beat of taiko drums, and then on a separate stage we saw fire dancing. Some were twirling sticks of flames, others rings of flame. There were different types of singers, some singing folk music. There was even a lady playing a xylophone, and wailing/singing at the same time, some improv melodic tune. They provided us with home-cooked meals and pizza. ("Kū Holo Komohana: 2007 Voyage to Japan," Uwajima, May 28–June 4, *Hawaiian Voyaging Tradition*)

The Japanese fans who put on this event had gathered after meeting each other on the Internet while following the progress of the canoe. When *Hōkūleʻa* arrived in Yokohama a week later, a crowd of several hundred greeted her, including city officials and civic groups, Japanese hula performers, and Miss Yokohama, in a kimono. *Hōkūleʻa* docked at Minato Mirai 21, a twenty-first century waterfront development of train and subway hubs, high-rise condos and hotels, shopping malls and restaurants, and an amusement park with a giant ferris wheel.

Hōkūleʻa was not out of place in Yokohama and the other Japanese ports she visited, where the crew was welcomed warmly and crowds lined up dockside to tour the canoe. Internationalism and multiculturalism are trendy, and cross-cultural exhibits and events are common. During the summer festival season in 2007, for example, a gathering on Sado Island off the coast of Niigata hosted by a local taiko group featured performances by Indian tabla master Zakir Hussain, Puerto Rican percussionist Giovanni Hidalgo, and French Guianese tap dancer Tamango.

Before American and European nations forced Japan to open its ports to shipping and trade in 1854, Yokohama (Side Beach) was a small fishing village with a population of 400 on the west side of Edo Bay. But in 1859, the village was designated as a port of entry for international shipping, and it developed into Tōkyō's maritime gateway to the world. Today, Yokohama is one of Japan's largest cities, with a population of 3.7 million, and also one of its most cosmopolitan, with 80,000 foreign residents. The wharf district is lined with Western buildings dating from the nineteenth and early twentieth century,

Hōkūle'a *arriving in Yokohama*

spared from American bombs in 1945 so that the facilities could be used by the occupation forces after the war.

The welcome for *Hōkūle'a* included a new-age group of hula dancers and musicians, led by a woman of Japanese, Spanish, and American ancestry who goes by the name of Sandii and who teaches Tahitian and Hawaiian dance in Tōkyō and Yokohama. Her program opened with a conch shell blown by a performer in a traditional mountain-priest outfit. One of the band members played a didjeridoo (an Australian aborigine wind instrument). The music on Sandii's recent CD, which she distributed as gifts to the crew, included keyboards, guitars, flutes, accordion, ukulele, piano, Tahitian banjo, Polynesian percussion (pahu, puniu, toere), and Brazilian percussion (zabumba and marimba).

Over a century before *Hōkūle'a*'s visit, Hawaiian King David Kalākaua arrived in Yokohama in March 1881, on the RMS *Oceanic* out of San Francisco. The first ruling monarch in history to visit Japan, Kalākaua was welcomed with pomp and ceremony, including "twenty-one-gun salutes by Japanese and foreign warships anchored in the bay":

When the boat sent by the Japanese to take the Hawaiians from the *Oceanic* to their hotel touched shore, they heard the Hawaiian national anthem, played with explosive vigor by a Japanese military band. They were astonished that the Japanese musicians had learned the anthem of so remote and unimportant a country. The king and the others of his retinue, touched, were all but in tears. Along the way to the palace where they were to stay, they noticed that the houses of Yokohama were decorated with crossed Japanese and Hawaiian flags. The king and his party were stunned by the welcome. (Keene 346)

The visit had a transformative impact on the population and culture of Hawaiʻi. The native population of Kalākaua's islands had been decimated by diseases introduced by foreign settlers, and the King went to Japan to ask Emperor Meiji to allow Japanese workers to emigrate to Hawaiʻi. His strategy was to repeople his kingdom with a "cognate race," whose values were similar to those of his native people, making the new settlers "compatible with the Hawaiian character" (Kanahele 326). The Japanese, the King believed, would eventually mix in and merge with native Hawaiians (Kuykendall 159–160). Repopulating his kingdom was essential to strengthening its economy and defending its sovereignty from Britain, France, and America, all three seeing it as a key outpost for controlling the North Pacific.

In 1885, four years after the King's visit, about a thousand Japanese men, women, and children arrived in Honolulu Harbor on the four-masted SS *City of Tokio*. The arrival was an occasion for the first formal cultural exchange between the two nations: the immigrants were greeted by hula dancers and the

King David Kalākaua (1836–1891)   *Emperor Meiji (1852–1912)*

Royal Hawaiian Band. Three days later, the Japanese delegation hosted the King at festivities on the lawn of 'Iolani Palace, with acrobatics on bamboo ladders (hashigo-nori), traditionally performed by Japanese firefighters; exhibitions of sumo and kendō (fencing with wooden swords); and saké toasting after the breaking open of barrels of brew for the celebration (Kotani 13–15, Ono).

Between 1885 and 1893, immigrants from Japan and other countries continued to arrive to repeople Kalākaua's kingdom. But the King passed away in 1891, and just two years after his death, American settlers with the backing of a contingent of US marines, forced his sister, Queen Lili'uokalani, to relinquish her authority to rule. The settlers established a provisional government, hoping to be annexed by the US. When annexation didn't happen, they formed the Republic of Hawai'i. The Queen hoped that the US would restore the Kingdom; when restoration didn't happen, an armed band of her supporters attempted in 1895 to return her to the throne, but the counter-revolutionists, including the Queen, were arrested and imprisoned. The Queen was freed in 1896 and went to Washington, D.C., to make her case again for restoration of her nation, to no avail. An annexation treaty was signed between the Republic and the US in 1898, and two years later, Hawai'i became a US Territory.

Immigrants from Japan and other countries continued to arrive in the US Territory as laborers and settlers, and a multiethnic community developed. In "What Was Dear to My Heart," Hawaiian writer John Dominis Holt (1919–1993), who grew up in the "multilingual and ethnically diverse" neighborhood of Kalihi during the 1920s and 30s, recalls with relish the foods he enjoyed—native poi and kalua pua'a (pig cooked in an underground oven) as well as Chinese broiled squab, hum hah pork, and lop cheong; Portuguese pickled pork and malasadas; Puerto Rican pigeon peas and pateles; Filipino chicken and pork adobo, and Japanese mochi and steamed or raw fish:

> The Japanese, at New Year's, would spend a half-year's wages on wonderfully decorative and imaginative delicacies. Sweet rice-paste cakes called mochi were filled with a black bean mixture called black sugar. Fish was prepared in the most stylish and incredible ways; a simulated net carved from a great turnip would cover a whole fish. This splendid display would be given a final embellishment of flower-like decorations carved from carrots and radishes. (*Recollections*)

Holt recalls the store and house of the Japanese merchant U. Yamane, on King Street in Kalihi, where, as a young boy, he tasted the New Year's food:

> His store was crowded with imports from Japan, canned goods, and pickled vegetables packed in large tubs. I can still see the long radishes colored yellow called takwan being pulled out of their wooden buckets

and weighed when purchased. Mr. Yamane was a short, stocky man who came as a merchant with early immigrants from Japan. He was impressive looking, with a short-cropped moustache and short hair. He usually wore grey suits and would remove his coat and tie as the day's activities progressed. The commodious Yamane home sat facing King Street opposite the family's variety store. Their yard, the largest in the neighborhood, was filled with fruit trees—mango, avocado, lichee and soursop. ("Kalihi," *Recollections*)

Holt also grieves in his essay over the loss of native culture and community due to Westernization in the US territory, a loss symbolized for him by the "forlorn, destitute look" of Kona on the Big Island, a traditional farming and fishing district that thrived before changes brought about by a capitalist economy based on wage labor:

> For a span of years between my childhood and shortly after World War II, before the great hotel and tourist explosion took place, Kona lost many of its kama'āina [native people, lit. "children of the land"], who migrated to other places. It was a period of heart-breaking loneliness and destitution. The little kuleana houses remained in various stages of disintegration and were rather brutal reminders of a once flourishing community no longer able to contain or support its native Hawaiian population. ("What Was Dear to My Heart," *Recollections*)

When Hawai'i became the fiftieth American state in 1959, it had the most diverse population of all the states, with no majority group. By the beginning of the twenty-first century, out of a population of 1.37 million, people with Hawaiian ancestry numbered 330,169 (24%) and people with Japanese ancestry 243,533 (18%), followed by people with Caucasian ancestry (235,374, 17%) and Filipino ancestry (182,457, 13%). The mixing and merging that Kalākaua had envisioned had taken place: inter-ethnic marriage was commonplace, and people of mixed ancestry were the largest and fastest growing group. (Ethnic Stock by County, 2011, *State of Hawaii Data Book*.)

Kalākaua's 1881 visit to Tōkyō, on the other hand, had little impact on Japan's population and culture. At the time, Japan was turning inward, industrializing, militarizing, and embarking on a nationalistic path to defend its sovereignty against the West, a path that would lead it to invade Asian countries, attack the US naval base in Hawai'i, and wage a war against America and its allies.

After Japan's surrender in 1945, the culture of the Hawaiian islands was introduced to Japan during the American Occupation (1945–1952), but the culture brought from Hawai'i was not traditional Hawaiian culture. It was a

Westernized version for tourists, popularized by Hollywood. During the 1950s, aloha shirts became youth fashion in Tōkyō. Yukio Mishima, a novelist and film actor, writes in his autobiographical novel *Confessions of a Mask*: "One of the boys was wearing an aloha shirt, a garment much in vogue among gangs of young toughs in the city" (251). In an interview, Mishima "assumed a pose of insouciance" and joked, "My ideal is to live in a house where I sit on a rococo chair wearing an aloha shirt and blue jeans" (Stokes 122).

During the 1960s, the Hawaiian sport of surfing, popularized in America after it was transplanted to California, was brought to Japan by US servicemen stationed at American bases in Japan, and surfers in wet suits could be seen in the surf off beach towns like Kamakura.

By the 1960s and 1970s, as Japan's economy recovered from the war and prospered, Hawai'i became a favorite destination for well-to-do Japanese and a dream vacation for the masses. The Japanese not only listened to hapa-haole hula and music, they began performing them in Japan as well. The 2006 movie *Hula Girls*, based loosely on real events in Iwaki, Fukushima, in the mid-1960s, depicts how a "Hawaiian" resort came to be established there. When the nation began switching from domestic coal to cheaper imported oil and nuclear power to generate electricity, a coal-mining company dreams up a plan to develop a Hawaiian-themed resort featuring hula. A Japanese dance instructor from Tōkyō is hired, and girls in the town start taking lessons. Despite opposition to the "heathen" dance by some of the older folks—including one father who beats his daughter, destroys her costume, and cuts off her hair—the resort opens and the dancers put on a show. The resort's hula is, of course, a takeoff on tourism-based hula. More recently, Japanese students of traditional hula have traveled to Hawai'i to learn dancing and chanting from Hawaiian kumu, or teachers, and have brought their kumu to Japan to provide additional training.

By the 1970s, the native people of Hawai'i began turning away from tourism-based hula and looking back to and revitalizing their ancient cultural traditions. In 1975, at the dawn of the revival of native culture and language taught in immersion schools, the Polynesian Voyaging Society launched *Hōkūle'a*, and in 1976, sailed her from Hawai'i to the ancestral homeland of Tahiti. Hawaiians hadn't voyaged across the 2,500 miles of open ocean in double-hulled canoes for hundreds of years. After Tahitians and other Polynesians settled Hawai'i during the twelfth and thirteenth centuries and flourished in their new North Pacific home, voyaging back to the South Pacific islands had ceased.

To navigate to Tahiti in a traditional way, without modern instruments, a Micronesian master navigator, Mau Piailug, was invited to Hawai'i to guide

Hōkūleʻa on her first voyage. Mau had learned traditional navigation from his grandfather and could guide a canoe on the open ocean. He used rising and setting celestial bodies, winds, and ocean swells as directional guides and the flight of land-based seabirds and other natural signs to locate islands. Following the successful 1976 voyage to Tahiti, Mau agreed to train Hawaiians as navigators, even though some in his home islands saw teaching their ancient tradition to outsiders as a betrayal of their ancestors. Nainoa Thompson, the navigator who brought *Hōkūleʻa* to Japan, was one of Mau's first Hawaiian students.

On her way to Japan in 2007, *Hōkūleʻa* visited the remote Carolinian atoll of Satawal, Mau's home, bringing with her a newly built Hawaiian-style voyaging canoe, *Alingano Maisu*, constructed by voyagers on the Big Island of Hawaiʻi as a gift to Mau in gratitude for his teachings and to help him and his family teach navigation on their home island. Mau had told Nainoa that he taught the Hawaiians his navigation so that one day they might help him perpetuate it among his own people, who were losing their traditional culture in the wake of the Westernization of their islands. While the *Hōkūleʻa* crew was on Satawal, Mau conducted a rite-of-passage ceremony graduating eleven sons of Satawal (including Mau's own son Sesario) and five Hawaiians (including Nainoa) to the rank of pwo (the ninth of fifteen degrees in the Weriyeng School of Navigation of Micronesia) ("Canoe Builders and Voyagers," *Hawaiian Voyaging Traditions*).[1]

Nainoa had been the leader of the revival of traditional voyaging in Polynesia since 1980, when he became the first Hawaiian in centuries to navigate from Hawaiʻi to Tahiti and back without modern instruments. The story of Nainoa's achievement and *Hōkūleʻa* had been told in Japan; less well known was Nainoa's connection to Kalākaua's 1881 visit to Japan: Nainoa is the great grandson of Isaac Harbottle (1871–1948), one of two boys of chiefly lineage, aged eleven and ten, whom Kalākaua sent to Japan in 1882 as participants in Hawaiʻi's first study abroad program. Kalākaua sponsored young Hawaiian scholars to study not just in Japan, but in China, Britain, Scotland, Italy, and America, so they

Nainoa in Yokohama (Photo: Jin Takuma)

could gain global knowledge and experience that would help him conduct his diplomatic affairs. Harbottle and his younger brother James Haku'ole learned Japanese language and culture at Gakushuin University in Tōkyō, also known as the Nobles School (Kuwazoku Gakkō), where the future Emperor Taishō was also enrolled. After a couple of years of study, both boys, "contented and happy," became "very proficient in their knowledge of the Japanese language and customs." Kalākaua's hope was that one day they would "aid in the government's immigration plans" (Quigg 195–197).

In 1997, Tiger Espere, who helped build and sail *Hōkūle'a* and *Makali'i* (a Big Island voyaging canoe launched in 1995), went to Japan on a mission given to him by his Tahitian elders to "verify the ancestral connection between Japan's pre-Buddhist settlers and native Hawaiians" (Gee). Tiger, a well-known big-wave surfer and fisherman, lived in and taught Hawaiian culture in Kamakura. Before passing away in 2005, he established the Japan-Hawaiian Voyaging Society, with plans to build a canoe and sail it to Hawai'i to reconnect the two island cultures.

Tiger hoped that one day *Hōkūle'a* would visit Kamakura to inspire his Japanese followers to build the canoe for their voyage. Before going to Yokohama in 2007, *Hōkūle'a* anchored off of Yuigahama Beach in Kamakura to pay tribute to her former crew member's mission. Tiger's brother, Loui Kaninau-Cabebe, joined the crew. Loui told us that for Tiger the voyaging canoe was not a physical artifact but a spiritual way, and that he wanted to

Hōkūle'a *greeted by canoe paddlers and surfers, Kamakura (Photo: Jin Takuma)*

189

carry on Tiger's dream of teaching Hawaiian culture to the world. As *Hōkūleʻa* approached the beach, she was greeted by sixty or so Japanese surfers and paddle boarders and six outrigger canoes, accompanied by jet skis. Loui chanted from the canoe, and members of the hula halau Tiger established in Japan responded on shore with chanting and dancing.

The opening of Japan to international shipping in the nineteenth century, after 260 years of isolation under the Tokugawa Shogunate, ignited a national debate over how much influence from outside cultures was desirable for the nation. Some advocated the adoption of ideas and practices from the West in order to modernize Japan; others urged "sonnō jōi" (respect the emperor, expel the barbarians). A movement to bring native and foreign elements together in a new mixed culture used the slogan "wakon josai" (Japanese heart, Western intellect), based on the paradoxical premise that Japan had to Westernize in order to preserve its traditional identity and culture. In the end, compromise and paradox prevailed, with both the restoration of Emperor Meiji in 1868 and the Westernization of Japan.

A national identity had begun to emerge during the Edo Period (1603–1868), after Ieyasu Tokugawa unified the country. Previously, regional domains ruled by warlords and isolated farming communities had their own local traditions and family loyalties and identities. After unification, the culture of the Tokugawa capital city, Edo, began to dominate. Many of the practices and traditions of this culture were originally brought from China and Korea and adopted by the Yamato court in the capitals of Nara and Kyōto during the Classical Period (538–1185). The imported cultural practices eventually took on a Japanese character and spread from the court to the warlords and samurai who became the ruling class during the Kamakura Period (1185–1333) and then to the merchants and trade people who prospered in towns and cities during the Edo Period. The culture depicted in the woodblock prints of that period, considered quaint by contemporary Japanese, still epitomize Japanese culture and identity for many foreigners.

During the Meiji Period (1868–1912), a unified national identity became a priority in response to the threat from the West. To fortify the nation in defense of the homeland, the government used the state-controlled education system to instill the belief that Japan was a Confucian family headed by an emperor who was descended from the Shintō sun goddess Amaterasu. As children of a divine emperor, the Japanese were taught that they were superior to other races and destined to rule Asia, if not the world. Bushidō (the warrior code of the samurai) was instilled in the masses to encourage loyalty to the nation and willingness to live, work, fight, and die for it.

Alternative identities were suppressed in favor of one nation, one race, one culture, one language; in a Confucian state bent on empire-building, there was little tolerance of multiculturalism, regionalism, or class identities. Although bushidō was an important component of the national identity, the samurai class itself was abolished. After Hokkaidō was declared imperial lands in 1879, the Ainu, descendants of pre-Yamato settlers, were subjected to oppressive policies of assimilation. Even Buddhism, originally from India via China and Korea but integrated into Japanese culture for over a thousand years, was deemed foreign and attacked. (Ironically, the thirteenth-century Nichiren sect of Buddhism, equated faith in its teachings with national salvation, and Meiji-period adherents preached ultranationalism.)

The monocultural view of Japan, founded on Shintō myth, was at odds with scientific evidence. Shintō itself, the so-called indigenous religion of Japan, was a mix of East Asian animism, Taoism, Buddhism, and Confucianism. Genetic, linguistic, archaeological, and historical evidence tells a story of a mixing of cultural groups.

The Japanese archipelago was inhabited for thousands of years by hunter and gatherers who left behind stone tools (the earliest dates exceed 30,000 years ago). The people may have arrived by a land or ice bridge to Hokkaidō and from there, across the Tsugaru Strait to Honshū by boat; or they may have come across the Korean-Tsushima Straits from the Korean Peninsula; or island-hopping from southern China, to Kyūshū. By 10,000 BC, a cord-imprinted pottery was being produced by the hunters and gatherers; fishing and eventually some plant cultivation supplemented their food supply. The people are now referred to as the Jōmon ("cord-mark," a term first applied to their distinctive pottery). These pottery-makers lived in pit dwellings, with store houses raised on posts.

Some scholars speculate that the ancestors of the Jōmon came "from Southeast Asia and/or south China sometime during the Pleistocene" (Hudson 3). In the late 1970s, after *Hōkūle'a* made her first voyage to Tahiti, "a group of Japanese built a primitive longboat to sail from northern Luzon in the Philippines to the southern tip of Kyushu" (Smith 198). The so-called southern influence on Japanese culture, discernible mainly in Okinawa and the other islands south of Kyūshū, prompted one scholar to argue that the Japanese can find an authentic version of themselves in Okinawans, who represent what the "Japanese" were before settlers from East Asia transformed the islands (Smith 283). (Other scholars point out, however, that similarities between Southeast Asian and Okinawan cultures may be due to later influences, as the Kingdom of Ryūkyū, which was annexed to Japan in 1872 and renamed Okinawa in 1879, traded with Southeast Asia, as far south as Thailand, during historical times.)

Around 300 BC, settlers from the Korean Peninsula introduced wet-rice agriculture, which had developed in southern China and was later adapted to a temperate climate as it spread north. This wet-rice-growing culture in Japan is called Yayoi, after a neighborhood in Tōkyō where a plain-style of pottery associated with rice cultivation tools was first discovered. The high productivity of Yayoi rice farming triggered population growth, and along with it, occupational specialization and social stratification. Genetic evidence indicates that mixing took place between the Jōmon and Yayoi populations.

By the late third century, chieftains in the Kinai area (Nara-Kyōto-Ōsaka-Hyōgo) began building keyhole-shaped burial mounds called kofun, which became increasingly larger and more lavishly supplied with prestige goods, indicating the emergence of a ruling class. Kofun culture spread from Kinai across the archipelago, south to Kyūshū and east to Kantō. Although the origins of the kofun have not been specifically determined, burial mounds are common throughout East Asia. One family with roots in Kyūshū eventually established a state called Yamato in the Kinai area and began to extend its rule from Kyūshū to Tōhoku (northeastern Honshū); it became Japan's Imperial Family.

The new settlers during the Yayoi Period (300 BC–AD 250) and Kofun Period (250–538) apparently adopted the language of the earlier settlers. Japanese is related to languages of the Altaic family, with roots in Central Asia. Modern Korean and Japanese share grammatical features and about 15% of their basic vocabularies, but the two languages are different enough to have diverged an estimated four millennia ago.

During the Classical Period (538–1185), travelers, traders, immigrants, and refugees from the continent introduced Buddhism, Taoism, and Confucianism, as well as Chinese music, arts, writing, medicine, costumes, rituals, and astronomy. The imperial court adopted the Chinese lunisolar calendar to organize time and feng shui to organize space. The capitals of Nara and later Kyōto were modeled on Chang'an, the capital of T'ang China (618–907).

The Yamato court labeled older settlers "Ezo" or "Emishi," "inhabitants of the northern lands." These were Jōmon survivors mixed with early Yayoi settlers who had been driven out of the central areas. The Ezo were considered barbarians, and the Yamato rulers sent expeditions to bring them under the control of the court.

The expansion of the rice-growing culture stopped in Tōhoku because rice did not grow well farther north. Around 600–700, a new type of pottery called Satsumon (Brushed-pattern) appeared in Tōhoku, produced by a people with cultural traits of both Jōmon and Yamato. The Satsumon cultivated dry-land rice as well as barley, millet, wheat, buckwheat, melons, and azuki beans.

Satsumon culture spread across the Tsugaru Strait to Hokkaidō, which was known as Ezo-chi (Barbarian Lands).

On Hokkaidō, the Satsumon encountered the Okhotsk, who migrated in the fifth century from the Amur River basin on the east coast of Asia and south on Sakhalin Island to Hokkaidō (Hudson 225–226). The Okhotsk settled along the north coast of Hokkaidō from Rebun and Rishiri Islands to Rausu, and on the Kuril Islands. The Okhotsk lived in hexagonal pit-dwellings and fished and hunted sea mammals (whales, porpoises, and seals) as well as bear, whose skulls have been found in their dwellings. The Okhotsk also kept dogs and pigs. The Moyoro shell mound in Abashiri (north Hokkaidō) is the largest Okhotsk site discovered so far. Okhotsk pottery was decorated with strings of clay rather than impressed with cord, making it distinct from Jōmon and Satsumon pottery.

The Okhotsk have cultural affinities with other maritime groups of the north Pacific, from Sakhalin and Amur to Kamchatka and Alaska. All these groups use toggle-head harpoons for hunting sea mammals and have whale-bone cases to hold and protect needles for sewing fitted, weather-proof clothing from sea-mammal skins.

A mixed Okhotsk-Satsumon culture developed in eastern Hokkaidō. By the thirteenth century, the Okhotsk were no longer present as a distinctive group on the island. At the same time, a proto-Ainu culture emerged from the Satsumon culture, with shifts from pit-dwellings to houses on pillars and from pottery to iron cooking ware (Imamura 203). Although the Ainu share some cultural beliefs with the people of Yamato and traded goods with them, the Ainu were not rice farmers; they hunted deer, bear, and rabbits; fished for trout (summer) and salmon (fall); gathered wild plants; and cultivated non-rice grains and vegetables. They called their lands "Ainu Mosir," "land of people" (as opposed to the land of kamuy, or gods).

The Ainu inhabited small villages called kotan and their territory extended from Ainu Mosir to the Kuril Islands (which the Japanese call Chishima) and southern Sakhalin (which the Japanese call Karafuto). According to a tale recorded by Batchelor, the Ainu believe that the original inhabitants of Ainu Mosir were a race of tiny people who lived in pit-dwellings and who were exterminated by the Ainu. The legend suggests that the Ainu admired these tiny people for their ability to fish for herring (five or ten men were needed to pull in a single herring) and hunt whales: "Surely these pit-dwellers were gods" (12–13).

After several centuries of conflict with the Ainu and fearing that Russia would seize Ainu Mosir, Japan annexed the island in 1868 and sent settlers to colonize and develop it. The Ainu were unable to stop the Japanese settlement. Ainu scholar Kayano Shigeru writes:

We were a nation who lived in Hokkaidō, on the national land called Ainu Mosir, which means "a peaceful land for humans." The "Japanese people" [Nihonjin] invaded our national land. (59)

The Ainu have not intentionally forgotten their culture and their language. It is the modern Japanese state that, from the Meiji era on, usurped our land, destroyed our culture, and deprived us of our language under the euphemism of assimilation. In the space of a mere 100 years, they nearly decimated the Ainu culture and language that had taken tens of thousands of years to come into being on this earth (153).

When *Hōkūle'a* arrived in Yokohama, a delegation of Ainu came to greet the crew and conduct a prayer ceremony in solidarity over shared concerns of native peoples whose lands had been colonized. Like native groups in Hawai'i working for recognition of the sovereign nation that America illegally participated in overthrowing in 1893, Ainu activists have pressed Japan for recognition as an indigenous people entitled by international law to self-determination in regards to land, resources and politics. The government has so far refused to grant that recognition to the Ainu. And discussions over the restoration of Hawaiian sovereignty have yet to bear fruit, in part because native groups continue to debate the form that sovereignty should take.

After Japan surrendered to end World War II and Emperor Shōwa renounced his divinity, the nation focused on rebuilding its economy, a project that gave birth to a new national identity: competitive, determined, single-minded entrepreneurs and salary men touted as economic exemplars of bushidō, or "corporate samurai." (Ironically, the samurai class traditionally looked down on the upstart merchant class.)

By the 1980s, however, after Japan's economy emerged as the second largest in the world, the corporate samurai identity became passé, and a new debate over identity ensued. Some who viewed the newly rich as crass and soulless consumers looked back to the past. Novelist Yukio Mishima (1925–1970), once "a frail youth, 'ashamed of my thin chest, of my bony, pallid arms'" (Stokes 74), began body-building and training in swordsmanship. He was a descendant of the samurai and formed a small private army. In 1970, at a Self-Defense Force headquarters in Tōkyō, he had the commander tied up, then addressed the soldiers in a speech calling for an uprising to restore the emperor's rule. The soldiers were unresponsive to his appeal, mocking him and jeering as he spoke. Mishima withdrew into the building and committed ritual suicide. Four months earlier, Mishima had lamented, "Japan is no more. In its place is a spiritless, empty, neutral, rich, calculating, economic superpower." While he is recognized for his literary genius and his writings remain popular, the mainstream viewed his foray into politics and his suicide as a tragic sideshow in its march toward modernization and globalization.

Not everyone became devotees of consumerism. Diverse religions continue to provide identities for those inclined to spiritualism: Shintō, Buddhism, and Shugendō (mountain asceticism blending Buddhism and Shintō), as well as a host of new sects and religions, have dedicated followers. Others find their identities in practicing Edo-period arts like haiku poetry, kabuki and nō theater, flower arranging, and calligraphy; or perpetuating traditional economic activities like rice farming, fishing, carpentry, saké brewing, paper making, and ceramics. Stories about young people re-learning ancient arts or returning to their furusato (ancestral home) to revive family farms or saké breweries are popular features in the media. But such traditional pursuits are specialties for relatively few and don't provide meaningful identities for the masses, who have taken on the modern occupational identities of global society—government worker, educator, nurse, accountant, etc.

A woman who worked on organizing events for *Hōkūle'a*'s visit expressed via email her anxiety over her lack of an identity. She was a volunteer in Japanese-American relations at the American military base at Iwakuni and confessed that when an American serviceman insulted her by calling her "Jap," she felt a sense of inferiority, which was perhaps rooted in Japan's defeat in World War II and the subsequent American Occupation. *Hōkūle'a*'s arrival and mission of cultural revival prompted her to ask, "Have I ever thought about who I am?" Her answer was no. "Do I have knowledge to take over something important in our heritage?" Again, her answer was no. However, she felt inspired by *Hōkūle'a* to reflect on her identity and was hopeful that she could one day somehow contribute to perpetuating Japanese culture.

Avant-garde dramatist Hideki Noda (b. 1955), however, questions the assumption that traditional culture can be perpetuated: "I met some ro-kyoku singers [traditional Japanese narration with musical accompaniment], and one of them said, sadly, that the ro-kyoku tradition is becoming extinct." It has to compete with many modern forms of entertainment and draws only small audiences. Noda comments that arts like ro-kyoku can survive only by adapting to the new global context:

> I think that the person's old style is probably finished, but new styles of ro-kyoku will survive. So, it's inevitable that art forms and culture change over time. Nothing stays at the same point, especially regarding culture. (Tanaka)

He argues that Japan needs to become multicultural in order to revitalize its native culture:

> It's time to open up to the outside world and mix with others in this 21st century. Most unmixed, full-blooded things die out anyway, and in history those who shut the door on outside influences become extinct. (Tanaka)

Noda directs kabuki plays while also writing, producing, directing, and acting in his own works on contemporary themes, like the world after the 9/11 attack on New York. He took a year off to live in London before returning to Japan to continue his theater work and teach.[2]

Unlike Noda, writer Ryū Murakami sees no future in blending the past with the future: the building of a global economy has transformed the country to the extent that there is nothing uniquely Japanese left. His novel *69*, an adolescent love story set in 1969, depicts a group of high school seniors who feel more comfortable in American pop culture rather than in Japanese tradition. A reviewer on Amazon.com comments: "Murakami's tale of high-school high jinks and adolescent angst in Sasebo, Kyushu, Japan, in the year of Woodstock and Yellow Submarine could, with only minor adjustments, be moved to Oxnard or Omaha or Oxford, Mississippi or the U.K."

Murakami believes the Japanese should be like Americans and strive to become more individual, to follow personal dreams, without limiting themselves to being Japanese. The teenagers in *69* rebel against their parents and would rather plan a protest or a festival than worry about getting good grades in school or planning for college, careers, marriage, and children. The thirty-two-year-old narrator, looking back on his senior year, sums up the outcome: "I always seem to be on the lookout for new excuses, and new ways, to celebrate." The drum rhythm of the Obon festival of his childhood turned into

> the jazz of the fifties and the rock of the sixties, and in one form or another [the music has] led me all over the planet in search of bigger and better thrills.
>
> What exactly that rhythm meant to me, I'm not sure, but I suspect it was just the promise of endless fun. (181)

The climax of *69* is a multi-genre youth festival, with music, film, and theater—a clone of the festivals that were taking place in the 1960s in America, from Haight-Ashbury and Golden Gate Park to Woodstock and the Sunshine Festivals in Diamond Head Crater in Honolulu—the forerunners of the be-in event the *Hōkūle'a* crew attended almost four decades later, in 2007, in the mountains of outside of Uwajima, and of the summer music festivals still popular in Japan today.

Individualism is not new to Japan: in a lecture to students at Gakushūen University in 1914, Natsume Sōseki advocated individuality as a basis for fulfillment and happiness. But as Sōseki observed in his lecture, "[t]he individual's liberty contracts when the country is threatened and expands when the nation is at peace" (43). In the decades that followed his lecture, national mobilization and war intervened to restrict individualism. Only after World War II did various forms proliferate.

Some manifestations of post-war individualism were based on imitation rather than originality: the Japanese became consumers and promoters of American pop culture, like the teens in Murakami's *69*. Riding motorcycles in leather jackets, à la Marlon Brando in *The Wild One* (1953), endures as an identity for some Japanese males who came of age in the 50s, and they can still be seen riding around Japan on Harleys. Jazz, became popular after the war, followed by early rock (Elvis imitators belong to a Japanese rockabilly sub-culture), then folk, heavy metal, punk, hip-hop, and rap.

Cosplay (costume play) became fashionable in the 70s and 80s, with youngsters dressing up as their favorite characters from cartoons, fantasy movies, and video games or as their favorite J-pop singers. Supposedly, the cosplayers are being individualistic by "becoming" (temporarily, in fantasy) who they dream they want to be, rather than who society or their parents want them to be. But a teen dressing up like someone else is a copyist, not an individualist, and doesn't grow up to become whoever is being imitated; cosplay is fantasy and serves as a vehicle for social interaction and what Murakami's *69* narrator labels as "endless fun."[3]

For others, individualism entails becoming "the first Japanese to" or "the first person to"; these individualists, unlike the cosplay crowd, gain recognition for achievements in their selected activities. Smith observes that Japan nurtures

> an elaborate subculture of dreamer-achievers: mountain climbers, trekkers in Africa, arctic explorers, single-handed-sailors. Among the best known is Naomi Uemura, who soloed by sled to the North Pole, lived alone in Greenland, and rafted the Amazon by himself. (65)

Wildlife photographer Michio Hoshino left Japan and settled in Alaska to pursue his work. He's featured, along with *Hōkūle'a*'s navigator Nainoa Thompson, in the documentary *Gaia Symphony No. 3*, about environmentalists. Hoshino was killed by a bear on the Kamchatka Peninsula during a photography expedition in 1996, and *Gaia Symphony No. 3* is dedicated to him.

Post-war globalization has given Japanese with world-class talent a wide variety of options in pursuing individual professional goals, from playing baseball in New York, to singing opera in Italy, to painting in France, to writing poetry in Taos, New Mexico, to studying nyatiti (a traditional harp-like instrument of the Luo tribe) in Kenya.[4]

Takuji Araki, who crewed on *Hōkūle'a* from Palau to Yokohama, promoted Japanese individualism in his "Big Dream" project, which involved students sleeping on the canoe when she was docked. He challenged Japanese youth not to be satisfied with the paths society had laid out for them, but instead to think outside the box, to dream big, using the voyaging canoe and star navigation as metaphors for life. Another Japanese *Hōkūle'a* supporter, Kyoko Ikeda, describes Takuji's project:

> At each port, Takuji hosts a maximum of 10 students and teachers to spend overnight on the canoe. While on board, participants learn about life at sea on the *Hōkūle'a* and the basics of star navigation.... Takuji recalls what Captain Baybayan said to a group of students in Fukuoka: "Our biggest enemy is fear. And in order to overcome fear, you need a dream. A big dream will turn into courage that will then help you overcome your fear. Tonight, you sleep on the *Hōkūle'a* and think about your dream under the vast sky. In the morning, the dream will have turned into courage to push you forward." ("Kū Holo Komohana: 2007 Voyage to Japan," Uwajima, May 28–June 4, Taku's Big Dream Project, *Hawaiian Voyaging Tradition*)

Takuji is concerned that young people in Japan are growing up "devoid of hopes and dreams for the future," citing the relatively high suicide rate among young people in Japan. Having a dream, he believes, "will save the lives of children and the future of his country."

His own big dream led him to become Japan's National Champion of Lifesaving in the surf-ski category. He came to Hawai'i to compete in paddle board and outrigger canoe races, including the Moloka'i Channel crossing, considered the world championship of outrigger canoe racing, with competitors from across the Pacific (Tahitians, Maoris, and Australians). Returning to Japan, Takuji founded an outrigger canoe club. During his efforts to promote canoe paddling and sailing in Japan, he met Nainoa, paddled with him from a Japanese island to a Korean island in a cross-cultural event, and was invited to join the *Hōkūle'a* crew for the voyage to Japan.

Writer Haruki Murakami (not related to Ryū) explores the dark side of the individualism so prevalent in modern societies—the isolation and alienation individuals suffer after ties to family, community, or country are broken by globalization and the pursuit of individual dreams. The narrator in "A Folklore for My Generation: A Prehistory of Late-Stage Capitalism" (*Blind Willow, Sleeping Woman*) describes a 60s upbringing, based on Murakami's own rebellion against limiting himself to things Japanese during his college days:

> I was born in 1949, entered junior high in 1961, and college in 1967. And reached my long-awaited twentieth birthday—my intro into adulthood—during the height of the boisterous slapstick that was the student movement. Which I suppose qualifies me as a typical child of the sixties. So there I was, during the most vulnerable, most immature, and yet most precious period of life, breathing in everything about this live-for-the-moment decade, high on the wildness of it all. There were doors we had to kick in, right in front of us, and you better believe we kicked them in! With Jim Morrison, the Beatles, and Dylan blasting out the sound track to our lives. (H. Murakami 61)

Murakami's father was a Buddhist priest and taught Japanese literature. Haruki, on the other hand, chose to study Western literature:

> I think that my interest in [Western] things was partly due to wanting to rebel against my father and against other Japanese orthodoxies. So when I was sixteen I stopped reading Japanese novels and began reading Russian and French novelists, such as Dostoyevsky, Stendhal, and Balzac, in translation. After studying English for four years in high school, I began reading American books at used bookstores. By reading American novels I could escape out of my loneliness into a different world. It felt like visiting Mars at first, but gradually I began to feel comfortable there. (Gregory et al.)

After graduating from Waseda University and before becoming a writer, he ran a jazz club called "Peter Cat" in Tōkyō, from 1974–1982.

Murakami appears comfortable in his role as a rebel against orthodoxy, but his tales of fissures in family and culture dwell on the loneliness of his characters. "Man-eating Cats" opens with a news story about a Greek woman living alone in Athens. She dies of a heart attack. With no companion to inform anyone of her death, her cats, trapped in her apartment without food, end up feeding on her corpse. The news article is read by one of two Japanese lovers, romantic individualists who abandon their marriages and families in Japan to live together in Greece. The woman studies Greek; the man sketches. They sip wine and make love. They have no obligations, no commitments, no community, adrift in a modernist void. In the end, the woman disappears and the man is left alone, wondering "So where is the real me?" He imagines himself dying alone and being devoured by cats (H. Murakami 123).

"Tony Takitani" is a longer tale of isolation and loneliness, in the context of Japan's historical encounters with the world beyond. The story begins, "Tony Takitani's real name was really that: Tony Takitani" (H. Murakami 175). The name in Japanese embodies disjunction: "Tony," written in katakana (the script used for rendering Western words and names), doesn't fit comfortably with "Takitani" (in kanji, his Japanese surname). Murakami, who vacations in Hawai'i, borrowed the name from a mixed-ancestry politician from Maui, Hawai'i, where such mixed names are common; when he heard the name, Murakami says, it "cried out" for a story to be told.

The fictional Tony's father, Shozaburō Takitani, is a jazz musician. On the eve of World War II, after trouble with a woman, he flees to Shanghai, which is occupied by the Japanese army. When the war ends with Japan's defeat, he spends a year in a Chinese prison. The Chinese army is executing its Japanese prisoners, and Shozaburō is resigned to death. (In his 1995 novel *The Wind-Up Bird Chronicle*, Murakami describes "the horrific violence inflicted on the Chinese during [Japan's] invasion of Manchuria during the 1930s" and acknowledges in an interview, "the Japanese people were the aggressors in the war and thus we are responsible for our many atrocities"; Qtd. in Gregory et al.)

When Shozaburō returns to Japan, he discovers his parents have been killed, and his brother has disappeared in the Burmese front. He marries a distant cousin and has a son. His wife dies a few days after childbirth.

During the American Occupation, Shozaburō becomes friends with an Italian-American major named Tony, since both are interested in jazz. Tony becomes godfather of Shozaburō's son, who is given the name Tony. But the American name becomes problematic for his son:

> ... living with a name like that was not much fun. The other kids at school called him a "half-breed," and whenever he told people his name they responded with a look of puzzlement or distaste. Some people thought it was a bad joke, and others reacted with anger. For certain people, coming face to face with a child called Tony Takitani was all it took to reopen old wounds. (H. Murakami 179)

Earlier in the story, we are told "Because of his name and his curly hair and his deeply sculpted features, he was often assumed to be a mixed-blood child" (175). (The reference to his kinky hair reminds me of one of my brother's high school friends, a Japanese boy with kinky hair, which made him something of an oddity, but not an outcast.)

With his father often on the road playing jazz, Tony spends a lot of time alone and gets used to a "habitual solitude." He spends his youth drawing meticulous renditions of non-human objects and eventually becomes a highly paid illustrator. He finally falls in love and gets married. But while it's a happy marriage, his wife is a child of Japan's consumer society, an empty shell whose identity is derived from buying and wearing expensive Western clothing, for which she compulsively shops. After she fills her large closet-room with clothes and shoes, Tony asks her to try to control her habit. As she heads back to a store to repurchase some clothes she has just returned, she dies in a car accident.

Tony's father dies two years after Tony's wife, leaving his son with a jazz record collection. Tony eventually sells the moldy vinyl to a used record dealer, thus severing his last link to family and past: "Once the records had disappeared from his house, Tony Takitani was really alone."

Like other writers of his generation, the 1994 Nobel Literature Prize winner Kenzaburō Ōe (b. 1935) wonders, "What kind of identity as a Japanese should I seek?" ("Japan, The Ambiguous, and Myself"). In a society both globalized and individualized, he acknowledges that traditional Japanese identity "has withered away":

> From the European and American vantage, we appear to be Japanese. But inside ourselves, who are we? What basis do we have for building our identity? In the past, we had awe and reverence for our fathers and ancestors. This is still powerful in Korea and in China. But in Japan the family has come apart, and our sense of community has also disappeared. Now we have nothing but the reflection of ourselves we see in the eyes of the West. We are confused and lost. (Qtd. in Nathan 150)

Awe and reverence for ancestors was still possible when Ōe was a child growing up before the war in Ōse, a small town in western Shikoku. In "The Day the Emperor Spoke in a Human Voice," he describes a womb-like pool where he felt an identity rooted in family, community, and place: the pool was in "a V-shaped hollow wedged between boulders and a bamboo grove—my private inlet." As a boy, laying there on his back, naked in the lukewarm water, Ōe envisioned "above the deep green of the hillside, a gigantic woman with a little man standing close by her side": the woman is Oshikome, the maternal ancestor of the village, and her companion is Meisuke, a trickster armed with a sword and a musket, who protected the valley against outsiders, including "the feudal lords of the region and the authority of the imperial system."

Ōe's traditional identity began to wither when his teacher at the national school mocked his drawing of Oshikome and Meisuke presiding over his world, and "the students whose parents had fled here from the air raids on the cities laughed at [him]"—an "ignorant country bumpkin." The drawing of the world on the blackboard depicted the emperor and empress ruling the world, "mounted on a cloud." Ōe comments, "[t]heir Imperial Highnesses had banished folklore from our region." Ashamed from being mocked, Ōe retreated to his pool and "became a lowly bug of a Meisuke and fastened my lips to Oshikome's large, peach-colored nipple."

Ōe's grandmother, who taught him the folklore of the village, died in 1944, and that same year, his father was killed in the war. After the war's end, the emperor himself was no longer a viable source of Japanese identity or authority, having been forced to renounce his divinity. Japan's defeat made Ōe feel that "imagining survival as an individual Japanese" was now impossible ("The Day the Emperor Spoke").

During childhood and adolescence, under the care of his mother, the Western literary influences to which she introduced him began to wean him away from his village identity. In his Noble Literature Prize lecture, he cites *Huckleberry Finn* and a Swedish fairy tale as two works that lifted his spirits and gave him confidence in himself. Ōe attended Tōkyō University and studied French literature, and since then, has been inspired in his search for an identity based on humanist values by French writers, like Rabelais and Sartre, as well as British and American writers, like Yeats, Orwell, Auden, Faulkner, and Flannery O'Connor.

In his Nobel prize lecture, he declares Japan's post-war culture "aimai," which he translates as "ambiguous," but which also suggests "evasive" and "equivocal": divided and pulled between East and West and guilt-ridden over the war, people are uncertain about who they are, what they believe, or where their loyalties lie.[5] His novel *Man'en gannen no futoboru* ("Soccer in the First Year of Man'en [1860]," the English translation titled *The Silent Cry*) is a complex narrative about the search for identity in an "aimai" post-war Japan. Two brothers Nedokoro (Root-place) return to their hometown of Okubo, a fictional version of Ōe's hometown of Ōse. Like the Japanese people, the two brothers are trying to come to terms with past moral failings in hopes of redeeming their future.

The older brother, Mitsusaburo (Mitsu for short), is fleeing Tōkyō, traumatized and confused by the gruesome suicide of his best friend from college and the birth of a son with a severe defect, whom he and his wife, Natsumi, shirking their parental responsibility, have placed in an institution. Mitsu hopes to find in Okubo the self he once was, so he can start life anew. His younger brother, Takashi, suffers from shame: he returns to Japan after having gone to America with a theater group to perform a play called *Ours Was the Shame*, intended to apologize to America for the protests that prevented President Eisenhower's visit for the ratification of the 1960 Treaty of Mutual Cooperation and Security. Leftist students like Takashi opposed the treaty because it allowed for the continued presence of US military bases in Japan; but Takashi apparently feels remorse for his ingratitude toward America, which aided in rebuilding Japan and now defends it.

In America, the repentant Takashi meets the owner of a chain of supermarkets on Shikoku, including one in Okubo that wasn't there when the two boys were growing up. The entrepreneur, who turns out to be from Okubo, offers to buy the Nedokoros' dilapidated, hundred-year-old ancestral kura-yashiki (storehouse and residence), which he wants to transport to Tōkyō to open a country-food restaurant (38). Takashi suggests the two brothers return to Okubo to sell the unused building.

When Mitsu and his wife, Natsumi, arrive in Okubo, Takashi meets them, and they stop for a drink at a spring where the village boys once played. Mitsu's hope of finding his former self quickly vanishes as he peers into the water:

> … the "I" bending down there now was not the child who had once bent his bare knees there, … there was no continuity, no consistency between the two "I's," … the "I" now bending down there was a remote stranger. The present "I" had lost all true identity. Nothing, either within me or without, offered any hope of recovery.
>
> I could hear the transparent ripples on the pool tinkling, accusing me of being no better than a rat. (58)

The village is also no longer what it once was. The supermarket, convenient and well-stocked with cheap packaged foods and modern appliances, has driven small family shops out of business. The tradition of pounding steamed rice in a wooden mortar with a large mallet to make mochi (rice cakes) has been lost because the supermarket sells packaged mochi. And Jin Kanaki, the woman who cared for Mitsu during his childhood, has a mysterious disease that causes her to eat constantly, turning her into the fattest woman in Japan—a sign of the declining health of the village addicted to cheap, abundant, processed food.

The supermarket magnate, we learn, is Sun-gi Paek, a Korean who was conscripted and shipped to Japan to cut lumber in the forest of Okubo during the war. Paek is called the emperor, an allusion to the fact that the Imperial Family, viewed as outsiders and oppressors by the villagers, has roots in a Korean kingdom.[6] Takashi decides to recreate the 1860 uprising led by a great grand uncle, whom Takashi believes is a hero of resistance against wealthy landowners and the regional lord. Now, Takashi asserts, the oppressor is the

Korean supermarket magnate, so, like his ancestor who trained and led the uprising, he organizes the hometown boys into a soccer team, then incites them to loot Paek's store.

Fat Jin rails against Koreans in general, justifying the looting of Paek's store: "The valley folk have had nothing but trouble ever since the Koreans came here. ... After the war ended, they climbed up in the world by grabbing the valley's land and money. We're only trying to get a bit of it back" (188). She also points out that Mitsu's brother S was killed by the Koreans in the village. After Mitsu points out that the Koreans were conscripted to labor in the village, that no villager lost any land after the war, and that his brother S was killed in revenge for S's friends' killing a Korean worker, Jin blurts out, "Everybody feels things have gone to pieces since the Koreans came. They should kill 'em all off!" (188). Mitsu counters Jin's racist rant:

> But Jin, the Koreans have never willingly inflicted any harm on people living here. The trouble just after the war was the fault of both sides. Why say such things when you know the facts as well as I do?

After his rebellion peters out, Takashi tries to make it appear as if he has murdered a young girl who dies accidentally. When Mitsu catches him in his lie, Takashi confesses the real reason for his desire to be punished—it's not for his anti-war protests or the failure of the rebellion led by their ancestor, but a dark secret from his past: as a teenager, Takashi had an incestuous relationship with their retarded sister, and she became pregnant. The child of incest is aborted and while his sister recovers, Takashi pushes off her sexual advances. Unable to take the rejection, his sister commits suicide. Ever since then, Takashi has been trying to find some way to punish himself for his sin. His actions in the village are intended to get himself executed.

After Mitsu exposes his lie, Takashi offers to donate an eye to his brother, who was blinded in one eye when a hysterical child, in an unprovoked fit, hurled a stone at his face. Deformed or violated heads, as Yoshida points out, are among "Ōe's archetypal metaphors"—Ōe's real son, Hikari, and Mitsu's fictional son are born with deformed heads. Mitsu's college friend is hit in the head during an anti-war protest and later hangs himself naked after painting his head red. The imagery suggests the constant danger faced by the part of the human body encasing the organ used for seeking out the truth and solving problems. Symbolically, Takashi offers to help the half-blind Mitsu see better and find his way out of the family's misfortunes. But Mitsu refuses Takashi's desperate, bizarre offer. Takashi then rigs a shotgun and fires it into his own face.

Are the Nedokoro family (and, figuratively, the Japanese people) doomed by the moral failings of their ancestors? Early in the novel, Takashi repeats a rumor that their great grandfather killed a younger brother who started a peasant uprising against the local lord, then ate a piece of his brother's thigh to prove that he wasn't involved in the attack on authority (38). Mitsu later gives his mother's version of events: the younger brother was a madman who led the farmers against his own family (104–105). The priest in the village offers a more convoluted version that suggests that the Nedokoro family are self-serving deceivers who plotted a controlled uprising of unhappy, overtaxed farmers to give the farmers an outlet for their discontent, fearing that if they allowed it to fester, the farmers might attack the wealthy villagers, like the Nedokoro family. The younger brother is chosen to lead the uprising of mostly second and third sons, considered expendable. After the uprising succeeds in getting the local lord's taxes abolished, the rebels hole up in great grandfather's storehouse to escape punishment. Great grandfather tricks them into coming out and getting drunk, and the rebels are captured and beheaded; only his younger brother escapes, as planned. Mitsu laments, "it seems as if I'm descended from a line of traitors" (113–115).

Mitsu, however, is able to salvage a new version of events from his hometown stay: after Paek begins dismantling the Nedokoro's kura-yashiki, Mitsu finds documents in the cellar that suggest that their great grand uncle who led the rebellion actually remained in the village, hiding from the authorities in the cellar of the kura-yashiki in self-imposed imprisonment and penance. Then a decade after the rebellion, he emerged from hiding and redeemed himself by leading a successful and bloodless uprising to improve the conditions for the farmers (260–264). Whether entirely true or not, this version gives Mitsu hope that his family is not doomed by its self-serving deceit, cowardice, and incest.[7]

Ironically, after his suicide, Takashi also achieves something of the redemption he was seeking: he is memorialized when the village tatami-mat maker carves a wooden mask depicting a shot-gunned face, to be worn by one of the participants in the annual Obon festival: "[The mask] represented a human face like a split pomegranate, and the closed eyes were studded with countless nails." As part of the festival dance procession, his unhappy spirit and other unhappy spirits of the village are placated. Mitsu and his wife, Natsumi, decide to start over again by taking responsibility for their deformed child, bringing him out of the institution to raise him, and also by raising the child with whom Natsumi is pregnant after an affair with Takashi. Natsumi plans to live with her parents for a while and encourages Mitsu to take a job in Africa, where he may be able to get his head together to restart his life.

Like Ōe, Mitsu realizes that he can neither break away from the past nor return to it ("in all probability, we would never set foot again in the valley");

but Mitsu needs, to the best of his ability, to discover the truth of that past and to be true to that truth, however piecemeal he can know it and however painful it might be. That Mitsu is heading to Africa to heal himself, rather than doing something traditional, like climbing one of the sacred mountains of Japan or going on a shrine pilgrimage, suggests that the traditional Japanese identity based on the emperor's mythic descent from Amaterasu needs to be replaced by a new story, based on genetic evidence, that the human race has a common ancestry in Africa, where Homo sapiens emerged, and through successive migrations into diverse homelands, settled the planet, including Japan. It's Ōe's way of suggesting the Japanese need to reconnect with the rest of humanity.

The prejudice and hostility toward Koreans expressed by Fat Jin and other villagers in Ōe's novel is a reminder of the historical and contemporary tensions and conflicts between Japan and its close neighbor. After the emperor of Japan and the emperor of Korea signed an annexation treaty in 1910, Japan ruled Korea until the end of the war in 1945. Koreans became citizens of the Japanese Empire, and the colonial government began forcing them to assimilate with oppressive measures such as mandating Japanese be taught in Korean schools and requiring Koreans to take on Japanese names and worship at Shintō shrines. The military also seized lands and businesses. Korean resistance against colonization emerged and persisted throughout the period of annexation.

After the annexation treaty was signed, Koreans began migrating to Japan to find work, and by 1930, over 400,000 Koreans resided there, mainly in poor city quarters, while working at "dangerous and ill-paying jobs" (Gordon 154). After an earthquake struck Yokohama and Tōkyō in 1923 and devastating fires broke out, Koreans were accused of "setting the fires, poisoning wells, throwing bombs, raping Japanese women, and looting Japanese shops" (Smith 268); they were also suspected of plotting rebellion with socialists. Although there was no evidence of crimes or treason, "neighborhood vigilante groups, along with police and army units ... began a rampage of executions" (Smith 268). Estimates of deaths range from 3,000 to 6,000, including "several hundred" arrested and executed by police and soldiers (Gordon 154).

During World War II, the Japanese Empire conscripted its Korean citizens as soldiers and workers. Over 5 million Koreans served the colonial empire, 200,000 as soldiers. About 670,000 workers were shipped to Japan. At the end of the war, an estimated 2 million Koreans were in Japan. The majority were repatriated, and by 1947, the number had fallen to around 600,000. In 1952, when the post-war American Occupation ended, Koreans in Japan were recognized as permanent foreign residents and could become naturalized citizens of Japan or obtain citizenship in either South or North Korea, two independent nations since 1948. Many Korean residents opted out of naturalization or assimilation for various reasons, including a desire to preserve their Korean identity or citizenship.

By the middle of the first decade of the twenty-first century, naturalized citizens of Korean ancestry in Japan numbered 284,840, with 10,000 or so naturalizing each year. But Chongryon, an organization of Korean residents aligned with and financially supported by communist North Korea, actively opposes naturalization and assimilation of its members. They operate Korean language schools and discourage members from marrying Japanese. Their position, based on ethnic pride as well as politics, has drawn the hostility of racist Japanese, who engage in narrow-minded, petty harassment. For example, in 2009,

> demonstrators appeared one day in December, just as children at an elementary school for ethnic Koreans were cleaning up for lunch. The group of about a dozen Japanese men gathered in front of the school gate, using bullhorns to call the students cockroaches and Korean spies. (Fackler)

The hecklers belong to what has been dubbed the Net Right, ultra-nationalistic malcontents who organize via the Internet. The largest of these groups, calling itself Zaitokukai (short for "Citizens Group Against Special Rights for Permanent Residents without Citizenship"), blames not just Koreans, but Chinese and other foreigners "for Japan's growing crime and unemployment." The hostility has been exacerbated by economic stagnation in Japan and competition from South Korea and China. A Zaitokukai member complains, "Japan has a shrinking pie. Should we be sharing it with foreigners at a time when Japanese are suffering?" (Qtd. in Fackler).

Anti-Korean demonstrations are often incited by invectives posted on the Internet by both sides and triggered by flare-ups of ongoing disputes, like the one over the Dokdo/Takeshima Islets, claimed by Japan in 1905 at the start of the Russo-Japanese war, and reclaimed and controlled by South Korea since 1952. The rhetoric gets ugly, with Japanese racists calling for Korean residents to be "holocausted" (Osaki).

The inflammatory rhetoric has prompted the prime minister and his justice minister to speak out against hate speech:

> Prime Minister Shinzo Abe has voiced concern over a further spread of race-based invectives, saying it runs counter to Japanese people's traditional pursuit of tolerance and harmony with others. Justice

Minister Sadakazu Tanigaki has meanwhile condemned the repeated use of hate speech in recent anti-Korean demonstrations. (Osaki)

Not all the aggravating commentary comes from fringe groups. In 2013, the mayor of Osaka was criticized locally and internationally for trying to justify the military's World War II practice of abducting or purchasing from impoverished families Korean girls and women for use as sex slaves in brothels for Japanese soldiers. One of the mayor's supporters, known for his ethnocentrism and sexism, blurted out in the mayor's defense that there were "swarms of South Korean prostitutes" living in Japan today. While the supporter was expelled from the mayor's party (Nippon Ishin, or Japan Restoration), the mayor continued to defend his views on "comfort women" ("Nippon Ishin to oust member").

In the twenty-first century, with Japan facing worker shortages, a low birth rate, and a shrinking population projected to be one-third smaller by mid-century, and two-thirds smaller by the end of the century, it's not surprising that the number of foreign residents, mainly workers, has increased in Japan, from about 1 million in 1990 to over 2 million by 2012. The largest increases have been among immigrants from China, the Philippines, and Brazil, with the Chinese emerging as the largest group of foreign residents, surpassing Koreans. Despite the increases, foreigners represent just 1.6% of the population of 128 million.

The government, however, remains ambivalent about bringing in more immigrant workers. When it went recruiting in the 1990s to fill jobs in factories and construction considered "kitsui, kitanai, kiken—hard, dirty, and dangerous" (Tabuchi), the government sought immigrants whom it thought would be compatible with the Japanese and offered special work visas based on ancestry to the descendants of Japanese workers who emigrated to Brazil and Peru in the late nineteenth and early twentieth century. By 2009, 366,000 immigrants from Brazil and Peru resided in Japan. During the global recession of 2008–2009, however, as unemployment rose, prejudices and resentment surfaced against the workers and their families because immigrants weren't fluent in the native language or knowledgeable about cultural and social practices (Onishi). The government made an offer to pay airfares for the immigrants to return to Brazil or Peru with the stipulation that they couldn't reapply for special work visas to return. Critics called the offer cold-hearted and disgraceful, as well as short-sighted, given the probability that the economy would revive at some point. The government countered that it was planning to change its immigration policy to recruit professional and highly skilled foreign workers rather than unskilled labor (Tabuchi).

Ironically, in 2008, a group of lawmakers proposed a plan to increase immigration to counteract the impending depopulation and worker shortages. Japan, the group suggested, should allow the percentage of non-Japanese residents to rise from 1.6% to around 10% by 2050, when the population is projected to have fallen to 90 million (Masutani). The lawmakers argued,

> The only effective treatment to save Japan from a population crisis is to accept people from abroad. For Japan to survive, it needs to open its doors as an international state passable to the world and shift toward establishing an "immigrant nation" by accepting immigrants and revitalizing Japan. (Qtd. in Ito)

The proposal also called for establishing an immigration agency to manage "legal issues such as nationality and immigration control" and offered a plan for citizenship for long-time and permanent residents (Ito and Kamiya).

In a surprising statement in 2011, Tōkyō governor Shintaro Ishihara, known for his xenophobia, acknowledged the mixed ethnic ancestry of the Japanese people and expressed support for more immigration:

> Japanese are not a homogenous people, because their ancestors can be traced back to Korea, Mongolia, China, Melanesia and even what is now Bangladesh, Ishihara said. "Since we are a mixed people, whether the number of foreigners increases or not in Japan is irrelevant. (The increase) [would be] a very good thing." (Qtd. in Fukada)

But the Japanese government is not ready to commit to a strategy that, like Kalākaua's recruitment of a large number of immigrants to Hawai'i in the nineteenth century, would increase the labor force, but also begin to establish a multiethnic state.[8] When not feeling threatened, the Japanese can be welcoming to foreigners, as they were when Kalākaua and his entourage arrived. Over a century later, the crew of *Hōkūle'a* was warmly hosted wherever the canoe docked ("Kū Holo Komohana," Yokohama, June 4–June 23, *Hawaiian Voyaging Traditions*). But despite the trendy multiculturalism and globalization of urban Japan and the many Japanese nationals searching for new identities as individuals outside of Japanese traditions, prejudicial attitudes and actions toward foreign workers, even those with Japanese ancestry, suggest that the insularity and ethnocentrism of the Edo and Meiji Periods remain deeply rooted; conformity and homogeneity are highly valued, to the extent that even those who grew up in Japan but have lived abroad feel discrimination when they return home.

In his story of the Nedokoro family, Ōe offers a parable of hope for openness to cultural change. When Natsumi, Mitsu's wife, makes traditional steamed rice dumplings in bamboo leaves, Mitsu notices the garlic in the pork-and-mushroom filling: "When I was living here, people never put garlic in any food, let alone dumplings." His wife is surprised: "What? ... Jin told me [']specially to put some garlic in" (111).

A Korean immigrant recalls that when he attended school in the early twentieth century and opened his garlicky lunch, he was taunted by his Japanese classmates, "Garlic, garlic. ... Oh, it stinks!" Humiliated, the Korean boy "never took lunch to school again" (Ienaga).

Ōe makes his racist Fat Jin responsible for introducing garlic into the dumplings in Okubo. Via the character of a Buddhist priest, Ōe provides a historical context for the change:

> Before the war, garlic played no part in village life at all. I don't suppose most people even knew there was such a plant. But the villagers discovered it when the war began, all because of the settlement built by the Korean laborers who came to fell timber in the forest. It was the villagers' contempt for a people who could eat such a smelly root that first made them aware of garlic. ... when the villagers took the Koreans to do forced labor in the forest, they told them some nonsense about not being allowed into the forest unless they took some dumplings with them. It was a way of asserting their superiority. So the Koreans began to make dumplings too, and hit on the idea of putting garlic in to suit their own taste. That influenced the villagers in reverse, who started using it for flavoring dumplings they made themselves. It just shows how the locals' stupid pride and lack of principles bring about changes in the customs of the valley. ... now it's a best seller at the supermarket. So the Emperor has double or triple cause to be pleased with himself. (111–112)

Mitsu notes that the "usual sentimental assessment" in the village now is that the garlic-flavored dumplings taste better than the ones his mother used to make; and the priest agrees. The ironic acceptance of a small change like garlic in dumplings is far short of the exuberant celebration of multiethnic cuisines by Hawaiian writer J.D. Holt in his essay "What Was Dear to My Heart" (quoted earlier in this essay); but it's a step toward openness to change for the narrow-minded.

Ōe ridicules those like Mishima and the new Net right who seek to fill the void of Japanese identity by reviving an ethnocentrism and nationalism: "The state becomes a crutch for those who are no longer able to stand alone, like plastic implanted in a dysfunctional penis" (Qtd. in Nathan 250–251).[9] Ōe feels an affinity to post-war writers who are both "deeply wounded by the catastrophe [of war]," yet hopeful of redemption and rebirth based not on a myth of divine ancestry, but on moral action and humane politics:

> They tried with great pains to make up for the inhuman atrocities committed by Japanese military forces in Asian countries, as well as to bridge the profound gaps that existed not only between the developed countries of the West and Japan but also between African and Latin American countries and Japan. ("Japan, The Ambiguous, and Myself")

For Japanese aspiring to such a redemption and rebirth, Ōe believes "the idea of democracy" and "the principle of eternal peace" embodied in Japan's post-war Constitution as important "moral props." But he also advocates a less abstract foundation in literature that helps people cross into one another's cultures to establish a common ground and achieve a true humanity. In his effort to reach out to the people against whom his country inflicted widespread suffering and devastation, Ōe has aligned himself with writers who have advocated for human rights, at the risk of persecution, in South Korea and China ("Japan, The Ambiguous, and Myself").

Ōe cites as one of his early inspirations Kazuo Watanabe (1901–1975), a French professor at Tōkyō University, who studied in Paris before the war and began planning to translate the untranslatable Renaissance humanist Rabelais into Japanese (a translation not completed until 1964). Of Watanabe's work, Ōe writes:

> Surrounded by the insane ardour of patriotism on the eve and in the middle of the Second World War, Watanabe had a lonely dream of grafting the humanist view of man on to the traditional Japanese sense of beauty and sensitivity to Nature, which fortunately had not been entirely eradicated. ("Japan, The Ambiguous, and Myself")

Watanabe wrote biographies of French humanists hoping "to teach the Japanese about humanism, about the importance of tolerance, about man's vulnerability to his preconceptions or machines of his own making" ("Japan, The Ambiguous, and Myself"). It's the sort of effort that people of good will have always engaged in.

Also on a mission to cross cultures to gain a deeper understanding of humanity, Nainoa Thompson and the Polynesian Voyaging Society sailed *Hōkūle'a* to Japan in 2007. Inspired by their discovery of common bonds and purposes with peoples throughout the Pacific, including Micronesia and Japan, the Hawaiian voyagers of *Hōkūle'a* have embarked on a new journey in 2014, to sail *Hōkūle'a* around the world to promote peace, protection of the oceans, and the survival of indigenous island cultures threatened by Westernization and the rising sea levels of global industrialization.[10]

NOTES

1. Coincidentally, in the summer of *Hōkūle'a*'s visit to Japan, a festival in Tōkyō celebrated an earlier Hawaiian-Japanese-Micronesian connection: "Towards the Islands—Sounds Across the Sea" featured music and dance from the Ogasawara Islands (Bonin Islands), halfway between Tōkyō and the Northern Marianas. The Ogasawaran dance, called nan'yo odori (dance with southern influence), has its roots in hula (Kakuchi).

A Spanish explorer recorded a visit to the islands in 1543, but the islands were not permanently inhabited until 1830, when a group of thirty from Honolulu settled there, including seven men and thirteen women who were natives of the Kingdom of Hawai'i. The group's leaders had heard about the islands from British and American whalers who had stopped there for fresh fruit, fish, and turtles in the 1820s. The whalers reported that the climate was warm and pleasant (Cholmondeley).

Japan occupied the islands in 1875 and named them Ogasawara after a samurai who is said (apparently falsely) to have discovered them in 1593. During World War II, the Allied forces captured the Japanese airfield on Iwo Jima, one of the islands. After the war, America occupied the islands, but returned them to Japan in 1968.

The languages of Ogasawara include Japanese, English (taught during the American Occupation after World War II), and a pidgin, with Hawaiian words of Hawaiian origin, brought by the first permanent settlers, such as the following: "tamana," from "kamani" (a hardwood tree); "ūfū" or "uhu," from uhu (parrotfish); "rahaina," from "lahaina" (a type of sugar cane); "rawara," from "lau hala" (pandanus leaf); "moe-moe" (having sex), from "moe" (sleep, or metaphorically, have sex) (Long). Musicology professor Junko Konishi notes, "the Ogasawaras flourished as a staging point between mainland Japan and Micronesia between 1914 and 1945. The movement of Ogasawarans visiting or migrating to and returning from Micronesia, and farther southwest, the islands of Palau, resulted in a wide exchange of musical styles" (Kakuchi).

The Ogasawaran music, dance, and chants are linguistically and culturally mixed. The chants have been influenced by "indigenous shamanism practiced on the Ogasawaras"; Shintō religion, which "trickled in through the Japanese who settled on the islands from Hachijojima Island, 700 km [435 miles] to the north, in the late 1830s"; and English "elementary-school songs sung in Japanese schools before World War II," some of the songs with Christian origins (Kakuchi). Instruments include the kaka (a Hawaiian drum, carved out of tamana wood in the Ogasawaras) and the ukulele, both of which accompany the singing. The title of Kakuchi's article suggests that the music and dance of these small, remote outliers "busts [the] myth of monocultural Japan."

2. Journalist Patrick Smith cites architects Hiroshi Teshigahara and Tadao Ando as examples of artists adapting native traditions to modern contexts. Son of a master of ikebana (flower arranging), Teshigahara applies the principles of that traditional art to designing buildings and bridges (e.g., Ayatori, or Cat's Cradle, a modern steel bridge with an S-curved walkway inside an inverted triangular frame, over the Daishōji River, in Yamanaka). In *Woman in the Dunes*, a film based on a novel by Kobo Abe, Teshigahara also applies traditional ikebana aesthetics in his cinematic art.

Ando designs buildings in raw concrete and glass rather than wood and paper, but allows nature (sunlight, rain, wind) into the enclosed spaces, as in traditional Japanese houses, so inhabitants can remain in touch with nature. He designed a subway station in Tōkyō so that speeding trains would suck fresh air a hundred feet underground to commuters. His vision for the metropolis includes a central area with no cars and a forest the size of a golf course planted on reclaimed land composed of garbage.

3. Some of Ryū Murakami's other works, filled with outlandish psychopaths and graphic, extreme sex and violence, introduce the reader to a dark side of Japan's brave, new world. When translator Ralph McCarthy asks Murakami about the significance of the "sick, damaged [characters in Murakami's novels] searching for meaning in a society that is increasingly materialistic and shallow," Murakami responds, "Every society has people who can't adapt, and their 'sickness,' if you will, their inability to adapt, can hold a mirror up to that society."

4. Cross-cultural identities go both ways: non-Japanese have entered traditional Japanese arts and sports. In 2008, *The Japan Times* published features of an Irishman who played the biwa (a Japanese stringed instrument); an Australian woman who became a geisha; an African-American enka singer (his mother is half-Japanese); and a Canadian woodblock print artist working in the style of Hiroshige and Hokusai. Sword making, Zen archery, and judo have non-Japanese practitioners recognized as masters. And "[i]n the world of sumo wrestling, Japan's venerable national sport, … 15 of the 42 top-division athletes

are non-Japanese, with the two yokozuna (highest-ranked) champions—Asashoryu and Hakuho—both hailing from Mongolia" (Otake). Earlier, at the end of the twentieth century, Akebono, of Hawaiian ancestry, and Musashimaru, of Polynesian ancestry, competed as yokozuna.

5. Ōe titled his 1994 Nobel Literature Prize lecture "Aimai na Nihon No Watashi" ("Japan, The Ambiguous, and Myself") to contrast his view of Japanese identity with that of Yasunari Kawabata, the 1968 recipient of the same prize. Kawabata titled his lecture "Utsukushii Nihon No Watashi" ("Japan, The Beautiful and Myself"), which cites the Zen aesthetics of the Buddhist priest Dōgen and the idea of emptiness as inspiration for his art; Ōe, on the other hand, is inspired by Western writers like Rabelais and George Orwell; what's important to Ōe is that human beings strive for decency and humanity.

6. The mother of Emperor Kammu, the fiftieth imperial head (r. 781–806), was Takano no Niigasa, a princess whose father was a descendant of King Muryeong of Baekje, on the Korean Peninsula. In 2001, as Japan and Korea were preparing to host jointly the 2002 World Cup of Soccer, Emperor Akihito, in a gesture of good will, acknowledged the Korean ancestor in the Imperial Family, although the Japanese media "played down the emperor's statement" (Takayama).

7. In "The Day the Emperor Spoke," Ōe mentions that after the war, the villagers of Ōse hid weapons in the forest in anticipation of the American Occupation and alludes to two historical uprisings in which his family participated, similar to the ones Ōe describes in *The Silent Cry*: "From my own house my mother carried up to the forest a sword that men of the family had used a hundred years earlier in two uprisings involving our local farmers, the first time as village elders, to suppress the violence, the second time as leaders of the rebel party."

The cannibalism, cowardice, and deceit rumored in various versions of the rebellion that Ōe describes in the novel may allude to moral failings of the Japanese during World War II. Takahi's incest with his sister echoes an incident of incest recorded in *Kojiki*, the narrative of the ancestors of the Imperial Family: Crown Prince Ki-nashi-no-karu "fell in love with and seduced his younger sister Karu-no-ō-kira-tsume" and is discovered and banished. "Unable to stop loving her brother, Princess Karu follows him into exile and there they kill themselves" (F. Murakami 463).

8. While immigration is an obvious strategy to mitigate depopulation, and many developed nations have more open immigration policies than Japan,

for now, the government hasn't acted on the 2008 proposal to allow foreign residents to make up 10% of the population by 2050. Immigration continues to be part of the economic plan, but the government is also implementing other strategies for meeting work force needs, like increasing labor productivity, employing more women (including mothers), developing robots to do routine work, building factories overseas, and outsourcing work. Other options include extending the work life of healthy retirees and establishing colonies of elderly in countries where healthcare workers are more available (Eberstadt 36–37). Local governments in rural areas particularly hard hit by depopulation have programs to promote marriage and families.

Some question the assumption that a nation needs to expand its population, production, and consumption to remain strong and healthy, an assumption that has driven Japan and the rest of the developed and developing world since the advent of global capitalism in the nineteenth century. A more sustainable model for societies might entail reducing populations, with less emphasis on increasing wealth and more on improving the quality of life in a healthy environment—a strategy that appeals to environmentalists (Eberstadt 36).

9. Ōe's satiric novella *The Day He Himself Shall Wipe My Tears Away* (1972) has been interpreted as a parody based on Yukio Mishima's 1970 failure to rally Japan's Self-Defense Forces to restore the emperor to power. The novella explores themes similar to *The Silent Cry* (1967), in particular, the obsession with self-constructed myths to protect the ego from the truth. The main character is the son of a man who at the end of World War II, on the day after the emperor's surrender speech, leads a group of army deserters who oppose the surrender and want to continue to war; they enter a town and are killed by soldiers. As the story is being told, the son is lying in a hospital bed wearing a pair of underwater goggles covered with cellophane and claiming to be dying of liver cancer (though he isn't).

The son wants to "remember" his father's death as an insurrection in which the group hijacks airplanes, disguises them as American, and bombs the Imperial Palace, killing the emperor "in order that the dignity of our national essence be elevated once again," by this "ritual purification of death by bombing at the hands of martyrs in a plane" (98). After his death, the emperor would be revived as a "ubiquitous chrysanthemum" (the imperial seal) that would "cover Japan and all her people" (98) and save the nation.

That the group was apparently gunned down in front of a bank doesn't matter to the son. He prefers to believe that his father was machine-gunned "by a plane disguised to look like a Japanese fighter but flown by an American" (99), turning his father's head into "a bright red pomegranate full of cracks"

(100); the son then envisions the huge shining gold chrysanthemum surrounded by a purple aurora appear in the sky, "rendered manifest" by his father's martydom and giving imperial blessing to it (99). The huge chrysanthemum spreading overhead suggests the mushroom clouds of the atomic bomb blasts over Hiroshima and Nagasaki, but the chrysanthemum "is not blocking the light as would a cloud but even managing to increase the glittering radiance of the sun in the blue, midsummer sky" (100).

If the father represents a Mishima in this parody (but one grown fat from isolation in his storehouse rather than muscular from training as a swordman), the son represents his Japanese followers who have fallen for his mythic views of the past. However, just as Mitsu confronts Takashi with the truth, the mother tells her son that he survived the incident at the bank only because he had fled before the massacre started. "Sooner or later the Japanese are going to change their attitude about what happened and I intend to live to see it, yessir" (105). The son, however, chooses to retreat deeper into his fantasy of his father's martyrdom by putting on a set of earphones and listening to the Bach cantata from which the novella gets it title ("Come, O death, brother of sleep, come and lead me forth; my saviour himself shall wipe my tears away"), while at the same time singing the American pop song, "Happy Days are here again!"

10. *Hōkuleʻa*'s worldwide voyage follows in the wake of King Kalākaua's round-the-world tour following his visit to Emperor Meiji in 1881. Kalākaua undertook his journey in more desperate times; he feared that his kingdom would be swallowed up by predatory nations like America, Britain, and France, which saw the islands as a key shipping and military outpost in the mid-Pacific. To counter the threat to his kingdom, Kalākaua planned to recruit immigrants of "cognate races" who would be compatible with his native people in order to repopulate his nation, strengthen its economy, and defend its sovereignty. In addition to asking Emperor Meiji to allow Japanese citizens to emigrate to Hawaiʻi, he also inquired if Meiji would serve as head of an alliance of Eastern nations to oppose Western imperialism in Asia and the Pacific. Meiji declined the following year, and Kalākaua passed away before he could revitalize his kingdom, which was overthrown by American settlers and US Marines two years after his death in 1891.

SOURCES

Batchelor, John. *The Ainu and Their Folk-lore*. London: Religious Tract Society, 1892.

Cholmondeley, Lionel Berners. *The History of the Bonin Islands from the Year 1827 to the Year 1876.* London: Constable & Co. LTD, 1915.

Eberstadt, Nicholas. "Shrinking Japan." *The Wilson Quarterly* Spring 2002. 30–37.

Ethnic Stock by County, 2011. *State of Hawaii Data Book.* State of Hawaiʻi, 2012. Web.

Fackler, Martin. "New Dissent in Japan Is Loudly Anti-Foreign." *New York Times.* New York Times, 28 Aug. 2010. Web.

Fukada, Takahiro. "Ishihara comes out for more immigration." *Japan Times.* Japan Times, 4 Feb. 2011. Web.

Gee, Pat. "Clement 'Tiger' Espere / 1946–2005: Canoe builder embodied many facets of Hawaiian culture." *Honolulu Star-Bulletin.* Honolulu Star-Bulletin, 30 July 2005. Web.

Gordon, Andrew. *A Modern History of Japan: From Tokugawa Times to the Present.* New York: Oxford, 2003.

Gregory, Sinda, Toshifumi Miyawaki, and Larry McCaffery. "It Don't Mean a Thing, If it Ain't Got That Swing: An Interview with Haruki Murakami." *Review of Contemporary Fiction* 22.2 (2002). Web.

Holt, John Dominis. "Kalihi." *Recollections: Memoirs of John Dominis Holt.* Honolulu: Kupaʻa, 1993.

---. "What Was Dear to My Heart," *Recollections: Memoirs of John Dominis Holt.* Honolulu: Kupaʻa, 1993.

Hudson, Mark. *Ruins of Identity: Ethnogenesis in the Japanese Islands.* Honolulu: U of Hawaiʻi, 1999.

Ienaga, Saburo. *Pacific War, 1931–1945.* New York: Random House, 1978.

Imamura, Keiji. *Prehistoric Japan.* Honolulu: U of Hawaiʻi, 1996.

Ito, Masami. "Will open-door immigration plan die after Fukuda?" *Japan Times.* Japan Times, 19 Sept. 2008 Web.

Ito, Masami and Setsuko Kamiya. "Let 10% of Japan be foreigners: Nakagawa." *Japan Times.* Japan Times, 13 June 2008. Web.

Kakuchi, Suvendrini. "Music busts myth of monocultural Japan." *Japan Times.* Japan Times, 19 July 2007. Web.

Kanahele, George. *Emma: Hawaii's Remarkable Queen.* Honolulu: U of Hawaiʻi, 1999.

Kayano, Shigeru. *Our Land was a Forest: An Ainu Memoir.* Boulder, CO: Westview Press, Nd.

Keene, Donald. *Emperor of Japan: Meiji and his World, 1852–1912.* New York: Columbia UP, 2002.

Kotani, Roland. *The Japanese in Hawaii: A Century of Struggle.* Honolulu: Hawaii Hochi, 1985.

"Kū Holo Komohana: 2007 Voyage to Japan." *Hawaiian Voyaging Traditions*. Asia Pacific Digital Library, Kapiʻolani Community College, n.d. Web.

Kuykendall, Ralph. T*he Hawaiian Kingdom, Volume III, 1974–1893. The Kalakaua Dynasty*. Honolulu: U of Hawaiʻi, 1967.

Long, Daniel. "English on the Bonin (Ogasawara) Islands." Publication of the American Dialect Society, no. 91; Supplement to *American Speech*, vol. 81. Duke UP, 2007.

Masutani, Minoru. "Keidanren: Immigrant worker influx vital to halt labor shortage." *Japan Times*. Japan Times, 15 Oct. 2008. Web.

McCarthy, Ralph. "Ryu & Me." *Kyoto Journal: Perspectives from Asia* 49 (2001). Web.

Mishima, Yukio. *Confessions of a Mask*. New York: New Directions, 1958.

Murakami, Fuminobu. "Incest and Rebirth in *Kojiki*." *Monumenta Nipponica* 43.4 (Winter, 1988): 455–463.

Murakami, Haruki. *Blind Willow, Sleeping Woman*. New York: Knopf. 2006.

Murakami, Ryū. *69*. Tōkyō: Kodansha, 1993.

Nathan, John. *Japan Unbound: A Volatile Nation's Quest for Pride and Purpose*. Boston: Houghton Mifflin, 2004.

"Nippon Ishin to oust member over South Korean prostitute claim." *Japan Times*. Japan Times, 18 May 2013. Web.

Ōe, Kenzaburō. "The Day He Himself Shall Wipe My Tears Away." *Teach Us to Outgrow Our Madness*. Trans. John Nathan. New York: Grove, 1977.

---. "The Day the Emperor Spoke in a Human Voice." *New York Times*. New York Times, 7 May 1995. Web.

---. "Japan The Ambiguous, and Myself." *Nobelprize.org*. Nobelprize.org, 7 December 1994. Web.

---. *The Silent Cry*. Trans. John Bester. Tōkyō: Kodansha, 1968.

Onishi, Norimitsu. "An Enclave of Brazilians is Testing Insular Japan." *ew York Times*. New York Times, 2 Nov. 2008. Web.

Ono, Philbert. "Robert Walker Irwin." *Photoguide.JP*. N.p., 24 Apr. 2014. Web.

Osaki, Tomohiro. "Nationalism rearing ugly head with greater frequency." *Japan Times*. Japan Times, May 23, 2013. Web.

Otake, Tomoko. "Foreigners flourish in the realm of Japanese arts." *Japan Times*. Japan Times, 29 June 2008. Web.

Quigg, Agnes. "Kalākaua's Hawaiian Studies Abroad Program." *The Hawaiian Journal of History* 22 (1988): 170–207.

Smith, Patrick. *Japan: A Reinterpretation*. New York: Libri, 1998.

Stokes, Henry Scott. *The Life and Death of Yukio Mishima*. New York: Farrar Strauss & Giroux, 1995.

Sōseki, Natsume. "My Individualism." *Monumenta Nipponica* 34.1 (1979): 21–48.

Tabuchi, Hiroko. "Japan Pays Foreign Workers to Go Home." *New York Times*. New York Times, 22 Apr. 2009. Web.

Takayama, Hideo. "The Ties That Bind." *Daily Beast/Newsweek*. Daily Beat, 17 March 2002. Web.

Tanaka, Nobuko. "Hideki Noda: Acting with joy in his soul." *Japan Times*. Japan Times, 4 May 2008. Web.

Yoshida, Sanroku, "The Burning Tree: the Spatialized World of Kenzaburo Ōe." *World Literature Today* 69 (1995). Web.

Overview of Japanese Historical Periods

Paleolithic Period (before 30,000 BC to around 10,000 BC): Hunters and gatherers from Asia settled the Japanese archipelago. Stone tools were first discovered shortly after the end of World War II, in Iwajuku, Gunma Prefecture.

Jōmon Period (~10,000 BC–300 BC): The inhabitants began producing ceramic pots and ritual figures. Archaeologists named the people "Jōmon" (cord-marks), from the imprint technique used on their pottery. Fishing and plant cultivation added to their food supply.

Yayoi Period (~300 BC–AD 250): New settlers from Asia, crossing the sea from the Korean peninsula to northern Kyūshū and western Honshu, brought wet-rice agriculture, weaving, bronze and iron tools and weapons, and a plain style of pottery. Yayoi is an area in Tōkyō where fragments of the new style of pottery was first discovered, in 1884.

Kofun Period (250–538): Ever larger keyhole-shaped burial mounds (kofun), filled with prestige goods, indicate the rise of a ruling class. Writing (Chinese kanji) was introduced in 405.

Classical Period (538-1185): The Imperial Family emerged as rulers of a centralized state, with a capital in Yamato (Nara Prefecture). Buddhism, architecture, arts, and literature, introduced from China and the kingdoms of the Korean peninsula, flourished. Three successive locations of the imperial court give names to three periods included in the Classical Period: **Asuka (538 – 710)**, **Nara (710 – 794)**, and **Heian (794–1185)**.

Medieval Period (1185–1573): The Minamoto, a samurai family, rose to power during the **Kamakura Period (1185–1333)**. In 1192 Yoritomo no Minamoto was appointed shogun by the emperor, and the shogunate Yoritomo established governed for a century and a half from the town of Kamakura. After a brief restoration of imperial rule (1333–1336), a shogun from the Ashikaga samurai family was appointed. The **Muromachi Period (1338 –1573)** is named after a street and district in Kyōto where the third Ashikaga shogun built his palace. The period from 1467–1573 is called **Warring States** (Sengoku) because daimyō (regional feudal lords), each with an army of loyal warriors and a land-base of rice fields worked by peasants, battled for supremacy.

Azuchi–Momoyama Period (1573–1600): The unification of the country took place under three successive daimyō: Nobunaga Oda (1534–1582), Hideyoshi

Toyotomi (1536–1598), and Ieyasu Tokugawa (1543–1616). The period began with decisive victories by Nobunaga over his rivals and ended with Ieyasu's defeat of the forces of Hideyoshi's son at the battle of Sekigahara in 1600. **Azuchi** was the site of Nobunaga's castle in Omi, on the southeastern shore of Lake Biwa. **Momoyama** was Hideyoshi's castle in Fushimi, south of Kyōto.

Edo Period (1603–1868): After defeating the Toyotomi forces, Ieyasu established the Tokugawa Shogunate in 1603, in Edo (later named Tōkyō, or Eastern Capital). The Tokugawa family ruled a unified nation for 265 years of peace and isolation.

Meiji Period (1868–1912): Unhappy with the Tokugawa Shogunate's weak response to the intrusion of American warships into Japanese waters and ports, a coalition of regional lords overthrew the shogunate and placed Emperor Meiji at the head of the government. During the so-called Meiji Restoration, the nation industrialized and militarized rapidly in order to compete with and defend itself against the West. It adopted an imperialistic foreign policy and went to war with China, acquired Taiwan, defeated Russia, and annexed Korea.

Taishō Period (1912–1926): Under the short-lived Emperor Taishō, Japan experienced a period of prosperity, a nascent democracy, and openness to Western cultural influences; but the period was also marked by inflation and conflicts between labor and capital. Civilian and military leaders vied for control of governance and policy.

Shōwa Period (1926–1989): Calls for military actions to solve economic problems grew stronger. Under Emperor Hirohito (posthumously Shōwa), Japan invaded China, occupied Southeast Asia, and in 1941, attacked the American naval base at Pearl Harbor. The Pacific War ensued. After the atomic bombings of Hiroshima and Nagasaki in 1945, Japan surrendered. It began rebuilding its economy and social institutions during a seven-year-long post-war occupation by America and its allies. A broadly democratic government with a pacifist constitution was established.

By 1978, "corporate samurai" had rebuilt the economy into the second largest in the world (behind the US) and maintained the position until 2010, when China overtook Japan. However, Japan's bubble economy (price-inflated assets) had already burst early in the 1990s, and in the post-bubble era, individuals began questioning old identities and searching for new ones.

The searching continues in the current period, called **Heisei** (Attaining Peace).

Author's Note

Roads of Oku: Journeys in the Heartland is the third in a trilogy of essay collections. The first two are about journeys at home—*Storied Landscapes: Hawaiian Literature and Place* (1999) and *Local Geography: Essays on Multicultural Hawai'i* (2004). *Roads of Oku* connects home and ancestral homeland.

Between 2004 and 2014, Karen and I made a dozen trips to Japan, to revisit places I went to on my first trip in 1970 and to go to places related to family and ancestral histories and myths, "places ears had heard of, eyes never seen." Inspired by the travels of the seventeenth-century poets Bashō and Sora, we logged over 20,000 miles across the four main islands, mainly by car, crossing straits by ferries and bridges, up to Cape Soya, at the northern tip of Hokkaidō, and down to Cape Kasasa, at the southwestern corner of Kyūshū.

Narratives and photos of the journeys are online at *Roads of Oku: Travels in Japan*, in Kapi'olani Community College's Asian-Pacific Digital Library. Blogs of my days on the double-hulled canoe *Hōkūle'a* from Uwajima to Yokohama are also online at the College, at *Hawaiian Voyaging Traditions*.

Two travelers, one path, across a bridge of dreams. Kintai Bridge, Yamaguchi

Kintai Bridge, under an eight-day-old moon, June 1, 2009

www.ingramcontent.com/pod-product-compliance
Lightning Source LLC
Chambersburg PA
CBHW060429180626
46817CB00007B/2730